Knight's Pawn

Knight's
Pawn

A. L. Kucherenko

Cuidono • Brooklyn

Cover Images: Details of the Bayeux Tapestry – 11th Century
Photographic credit: City of Bayeux

ISBN 978-1-944453-20-6
eISBN 978-1-944453-21-3

Cuidono Press
Brooklyn NY
www.cuidono.com

To my most beloveds:
Ilya and Natasha, who,
from the moment of their birth,
have made history every day
of their extraordinary lives.

Characters

* indicates people in recorded history

Ewyas, Englelond

Alaric the Norman of Ewyas, a mercenary born in Englelond
Simeon "the Brave" d'Évreux, bastard son of Archbishop Robert de Rouen,
    and cousin to William of Normandie; and Julienne, "the Fair,"
    Alaric's parents
Rannulf, Alaric's younger brother
Leota, niece of Harold Godwinson, married to Rannulf
Goda, Leota's nurse
Edo de Lens, Gilbert "the Monkman" fitz Gilbert, Johan de Vaux, Roderick
    d'Ivry, Alaric's boyhood friends
Marguerite d'Hesdins, a widowed noblewoman, later Alaric's mistress
Pierre, a Norman priest and scribe, serving Alaric's family
* Osbern "the Pentecost" d'Eu, Norman castellan of Ewyas during King
    Edward's reign

Boulogne & Francia

Genevieve Elysia de Fontenay, privately known as Elise, a Norman countess;
    kin of King Philip of Francia and Count Eustace II de Boulogne
Marie de Mortemer, Elise's younger sister
Hortense de Tourny, their aunt
* Guillaume d'Arques, son of Duke Richard II of Normandie and uncle to
    Duke William of Normandie, Elise's titular guardian
* Walter Arquesson, Guillaume's son
Philip, King of the Franks
Thierry de Châlons, King Philip's advisor
Juhel de Ponthieu, abbot of Clarion in Normandie, kin of Elise
Roland de Rennes, a count of Brittany, who fostered with Elise's family
Tristan de Vannes, Bertrand the Stammerer, Giles, and Yves, Roland de
    Rennes' companions

The Normans & Allies

* William of Normandie, duke of Normandie, later king of Englelond
    (1066–1087), known later as "William the Bastard," and
    "William the Conqueror"
* Guillaume Malet, a Norman with an English mother, thought to have
    lived in Englelond prior to the invasion
* Eustace II count of Boulogne also known as Eustace aux Gernons,
    Elise's uncle
Brian "le Dogue" Dubec, Eustace's henchman
Dreux Marchand de Ville, Alaric's best friend, later aligned with
    Bishop Odo
* Alain le Roux, also known as Alan the Red and Rufus, son of a count
    of Brittany
* Odo, Bishop of Bayeux, half brother of Duke William, later earl of Kent
* Robert de Mortain, half brother of Duke William
* Matilda of Flanders, William's wife, duchess of Normandie and queen
    of Englelond
* Guillaume fitz Osbern, Duke William's seneschal, later earl of Hereford
* Guillaume d'Évreux, son of Count Richard d'Évreux and cousin of
    Duke William, later Count of Évreux
* Hewisa de Nevers, wife of Guillaume d'Évreux
* Henri de Beaumont, Norman follower of William of Normandie
Picot de Cussy, one of William's commanders
Richard de Rupierre, a knight and commander, later aligned with
    Bishop Odo

The English & Allies

* Harold Godwinson, King of Englelond, Jan 6, 1066 to October 14, 1066
* Edgar the Atheling, the last surviving heir to the Wessex royal house of
    Cerdic, grandson of King Edmund Ironside, and nephew of King
    Edward the Confessor
* Agatha of Wessex, mother of Edgar the Atheling and Margaret of Wessex
* Malcolm III "Canmore" king of Scotia
Clare of Wolenbroth, daughter of an English thegn

Tutbury, Englelond

Derrick, a Mercian monk from Burton Abbey
Frigga, a former abbess living in Needwood Forest
Herluin "the mute" de Lessay, a Norman monk
Jeoffroi d'Ardain, an elderly captain of Alaric's garrison
Serilda, Frigga's granddaughter

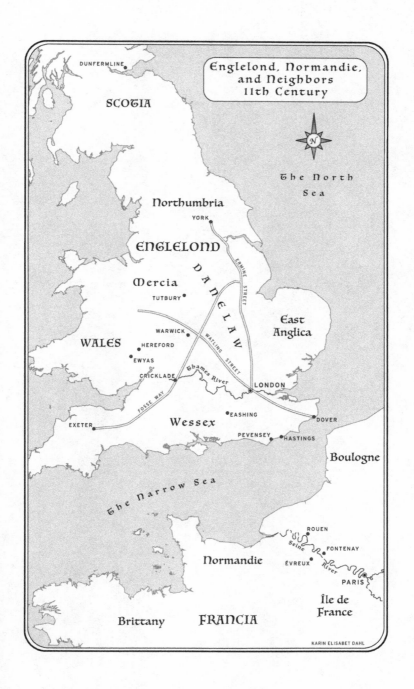

Englelond, Normandie,
and Neighbors
11th Century

SCOTIA

DUNFERMLINE

The North
Sea

Northumbria

YORK

ENGLELOND

DANELAW

Mercia

ERMINE STREET

TUTBURY

East
Anglica

WARWICK

WATLING STREET

HEREFORD

WALES

EWYAS

CRICKLADE

Thames River

LONDON

FOSSE WAY

EASHING

DOVER

EXETER

Wessex

PEVENSEY

HASTINGS

Boulogne

The Narrow Sea

ROUEN

Seine

FONTENAY

Normandie

ÉVREUX

River

PARIS

Île de
France

Brittany

FRANCIA

KARIN ELISABET DAHL

Prologue

September 1052, Ewyas, Herefordshire

Distant horns bellowed, deep and long, threading into Alaric's dream, drawing him from misty ghosts to his future. Blinking at the glare of a flickering rushlight, he pushed the hounds away and wiped smoky grit from his eyes. A few infants whimpered, and the longhouse trembled as men ran down from the loft. He searched for his parents and found them when a torch flared to life. Standing beside the doorway open to full night, they exchanged a few words. His father, fully armed and looking grim, snapped his sword into its hilt before vanishing into the darkness.

"Wake up! Wake up!" Alaric whispered to his younger brother, shaking him hard.

Rannulf protested briefly, burrowing into his furs until he recognized the sounds.

They scrambled from their pallets and dressed. They had been trained to be quick and quiet. Silence, their father had taught, was often the difference between life and death. They were all warriors, and, from birth, the warrior's belligerence and instincts had been bred into them.

"Riders coming," his mother said, joining them, waking their younger brothers.

At once, Alaric understood. The scouts who patrolled the valleys around Ewyas Castle had spotted horsemen and warned the garrison.

Alaric and his brother stepped out into the brisk September air, into the coming dawn's silvery light. Searching the walled courtyard for his father, Simeon, he spotted him on the ramparts near the gate. Urging his brother on, Alaric headed to the wooden tower, the core of the compound where the fort's inhabitants were gathering and where the castellan, Osbern "the Pentecost" d'Eu, waited with his captains. Alaric's friends—Roderick, Edo, Johan, and Gilbert, all boys near his age—joined them. They jostled each other to glimpse the castellan. Osbern whipped his deeply scarred face from side to side, growling at his captains and gesturing wildly.

"Who goes there?" a sentry shouted to the riders approaching the closed gates. Alaric watched his father run along the edge of the palisade to the gate tower and peer down at them.

"Mile de Reviers," came the answer, "from London. In peace and with my life, for as long as God grants it. I bring urgent news."

"Open the gates," Simeon ordered.

"Advance!" a guard called.

Alaric's father hurried down from the ramparts and joined Osbern and his fellow captains who had separated themselves from the crowd to hear the news privately. As the gates closed, the riders, their horses spraying foam over the people pressing near, approached the tower.

At nine winters, Alaric, small and agile, ducked and darted through the throng and squeezed between the salt-pork barrels stacked near the tower steps. He crouched close enough to hear the messengers panting and all speaking at once.

"Again!" Osbern demanded.

"The Godwins are back!" Mile said, breathing heavily.

"When?"

"Days ago. Godwin surrounded the king. Edward absolved them and proclaimed the bishops of London and Dorchester, and the Archbishop of Canterbury outlaws. As are we, by Godwin's demand. All French speakers," he said, "especially those who supported Eustace and gave the king bad advice."

"The Godwins are traitors! The king will not sanction this action against us all."

"No," Mile said. "His nephew is safe. As are some of the king's hunting partners, his chamberlain, and those approved by Godwin or his sons."

"Archbishop Robert?" Osbern asked.

"He fought his way out of East Gate and barely escaped," Mile said. "A heavy purse is on *your* head, Osbern d'Eu. Harold Godwinson comes for you himself and vows to destroy Ewyas."

"He would not dare. Besides, I will have time to—"

"You have no time!" Mile said. "Godwin forced the king to revoke the five-days' grace. Harold's ships and thegns sealed off the routes to Normandie, and he sent out a call-to-arms before King Edward's proclamation. We skirted Harold's forces on our way here, but they are only hours from Ewyas."

"Impossible!" Osbern said.

"We fled as soon as word got out. Norman blood flows in London streets and along the roads. Get out if you can, for they mean to kill us all." Without waiting, Mile rose on his stirrups and shouted to the crowd. "Normans are outlawed! Harold comes to slaughter you. Run for your lives!" The messengers wheeled their horses and left as quickly as they had arrived.

The castle's inhabitants ran after them, screaming, crying. Fights broke out. Osbern turned to his men. "Get your weapons and gear. We leave for Scotia before dawn. Travel light. No carts, no sumpters."

Simeon grabbed Osbern's arm. "You cannot leave. There are families here, cooks, the foot soldiers."

"Unhand me, d'Évreux!" Osbern yanked his arm free. "These creatures do not concern me. Normans must die to satisfy Godwin. Killing them will slow Harold. No Godwin will ever put his hand on me!"

"You command this post. You must see to their safety."

"The king relieved me from that duty when he surrendered to Godwin." Osbern pushed Simeon away. "Take command of these underlings if it pleases you."

As Osbern entered the tower, Simeon's face hardened. Without turning, he said, "I need runners, Alaric. Gather your compeers and meet me at the watchtower."

Alaric worked his way through the crowd. People pushed and shoved, grabbing what they could. Armor clanked like the sound of a dozen smithies. Women scrambled to gather their children and their goods. Foot soldiers loaded a cart with weapons and the farrier grabbed his tools. Alaric found his friends and sent them to his father. He dragged his brother from the path of a horse-drawn wagon, and shoved him into a niche beside the chapel where he would stay until summoned. Alaric ran to join his father, who gave each boy instructions for the men under his command.

When Osbern and his company began to leave, a collective shriek rose throughout the castle. The mob surged and charged the troops, begging them to stay and protect their escape. The knights kicked and slashed at the crowd with their whips and swords, rearing their horses to clear a path. Osbern and his men raced through the gates, trampling anyone in the way, leaving behind those they had wounded or killed and even their own women and children.

The sky began to lighten, and with it came a hurried calm. As the sun rose, and throughout the morning, Alaric and his friends ran back and forth, conveying messages. Simeon directed an orderly evacuation, urging people to leave their goods behind and follow Osbern north. As people left the castle, the embittered villagers had gathered near the bridge at Dulas Brook. They jeered and shouted and called out their hatred, for they had long resented the French-speaking foreigners in their midst.

Only a handful of soldiers and their families remained behind with Simeon and his family. Among them were Alaric's friends who fostered with his parents. When the last wagon departed, Simeon had the gates shut to keep the villagers out. Alaric retrieved his brother Rannulf and both joined their parents in the bailey. They did not wait long. When the shout came, Simeon turned to his wife, Julienne.

"You know what to do," he said.

She nodded, cupped Alaric's cheek with her palm a moment before taking Rannulf with her to the other children.

"Come," Simeon said to Alaric.

He stood beside his father on the ramparts as Harold's army crested a nearby ridge. With a battle roar, hundreds of soldiers afoot charged down into the valley. Within an hour, they had surrounded the castle and stood now in deathly silence. A score of mounted warriors rode slowly through the ranks toward the castle, flags waving, lances poised.

In unison, the foot soldiers began to beat their weapons against their shields sending forth a tumultuous, thundering rumble.

"Open the gates," Simeon commanded. Alaric scrambled to keep pace with his father as he pounded down the watchtower steps and ran into the courtyard. They joined the small group of unarmed soldiers, who stepped aside to let Simeon and Alaric take the lead position facing the entrance to the walled compound. Alaric had a sudden urge to urinate, his mouth dried, and his heart throbbed so hard he felt his eyes and ears pulse with each beat.

Simeon put a hand on his shoulder. "Steady, boy."

As the riders entered the courtyard, the ground beneath Alaric trembled, and he twisted the rolled pennons in his hands while his father unbelted his sword. The soldiers behind Simeon stood quietly.

With his retinue ready for the kill, Harold galloped through the castle gates. The sun reflected off his helmet and nose guard. Shoulder-length blond hair flew behind him, and he rose like a giant on his enormous gray speckled horse. Encased in linked metal rings, his chest appeared massive. Alaric held his breath. They would all die in moments. Harold's stallion stopped abruptly, reared, and steadied. Alaric's gaze traveled from the hooves of Harold's great steed up its broad chest, over a wooden saddle to Harold's large hand gripping his reins. Daring to look further, Alaric saw Harold's fierce eyes blazing at Simeon before he dismounted.

Urged by his father, Alaric stepped forward. "*On Eadward kyng's halve*," he said in Saxon, as fearlessly, he hoped, as his father stood before Harold.

Harold's bushy eyebrows twitched as he focused his intense gaze on Alaric.

"*On Eadward kyng's halve, my fathur*, Simeon d'Évreux, *gifs you Ewyas burgh.*" Alaric's hands shook as he handed over the pennons that had flown above the tower.

Harold growled and threw the flags on the ground. Alaric watched his father's composed features as he gave his sheathed sword to Harold. The two stared at each other with unflinching eyes. After tossing Simeon's sword to one of his soldiers, Harold slowly drew his blade. Alaric cringed as Harold spoke.

"*Yer either vera dumb or vera fraidless, Symon Defru.*"

Chapter One

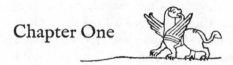

January 1066, Ewyas, Herefordshire

Toss the bones, Monkman," Alaric, the Norman of Ewyas, laughed and clapped a hand on his friend's shoulder. "They did not come from your saints." Flames from a nearby torch sputtered, bringing stark shadows to Alaric's clean-shaven face and to his men tossing coins onto the dicing table. A familiar dread, like rats in the thatching, nibbled at his outward calm. This morning, couriers, as exhausted and muddied, as cold and haggard as their horses had arrived. They'd made the five-day winter journey from London in half the time to deliver a terse message: *Stay at Ewyas until I arrive. It's urgent!*

"I marked the ox knuckles myself," said Roderick, Alaric's second-in-command. He tapped his fist against his breastbone before his injured expression dissolved, making him look like a bear scratching his hairy chest.

Gilbert the Monkman cautiously took the marked bones in his hand as the others crowded around him, eager to start the game. He shook the dice in his palm and crossed himself.

Alaric slapped him on the back. "Bless them while you're at it. Edo here needs coins. He owes me money."

"And me," Johan said, leaning his long, thin body against the table.

"And me," shouted Alaric's younger brother, Rannulf, from across the room. They all laughed.

As Edo hunched down and rubbed his hands together, five riders raced across the meadow, through a thick mist hugging the valley floor. Hooves churned the muddy road, tossing clods in their wake. Harnesses creaked, horses wheezed like giant bellows stoking a funeral pyre, lather gathered along their necks and flanks. Before night claimed Englelond's western border near Wales, the riders, eager to reach their destination, leaned forward, whipping their horses on. Cloaks flared and snapped like winged beasts flying low, hunting prey.

A damp chill seeped into the fort overlooking the village where Alaric hosted his family and friends for Christmastide, hoping they would stay until Candlemas. After Gilbert rolled the dice, Alaric walked through thick smoke to the back wall and grabbed the iron tongs hanging among the battered pots and utensils spiked to the timbers.

"It does not bode well," Rannulf said, joining him. He unhooked a ball of cheese hanging with the herbs and meats curing for the winter.

"We shall see," Alaric said. His men roared at a pair of rolled spots.

"The day wanes." Rannulf dug his thumbnail into the cheese and sniffed. "The journey becomes more difficult at night."

"Malet will come," Alaric said. "He most likely left soon after his messengers."

"Think we are outlawed again?" Rannulf replaced the cheese.

"Possibly." Alaric approached the fire pit where one end of a tree trunk as thick as his thigh burned furiously on a bed of embers. Using tongs, he slid the cooking racks along the iron bars bordering the stone pit. Bracing one boot on the hearth, he grabbed the cord that dangled from the vent hole and adjusted the slats. Smoke swirled and filtered out of the thatched roof. "Maybe it's a call to arms. An invasion, the Danes on the North Sea, or the Scots."

"You are exceedingly calm," Rannulf said. "Even Father is inspecting his armor tonight. Are you not worried about losing your . . . your castle?"

Alaric's steely gaze checked his brother's ridicule. "You and father, with your lands and titles, will be fine no matter what comes."

"You could have received a thegnland, too."

"I could have, but you wanted Leota, not I. Are we going over that again? It's settled between us."

"There's Marguerite."

Alaric looked across the room. "To bed, not wed." Lady Marguerite d'Hesdins, draped in a pale green tunic that heightened her rosy cheeks, talked with Rannulf's wife. Married at twelve, a childless widow at fifteen, now at eighteen she sought a protector, a lover, an escape from boredom—possibly a husband. Just this eve, she had invited Alaric to her bed. She had surreptitiously watched him all night. Now, as if sensing his gaze, she glanced at him sideways.

He gave her a slow, meaningful smile. Marguerite's eyes flashed. A faint curve appeared at the corner of her mouth, and a flush rose on her cheeks before she looked away. No, not to wed, he thought.

"On your feet, you hell-tarnished ass!" Johan's curse drew Alaric's attention. Johan grabbed Edo's tunic and yanked him to his feet. Roderick reached across the table and slammed his fist into Johan's face, sending him flying. Edo growled at Roderick's interference and swung a jug into the giant, overturning the boards in the process. Gilbert looked on, wincing as his friends exchanged blows.

Alaric's father, Simeon, expressed approval by banging his shield with the hilt of a sword. Rannulf threw a bench into the melee, where it crashed and splintered against the stone hearth. Leota and Marguerite scrambled out of the way. The priest, gripping his drinking horn, scurried over and around the combatants toward Alaric's parents.

Alaric recognized the sharper edge to this nightly brawl. Guillaume Malet, a royal envoy and Simeon's long-time friend, had intended to join them all for Christmastide but had been called to court. Now, awaiting his arrival, the men sought anxious entertainments.

Roderick rolled out from beneath the other two, bounded to his feet, and tossed Edo across the room. A dazed Johan crawled on the ground until Roderick lifted him, dusted his tunic with his broad hand, and shoved him toward the table. Edo staggered to his feet and gave Alaric a bloody grin. He yanked out a tooth loosened in the fray and tossed it into the fire. The men reassembled the table and resumed their game. Everyone settled back to wait.

Alaric turned to his brother. "Leota is frightened. Go to your bride until Malet arrives."

As Rannulf rejoined the women, Alaric sliced off a piece of roasted boar from the skewered remains at the edge of the fire. He popped the meat into his mouth and wiped the blade and his fingers on his tunic. Reaching for a pitcher, he caught Father Pierre's eye. The family priest and scribe nodded in return.

"Although my spiritual brothers forego wine," Father Pierre mumbled to Alaric, lifting his drinking horn, "I, a sinner, rejoice to drink more." Alaric grinned at the intoxicated priest and filled the vessel. After he refilled his father's beaker, his mother set her spindle and distaff aside and grabbed a black tunic she'd made. Julienne stood and measured it against Alaric's back, chiding him that he had surpassed the height of his father. "Black suits you," she said.

"You noticed," Alaric teased with a grin. He usually clothed his lean body within black leggings and tunic.

"Do you remember your ninth year?" Simeon asked, oiling his shield. "When last we received urgent news from London?"

"I do." Memories flashed in Alaric's mind: a brisk fall dawn, the jeering villagers, Harold's sword. It was the only time he and his father had stood unarmed, waiting for the deathblow. Alaric now held his father's somber gaze, remembering the moment Harold had dubbed his father Simeon the Brave. He nodded before crossing the room to settle on a bench.

Picking a piece of gristle from his teeth, he gazed critically around his hall, a converted barn. Pools of light from a torch and a rushlight left deep black shadows. Above the fire, flames lighted the rough-hewn beams and thatching, and across the room, he could barely see the thickly timbered door and the iron latch. His defenses: a wooden palisade, some huts, a small garrison, mostly cavalry and bowmen, that occupied the site of the old Norman castle. They could not hold off an attack for long, he thought, drinking from his beaker.

He and Rannulf had been born here, in the timber tower that once sat atop the earthwork mound overlooking Ewyas. They'd grown up among the rugged, tenacious, and proud English, adopting their dress, learning their Saxon speech, their legends, and songs. English warriors taught Alaric how to surprise and track an enemy, how to kill with stone and sling, how to disappear in the woods, how to lock a shield wall, and how to swear in Gaelic.

When Normans were outlawed, his father sent them across the water to Évreux for safety. For a year, they lived with their uncle,

Count Richard d'Évreux—Simeon's younger, legitimate brother—who had stolen Simeon's estates. The experience taught Alaric about land, wealth, and power, and why Simeon had come with King Edward's Norman cadre rather than stay in subservient vassalage to his half-brother.

Alaric and Rannulf began their military training under Duke William. Although fluent in French, Alaric and Rannulf spoke Saxon to each other, infuriating their Norman peers and drawing ridicule. At first, Alaric saw Normans through outlander's eyes, comparing every aspect of Norman life with his early years in Ewyas. He resented Norman presumed excellence and knew an English warrior with a good sling could take out a Norman knight in the right circumstances. Yet, as the years passed, Alaric absorbed Norman customs and took pride in his heritage.

Now, recalling those dangerous, frustrating days with pleasure, Alaric felt the scar on his palm. He missed his friend, who bore a similar scar. They had seen plenty of action together. Alaric could have joined Duke William's garrisons, but he yearned for the Black Mountains, their solitude, the reckless Welsh, and the old tales.

He had returned three years ago, his brother followed a year later. Both hired swords, they'd fought for Earl Harold Godwinson. Impressed by Alaric's natural leadership, Harold had retained Alaric to command this post—ironically, choosing a Norman to reestablish a small Norman fort at the very site that had spawned the earl's exile years before.

Now, at twenty-two, Alaric, a Norman, protected the English who despised him from the Welsh who would kill him. Like his friends at the dicing table, he faced a narrow, landless future. He watched the dice roll, jump, and spin across the table, knowing his future could change as erratically.

Horns wailed a startling alarm: riders approaching Ewyas. The muted sounds, one deep moan and two short blasts, filtered beneath the laughter and conversations in the hall. Everyone stiffened as they heard Alaric's guards running to the walls surrounding the compound.

Alaric rose calmly from his bench and went to the hearth. Crouching down, he rolled the thick log, and shoved it half an arm's length onto the embers. He donned his mantle and slipped from the dark hall, blinking into the still-bright dusk and flinching from the icy wind spiking his face.

He wove through open fires dotting the bailey, the courtyard enclosed by timbered defense walls. Joining his guards at the gate tower, he saw two torches in the distance. After giving orders to his captain, he descended from the parapets to wait near the hall.

Heavy clouds poured through the Golden Valley and swirled over the low-hung thatched roofs huddled together as if shivering from the cold. The riders galloped down the village road, dogs barked, chickens squawked, but the villagers, having abandoned their bonfires, hid behind shuttered doors. The horses thundered across the wooden bridge spanning Dulas Brook, climbed a narrow spiral road, and drew up before the large wooden gates flanked by guard towers.

A torch on a long pole waved before them, a fiery flag. "Who breaches God's peace?" a guard demanded.

"Guillaume Malet, Seigneur de Graville, with an urgent message for Alaric, castellan of Ewyas." His horse pranced sideways, its head thrown back as if about to rear.

A small door within the wide gate opened. The five horsemen ducked their heads and rode single file into the compound. Guards led them through the bailey. Archers with loaded weapons stood on the parapets, tracking their progress past small open fires surrounded by wary, alert castle inhabitants, past the kitchens, the garrisons, the smithy, and armory. Amid jangling harnesses and booted thumps on the ground, Malet and his men dismounted near the hall. Alaric grinned a welcome to his friend. As they clasped arms in greeting, grooms led the horses to the stables, and squires took Malet's four men to a small hut.

Now enveloped in the dark, the two men ran to the hall, huffing a trail of steamy moisture into the silent cold about them. The thick-timbered doors opened wide, their weight scraping on iron pintles. Alaric and Malet entered the whitewashed hall. The room, brightened by several fresh torches, smelled of pine smoke, cinnamon, and a trace of the last meal. The doors closed behind them with a slow grating clank, and the iron latch fell into place.

Alaric found everyone standing near the fire pit, suspended like a group of statues. "You know everyone here, Guillaume."

"Indeed," Malet said.

Alaric's parents, Simeon the Brave and Julienne the Fair, smiled a greeting. Beside them, Rannulf, a muscle pulsing in his cheek, rested his hand on the shoulder of a wary fourteen-year-old Leota. Father Pierre and Lady Marguerite waited near Alaric's four trusted men, who stood within reach of their mounted weapons and shields, fully alert, ready to defend.

"Come," Alaric said. He strode toward the central hearth, pulled his mantle from his shoulders and tossed it onto a bench, where it slithered to the hard-packed dirt floor.

Malet followed. Vapor rose from his damp, green cloak, and lingering fog seemed to swirl about his thickly wrapped legs. Dirt and sweat confirmed his difficult journey. Malet threw back his hood, revealing short hair, more gray than black. Immediately his cheeks and ears reddened from the warm room.

Alaric filled a mazer from a large pitcher. "Before you speak of London, drink this. It will warm your soul. The Benedictines, your *favorites*, blessed it."

Guillaume Malet, tall, thin and haggard from his hard ride, chuckled. He gulped the potent concoction: wine seasoned with apples and rare *clou de girofle*, and wiped his lips with a single knuckle.

He returned the wooden bowl with a nod of thanks and spoke, his voice cracking at first.

"Edward is dead. Harold is king, and William claims the throne."

No one said a word, although some looked at Simeon, the eldest and highest ranking member of the assemblage.

"In what manner is William's challenge?" Simeon asked.

"He sent messengers to Harold. He asserts his hereditary claim through Emma of Normandie, his great aunt, Edward's mother. He reminds Harold that Edward chose William his heir and that Harold swore a sacred oath to uphold William's succession. He demands Harold relinquish the crown."

At Alaric's gesture, everyone sat near the fire. He handed Malet a trencher, and between nibbles, Malet continued. With each word, Alaric's stomach tightened. Of course, they'd known King Edward had taken ill, and rumors had spread that once—years ago—Edward had named William his heir to the throne. Alaric recalled the large, strong duke he had trained under as he had seen him last in Rouen. William himself had often proclaimed to everyone that he would wear the crown one day. It hardly surprised Alaric that the vibrant Earl Harold, King Edward's brother-in-marriage, possessed the English throne. But had Harold ever agreed to William's claim? It mattered not. This meant war. He lowered his head and watched his father from beneath his eyebrows.

"Harold's response?" Simeon asked.

"The Witan refuse, and so does Harold, claiming the Witan has chosen him," Malet said, leaning over the hearth and stretching his palms toward the red embers. The Witan, thought Alaric, those crafty old ravens. Those "wise men," an English contrivance, this council of prelates and nobles who counseled the king, would, of course, choose Harold for their king.

With little prodding, Malet told everyone about the Christmas court near London instead of Gloucester to accommodate the king's failing health, about Edward's delirium, visions, deathbed ambiguities. He told them Harold had been with Edward throughout the last days, along with his sister, the queen, and noted those present when the king died. He described Edward's burial and Harold's coronation at the newly consecrated West St. Peter's Minster Abbey and the messages sent to Duke William reporting Harold's coronation.

Malet, himself a close friend of Harold Godwinson, answered all their queries with precise information, sharing his impressions about the whisperings in the palace halls. He told them the alignment of the bishops, which nobles had already promised to stand with Harold. They discussed what steps Harold would take to solidify his hold on the throne.

Malet turned to Simeon. "Harold expects a show of allegiance from all his vassals."

Simeon nodded. "It has been a long day. Let us retire." He rose and placed a hand on Malet's shoulder. "Thank you, Guillaume. Join the family in Alaric's chamber for a moment before resting this night. Tomorrow we shall ride with you to Hereford and spread the news to others. Come, Julienne."

Alaric waited until his family had retired to his private chamber, separated by thick hides. He spoke to his men and they began disassembling the table and stumps to make way for their pallets.

"It matters little to me who rivals for the English throne," Roderick said. "I stand with you, Alaric."

"Both Harold and William are strong. Make your own choice, Roddy, as each man should."

"I already have," Roderick said, lifting a bench. "I'll cover your arse—as usual."

As Edo set up a private alcove behind a screen for Marguerite, Alaric poured her a mazer of sweet wine. Her eyes glistened as he handed it to her.

"Have you considered my proposal, Alaric?"

"Yes, it's difficult to think of anything else." He smiled as his eyes roamed over her breasts, just barely imaginable beneath her thick winter's garb. "I will not marry you, Marguerite."

"Nor I you," she said firmly. "And you can be sure there will be no bastards."

He stroked her soft cheek, letting his thumb rub against her lower lip. "You could, you should remarry . . . ."

"I shall when I am ready. Perhaps I will choose . . . a bishop."

Alaric chuckled, folding his arms before his chest.

She sighed in annoyance. "Alaric, I have my own land. I am barren as I found after three years with a rutting husband." She put her hands on her hips at his teasing grin. "I offer you a dalliance, as long as you wish to keep me, and I am not pleased you are taking so long to accept my gifts."

He threw his head back and laughed, raising his arms in surrender. "I accept," he said, smiling and then sobering. "You understand that you or I may cease this liaison at any time?"

"Of course." She nodded her head in finality. "Tonight?"

He smiled. "Yes, I shall come to your pallet." He winked and turned toward his private chamber, instantly forgetting Marguerite and shifting his full attention to Malet's news.

Chapter Two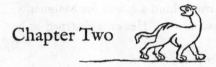

Malet reached down to loosen the leather straps crisscrossing his leggings. "The duke will have most of the Norman lords, but some, like those near Flanders or those sharing a border with Francia, might oppose the action. It would leave Normandie vulnerable to attack."

Alaric's family huddled with Guillaume Malet around a brazier. The dim room, no larger than a couple of horse stalls, glowed from the red embers. They spoke in French as Rannulf translated softly to his wife. Alaric sat on a stool, his elbows on his knees, leaning forward to hear every word.

"Your brother?" Julienne asked Simeon, coaxing the wicks of bundled reeds to flame for the rushlight.

"Richard will come," Simeon said. "He will bring his son. Do you boys remember your cousin, Guillaume?"

Alaric glanced at Rannulf and nodded, remembering their tormenter, a tall, gangly youth strutting about with his whip. *On your knees, you odious pig-rats!*

"Who else will join?" Rannulf asked.

"The Bretons—Alain le Roux and his brothers," Malet said, running his hand through still-damp hair. "Eustace de Boulogne will come—for strictly personal reasons."

Julienne's gasp drew Alaric's attention.

"On the maiden voyage?" Simeon asked, taking her hand.

"Yes," Malet said. "He would like to crush Harold for snatching Dover from his grasp years ago. But William would be wise to take Eustace's son hostage, surety against a rival claim."

"What about Harold's brother, Tostig?" Alaric asked, puzzled by his mother's pale face. "Would he, too, claim the crown?"

Malet yawned and eased his back against the wall. "Since Harold forced him from Northumbria, Tostig has few coins and fewer followers. He's begging arms from Normandie to retake his earldom. Although he and Duke William are related through their Flemish wives, William would never give arms to anyone who could turn against him. Unless Tostig finds support abroad, he will slither into hell's crevices where he belongs."

Simeon grunted. "William will be generous to those who support him."

"And give land and coin to all who distinguish themselves in battle," Malet said. "He will draw mercenaries from Picardy, Burgundy, and from the farthermost reaches of Christendom's Empire, including the Normans now living near Rome." Malet rubbed his nape before continuing. "And after arms have been assembled, after coins are disbursed, after the ships are built, others, like flies drawn to dung, will swarm with radiant ceremony to join the fight."

"Anyone in particular?" Simeon asked, chuckling.

"You know them as well as I."

Leota asked Rannulf when the fighting would begin.

"After the babe comes," he answered in Saxon, "after St. John's Day in June."

In French, Simeon said, "Before winter. Late August, perhaps."

Malet agreed. "Much depends on the duke's ability to solidify his vassals. It will be an enormous undertaking and may not be practical."

"Is it an idle threat?" Rannulf asked.

"William's threats are never idle," Simeon said. "He means to have the throne."

"Have you decided which man to support?" Rannulf asked Malet.

"No. Harold is my friend, and yours, too." He glanced at Simeon, who nodded. "Harold hopes I will choose him, but he knows my heart lies with Rouen—although I am English, too. I must also consider my son and his future." Malet pinched the bridge of his nose between his thumb and forefinger. "Duke William and I have much trust between us. Still, I cannot say he would rule the English better than Harold." Malet shrugged. "Sometimes, I think I am too old for these wars."

Alaric ushered Malet to his pallet and returned to his chamber. As his mother opened the pincers to lengthen the flaming rushes, he relaxed against the wall and listened to his brother and father weigh the news. Watching the shadows flicker about the room, he felt his mother's intense gaze, asking the same question he asked.

Having fought with both Harold and William, Alaric thought Harold the more powerful of the two. One to one, he could destroy William, like crushing a fly in his palm. But Harold's strength existed in the South, from Cornwall to Canterbury, where his thegns were loyal.

Since Alaric's return as a hired sword, he had traveled through the remnant kingdoms of Wessex and Mercia, skirted the edges of Northumbria and East Anglia. He knew the land bisected by the northern frontier, where Danish law prevailed. Although King Edward had paid annual tribute to keep the Danes from invading, they regularly attacked along the eastern coast. Yearly, they crept deeper into the Humber to control the rivers, to blockade major waterways, or to pillage the riches of the ancient kingdom of York. Alaric had seen the River Severn lost to Viking longships raiding deep into the Midlands, and had fought the Welsh who invaded annually along the western border. He'd found a land divided by race, language, and custom. A land surrounded by vultures, waiting to pluck out Harold's eyes and pick at his bones. Normans, Welsh, Danes, Swedes, Norwegians, Scots, and—Harold's own brother, Tostig—all wanted to devour the land. Harold could not fight them all.

Could William? During his decade in training with William, the duchy had coalesced into a distinct province—spurred by William's sword. The duke's unrelenting energy and his ruthless and aggressive military actions had united his contentious lords. Now, all spoke Norman-French. Under William, Normans adapted innovations from distant lands, and opened new trade routes. Despite Frankish pagans still worshiping in the woodlands, Normans had exchanged Thor for Christ, and built new churches and monasteries throughout. But could William unite a land dominated by Angles and Saxons, a land filled with people who spoke different languages, who still fought to preserve the shards of their ancient kingdoms? To Alaric, the question was vital to his homeland's future, and his own.

As his father and brother talked, Alaric studied his father. Simeon and Duke William were both bastards—and first cousins. But when Edward, who'd lived in Normandie for more than twenty-five years, returned to Englelond, he took a cadre of Norman soldiers, administrators, and clerics with him. Simeon and other knights in Edward's elite retinue had established Norman castles along the western border to defend his kingdom from Welsh raiders. But now, armed Normans on any border could menace Harold Godwinson, the new English king. Alaric knew his father would never return to Normandie. Years ago, when Edward had outlawed Normans, when they were killed for bounty, Harold Godwinson had let Simeon and his family live in exchange for Simeon's fealty. He would honor his vow and serve Harold.

Shifting his gaze to Rannulf, Alaric felt an overwhelming urge to protect his younger brother as he had for years. They were the last of Julienne's children to survive childhood injuries and maladies. Rannulf had married Harold's niece. Now related by marriage to the king, he, too, would support Harold. He might argue that old King Edward had not promised his crown to William, or that the Witan's decision to crown Harold should be upheld. But if he supported William, Rannulf would forfeit his thegnland and titles. He would return to Évreux a landless warrior, with an English bride who would be ill-treated, and a child who would never make a favorable marriage.

It could be a long and nasty war. In the end, nearly all of Harold's family could be killed. If Leota had a boy, Rannulf's son might be the only heir to a disputed throne—an heir who would never survive its infancy as the past had shown so clearly.

Alaric looked down at the ashes gathering on the firestone and decided his own course. He lifted his eyes and met his mother's knowing gaze.

Shortly after leaving Ewyas, Malet relinquished all his English lands and returned to Rouen to join Duke William. In February and March, Alaric and his soldiers made short forays into Wales keeping the loosely organized bands of raiders too busy to overrun the border.

By early April, King Harold had yet to summon Alaric's family. Alaric told his most loyal warriors his plan to join Duke William, and two dozen decided to follow. He sent all but his four closest friends to join Malet, vowing to meet them in Rouen before Pentecost. Taking Marguerite d'Hesdins with him, he traveled to Hereford to join his family for Easter. As if suspecting his intentions, Marguerite became nearly frantic in her attentions, brazenly seductive one moment, caustic the next, then coquettish, or sullen when he remained silent.

Alaric and his family celebrated Easter in the Norman chapel at Hereford—not in the crowded, noisy village church. As in previous years, Alaric and his family went to mass each night of Holy Week amid the heady sweet smell of frankincense. When they reenacted Christ's entrance to Jerusalem, Alaric helped his brother carry the cross. He and his father held an all-night vigil in front of the sepulcher. His mother stood beside him as the four monks searched through the crowd, and clasped his arm when the candle burst into flame. Afterward, during the festivities, a subdued Alaric watched his family.

Two days later, Alaric leveled his eyes at Simeon and spoke softly. "Father, I relinquished Ewyas and returned Harold's patent and coins. I leave in the morning to join William."

April 1066, The Brecons, Wales

At dusk, Alaric and his friends urged their horses stealthily up the narrow track climbing through the woods toward Pen-y-Fan, the highest ridge of the Brecons in Wales. The fog seeped into the ash, beech, and oak, and as their horses thudded a hollow rhythm on the damp forest floor, a dense, musky perfume, pungent in the first whispering pulse of spring, infused them. A fitful wind shook the trees, and a fine mist sprayed the riders.

Alaric adjusted his cloak. Water dripped from his hood as his body rocked easily with the sway of his horse and the creaking rhythm of leather harnesses. From travelers, he had learned about a great heavenly omen, a sign of Harold's demise. He led his men up the mountains, into enemy territory, to see this harbinger hidden by low clouds over Hereford.

Above the trees, he followed a trail along the spine of the wind-swept mountain. Emerging from the fog, he found the moonless night luminous. Alaric reined in his horse, and instantly his men moved into a tight formation, swords drawn, horses facing outward. Fog washed over the lower mountains like waves, pouring into the valleys, swirling over and through the woods below, pooling like vaporous eddies. Above, glittering stars, like drops of spray, hung in an invisible web.

Turning to see the whole sky, Alaric sighted a blue-white flare suspended in the canopy. As if alive it flickered, so bright it nearly blinded him, its tails floating like a woman's long tresses across an effervescent sea.

Alaric dismounted. His companions sheathed their swords and did likewise. Monkman crossed himself, Roderick emitted a low whistle, Edo gaped, and Johan seemed to measure the distance spanned by this strange object.

Throwing back his hood, Alaric climbed up the flat stones protruding at the crest close to the edge where the mountain dropped to the basin. The wind ruffled his hair and teased his damp cloak. Of all the nights he had studied the skies, learning their seasonal patterns, listening to his father's stories, he'd never seen such a thing. Fascinated and terrified at once, Alaric thought it spoke to him alone. There would be fire and war—as King Edward had seen on his deathbed. And worse, for Alaric felt the omen foretold the death and destruction he would bring to his homeland.

His father had always said, *Choose a virtuous man.* He had chosen William, a man whose virtue he could not assess. He believed only that William could unify and protect his birth land from predators. Yet, in following William he might put his family in danger. At the thought, he wanted to stay here on the edge of this cliff, suspended in the sky, balanced between heaven and hell, between war and peace, between life and death. He wanted to freeze his heart against the memory of his brother's horror a fortnight ago when Alaric had suggested Normans might plunder his wife's lands.

Rannulf had exploded. "How can you say that, when you are more English than Norman? You and I both are. We were born here. This is our home. Would you plunder a people you have protected?"

"Would I plunder Godwins' riches?" he asked, looking directly at

Leota. "Yes. That may be the only way to keep your land from falling to others. Leota, would you prefer Rannulf as a Norman lord to live in your father's house—or another Norman, who cares nothing for you and your family?"

"That is dishonorable question, Alaric," Rannulf snarled.

"But it must be asked, for it may come to pass."

Leota rose, her body large with child, and she glared at Alaric, tears welling in her eyes. "If you ever set foot on my father's land, I pray they burn you alive, and may the wind blow your ashes away." As she left the room, Rannulf and Alaric watched each other warily, until Rannulf broke the tension with a chuckle.

"You look English, even without a beard," he said, shaking his head. "You could shave more often. And cut your hair."

Alaric grinned, rubbing his stubble with his knuckles. Sobering, he leaned forward. "You're in danger, Rannulf. Your only chance may be to join William."

"If you truly think so," Rannulf said, his knowing eyes intense on Alaric, "you and I will face each other in battle."

Looking at the comet again, Alaric next remembered the pure joy of his mother's smile. Julienne the Fair, he thought, an apt name, even with eyes brightened by unshed tears. *I shall miss you, more than you know, Alaric. I pray God protects you.* She gave him the hammered bronze cross he now wore around his neck. And Alaric recalled the feel of his father's steadying hand on his arm as Rannulf shouted. *Are we not obligated to hold Alaric? He is a traitor to King Harold!*

Now, the sound of a wolf howling in the distance drew Alaric from his memories. The long, soulful wail pulled at something deep inside him. He cupped his hands around his mouth and answered, letting his voice slowly rise and fall, feeling the deep timbre of his own song. The hair at his nape rose as the single note floated above the valley. A lament, an offering to God.

The echoing howl soothed him. Like this hairy star, he, too, drifted to wherever God sent him. He had made the right choice. He had weighed it, again and again, not wanting to be frivolous on so critical a decision, knowing the lure of adventure lay heavily on one side.

Chapter Three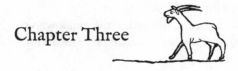

S top scratching," Alaric growled as they walked to a brewer's cottage outside Dover nearly four weeks later. "You're drawing everyone's attention."

"My bloody beard itches!" Roderick scowled as he followed Alaric into the hovel serving as a makeshift alehouse. They casually looked about the crowded room as two serving wenches sidled up to Alaric with a jug and two cups. Roderick wagged his abundant eyebrows and gave the women a leering grin to attract their attention, but they had eyes only for Alaric. He sighed and shook his head as Alaric sent them on their way with an appreciative smile.

In the weeks since seeing the comet, subterfuge had filled their days. Harold had begun to assemble his army and ships, and the movement of soldiers and supplies gave Alaric an opportunity to assess the location and distribution of Harold's defenses. He and his four friends, all knowing the language and customs, blended in with the fyrds, the armed citizen army, farmer-soldiers, traveling to their posts. Each going to a different area, they reconnoitered the southern regions and surveyed the coastline making detailed maps, taking crude measurements. They overheard gossiping villagers, talked to fishers about tides and to steersmen about currents, charted the harbors where hundreds of ships might shelter, and found routes leading inland that could support a mounted army and heavy carts loaded with weapons. They had agreed to meet in Dover by the ides of May, at the beach below the old Roman lighthouse. So far, only Roderick and Alaric had shown up.

"*A curse on Geeyome bastardus,*" growled one of the patrons in Saxon before he spat on the dirt floor. "*I seys the bastard es a devil. Yer wifs, yer gels, and . . . and even yer sons will be prikked by those evil Northmen.*" He glared at everyone in the room. "*If troth be telt,*" he said, lowering his voice, "*the Northmen rapen nuns and priests, too!*" The pronouncement set off a flurry of boastful threats.

Over the rumbling crowd, someone shouted to the monk who sat in a corner with a bowl of mead. "*Brothur, a blessan fur Harold kyng?*" The others cheered.

The monk, his long yellow robe gray from walking the dusty roads and wet where mead had dribbled down his chest, raised his bowl to the crowd and sipped. Putting the bowl down, he clasped his hands together. "*Gott in heafen,*" he began, bowing his tonsured head. "We pray Harold king is saved from them that make wars and burn churches. Turn the Northmen into a nest of dragons and strike them down. May Harold king tie the Norman bastard to the gib and feed the kites and griffons."

The patrons exploded with shouts of approval and calls for more blessings.

Raising his voice and his arms, the monk said, "May Harold king raise up his sword, unsheathed and wielded by God, to save us from this evil."

Alaric lifted his bowl and signaled to Roderick, who slipped out of the inn. A moment or two later they met in the crowded street.

"We've got to get out of here," Roderick whispered. "It's too dangerous."

Alaric, walking beside him, agreed. Behind them, horns blasted. People began to shout and whoop as carts bearing lances and bows came from inside the gates of Dover with a company of housecarls who lodged within the fortified town. Without a word, Alaric and Roderick separated and merged into the crowds gathering outside the walls. Here, the small village had nearly tripled in size as tents and thatched cottages had been raised overnight. People had come seeking passage out of the kingdom. Others had come to provide goods and services to Harold's warriors—arriving daily on foot, by horse or mule, in carts, by boat. Everywhere Alaric turned, someone hammered on weapons or armor, hawked bread or clothing, made leather harnesses, or repaired carts. Dover prepared for war.

Alaric wondered if Johan, Edo, and Gilbert would make the rendezvous. He thought it dangerous to wait even one more day. Just then, a couple of fyrds stumbled out of another alehouse before he could avoid them. One of the hooded, bearded men threw his arm around Alaric's neck, grabbing him in a kind of stranglehold, dragging him backward nearly off his feet. Alaric clawed at the thick arm, trying to escape the men, whose short tunics reeked of manure and ale. Together, all three staggered along a few steps and stopped, swaying on unsteady feet in the middle of the narrow road jammed with carts and horses, and people. Alaric struggled to pull free of the chokehold; but before he could free himself, he felt the hot splattering of urine on his leggings.

Tottering and pissing in the street, the farmer-soldiers talked between themselves.

"Ah, yer prick's a picked eel all yellow with brine. 'Tis a wonder yer never lost it in a goose-girl afore now." The hint of a Welsh accent, grabbed Alaric's full attention. "'Twill fall off any day now."

"Nay," said the other, squeezing Alaric tighter to his chest. "'Tis me old and dearest friend. Yellow though he might be, he's a might bigger than yourn."

Suddenly, Alaric recognized Johan and Gilbert. He barked a laugh and elbowed Johan in the ribs, winning his quick release. "Ye gads, yer sure to drown the village with yer piss. Or destroy the whole Norman host with yer stench!"

Together, all three linked arms and began to sing an old Saxon drinking song about the famous goat from Clee as they lurched drunkenly away from the crowds.

That night the four men huddled on the beach beside the remains of an old longship half buried in the gravel before the lighthouse. Only a few unbroken ribs and strakes protected them from the wind. Tied to the cracked, weathered stem-post, their horses faced the wind. Alaric spoke softly as he shivered in the damp mist.

"We'll make one more sweep of the area, but we have to leave. We can't wait for—"

Someone shouted, and they heard the sound of horses in hot pursuit. They leaped from their shelter and looked down the beach at the source. A woman chased by three riders ran on foot holding her skirt above her bare knees. Her cloak flew out behind her, and she frantically waved her free arm. What? Alaric thought incredulously as the woman kept shouting and racing toward them. He heard his name.

"Let's go," Alaric shouted.

Mounted, they headed toward the woman. Roderick, the largest of the four, reached down and plucked the woman from the beach. With drawn swords, the others intercepted the soldiers. After a brief skirmish, Alaric and all of his men turned their horses and raced for the docks—as more soldiers joined in pursuit.

May 1066, Rouen, Normandie

Actually," grinned Alaric, "we stole a boat!"

"Yes, a stinking boat filled with fish and just barely seaworthy," Edo grumbled, his shudder recalling fish slithering into their leggings and wiggling down their braies. Everyone roared at his discomfort.

Alaric and his men had arrived at the ducal palace in Rouen, the seat of Normandie. They sat around a table in one of the duke's towers drinking with Alaric's best friend, Dreux Marchand de Ville. They related the story of their close escape, and how Edo had followed Gyrth, Harold's brother as he trekked through the southern shires setting up defenses. The night Gyrth had arrived in Dover, Edo found an opportunity to steal the missives, maps, and everything Gyrth carried with him, by dressing as a woman selling her womanly wares. The story concluded with laughter and ribald comments about Edo and his comely figure galloping across the beach.

One by one, the men drifted away until only Alaric and Dreux remained at a corner table, a smoky tallow burned nearly to its base. Around them, everyone had taken to their beds. Familiar sounds embraced them—a woman's soft giggle, a fitful snore, the rasping of a body turning on a straw pallet.

Dreux, with a lazy smile on his bronzed face, looked over at Alaric and shook his head. "You were always getting into trouble, even as a boy."

"It is my nature." Alaric grinned at Dreux whose hair was still blond, nearly white. His intense eyes were the same pale blue, and his lips curved upward, as always, a twitch away from a smile. "By God's own sword, it's good to see you again, Dreux!"

"It's been nearly five years."

"Yes." Alaric smiled. They'd hated each other when they first met. At fourteen winters, although opposites in appearance, they were equally matched in height, weight, strength, skill, ambition, and impudence. Duke William had used their mutual hostility to train them. He thrust them together, made them compete with one another, pushing them harder and harder. When they were old enough for battle, he forced them to protect each other's backs, and in the process, they had come to an understanding. Wary and tolerant at first, and then painstakingly professional, until, finally, they were friends. Alaric fingered the scar on the palm of his hand, the remnant of their blood-bond made on the eve of his return to Ewyas.

Alaric and Dreux were both twenty-three and landless. Dreux, the youngest of four sons, had not joined the Church, nor had he followed his brothers to join the Normans in Sicily.

"Have you a liege lord?" Alaric asked.

"I'm one of Bishop Odo's men." Dreux scratched his head. "But no title or land. My eyes are on *Anglia*." Alaric smiled. He, too, hoped this war would reward him.

"And you?" Dreux asked. "Will you serve under Malet?"

"Possibly," Alaric said. "Malet and I are working with William's steersmen and the monks who'd once lived near the Wessex coast. We've pointed out possible landing sites and revealed what we know about Harold's preparations. Daily, I thank God's generosity, else William would not have taken me back into his fold."

"He would have taken you back, Alaric. If for no other reason than to have you slay everyone within a three-horse radius." They laughed remembering a bet they had made once a long time ago on one of the duke's sorties.

Dreux next told Alaric how William intended to transport three thousand horses across the Narrow Sea.

"God's shield!" Alaric said. "Battle-ready horses on ships in open waters?" Their ships would have no rowers. Loaded with heavy cargo, they would tack against an unfavorable wind. He imagined nervous stallions drifting for days on a choppy sea. After such a voyage, the beasts could not fight immediately. "Can it be done?"

"We shall see," Dreux chuckled. "Normans now living near Sicily counsel William. They ship horses all the time on the Middle Sea. Learned how from Romans and Greeks."

"Did any of your brothers come?" Alaric asked.

"No. Their fortunes will be made in Sicily." Dreux changed the subject. "I hear you're meeting with Gundulf, the mad monk from Bec."

"Yes," Alaric smiled, knowing the reputation of William's architect who talked aloud to himself and shouted insults to no one in particular. "I've told him and the steersmen where the old, still usable forts are located along the coast. We are building a wooden castle in sections to transport. As soon as troops land, the notched timbers and frames will be reassembled, either to stand alone or to reinforce the old forts. We will need the protection. The English will see us coming and are likely to charge as soon as we touch the shore."

Dreux nodded.

Gundulf's fortresses were not the great stone strongholds in the heart of Normandie that took years to erect. Alaric had learned to construct the expeditious castles built throughout the duchy: timbered tower and ramparts atop a natural or man-made rise, a defensible courtyard, ringed with a timber wall and a moat or ditch. With enough labor, these strongholds could be raised in days or weeks and could pin down an enemy for years.

"Then what?" Dreux asked.

Alaric winced. "I will visit my uncle and cousin."

Dreux laughed. "They'll eat you alive, Alaric, just like they did, what, ten winters ago?"

"Maybe," he said, smiling. "But now I bite back."

Dreux raised his eyebrow at Alaric's unmistakable intention.

"I'll only stay a short time. The duke wants me to cross the Narrow Sea ahead of his fleet."

"Dangerous," Dreux said.

"So is war." Alaric yawned and drained his wooden drinking bowl.

"Rannulf did not come?"

"No." Alaric looked down at his empty bowl and explained.

"So," Dreux said. "We're going to save his arse, again, eh?"

Alaric nodded, grateful for Dreux's understanding. "Afraid so," he said, remembering the last time he had seen his brother.

Rannulf, although still furious at Alaric for leaving Hereford, had ridden hard to catch up with him. They had dismounted and walked their horses together in silence.

"If I could tie you to a tree and let you sit out the war, Alaric, I would."

"Come with me."

"You know I cannot."

Alaric nodded, and they fell silent again before he teased, "Watch the archers, little brother."

Rannulf chuckled. "And you be mindful of Harold's two-handed battle axes. 'Twill fell your horse and give a fearsome headache."

They laughed and sobered. "Alaric," Rannulf said, shrugging his shoulders, "if . . . if something should happen. Will you . . . will you protect Leota?"

"I swear by my saints," Alaric said. "I will!"

They embraced tightly for a moment and parted. When Alaric reached the valley's edge, he reigned in and looked back. Rannulf had waited for his final wave.

In June, Alaric learned Harold's brother Tostig threatened to invade Northumbria, and wondered if William had encouraged him. Norman counts, their military tenants, warhorses, armor, and weapons amassed. Soon William's fleet began to appear. Alaric and Dreux, working together with William's advisers, fell back into their old friendship. Alaric knew his brother and father would be likewise

engaged in defense preparations, and he sometimes wondered whether
Leota had given Rannulf a son or a daughter, for the child should have
come by now.

In July, after nearly ten years, Alaric returned to his uncle's home
in Évreux. He and his cousin Guillaume eyed each other. Alaric noted
their similarities: long, thin Norman faces and lean, tall bodies. But
Guillaume's blue eyes and reddish-blond hair, similar to Simeon's, did
not match Alaric's gray and black. His family treated him differently
after Guillaume tried to best him but ended up pinned beneath the
sharp tip of Alaric's sword. Perhaps it was his alliance with the duke.
Although Guillaume outfitted new ships for William's venture, Alaric
gave Duke William information, which might already have assured
victory. Still, Alaric felt deeply honored by his uncle's invitation to
confer on the Évreux preparations, and was surprised when he gave
him a superb black warhorse and his old suit of chainmail—expensive
gifts the equivalent of four *mansi,* enough land to feed several
households.

Chapter Four

After the Feast of the Assumption, Alaric and Guillaume Malet infiltrated back into Wessex with a few of their best men. They began to hear the weary, disgruntled voices of the militia guards stationed along the coast, who were tired of waiting for an invasion that never came and who complained about the lack of provisions and the boredom. The fyrd had already stayed beyond their two months' required service, and now they wanted to return home. Winter neared and with it cold and famine unless they could harvest their crops, cut logs, dry fish, and finish the hundreds of tasks waiting for them.

In early September, Harold dismissed his forces, sending the militia home. He and his housecarls retired to London. By mid-September, Harold had released nearly all the land forces along the southern coast. Alaric and Malet learned from travelers that Tostig and King Hardraada of Norwegia had attacked near York, and Harold had marched north to confront them.

Alaric and Malet dispersed their men to assess the strength of Harold's remaining forces. Speaking Saxon with round shields toggled on their backs and wandering on foot, they meandered the southern coast as if stragglers from the dismissed army, not quite willing to return to their small villages. Within days they rendezvoused, astonished by their findings: Nearly all the ports lay unguarded. They would wait until October as the duke had instructed. If the fleet had not yet arrived, they would sail back to William—if they could get out.

"There's been no southerly wind for nearly a month," Malet said as they walked together along the ridge skirting the coast. Alaric looked out over the channel. The winds blew *toward* Normandie, grazing the tops of choppy waves. He imagined the duke and his mariners feeling the spray blow into their faces as they looked across the sea, and how they would pray and scan the September sky for a favorable wind.

Malet sighed. "Fishermen say winter gales begin tomorrow on the equinox, and that no southerly wind will blow until spring. They say, no invader can cross the Narrow Sea in winter. What say you, Alaric?"

"I say," he grinned, "they have never met the duke."

September 1066, Sussex

An unseasonable southerly wind began to blow just at dusk six days after the autumnal equinox. Alaric stood atop a cliff bracing himself against the brisk wind and searched the sea. At night, a lighted torch could be seen from afar, and William's ship would carry a signal lantern.

Hours later, Alaric's men posted at Beachy Head lighted a small, sheltered beacon fire to alert him that they had spotted Duke William's signal. Through the night, he and his men watched for the lead ship and lighted more beacons along the coast for William's steersman. As the fleet neared, Alaric's men swung flaming torches in wide arcs to answer the pre-arranged signals.

As the sun rose, Alaric and Malet tracked the fleet along the coast to Pevensey. Alaric watched in awe as nearly a thousand ships approached the shore, skimming swiftly over the undulating water, their crane-head beaks pointing the way. Under full wind, the square sails slashed with colored stripes strained against their ropes. Shields angled along the bulwarks, and from within, a few men wearing armor glinted in the sun.

By the second hour of the day—after most of the ships had entered the mouth of Pevensey Bay—the wind died suddenly. Sails flapped, fell limp, and were quickly pulled down. With masts naked as a grove of winter birch, the fleet rode the high tide slowly into the harbor. William's ship touched the broad shore at mid-morning of Michaelmas Eve.

By the time Alaric and Malet had descended to the beach, the duke, robust at thirty-eight winters, had disembarked and trudged across the shingle toward them.

"By God's breath, Alaric, I would not have known you," the duke teased. He slapped an unshaven, long-haired Alaric on the back and greeted Malet.

Guillaume fitz Osbern, the duke's seneschal, had joined them and quickly thanked them for the information about the bay. "Perfect," he said to Malet, grinning from ear to ear.

"How fares my kingdom?" William asked, his eyes twinkling as he scanned the unguarded beach.

"It is yet to be seen," Malet said. "Harold fights Tostig and Hardraada in the North."

"Good, good," the duke murmured, nodding his head and smiling as his eyes traveled over the rising hills. He sent Malet to establish the contingents as they debarked from the ships. Meanwhile, he and Alaric walked along the beach surveying the Roman ruins where the troops would assemble. Most villagers had fled their homes, a few watched from the ridges. The duke's brother, Bishop Odo, and two men Alaric did not know joined them.

"We've heard nothing about the northern invasion," Alaric said as he watched grooms unload the warhorses, searching for his own. "We don't know whether Harold, Tostig or Hardraada prevailed, although the fighting must have ended by now."

"Land forces?" the duke asked.

"The militiamen went home a few weeks ago. We patrolled the coast from here to Dover, and only a handful of stragglers remain. Most of the local thegns went with Harold leaving only skeleton garrisons to protect the larger villages. No doubt messengers have already left with word of your landing."

"The fleet?"

"The bulk of Harold's fleet sank in a storm a fortnight ago. A few seaworthy ships remain guarding the Thames."

"Well done, Alaric!" the duke said smiling. He asked fitz Osbern for a map, and Alaric began to show the duke their location on the oilcloth. He indicated a Roman road and gestured toward a ridge. "It's the easiest route, once you get to it, although you could move along the marsh and from there up along the bluffs."

"Forgive me, William." A large, bald man standing beside the duke interrupted. Alaric's attention immediately turned to the noble who had spoken so familiarly to the duke.

"My friend, I caution you," the man continued, brushing his mustache with his thumbnail.

The duke raised his eyebrows. "Eustace?"

"The information provided by this . . . this outsider," Eustace said, raking his eyes over Alaric, "could be tainted."

The duke laughed. "Count Eustace de Boulogne, meet Alaric of Ewyas, my *cousin*," he said pointedly. "Alaric, son of Simeon the Brave, nephew of Count Richard d'Évreux, this is Eustace's captain, Brian Dubec, *le Dogue*."

Alaric nodded curtly to Eustace, and noted that Dubec indeed looked like a mastiff.

The count's eyes narrowed. "Simeon the Brave?"

"My father," Alaric offered, wondering at Eustace's surprise.

Eustace turned abruptly to the duke and said, "Cousin or no, this young buck has just now joined us. Can you be sure of his loyalty? His father supports Harold, and his brother is married to a Godwin."

Alaric looked closely at Count Eustace. How did this man from Boulogne, whom he had never met before, know so much about his family, and why would he challenge Alaric's loyalty to the duke?

"It would be easy to steer you into a trap, William. There may be no reason to trust him," Eustace said. "I merely advise caution."

"My lord?" Alaric asked respectfully.

William nodded, watching the two men closely.

"If I supported Harold," Alaric said to the duke, "it would have been easy to stop you here on this beach, before your guard surrounded you." Alaric lunged, grabbing Eustace around his neck. His *seax* pointed at the count's jugular vein. "Like this," he said calmly, his lips beside Eustace's ear.

William restrained the others, who had moved to protect the count.

Alaric grazed the short sword's point across the count's naked flesh before gently releasing his captive. Turning to Eustace with a crisp bow, Alaric spoke softly, his eyes intense. "I beg your forgiveness, my lord, and thank you for letting me demonstrate my intentions." He sheathed his weapon.

William threw back his head and laughed. He slapped Alaric on the back and urged Eustace to admire the clever way Alaric had very nearly slit his throat. "Alaric is with us. I have no doubts, Eustace, and neither should you." Placing an arm around Eustace's shoulders, he turned him away from Alaric. "Have your men situate the arms and mail."

He released Eustace abruptly and turned to the others. "Fitz, the horses. Odo, isolate the wine and food. Have your men capture the livestock, gather whatever food the villagers have left behind, and burn down all those cottages. Post sentries on the bluffs and send patrols to scout for approaching troops. Robert, your companies will assemble our fortress inside the old walls. Our combatants and non-combatants number more than eight thousand. Keep them busy. No one remains idle. See to the ditches and privies. Everything: men, horses, arms, supplies must be stored behind those walls before nightfall. Come, Alaric, show me the best route before we reconnoiter the area."

Eustace watched the duke and Alaric walk along the beach.

"Shall I kill him?" Dubec asked.

"Not yet," Eustace said as they turned toward the ships. "I may have use for him."

Chapter Five

Alaric's horse staggered amid a sea of bodies covering the field. Exhausted as his destrier, Alaric struggled to stay mounted and awake. Beneath his mail, his quilted padding oozed sweat. He hurt all over. His head buzzed from the blows he had received, his left shoulder screamed when he moved it. After almost nine hours, the battle had ended. Alaric and his men had fought in the center with the duke's brother Bishop Odo.

His sword, this morning smoothly sharpened, now hung in his loose grip, dulled, sticky with blood, as were his hose, boots, and horse, and his kite shield bore long gashes in the leather-covered wood. At a standstill, unable to rise in his stirrups for his trembling legs, he looked over the murky field.

A few isolated soldiers still fought on the edge of the main battle site. He watched a handful of knights chasing the enemy into a shadowed thicket, but he did not join this rout as he had the last, where William had nearly lost his footing in a hidden ravine. He nodded as sleep crept over him. Fear, simmering at the base of his spine all day, seeped through his pores. He jerked awake and vomited.

Swallowing thickly, he knew he would relive this day a thousand times. Already disjointed images and sounds echoed in his head: a restless night around the fire with the men who had followed him. They shared a fish broth, a little wine. They had agreed to rendezvous or leave word of their circumstances at Hereford when it became safe to do so. He had prayed with them, asking God to spare him from killing his own brother or father. He shaved his head for the helmet. He slept badly on a rocky bed. At dawn, a trumpet blasted. In the drowsy chaos, he faced the chilly wind, consuming a dry biscuit soaked in wine as they marched.

"Who goes there?" a voice in the misty morning demanded.

Alaric touched his chest where his mother's crucifix hung beneath his quilted *aketon*. A trumpet blared.

"Whoa!" A pennon snapped.

"Have they come already?" queried a nervous knight.

When their forces reached the small rise near the village, Hastings, he donned his armor and strapped on his sword. Once mounted on his warhorse, his squire offered up his shield and lance.

"Advance!" The columns began moving.

Keep moving, Alaric thought, keep moving.

"*Arrêtez!* Stop!" With others of his company, he looked up the hill.

Harold's warriors, fully assembled, had the advantage, surprising Alaric and the others, clustering in disarray. Waves of doubt rolled through him as the sun rose, as banners fluttered in the October wind. His gaze searched for and found Harold's Wessex Dragon, and he recognized a few flags belonging to men he'd fought with, but he could not find his father's or brother's pennons among so many others.

"God's sword! They've many more than we," an awed voice quivered in French. Harold's spearmen stood ready to hurl their weapons at William's foot soldiers. Dogs barked, horses reared.

A bowshot away, thought Alaric, or three.

A deep, thundering rumble began as Harold's men beat their shields.

William's archers and crossbowmen loaded their weapons and paused. Harold's troops fused into a solid wall, shields clattered and slapped into place. Alaric swallowed as a cloud of arrows streaked across the sky. Dull drumming, punctuated by sudden screams as arrows hit the shield wall and pierced exposed limbs. Blots flew wildly, splattering flesh, denting helmets.

"Foot!" called the order. Voices roared as under cover of arrows, they moved into position and ran up the gentle slope until the final clash when shields slammed against shields.

"*Ut! Ut!*" Out, out, the English chanted.

"Press them!" the command. Men pushed against each other hacking, stabbing blindly, a writhing blood-spurting mass.

"They hold, still!"

"Lances!" Banners snapped.

"Let's go!" Alaric shouted. His unit galloped toward the wall sparkling with raised axes.

"Kill them! Kill them all!"

At the wall, he threw his lance at an unshielded face and wheeled his horse. A powerful blow struck his back. He drew his sword, then swung it, severing the arms raising an axe. Blood spurted over him. A large stone hit his chest, another grazed his head. Blinded, he wielded his sword side to side, clearing, slashing, one after another, barely missing the knight beside him. Trumpets blared conflicting orders. He shouted commands to his men and wrenched his weapon from a body. He turned his horse out of reach to sense the direction of the battle.

"Give no ground! Behind you!" He shouted. Gritting his teeth, he brought his sword down and crushed a helmet. He heard fresh knights join the assault as he turned his horse aside.

"Pull back! Pull back! This way!"

Horses neighed, some reared. Several stumbled and fell.

"Move!" he'd shouted. "Move!"

And Edo. Dear God, Edo had wheeled his horse away, turning his head back to meet Alaric's eye. The axe came from behind. Blood spewed from his mouth as he went down.

The axe! God's breath, the axe!

Alaric blinked the specter away and glanced across the field to the campfires. Black smoke from the torches shimmered against a pale coral sky. Lances with streamers and arrows quivered in the breeze, stuck at awkward angles, skewering men and horses. Chargers with flailing legs tried to rise from beneath dead or wounded soldiers, others stumbled about riderless, their reins trailing. The sickly sweet smell hung low to the ground. Women picked their way among the fallen. Those detailed to collect armor threw shields, swords, mail, and helmets into the small carts they rolled up and over those they stripped. Victors, overcome by battle sleep, nested in groups among the dead. Separated from his men, he could not find Roderick or the others.

Despite excruciating pain at his left shoulder, Alaric relaxed his grip on the enarmes and let the shield hang to his side from the guige strapped around his neck. He wiped his bloody sword on a handful of his horse's mane, and with difficulty sheathed his blade. He heard his name.

Turning, he saw Dreux atop his horse approaching at a slow walk. Bloodied, muddied, he reined in beside Alaric, head to tail, sword arm to sword arm. Dreux's eyes still glazed in battle-lust, reflected the horror, the terror, the death surrounding them. Alaric clasped a firm hand on Dreux's near arm and held him tight, feeling him whole. Alive. Dreux reached over and clamped his free hand on Alaric's arm—strong, solid, steady.

With a nod, they broke off.

"Your . . ." Dreux's voice cracked, and he began again. "Your father? Rannulf?"

Alaric shook his head. He glanced over the field where they might lie dead or dying.

Behind him, Duke William hailed them. Alaric reined his horse around to greet William, and Bishop Odo.

"The kingdom is mine, is it not, Alaric?" Duke William asked.

"It's the first battle," Alaric answered, looking around, not knowing how many more battles like this they would face.

William chuckled grimly. "My cousin is a prudent man, is he not Odo?"

"Prudent? Anything but!" Bishop Odo turned in his saddle and shoved his club into its girdle. "You should have seen him, Brother. He fought like Odin's own—a black wolf, snarling and biting as if feasting on his prey."

"Is that right, *Black Wolf*?" the duke said, appraising Alaric.

"My saints!" Odo grinned. "I've never seen anything like it. You saved my life, Alaric." He shuddered. "The battle axe sliced through a man and his horse right next to me. I would have been next if *Black Wolf* had not come in for the kill."

Alaric met William's eyes, remembering he'd also blunted a sword aimed at William's head.

"And Dreux," Odo said, "led the feint, which turned the battle." He gestured to Alaric and Dreux. "These men served you well this day."

William smiled. "Remind me when I am crowned to enfeoff my most distinguished warriors," he said, giving Alaric and Dreux a grand compliment and the promise of land. "But our work is not yet done," he continued. "Odo, Dreux, send your companies to the nearby manors and hamlets. Burn them to prevent Harold's remaining forces from sheltering or regrouping for a night attack. Confiscate the food and anything of value the enemy can use. Take hostages, men of rank or their kin."

Alaric and Dreux exchanged glances. *Go with care*, Alaric thought.

"Come, Black Wolf. We must find Harold," William said. "He fell up there." The duke swept his gaze toward a pile of bodies.

Alaric spotted Malet waving at them. "There," he pointed.

They climbed the hill where the ground seemed alive for the large mound of moaning, writhing bodies. Malet, looking far older than his fifty-some years, knelt beside a mass of flesh, akin to a flayed haunch of boar.

Harold's head, without a nose, lay nearly severed. Among his dismembered limbs, a leg was missing, and a deep gouge marked where his manhood had been. Alaric and Malet exchanged dazed glances. Someone had mutilated an *anointed* king, God's chosen majesty.

Malet explained. "Edith searching . . . . My men took her back to Hastings."

Duke William grunted and looked over the battlefield. Alaric followed his gaze seeing the bodies—English, Normans, and others, brave men all, had fallen this day, and many others would die tonight or the next. William turned to Malet and Alaric. "Once, you both served Harold. Bury him," he ordered curtly. "Honor him. As a great *warrior*, a worthy adversary."

Not as king, Alaric noted, catching Malet's eye.

"I will speak to Edith," the duke said. "It was a cruel fate for her to find him so."

After William and his men left, Alaric asked in Saxon, "Who would do this?"

"Eustace did it," Malet answered in French. "I saw him and others I cannot now recall. They'd dismounted and . . ."

Alaric recalled the blood pouring from Eustace's nose and ears after taking a hard blow. "It is sacrilegious to mutilate a king, anointed and consecrated by the Church."

"Silence!" Malet ordered in Saxon, grabbing Alaric's arm and looking around to see if anyone had overheard. "We will never acknowledge Harold's reign. He usurped the throne. To William and the Pope, he was a lowly ruffian, a commoner who broke a sacred oath—a heinous crime deserving a heinous punishment. Take care with your words, lest others think you loyal to Harold instead of William."

Alaric nodded.

Malet crouched beside the remains of a man he had respected and honored. His shoulders stooped, his head swayed slowly from side to side.

"I'll get my men to help," Alaric said, a hand on Malet's shoulder. He scanned the field and saw Eustace's man, Brian *le dogue* Dubec. He sat atop his horse with his helmet off, laughing with his companion amid the dead and dying.

The sky glowed a pale salmon as Dreux and fifty knights rode into a nearby village and found it almost completely deserted. The few who remained lay bleeding in the streets or hobbled away in flight. Dreux dispatched his troops to begin firing the cottages. He and a handful of men walked their horses through the open gate of a compound enclosing a large, well-built house, a tower, and outbuildings marking a thegn's manor. Others had been here before him, as evident by the people slaughtered in the courtyard, the open hall doors, and the scattered goods dropped by fleeing looters.

He reined his horse around the remains of a woman distinguishable from her rich clothing as the manor's lady, killed—perhaps worse. He and his men dismounted and, with swords drawn, entered the hall. There, they discovered a cowering servant who could not answer their questions spoken in French. His men began grabbing plates, candleholders, weapons, and anything they could find. Others emptied chests, sliced through screens, overturned pots looking for coins and jewels.

Searching the loft, Dreux burst through the door onto a lookout deck ahead of his men and stopped, blocking his men with one arm. A young woman stood gazing at the field as if mesmerized by something in the distance. She did not turn her head to look at them. The wind pressed her tunic against her small body and teased her uncovered brown hair.

"A tasty morsel, this one," snorted one of his men, moving against Dreux's shoulder to reach her. Dreux shoved him into the others.

"Mine," he growled, daring them to contradict him.

They grumbled and, as one, turned and left him alone with her.

From three strides away, Dreux studied her expression and wondered what she contemplated.

"Are you cold?" he asked, his Saxon clumsy.

As if the gentleness of his voice surprised her, she turned to him. "No," she said.

Her hazel eyes glowed from the last rays of the sun blushing her face. Several shades of red and gold sparkled through her hair as the wind blew a loose strand across her cheek, across perfect, delicate skin, on a face as innocent as a child's, as wary, knowing, and proud as a woman's. A noblewoman, he thought, noting the gold and amethyst necklace, the garnets on her jeweled belt, and the elaborate gold brooch clasping her mantle.

"I'll take you with me," he said, informed by her gaze of the gore splattered over his body and face. "You'll be fed, protected, and when it is decided, ransomed to your family."

"My family has fallen this day," she said quietly. "I am your slave now, to sell or use as you wish." She turned again to look out at the valley as if seeing it for the last time.

"By English law, yes," Dreux said. "Not by Norman law." He sheathed his sword and stepped beside her. She stood no higher than his chest, yet she did not shrink away from him. "What do they call you?" he asked.

"Clare. Clare of Wolenbroth."

"Come, Clare. This place is to be torched."

"May I stay here?"

"And burn in the funeral pyre of your ancestors? No, little one," he said. Taking her arm gently, he led her down to the ransacked hall and issued orders to his men.

Leaving the hall, she cried out and tried to reach the dead noblewoman. Dreux pulled her away and lifted her atop his horse. Mounting behind, he blocked her view, and when she turned to see, he pulled her against his chest and spurred his horse out of the compound.

"What happened here?" Dreux shouted to a villager, sweeping his arm toward the hall.

The villager said soldiers from the battle reported that Clare's father, the thegn, and all her brothers were killed. Her two older sisters had escaped with the retreating warriors, leaving Clare's mother to protect their home from looters. The villager refused to say if the men who dragged her into the courtyard and cut her to pieces were English or Normans, soldiers or townsmen.

"She sent me to the loft," Clare said, choking on her words.

"She saved you," Dreux said, his head bent to hers. "I shall have her buried properly in consecrated soil." He found the priest, tossed him a few coins for the burial, and left the flaming village, taking Clare with him.

Chapter Six

During the weeks following Hastings, William waited for the English to surrender. To encourage them, he sent troops out to plunder the villages east and west along the southern coast.

One cold November morning, the day after St Martin's day, Malet and his troops joined Alaric's company and brought stunning news. Of the nearly four thousand warriors who had fought with Duke William about a third had died at Hastings. Alaric had lost nine, including Edo, whose body Gilbert had found. Johan and two others were missing. "Harold lost as many?"

"Perhaps fewer. They would have held the day had they not broken ranks."

Alaric nodded, remembering how William's forces had become discouraged, how Dreux's feint and chase finally opened the English to slaughter.

"There is more," Malet said. "Two of Matilda's ships landed at Romney instead of Pevensey. The villagers slaughtered everyone on board. William burned the village to the ground and killed every man, woman, and child he found there."

Alaric's stomach clenched. During his training years, he'd seen William unleash his savagery against small, unimportant Norman villages, which could ill defend themselves. He terrified his opponents by showing boundless brutality. He would have done far worse to the villagers who destroyed his wife's ships.

"And?" Alaric asked, knowing the English would begin to capitulate.

"Dover and Canterbury surrendered."

Alaric raised his eyebrows. He'd expected Canterbury to put up a fight. It annoyed him that the English had not offered greater resistance. "London?"

"Not yet. The Witan named Edgar the Atheling king."

"He's barely fourteen winters," Alaric said, recalling the boy he'd seen once. The last heir to the Wessex royal house had no chance against William. "The Witan is stalling for time."

"Yes," Malet said. "William will force them. He is leading the army around London to isolate it and sends small companies to assault the surrounding villages. We are to remain in the south."

Alaric recognized Malet's set expression. Both had lived in this land. They knew the people, their customs, and the terrain. They had chosen William over Harold, and they dreaded the days to come.

They entered Eashing that afternoon. The day before, a company of knights had slaughtered all the oxen, stolen the pigs and chickens, and taken all the grain and loot they could carry before burning the village to the ground.

Riding through the charred ruins, Alaric saw only a handful of listless people. One woman, in torn clothing, with a bloodied face, wailed. She pulled at her hair and rocked back and forth on her knees before the still smoking remains of the church. Alaric sent Gilbert the Monkman to question her.

"She won't speak," Gilbert said.

"Our beloved homeland is smoldering, Alaric," Malet said in Saxon, looking around in disgust. "Does it matter she does not speak?"

"No," Alaric said. No one would be punished for these acts, for they obeyed William's orders to harass the countryside. The occupation had just begun. In a matter of days, he and his men might very well do the same. Still, he could not fight the rage he felt for the slow hunger that would haunt the people this winter.

He knew this hamlet. It belonged to his brother's wife, Leota.

He and Rannulf had ridden here once to see if the old hill fort could be used. Alaric still did not know if brother or father had been at Hastings. It would be weeks before he could get a message to them at Hereford.

"Alaric," Roderick, his second-in-command, said with a strangled voice as lightning flashed in the darkening sky.

"Yes?" He saw Roderick's blanched face and followed his gaze to the small cemetery beside the smoldering church. Foreboding crept up his spine. Leota's nurse, Goda, the crone who had hated Rannulf, who had begged Leota not to marry him, sat atop one of the burial slabs, staring at the ground.

Alaric and Roderick dismounted and approached her. A clap of thunder crashed over his words. "Goda," he said. "Goda!" He shook her shoulder, commanding her attention. The lingering rumble stilled the air.

For a moment, her eyes blinked and when she saw him, she flinched, and covered her face. Then, as if recognizing him, she gave him a slow, toothless grin, and began to hum.

"Goda, what are you doing here?" he asked in Saxon, knowing Leota never went anywhere without her.

She shook her head back and forth vigorously as if trying to keep the sounds away. She stopped, her head bowed. Her shoulders began to shake, and Alaric put his hand on her arm in comfort. She lifted her face and cackled, squinting at him. He recoiled from her breath.

"Die, death, death, I say," she sniffed. "Wed and bed, and live you'll nay." Flicking her hands at Alaric, she said, "Away you beast, this day you feast, upon your own you dine and wine, upon your blood, you raise a shrine." She cackled again, clapped her hands and buried them in her skirts between her knees. She then grinned at Alaric and rocked back and forth. She pointed her nose at the charred ruins. "All, Normans, villagers, done by Normans torched for fun."

"You make no sense. Is Leota here, you old witch?"

She looked at him coldly. "Aye, Leota, the babe, your brother too. And Simeon, his wife, that old fool."

"What? Where are they, Goda, where?" Alaric growled, pulling her from the slab and shaking her hard.

She raised her arm and pointed a short, blunted finger to the church. Without another word, she glared at Alaric and twisted her mouth into a sneer.

Alaric staggered toward the church and pushed himself through the entrance still standing. He paused, bracing his bare hand on the hot stone. Ignoring the lingering heat, the smoke, and the smell of charred flesh wafting against his face, he stepped into the amorphous mass. An old man raked through the embers. Alaric searched among the shrunken, piled bodies still smoldering in the ashes. He could not tell men from women, although he could distinguish a blackened grimace, clawed hands, lumps of iron, part of a mail coat fused into a blackened body. His brother? His father?

He slowly dropped to one knee. His body trembled. His ears roared with the echo of one word: *no, no, no, no. No!* Dead? *No!* He remembered his family alive: his father clasping his arm in farewell, his mother holding back tears, his brother asking him to protect his pregnant wife. Looking at the twisted shapes huddled together, his gaze rested on one stiffened figure until he realized it crouched protectively over a charred infant.

Agony pierced him, stealing his breath. He pressed the heel of his palm on the searing mail rings to stop an anguished howl struggling for release. As the metal rings branded him, he hid the pain along with grief, his helplessness. His emptiness. A sudden gust of wind swirled the ashes and Alaric remembered the merciless irony of Leota's words: *May the wind blow your ashes away.*

The old villager related that Harold had sent Alaric's family to Eashing in the summer. Rannulf had ruled as thegn, Leota's son had been born, and together with Simeon and Julienne, all had lived in peace until yesterday. William's men had herded them and the villagers into the church and torched it. All but those who'd fled had perished.

Malet sent Alaric and his company back to their encampment and vowed to bury Alaric's family. As Alaric approached the field of tents, three dozen knights sallied forth to harass other villages. Alaric watched, coolly. *Who killed my family? How exactly will I avenge their deaths?*

Chapter Seven

For a knight in the king's elite service," Dreux said to Alaric, "you look sullen. Are you abstaining from women and drink?" he teased.

"Not likely," Alaric said, lifting his drink and saluting the noble-women smiling at him from across King's Hall.

The previous day, on Christmas, William, duke of Normandie, had been crowned. This morning, Alaric, Dreux, and twenty others were knighted, initiated into the king's royal order. All received enfeoffments, small land grants, to support their knight's service, and new swords inscribed, *in nomine domini*. Alaric now shared the bottom rung of the new Norman aristocracy with hundreds of others, clinging with slippery grips, clutching with toes, and clawing over each other for the next. He had not hoped for so much when he'd first joined William's venture. But now, despite the coronation festivities, it all seemed rather . . . empty.

"Is Blackwolf drunk?" Richard de Rupierre, asked, stumbling into Dreux.

"Sober enough to crush your skull," Alaric said by way of greeting.

"Ha!" Richard drained his cup and grabbed a jug from a passing servant. "I pray William feeds you to the hounds one day," he snarled.

Burly and blunt, with pale brown hair, Richard reminded Alaric of an ox. Thor's hammer, easily mistaken for a cross, marked the back of his sword hand. He was a year older than Alaric, a third son of an undistinguished family seeking his fortune in William's kingdom. They'd met in Rouen, where they parried insults instead of swords. At Hastings, Richard's unbridled ferocity had won Alaric's respect. With Dreux, Richard served the king's brother, Bishop Odo.

"Drink up," Richard said, filling everyone's cup. "We've won the kingdom."

"Total victory!" Dreux concurred.

Alaric looked into his cup and gave it a swirl. He knew better. Just a week ago, when he'd approached the River Fleet to enter London, he smelled the heads staked along Lud's Gate and on the hill. The townspeople, he heard, had tried to keep William out, and London's soldiers had fought so fiercely the river ran red. Alaric had battled with the English. He knew their tenacity. They were not defeated.

Still, looking at the crowd, he understood why others thought so. Most of the English nobility had fallen at Hastings. Harold's four brothers, the only men trained and capable of mounting resistance, were all dead. Harold's sons had fled. Nobles who had survived the battle had scattered to the woodlands. Perhaps they hoped to organize a rebellion among the freemen of substance.

"Jesu," Richard said, "those longhaired, bearded English look like dim-witted oafs, overdressed and uncultured."

Alaric rotated his left shoulder, injured at Hastings, and measured the earls and thegns who had not fought against William. Easily distinguished from shorn and shaved Normans, they wore their traditional garments of interwoven fine wool and gold, and about their necks hung thick, silver chains with pendants of carved wild-ox horns decorated with gems. The most prominent, the earls of Mercia and Northumbria embodied the highest-ranking nobles around whom disaffected English would gather.

"Each gave William their oaths and hostages," Alaric said.

Richard snickered. "For their lives. He'll let them keep their titles and lands as long as they remain his honored *guests*."

Biding their time, Alaric thought, watching them circulate King's Hall, ignoring each other as if afraid to be seen together, and moving like stiff-legged mules, always accompanied by William's men as if leashed.

Alaric's attention shifted to Guillaume d'Évreux, cutting through the crowd toward him. His richly embroidered attire reminded Alaric that Guillaume would inherit his father's title and all the land and wealth. If Alaric's father had been legitimate, Alaric would be the heir to Évreux. Both knew it. As boys, they'd exchanged blows over it.

"Please accept my lauds, Cousin," Guillaume said upon his arrival.

Alaric wondered if having deigned to cross the room and acknowledge him accounted for Guillaume's embarrassed look. He smiled, burying the animosity between them. "Thank you, Guillaume."

"I hope you understand your position, Alaric. May I speak to you as your cousin and hopefully your friend?"

"Go on."

"Your reputation since Hastings has grown." Guillaume looked across the room, his hands clasped behind his back as he rocked on the balls of his feet. "Even though they are small estates, William has been quick to reward you, and . . . more generously than anyone else."

Guillaume paused. "Without sounding covetous, I and others who paid for William's venture have yet to receive any estates."

Richard snorted and Dreux nodded. Alaric knew that Guillaume had given William eighty new and fully outfitted ships for the crossing. A fortune. Until Guillaume mentioned it, Alaric had not realized the king had so generously acknowledged him.

"Be careful. Enemies abound," Guillaume said cautiously.

"I appreciate the advice," Alaric said, seeing his cousin's shoulders relax.

"I am sorry about your family. Come to Évreux when you can." Guillaume clasped Alaric's arm and walked away.

"He is right," Malet said, who had joined Alaric and his companions. "About enemies. They are everywhere. In this very hall. As fortunes change, so do loyalties."

Alaric looked around the hall. At one end, William wore his bejeweled crown and a lavish scarlet tunic trimmed in gold braid. He appeared wholly absorbed in discussion with the men of his inner circle, his own brothers, his prelates, his best and most loyal men, including the Breton, Count Alain le Roux—a man whose acrimony Alaric had won. Throughout, he saw William's followers, noblemen who had come from Flanders, from Sicily, Picardy, and beyond, all adorned in their finest attire, all waiting like gulls for the king to toss them a morsel.

Laughter drew Alaric's attention to Count Eustace de Boulogne, the man who had challenged his loyalty on the beach at Pevensey. At Hastings, an axeman had knocked Eustace from his horse with a near-deadly blow. Now, apparently recovered from his injury, the count glided among the noble personages with a skill few possessed, gregarious and affable, with a smile, a quick laugh. His bald head reflected torchlight, and unlike Normans, who preferred clean-shaven faces, he wore a conspicuous mustache.

"Ah, the *kingmaker*," Malet said, the word ladened with fury.

"Who, Eustace?" Dreux asked.

"Yes, as his minions call him. They claim he gave William the crown. But have no doubt that he would have claimed the throne for his son had he sired a boy on King Edward's sister."

"Thank God," Richard said. "I've loathed the coward since Hastings, when he told William to concede."

Alaric recalled the long day of exhausting, bitter combat, the late afternoon, the desolate feeling as Eustace quit the field and took his men with him. Yet, when the battle shifted, Eustace returned with great pomp. And chopped Harold to bits.

Watching the count, Alaric flexed his shoulder again. He would not have fought for him had he sought the crown. As if hearing his thought, Eustace met his gaze and began shouldering through the crowd towards him.

"God's teeth!" Malet said. "I've no stomach for him."

"Nor have I," Richard said, leaving with Malet.

"You?" Alaric asked Dreux.

"I've a woman to woo." Dreux slapped him on the back and departed.

Alaric watched Eustace approach, wondering if the man's infectious laughter and robust frivolity disguised a keen, appraising mind. Anyone might have thought him a mere jongleur, were it not for his clothing, dazzling in gold and jewels, and the apparent influence he wielded as others gravitated to him, like sinners seeking dispensation.

Lifting his drinking bowl, Alaric offered a casual salute to Eustace's man, Brian Dubec, a fellow warrior in liege to a lord, but received no acknowledgement even when they presented themselves before him.

"Greetings, Alaric of Ewyas, son of Simeon. You proved yourself a fine soldier at Hastings," Eustace said smoothly.

"My lord," Alaric said. "Others fought as well."

"Modesty does you no justice. You are a bloodthirsty killer, and my most hardened soldiers are terrified of you. Isn't that so, Brian?" Dubec did not answer.

Alaric disliked Eustace's dubious compliment given at the expense of his captain.

"I'm impressed," Eustace said, "that the king gave you the task of burying Harold."

"I merely assisted Malet," said Alaric. Together they had carefully, reverently, scraped Harold's body from the battlefield. Even in death, Harold was an *anointed* king, chosen and blessed by God to rule. Alaric studied Eustace, thinking that only a desperate, depraved man would profane a king's sacred body. There was killing, and there was maiming. There was war, and there was murder.

"Harold's corpse had been mutilated—beyond mere battle wounds."

"Harold deserved his doom," Eustace replied.

"Some say he was a king."

"He was a commoner with no royal blood. Call him usurper, earl, villein—debt canceled."

"Debt?"

"His villagers at Dover insulted me."

Alaric frowned.

"Yes," Eustace said. "As I recall, your father served under Osbern the Pentecost near Wales."

"Yes," Alaric answered, unsure what that had to do with Dover.

"Osbern. A good and loyal friend," Eustace said. "Do you remember when he left Ewyas?"

"Vaguely. I was a boy," Alaric said.

At Eustace's gesture, his man stepped away, and they sat on a nearby bench.

"Years ago," Eustace said, "I visited my brother-in-marriage, King Edward. As I journeyed home, I stopped in Dover for the night. The villagers attacked my retinue and me. After defending ourselves, we informed the king of our ill-treatment. Since Dover belonged to Earl Godwin, the king ordered him to punish the villagers for abusing his sister's husband. Godwin, urged by his son Harold, refused, saying he would not punish villagers for defending themselves against raiding foreigners!"

The count swept his bejeweled hand over his smooth head and continued. "Edward floundered with indecision. Osbern, however, loudly charged Godwin and his sons with treason for disobeying Edward's order. With support from my French-speaking comrades in Edward's court, the king agreed. He exiled the entire Godwin family, including the queen, and seized all their land and possessions."

Eustace sipped his drink. "Normans controlled all the riches of Wessex. New taxes, new laws. We seized Godwin's wealth—"

"Godwin came back in less than a year," Alaric said.

"Yes. Edward marched to battle, and found himself surrounded. His men would not fight the Godwins. He reinstated the family and outlawed French-speaking foreigners. Across the land Harold hunted and murdered my allies for bounty."

Now, Alaric understood why riders had come to Ewyas, urging them to flee, and why Harold had not given Osbern five grace days.

"Norman heads," Alaric said, "men, women, and children were spiked at town gates throughout the kingdom."

"Not all. Harold spared you and your family. He dubbed your father, Simeon . . . *the Brave*, and sent him to Hereford where he served my stepson. It must have galled him."

"Galled who? My father? Or your stepson, Ralf the Timid?" It annoyed Alaric that this count knew so much about his family.

"No matter now," Eustace said, erasing the past with a cheerful smile. "I gave William ships, gold, and arms. William's reward will cancel Harold's injury to me completely." He glanced around the hall and chuckled. "But, I must say that after fifteen years, revenge tastes like fine wine."

"That's a long time to hold ill feelings," Alaric said.

Eustace turned to Alaric, all traces of the fool gone. "I never forget. Never." His gaze cut deeply into Alaric. "Until I receive full reparations." He laughed suddenly.

"Is revenge the reason you joined William's venture?"

"My dear boy!" Eustace shook his head. "The only reason I came on the maiden voyage was to best Harold. But like any honest man, I joined for the returns, my boy, the riches." He waved his arm as if sweeping from north to south. "While the rest of Christendom suffers from frequent famines, this land is lush. Ripe for the picking."

"That is one way to look at it," Alaric said.

"How do you see it?" Eustace stroked a thumb along his mustache.

"I think William will strengthen and unify the kingdom."

"Do you believe in fairies as well?"

The mockery startled Alaric. "You doubt William can protect his kingdom?"

Eustace laughed. "William can protect Englelond from everything but the Normans, and Normans will destroy her. This land is William's safeguard. It will distract young, highly trained killers—like you—who might otherwise get bored, restless, and take it upon themselves to disrupt William's duchy or join his rival, the king of Francia. It is safer to send all these second and third sons over here and isolate them on this island. Let them plunder, rape, and murder, far from Rouen, I say."

"The king has forbidden rape," Alaric said.

"William will never stop his followers from exercising a victor's rights."

Alaric remained silent. He disliked Eustace more each moment.

"After raping the kingdom," Eustace continued, "Normans will wring her dry. Revenues will feed and enrich we who paid for the invasion." Turning to Alaric, he said, "You disapprove. Do you cling to some exalted purpose? Like *honor* or *glory*, praised in ancient tales?" Eustace grunted. "Actually," he leaned toward Alaric conspiratorially, "I, too, would sacrifice my daughter for a favorable wind."

Alaric, confused by the reference, said, "I am only a warrior in service to the king."

"Truly? When you subdue the English, as I am sure you will, what reward would you seek?"

"No more that what the king has given me. The honor of serving him and enough revenue to support my knight's service."

"A fool like your father, I see." Eustace shook his head. "I suppose you think your father an *honorable* man."

Alaric checked his sudden urge to grab the man's throat for mocking his father. His violence would discredit Simeon and destroy William's trust. Was that Eustace's intention? He took a breath to calm his fury. "Simeon honored his vows."

"Do you?"

Alaric did not know how to answer that question.

"Surely you see the opportunities here. You have usurped all of William's closest supporters by gaining the king's confidence, yet you pretend to have no ambitions! Life, Alaric son of Simeon, is about influence, domination, and power."

"Is it?"

"Yes." Eustace said, his piercing gaze on Alaric. "I take great pleasure in mastering men and events, in bending men to my will. I can control a man's existence, his sleeping hours, his dawns and dusks, his generations to come, and his eternal life. I assure you there are fewer joys than influencing others to achieve my aims. That is why those wanting crowns seek me out."

"Isn't such power given by God?" Alaric asked.

"God doesn't give power," Eustace said. "It exists for men to seize as William has."

Is this true? Alaric wondered. William had sent his envoys to Rome as soon as he'd learned of Harold's coronation. Had he received the papal banner because he had swifter couriers than had Harold?

"Would you, son of Simeon, run from such potency—or grasp it?" Eustace asked. "Mastery over people and events is seductive, and like fine nectar, it sharpens the mind and makes you want more. I wonder what you would do to experience such pleasure."

"Such mastery demands deliberation and care, not pleasure," Alaric said.

Eustace smiled. "You do not yet understand." He rose and nodded to a group of nobles across the room who were motioning him to join them. "Perhaps, one day, I shall give you a demonstration." With Dubec following behind, Eustace walked toward the men who opened their circle to greet him.

Alaric watched the count address his admirers. The group exploded in laughter, and several nobles slapped him on the back. Alaric glanced down at his empty bowl and remembered when he and his father faced Harold, raising his sword for the death blow. The hostility between the Normans and the English had blossomed with the Dover incident. Harold would never have relinquished the throne to a Norman, especially after the degradation brought about by Eustace de Boulogne and his Norman puppets like Osbern the Pentecost.

How many lives had Eustace changed in Dover? His actions made armed conflict between Harold and William inevitable. Did he care? No. Eustace passed through life like a *trouveur*, singing his songs while behind him the earth trembled, buildings collapsed, dust and smoke rose, fire and death ranged, and still he walked on, waving a hand, skipping to his merry tune.

Alaric relaxed his jaw, realizing how tense he'd become talking with Eustace. He gazed at the sculpted wooden columns, the animals painted on plastered walls, and shuddered. God help me avoid further notice from Count Eustace de Boulogne.

Chapter Eight

As Alaric conversed with Eustace, Dreux worked his way through the crowd until he finally escaped the festivities in King's Hall. Now, eager to see Clare, he hurried to his quarters. Torches lighted the path. On the courtyard walls, he saw sentries, alert and watching, a few servants ran between buildings. Beside the palace, he saw a glow coming from the abbey and heard the resonant chants of solemn prayers.

Since October, Clare of Wolenbroth had been his captive. His claim assured no other man would touch her lest they face his sword. Under his protection, but with no family to ransom her, she began a new life more servant than honored hostage.

In the weeks before London accepted William's victory, Clare, along with cooks, baggage tenders, farriers, and others, moved with Dreux's company from village to village, from one confiscated manor to another as the Normans encircled the town.

Between his sorties, Dreux looked for her among the other captives. He saw her struggle to carry heavy pails sloshing with chamberpot muck. He noticed her hands became red, rough, and cracked from washing clothes in icy water. He saw her remain calm when people tripped her on purpose or pushed her into a wall. Seemingly reconciled to her fate, her acceptance provoked others to taunt her. "Here, you, the English Princess, take this pig fat to the bridler."

Once, Dreux had observed a prominent Mercian noble approach her. Recognition and elation filled her face as he spoke softly to her. She nodded and bowed her head. The man touched her shoulder. A few more words passed between them, and she left as the noble watched her, his own lips pressed together in apparent fury. After that encounter, Clare seemed even quieter than usual.

Dreux hoped to change her status tonight. He had ordered his servants to have Clare bathed, clothed in fine garments, and delivered to his quarters. From the moment he met her, he'd intended to bed her. But he eschewed the victor's right to plunder, pillage, and rape allowed until the Witan capitulated. As king, William now forbade those acts and made clear his disapproval of fornication. Although Dreux risked censure by making Clare his mistress, he needed to establish her indisputable position until he obtained William's permission to marry her.

He entered his quarters, warmed by a large brazier, and saw her wearing a soft woolen cotte, her hair brushed out and hanging loose down her back. She took his breath away.

Unable to speak, Dreux pulled off his mantle and crossed the room. He reached for her.

She put a hand on his chest and bowed her head. "My lord, please. There is no need to frighten me."

He eased his hold and stepped back. Putting a finger on her chin, he raised her face. He kissed the tears welling in her eyes and pulled her gently against his chest with a deep sigh. The Normans had forced English subjugation with brutish force, and more violence would follow. Despite his twenty-four winters, he felt weary, and . . . old.

"Can you find peace with me, though you are no longer a noblewoman?"

"I would rather be enslaved and have my family alive than to be a noblewoman with them all dead. It gives me hope to think my sisters may still live. God willing, I may see them again someday."

He took her tenderly. Neither expectation nor experience had prepared him for such a gift. In the burst of her first awakening, something profound and fragile happened to him. He opened his heart. Slowly, like wax poured into a mold, she filled all the crevices he had not known were empty.

The next morning, armed guards flanked Alaric and Dreux, and escorted them to the king's council chamber. Dreux's furrowed brow sharpened Alaric's apprehension. Had Dreux's liaison with Clare become known? Would it warrant such an abrupt summons? They entered a brightly lit chamber animated by angry shouts, whispered discussions, and wayward laughter among William's inner circle of advisors—closed to all but the king's intimates.

Alaric and Dreux waited, their heads bowed. From mumbled words, Alaric heard his name, paired with others: "Sympathizer . . . untrustworthy . . . ." Fury stiffened his spine. The loudest voice belonged to Count Alain le Roux of Brittany, known to the English as Alan the Red. Alaric called him Rufus, a name which irked the count. The night before Hastings, Rufus had mocked Harold and his forces. Alaric, who had fought with Harold, challenged the count's faulty assumptions and bad orders. Rufus told his men to ignore Alaric's inferior counsel. The next day, Rufus lost nearly half of his troops, and most of the survivors had openly disobeyed him to follow Alaric's tack. Since Hastings, Alaric had rarely seen the Breton, yet at each encounter, Rufus bristled and showered Alaric with loathing, especially after discovering they, like everyone close to William, were kinsmen. In recent weeks, le Roux's hostility had greater consequences, for he had pushed his own brothers out of the king's inner circle. Now, Rufus, William's chief advisor, accompanied the king everywhere—even to the privy, and his disparaging comments—and accusations—went directly into the king's ear.

"Quiet!" the king bellowed.

Alaric's alarm grew at the simmering silence. He felt the king's eyes bore into the top of his head, and his throat became dry. The fire crackled and snapped like breaking ice.

"Come forward, Knights!" William said.

As he and Dreux approached the advisors, Alaric felt them measuring him. Malet avoided his eyes. Several nobles circled behind him as if positioning themselves to lunge.

The king occupied the head of a long, narrow table, flanked by an English bishop and the king's youngest brother, Robert de Mortain. Behind them hung a red tapestry woven with the golden lions of Normandie brought over by a confident William.

The king studied Dreux for a long moment before turning his fiery gaze on Alaric. "Speak Odo."

The king's brother stepped beside Alaric, introduced him and Dreux to the council, and said, "The king's warriors have been given a much-needed rest until the Epiphany. The crown is William's. The challenge will be to hold it. You have been summoned because you men will take command of the king's forces."

Alaric blinked. Command? Surely, he had not heard correctly.

"God's breath!" le Roux cursed. "This is a mistake!"

"Leave it!" the king snapped.

Le Roux glared darkly at Alaric.

"We're here," Odo continued, "to decide how these troops will be deployed."

Dreux bowed, "We are honored."

"No honor is intended!" William's blunt statement hung in the chamber. He tested the sharpness of his dagger's blade with his thumb. After drawing blood, William continued. "I've trained you and know what you can do. You're both young enough—and hungry enough—to tame the land."

The king motioned them to approach the table. Dreux sat down. Alaric remained standing between Odo and the king's seneschal, Guillaume fitz Osbern.

"Some of our compeers," Odo said, "believe the king's choice of senior commanders foolish. Neither one of you has much experience in taking and holding the land. But those of us who are older and more experienced in these matters, have competing responsibilities in Normandie."

"Exactly," Robert de Mortain said. "Splitting our command would risk the kingdom to protect the duchy."

"This action," le Roux said, "will jeopardize your victory, my lord! De Ville, yes, but . . . ?" he gestured toward Alaric.

To Alaric, the king said, "You and your men know the terrain and the people—"

"As does Malet," le Roux injected.

"Malet knows the Witan, the treasury, how the kingdom is administered. He is needed at court. Besides, Malet would not know a Welshman if one kissed him. No offense, friend," the king said to Malet.

"True enough," Malet chuckled, stroking his upper lip. "I am a courtier, barely a soldier, and I know nothing of building timber forts as does Alaric."

The king nodded his agreement and directed his words to Alaric. "You've fought with the English against the Welsh. You know how they think, the countryside, and where they might launch attacks."

"—And *that* knowledge," le Roux interrupted, "can be used against you!" He raised his hands to forestall interruption. "Today, you establish two powerful, private armies, and you give one of these legions to your kinsman. But he has questionable loyalties. He can turn his knowledge against you, and now he will have the military might to strengthen your enemies."

William rose slowly. Robert de Mortain leaned away from his brother. "There are no *private* forces!" William drove his dagger into the table, just missing the hand of the bishop sitting beside him. The bishop shrieked and fainted. William wrenched his knife from the oak and ordered the guards to remove the overcome prelate.

Glaring at Alaric and Dreux, he said, "The men deployed under your command belong to *me*. Turn them against the king and . . . Need I discuss consequences?"

Alaric shook his head. The consequences would be worse than death.

"Do you stand with my decision?" William asked le Roux, fingering his dagger.

The Breton exhaled his surrender and sat down.

William grunted, reclaiming his seat. "Tell us about the western border."

Alaric glanced at the suspicious faces watching him. Except for Malet, no one else in the room had much knowledge of the land beyond Wessex. He began by explaining what he had learned on his reconnaissance before the invasion. He told them about the villages along the southern coast, and where Normans might encounter English raiders. He estimated the numbers and proficiency of the remaining enemy forces, told them which villages might be harder to subdue, and which harbors and shipping lanes were still open. He answered succinctly every question asked about the western land bordered by Wales.

Aggressively, le Roux shoved a wooden bowl of sand to the center of the table, spewing the contents over its sides. Accepting the challenge, Alaric moved around the table as the others made room for him. He spread more sand over the boards and marked out a crude map. "Here the Welsh mountains, the River Severn, Herefordshire." He marked the ancient hunting tracks and surmised the fleeing English would use the same. "The Welsh will begin raiding as soon as the weather permits, but inconsistently. Deadly raids will begin after the vernal equinox."

After clearing the marks, he drew a jagged line representing The Spine, the mountain chain running north and south. He sketched in the Danelaw, the Roman roads converging at London, and a few less frequently traveled roads bandits preferred. In answer to the king's questions, he explained the strategic importance of villages at major crossroads or rivers. Malet nodded his concurrence.

Alaric pointed out the sites needed for trade or resources such as the salt ponds, the woodlands, the farmlands, and navigable waterways. He told of the harsh and rugged conditions of the frontier land north of the Danelaw. He told them about York, an old Viking kingdom, the rich trading markets, annual raids, and that King Edward could not keep the Yorkshire or Northumbrian thegns loyal to him.

The discussion moved on to the regions where Alaric knew little. Malet took over and explained the Humber, the fens, the coastal areas frequently attacked by Danes and Norsemen, the traditional lines of allegiance, the reputed thegns, who had fallen at Stamford Bridge or Hastings, and about those yet to submit.

The Council discussed the advantages and disadvantages of keeping a standing force ready to move at a moment's notice, where such a force could be located—and fed. Everyone dove into the discussion except Alaric, who listened to the others.

"Small groups of knights," William said, "posted in well-placed castles would forestall the formation of a large enemy force."

Alaric inwardly agreed.

"Mounted contingents," William said, "could move into and get out of an area quickly."

"Taxes and land disputes can be administered from the castles, too," Malet supposed. "It would be easier to pay for the mercenaries if each castellan had the responsibility of feeding and paying for his own men. Local revenues instead of the king's coffers. And supply lines to the frontier could remain open if garrisons were posted to defend the roads."

"Excellent," William agreed. "We will plant tower fortresses first along the borders as we did in Normandie," William said, gesturing to Alaric.

"Here," Alaric said, differentiating the size of the garrison and the area's importance with coins. "Here," three coins at the mouth of the River Severn, two at Hereford, single coins along the Welsh border. Alaric felt the group's hostility toward him wane as Malet distributed coins likewise along the eastern coast—Dover, Thetford, York.

When the talking faltered, all turned to the king.

William studied the map as his seneschal reported the number of foot soldiers, knights, and archers remaining since Hastings, and the number of mercenaries among them. "I will keep one-third of these forces to secure the southlands." The remaining two-thirds would be commanded by Alaric and Dreux. He assigned Bishop Odo to provision Dreux's troops, send supplies and pay the mercenaries along the way, and fitz Osbern to likewise support Alaric.

Alaric dared not pull his eyes from the map. It was an astonishing number of men to command, to feed.

"You will march under your own banners as well as mine." William said. Alaric barely breathed. William's banners extended the king's authority: territorial, judicial, and administrative to Alaric and Dreux—rights and responsibilities given to no one else.

"Obtain formal submission from local magnates," William said. "Rout out any who give *armed* resistance." He reiterated the new restrictions placed on his followers: unarmed villagers will not be harmed. No rape, no pillaging. The vanquished will not be sold into slavery. For now, those currently enslaved will be appropriated to build defenses alongside villagers put to hard labor. Earls, thegns, burgess, and magistrates who did not fight at Hastings will retain their positions and land, and the churches and monasteries will remain untouched.

William met Alaric's eyes. "French-speaking men with lands and titles granted by King Edward will pay to keep their rights. Build fortresses and establish garrisons at your discretion, take hostages if needed, and arrange for villages to pay traditional geld."

William's gaze moved slowly over everyone in the room as if assessing them. He reached for two scrolls and displayed his royal seals to all. "Before these witnesses, here in this place, I bestow upon you tenancy-in-chiefdoms of the shires of Norfolk and Stafford respectively." He gave one scroll to Dreux and the other to Alaric. "These charters grant you special rights and obligations and establish your predominance above the English thegn."

In the ensuing silence, William turned to the members of the inner circle. "I will not distribute land to the rest of you until the borders are secure."

Everyone nodded.

Alaric turned the scroll to see the elaborate royal seal. He and Dreux had received the first titles, the first provinces distributed in William's kingdom, even before Rufus, the king's *pissoir* partner.

"When you finish your mission," the king said, returning to the map, "You may build castles on your lands. Lord Norfolk," he said, using Dreux's new title, "rebuild the fort at Thetford. Lord Stafford, put a castle beyond the Danelaw if you can to defend the frontier."

Alaric nodded.

"You will command," William continued, "both many soldiers and nobles of high rank in the duchy. I trust you will consult those more experienced in warfare when necessary. Choose your own captains, and leave as soon after Epiphany as you can. Secure the borders and meet Malet in York by the vernal equinox."

William looked to Malet, who nodded confirmation.

"As vicomte of Yorkshire, Malet and his garrison will stabilize the northern frontier."

"How far north?" Alaric asked.

William studied Alaric a moment. "What think you?" The others, including le Roux, turned to Alaric.

"The boundaries between Scotia and Englelond are . . . fluid," he said.

William smiled. "We will begin with York."

Chapter Nine

Alaric, Guillaume Malet, and Roderick stood in a niche behind a thick leather screen waiting for the king, who had summoned them for a private counsel. Roderick leaned against the wall cleaning his nails with his dining knife, and Malet complained of his aching joints. Alaric studied the coppery sheen of the beautifully tooled leather. He felt tired, and wanted a soft bed and a warm woman. He ran his hand through his short hair, annoyed it had not yet grown back.

Alaric heard the familiar voice of Brian Dubec, Eustace's man on the other side of the partition, faint at first, slowly increasing in volume. "Old King Edward almost gave Eustace Dover once."

"Why?" another voice asked.

"A suitable recompense for the insult shown to his brother-in-marriage," Dubec said.

"Agh! Eustace already controls Calais and Boulogne," the other said. "With Dover, he would possess the shortest route across the strait, the richest ports. Why would William now give him Dover?"

"Because Eustace gave William gold, ships, and soldiers for the invasion. Why else would Eustace come himself?" Dubec asked.

"To see the look on Harold's face when he saw Eustace again," Dubec's acquaintance teased.

"That, too," Dubec said. "It pleased him to cut Harold down."

"But ..." the other man said. "William is unpredictable. No one guessed he would give . . . *le Loup Noir* a title, so much land, and so many soldiers. You know the one."

"Alaric of Ewyas, Simeon's son," Dubec said, "the Black Wolf."

"Yes. Can he handle it?"

Hidden by the screen, Alaric grinned at Malet, who signaled they all remain quiet. He frowned at Roderick, who moved directly behind him.

"Black Wolf," Dubec continued, "is William's man. Deserted his family to join William. Did you know Simeon the Brave and his wife, Julienne the Fair?"

"No," the other chuckled, "but, no doubt, you did."

"In truth, I did not. But Eustace knew the bastard, Simeon, and his brother Count Richard d'Évreux."

"Ah, yes," the voice said. "A feud between the brothers, wasn't there?"

"One Eustace turned to his advantage," Dubec said. "Simeon and Eustace had trained together as youths."

Alaric raised an eyebrow because his father had never mentioned Eustace.

"But it was Julienne he remembers best. He was her first . . . Well . . ."

"Eustace was her *amour*?"

Alaric turned his questioning eyes to Malet, whose expression hardened.

"Eustace called her an exceptional woman," Dubec continued. "It seems Simeon and his brother both wanted to marry her. Eustace wanted to bed her. She rejected Richard, spurned Eustace, and chose Simeon. In retaliation, Richard seized Simeon's estates, and Eustace took what he wanted on the eve of her wedding."

"Willingly?"

"Eustace's will prevailed."

The men laughed.

Alaric stepped forward, ignoring Malet's restraining clasp. From behind, Roderick clamped one large hand over Alaric's mouth. Simultaneously, his other arm pinned both of Alaric's arms, and in one move, he lifted Alaric off the ground and held him pressed against his own massive chest.

"If you make one sound," Roderick whispered, "I swear, I will knock you cold. Understand?"

Alaric closed his eyes. His mother raped? A sickening horror seeped into him.

"Where is the fair lady now?"

"With her Savior," Dubec said. "All of Black Wolf's family died at Eashing. One might say Eustace executed them."

Alaric tried to move, but Roderick held him firm. Malet whispered to Alaric, "Stop. You must learn the truth." Alaric ceased his struggles.

"Eustace *killed* them?"

"Not personally!" Dubec said. "We rode into a village, met resistance, and burned the village down. The family died in the encounter."

"But how? The villagers raised arms?"

"Not exactly. Simeon and his son, the thegn, wearing armor and sheathed swords rode out to meet us," Dubec said. "Simeon told Eustace that they would not stop us from taking all we wanted, but they were honor-bound to protect the villagers from harm. Eustace asked Simeon if he thought Normans would not kill Normans, saying that he, a Boulonnais, had no such prohibitions. Eustace ordered us to put Simeon and his son in the church. We forced them from their horses and shoved them into the church. We herded the villagers there, too."

Alaric jerked despite Roderick's firm hold. He began to tremble.

Dubec continued. "Plunder alone could not appease Eustace's fury at facing his *honorable* enemy."

"Is that why Eustace killed him?" the voice inquired.

"Our mission was to harass the southern villages until the Witan recognized William. Once the villagers were in the church, we killed or took the livestock, all the grain, and everything else we wanted. Before riding out, Eustace gave orders to torch the village. He learned days later that his soldiers had fired the church without releasing the villagers."

"And Eustace was rid of his rival."

"Eustace feels no remorse," Dubec said. "He did not intend to kill them. The deed was done. God willed it. But he admitted that if he'd known they would all burn, he would have asked Julienne the Fair what she would do to save her family. He laughed, *Would she have come willingly to my bed? Would I have wanted her now after all these years, probably gray-haired, wrinkled, with a sagging, flabby body?*"

Dubec's companion chuckled. "Knowing him, he would have asked just to hear her plead."

Sweat dripped from Alaric's scalp. Without seeing, he stared at the leather shielding him from Dubec. Just days ago, Eustace had approached him, knowing he'd murdered Alaric's family. He'd mocked Simeon, probed Alaric's ambitions, had praised the joy of conquest and plunder. He'd toyed with Alaric.

"Truth is," Dubec said, "we will do worse yet."

"That we will," agreed Dubec's companion. "I am surprised the king raised Simeon's son. If Simeon stood against the Normans, would not Black Wolf turn against William when he learns about Eustace's deed?"

"Before his coronation, William gave us all, including Black Wolf, orders to destroy those villages refusing to submit, and to surround and isolate London, until it surrendered. When Simeon chose Harold, he became William's enemy. Like Harold, he was felled as he would have been had he fought at Hastings. Black Wolf himself might have cleaved Simeon's skull during the battle. This happens in war."

"What if Black Wolf seeks revenge?"

Dubec grunted. "The moment he tries to touch Eustace he will lose William's favor. Land, titles, and everything he has gained. Besides, William needs Eustace too much to censure his action."

"But," the other man said, "the king's ban will protect Eustace only for a while."

"Eustace will protect himself. Be sure of it." Both men laughed.

"Come," Dubec said, "let us find a slave girl infused with virtue. I hear there are some fine . . ." Dubec's voice faded.

Alaric stood rigidly, unaware that Roderick had released him. The words had hit him as if the blunt end of an axe had slammed into his stomach. He staggered to the edge of the screen looking for Dubec— or Eustace—in the milling crowd.

Malet grabbed him and pulled him back. "Any quarrel between you and Eustace must be settled in the king's court."

Alaric threw off Malet's hands and turned on his friend.

Malet gasped. "You cannot! You cannot touch him. The king protects Eustace."

Looking beyond Malet, Alaric again searched the crowd for Eustace de Boulogne.

"Lord Stafford, *Seigneur* Malet?" a page called. Alaric looked at the boy, who shrank upon seeing Alaric's expression. "The . . . the king," the page said hurriedly, "has countermanded his summons. He will send for you again."

"I must see the king now!" Alaric said. The boy ducked and said he would convey the message and quickly turned away.

"Choose, Alaric," Malet said, coolly. "You must choose now, to stay within the king's graces or challenge his rule and seek your personal revenge. If you say anything to William, he will cast you out. As Dubec said, Eustace did the king's bidding. You must leave Eustace to God's zeal."

"I am God's zeal!" Alaric turned to follow the page. Suddenly, Roddy pinned him up against the wall, as if he were nothing more than a small boy.

"My liege lord," Roderick said to Malet, "is a wise knight. He does not squawk like a tickled maiden. He never forces me to dunk him in a trough of icy water. He prefers to await the king's summons and to leave the premises on his own legs rather than over my shoulder like a sack of grain. He bids you farewell for now." He let Alaric go and stepped back. "Is that not so, my lord?"

Alaric glared at Roderick a moment and took a deep, shuddering breath before nodding.

Chapter Ten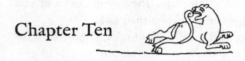

Royal priorities prevented Alaric from seeing the king for several days. By then, he'd absorbed the brutal knowledge of Eustace's iniquity and said nothing about the matter to William. Resolved to take action after his mission to York, he intended to use the intervening months to formulate an adequate reprisal. Meanwhile, Alaric worked hard and long until exhaustion let him sleep without envisioning his family's charred corpses, without being consumed in powerless rage.

On Twelfth Night, before the festivities, William summoned him again. When he arrived, everyone, the pages and scribes, the clerics, nobles, and guards, left. Only Guillaume fitz Osbern, and Count Eustace de Boulogne remained. Seeing Eustace, Alaric, curled his fingers over the mark of chainmail he'd branded onto his palm, recalling the armor fused to his father's or brother's charred corpse.

"Come forward," the king said, distractedly as he pressed his seal on a document and handed it to Eustace. Turning his attention to Alaric, he said, "We have arranged a marriage for you."

"A marriage?"

"Yes," the king replied, leaning back into his throne-like chair. "Count Eustace informed me you have no wife. He has given you his niece, a Norman countess."

"I will not take her!"

Fitz Osbern grunted. King William's cheek throbbed. Eustace stroked his mustache thoughtfully, and Alaric regretted, too late, the words he had blurted out.

The king leaned forward slowly, tilting his head, like an eagle sighting his prey. His eyes fixed on Alaric. "Have you forgotten the oath you swore to me, Knight?" he asked in a low voice.

Alaric cringed. Eleven days ago, Alaric had sworn his fealty to William. "My life belongs to you, my king." Alaric bowed and kept his eyes on the king's boots.

"The king expects nothing *less* than your life!"

The words fell like a whip across Alaric's head. His relationship with William changed when Alaric received command over the western forces. William still slept on the floor with his men and livestock, wrestled with his knights, and joined in an occasional brawl. Those among his inner circle called him by his first name or argued openly with him, often raising their voices. But the easy jests, the familiar smiles and friendly intimacies William had once bestowed on Alaric were gone. Now, as one of the king's commanders, their encounters became more formal and exacting. The change unsettled him.

"Well, Black Wolf?" the king roared.

"I wish to serve you, in all things, my lord," Alaric said, his eyes lowered.

"By God's breath, serve me you shall!" William leaped from his chair and paced the room. He spun on Alaric. "For a blade's width, you have received greater rewards than anyone else. Even my brothers have yet to receive land."

The king's voice pierced his ears. Startled, Alaric recalled the instant his sword had deflected a mortal blow aimed at William's head, a moment so brief, so chaotic as to be nearly forgotten amid the fierce battle. Alaric's anger flared. Did William begrudge owing his life to a lowly horseman, a minor kinsman?

"Look at me, Cousin!"

Alaric's head snapped up. William the Bastard, king of Englelond, studied him with a serrated intensity that ripped through his flesh and stole his breath away. As if from inside a dark, icy tunnel, his heart throbbed in terror. He withstood the king's long, speculative, angry gaze, knowing the king could order his death in a moment.

William resumed pacing. "Your knowledge of this land will expedite my triumph. You command an unprecedented number of soldiers, men of high birth—many ranking higher than you in Normandie—and ruthless mercenaries. I can only give such a force to someone I trust."

William threw himself into his chair and sat back stiffly. "My supporters question why I transferred such military might to you. No titles, no riches will be granted to my followers until we have control of the land. We will not know what we have to distribute until you and Dreux complete your surveys. The situation feeds impatience and breeds insurrection."

"Your peers," Fitz Osbern injected, "and you know them well, counsel the king that you will conspire with Harold's cubs. They argue that you, born and raised among the English, have no loyalty to your race. As mercenaries, you and your brother fought beside Harold. Harold retained you to command the garrison at one of his outposts. He made your brother a thegn, gave him titles, and his niece in marriage. Even after Harold usurped King William's throne, your father and brother served him. They say," his voice softened, "that, like your father who stood against Eustace's men at Eashing, you will stand against the king."

Alaric's gaze snapped to Eustace's unflinching eyes. Had his father and brother raised arms against Eustace? Had Eustace defamed them with a deliberate lie? Alaric could barely keep his hands from gripping Eustace's throat, even when he realized that the king knew Eustace had murdered his family!

"These doubts," Fitz Osbern said, drawing Alaric's attention from Eustace, "must be banished immediately."

"The events at Eashing," King William stated tersely, "were unfortunate. But now, all eyes are turned on you and Eustace—waiting. I will not tolerate private wars among my men. I must have unity to hold my kingdom, to fight our enemies, not each other."

William adjusted his cloak and said, "Eustace offers you a blood price—his niece in marriage. In exchange, you will relinquish all your rights to obtain further restitution or to punish Eustace in any way. This is not a request. Less than two weeks after my coronation, no one from within my forces or among my allies shall disobey me—least of all you, Alaric, my own blood kin. Marry the woman or face our maker."

Alaric blanched. He stood on the brink of destruction. *Choose a virtuous man*, his father had said. Only now he realized the cost of his decision. His king demanded that Alaric sacrifice his family's honor for his life. Dead, he could bring no honor or justice to his family. Outwardly, Alaric's acceptance of the blood price would demonstrate his absolute obedience to William—and inwardly corrode his loyalty.

"Sire," Alaric said, "pray forgive my brazen words. I wish to serve my king."

"So be it." The king snapped, gesturing to Eustace.

Eustace handed Alaric the parchment. "These are the betrothal offers."

Alaric took the parchments from Eustace and handed the documents to fitz Osbern, who read aloud the Norman land and wealth transferring to Alaric upon the marriage. Astonished, Alaric stared at William. The fertile land of the Aumale valley alone would make him a rich and powerful lord!

"You hold land in Staffordshire," William said, "and now you will hold land in Normandie. When I return to Rouen in the spring, you will remain here as one of my agents. My followers and your detractors would find it difficult to challenge your sympathies when your wealth is rooted in Norman land."

"Your proxy will seal the document properly," Eustace said. "You need only mark your consent." He handed Alaric the inked quill with a triumphant, mocking grin as if daring him to sign. He marked the parchment quickly, angrily.

"Welcome to my family, Alaric. You shall be like a son to me." Eustace handed Alaric a bowl of wine and sipped his own. "I give you a great gift. My niece will keep her title which outranks yours and she has her own wealth. Although she has been betrothed three times before, I promise you a virgin—a spinster virgin. I would not call her comely. Her mother was disposed to be thick. Most of her family died covered with pustules, a pestilence that killed most of her siblings when she was a child."

Eustace's description sparked Alaric's memory of Goda, pointing at the smoldering church where his family had died. At that moment, the crone's hideous features—a pox-marred face, bulbous nose, blackened teeth, and scabby tufted scalp—fused into Alaric's mind as the image of his future wife.

"While you secure the realm for King William," Eustace said, "my niece will tend to your wealth and property and seek my counsel on all things. She will rule your household with a discipline tempered like the finest Damascene sword. She will bring you revenue, perhaps bear you sons, and be your sacred companion for all of eternity."

If Alaric had not felt like jabbing his fingers into Eustace's eyes, he might have laughed—or wept. He understood now what Eustace meant when he had talked about the power to bend men's lives. Eternity. For all of his waking and sleeping hours, long after his death, Eustace's niece would be his wife, an iron band imprisoning his soul.

"The countess de Fontenay," William said, "has many of the same *attributes* as her esteemed uncle."

A warning? Alaric wondered.

Eustace smiled with a slight nod as if accepting a compliment.

"In time," Fitz Osbern said, "you may find her useful. Like Eustace, she is adept at influencing those around her, is cunningly astute in court craft, military stratagems, and the Church. She is likely to be . . . mannish would you not say, Eustace?"

"Despite her flaws, she will suit you." Eustace said, his eyes taunting Alaric.

"Thank you, Sire," Alaric said, bowing to William and controlling his voice. "I am, with sword and heart, your loyal vassal."

The king nodded and gestured Fitz Osburn to show Alaric out.

"Come," Fitz Osbern laughed, giving Alaric a friendly slap on his back. "We have not ruined you."

Beyond the royal chamber, Fitz Osbern sobered and pulled Alaric aside. "William warns you: a Countess with a character like Eustace would be a formidable woman. Never underestimate either."

Alaric searched Fitz Osbern's eyes.

"No law or custom," Fitz Osbern continued, "prevents a man from using his wife for a just cause. What happens between a man and his wife is no concern to the king, Alaric."

Alaric nodded. The king gave him a pawn with which to avenge his family's death. He will use her land and wealth to destroy Eustace. And when it pleased him, he might even strangle her with his bare hands.

I'll race you to York," Dreux challenged as they mounted their horses the morning after Epiphany.

Alaric scratched his chin with the edge of his stiff leather mitt. He squinted at the thin streak of golden light along the horizon where the sun would rise and hide in a layer of thick, black, storm clouds. The fiery horizon marked a rare January dawn, usually overcast with no hint of sunlight. An occasional snowflake swirled in the air. Alaric grinned at Dreux and shook his head, telling his friend he had no chance of getting there first. "Wagers?" he asked.

Dreux laughed. "The usual."

As youths in training, when they hated each other, they had wagered their horses. Each had hoped to cripple the other with a poorly trained, or absent, mount. Somehow, it was not long before another wager, and the lost horse was returned. Over the years, it had become a jest between them.

"Agreed," Alaric said.

March 1067, York

Both reached York before the vernal Equinox. Light snow covered the ground, and the wind, like shards of ice, spiked through their thin cloaks. Their combined forces had nearly surrounded York by the time Guillaume Malet joined them with his own soldiers.

Alaric and Dreux began a ritual repeated in all the villages they had seized on their way. Helmeted and armored, accompanied by deep-bellowing horns, they rode to the gates with a hundred horsemen. A couple dozen bowmen and foot soldiers ran alongside. The archers and foot took their places, the mounted soldiers moved into a line formation, five deep behind Alaric and Dreux.

Waiting for the townspeople to respond, Alaric recalled what he knew of York: once an ancient kingdom, the second largest town after London, with about eight thousand fiercely independent people stemming from Roman and Viking blood. The town, dark, brooding, gave sanctuary to rebels and inspired unrest. They had to be careful here. Looking at the walls, Alaric wondered what they would find inside the gate, especially since he saw only townspeople, no soldiers, on the ramparts.

One side of the broad, double gate opened, and the bishop, along with a crowd of townspeople, met them.

In French, Dreux began, "We come in peace to obtain your vows of loyalty to King William of Englelond."

The faces before them were pale, drawn, and blank.

Alaric spoke in Saxon, first to the bishop and then to the people. "*We cuman to getan yer oaths fur Geeyome Kyng of Anglicus.*"

"*Geeyome, thaet stincan bastardus,*" sneered a townsman.

Despite the barely understandable dialect, Alaric grasped the sentiment.

Murmurs rumbled among the crowd. In Saxon, another called out, "William seized Wessex only. He has no claim over York!" The crowd exploded in agreement.

"William is king," Alaric said in Saxon, "from Wessex to Northumbria."

Another yelled, "These foreigners butchered Harold, chosen by the Witan, by English laws, by *English* lords." The murmurs increased to shouts. Several people raised their fists, a stone whizzed by Dreux's head. He did not flinch.

"William is your *rightful* king," Alaric said, "chosen by King Edward, and anointed by the Church, by Archbishop Ealdred of York, who continues to serve his king." His loud voice and Saxon words silenced the crowd. "We come in peace," he said to the bishop, Ealdred's underling, "but we will quash any and all treason against our king."

"Whores of Satan!" someone else shouted as a rock hit Alaric's shield. Dreux calmly motioned the soldiers forward as he slowly drew his own sword.

Alaric looked down at the bishop, a middle-aged, sallow man who watched him suspiciously. Alaric pointed his arm toward the billowing black smoke drifting its wispy tendrils toward York. He'd given his men instructions to fire only the storehouse knowing the thatching, thicker than he was tall, would smoke as if an entire village burned. "Do you wish the same fate? In an instant, all of York would blaze."

Hostile silence greeted them. Another rock flew through the air, followed by a scream, which shattered the quiet. A watchful bowman had shot the man who had thrown the rock. A woman wailed over his crumpled body, and immediately the crowd erupted in angry shouts and threats. As one, the mob moved forward, throbbing.

At Dreux's signal, the archers ran forward and knelt in a row. Foot soldiers, carrying lighted torches, followed and lit the archers' oil-soaked missiles: loaded, nocked, and aimed high to sail over the walls and onto thatched roofs. They waited for Dreux's command.

The bishop stepped forward. Turning his back to the soldiers, he raised his arms to the townspeople. "William is king by grant of God. He carried papal banners, and Archbishop Ealdred anointed him with holy oil." He glanced at Alaric and back at the crowd. "Our English magnates through the Witenagemot, too, have chosen William," he said in a softer voice as his shoulders drooped. "All, including Prince Edgar and Earls Edwin, Morcar, and Waltheof have sworn fealty to William. Go to your homes, I beg you."

The crowd hesitated. Alaric watched as one man reached for a stone, another curled his lip and hunched forward. Dark and hostile eyes pierced the soldiers. Someone spat, another cursed. One woman held her man back, another urged hers forward. First, one retreated back inside the gates, then another and another, until only a handful of townspeople were left to face the soldiers, their lack of strength exposed and witnessed by all. In a few moments, both gates were thrown open.

The bishop turned again to Alaric, who nodded slowly. "Thank you, Lord Bishop. You saved many lives today."

"The day has just begun," the bishop said bitterly.

Within a week, York was tamed. As unsettled as the people, the weather fluctuated between rain, ice, snow, sunny days, followed by more of the same, and the wind, still icy cold, blew constantly. Scouts found no rebels or Scots within a day's ride from the town, nor spotted any longships patrolling the waterways.

Restless and eager to leave York, Alaric and Dreux rode out alone to patrol the area.

"Concluding your betrothal will be difficult," Dreux said, as they rode abreast through the Vale. "I dread both the discussions and being your proxy. I hope the king will reward my efforts by granting me permission to marry Clare of Wolenbroth."

"I envy you," Alaric said, "to marry a thegn's daughter, a woman of your own choice. I had hoped for an English heiress myself." He reined his horse around a marshy pond. "Get me fat cows, dense woods, and rich farms. Wear your armor. I've been told to use caution when dealing with anyone related to Eustace, and be forewarned: my betrothed is said to be old and pox-scarred."

They rode down into narrow gorges, up over high plains and through desolate land. Finally, the trail led them to a frozen waterfall, where they paused and looked at the jagged rock face covered with ice.

"Before sailing to meet your betrothed, I will stop in London to see Clare," Dreux said. "I hope she is with child, but I fear she is not safe there."

"Send her to Hereford," Alaric said as they began to walk their horses toward an ice-covered bridge at the edge of a gorge. "After the builders start my castle, I'll go to Hereford to arrange a mass for my family and pick up Johan, wounded at Hastings. She can travel with us to Tutbury, and I'll keep her safe until you meet us there in May."

Chapter Eleven

Across the Narrow Sea, in a small, impoverished hamlet at the edge of Boulogne, Genevieve Elysia de Fontenay, her sister Marie, and their Aunt Hortense waited in silent apprehension. Yesterday, they had retreated to the solar where, behind a thick wooden door and a sturdy metal latch, they'd spent a restless night jumping at sounds of rampage in the great room below.

This morning, the solar, long a sanctuary from the dark, brooding castle, was luminous. They sat beside three tall, narrow windows, and carded wool, spun thread, and embroidered. But the gentle light did nothing to take the chill from their spines when voices bellowed—or now, when startled by the thundering ferocity of someone pounding against their latched door.

"Lady de Fontenay," a gruff, demanding male yelled, beating on the door with enough force to jolt the thick boards. "You are summoned. Immediately."

Hortense leaped to her feet, poised for battle.

"Elise!" Marie cried, using her sister's familiar name.

Setting her embroidery aside, Elise stood. Calmly, she shook out the ankle-length skirt of her red cotte, richly embroidered with silver thread. "Our . . . *guardian* merely wants to demonstrate his authority," she said to Marie.

Hortense unlatched the door and opened it boldly, filling the doorway with her ample body. "God's peace, Sir!" she said. "Mind your manners, you're not in a bordel," she chided the hearth knight.

"God's blessings," Elise said to the messenger, stepping out into the damp, chilled gallery. She ignored his flustered greeting and turned instead to her handmaiden beside him, a fresh, red handprint on her cheek. With lowered eyes, the girl lifted a blue, ermine-lined cloak, which Elise accepted, furious her servant had been struck. Sweeping the mantle around her shoulders, she watched the soldier's quick departure. Whether it signaled his impatience or the urgency of her summons, she knew not.

Leaning carefully over the loose balustrade, Elise peered down into the cavernous hall, listening to the silence. She hoped the men, who'd arrived the night before, had exhausted Arques' revelry. His entertainments tended toward the depraved. As if seeking absolution for his excesses, he often summoned her after his debauchery and displayed an unpredictable and violent temper in her presence. Unable to control his warring impulses, Arques both desired and detested her.

Three years ago, her uncle Count Eustace de Boulogne took Elise and her sister from the abbey near Fontenay, the seat of Elise's estates. They had not seen him for more than a decade, and both knew the move meant he would soon barter them—through marriage—for lucrative alliances. He'd sent them to a small village edging Boulogne, near enough to be summoned quickly, far enough to ignore. Here they lived with their Aunt Hortense, Guillaume, the former count of Arques, and Walter, his son. Although Arques had no kinship to them, he was bound by ancient alliances to serve Eustace as the nominal lord of this castle and their token guardian.

Taking a lighted candle from the sconce, Elise kicked out her skirts and proceeded down the steep, narrow steps, careful to avoid the fate of a servant who recently lost his footing–and his life.

To her, this once-sturdy fortress bore the characteristic essence of Arques: the castle rotted from within. No pretext of grandeur, no fresh mortar, nor daub and mud could hide the dilapidating shell, the disintegrating timbers, the poorly thatched roof. Like their contentious relationships, the castle and its dark brooding turbulence bore heavily on its inhabitants.

She stepped off the last tread onto loose stones shifting beneath her feet. After setting the candle in a sconce, she scanned the room to gauge the degree of Arques' malice.

At one end, thin rays of weak sunlight streaked across the floor from the slit windows above the gallery. Instantly comforted, she saw Walter sitting beside the roaring fire in the center pit, though he sat with his head in his hands in apparent distress. Searching the corners of the room where Arques' thugs ruled, she found it unusually empty. A few servants darted about, and despite the fire, a chilly breeze billowed the heavy, faded red drapery, which swayed like tall, breathing pillars.

Fingering the silver trim at her wrist, she studied Guillaume Arques, sitting at a table beside the glowing hearth. A circle of bright light from a candelabrum illuminated the document in his hands. With a slightly amused look on his face, he studied the scroll, an important document, she inferred from the ribbons and seals. A pair of lethargic hounds flanked him. One raised his head to look at Elise and dropped it again to his paws, blinking against the fleas jumping about his face.

At fifty, Arques still looked the prince: tall and powerfully built. A startling plume of white hair flared above his right temple against thick, black locks framing a smoothly handsome face. The legendary Count d'Arques and his grandeur had once exemplified the ideal of Norman nobility and provoked awe among his peers. Now, the bitter, demeaned outcast personified ruination and provoked ridicule.

Walking toward the hearth, she watched Walter. His father's schemes had condemned Walter to destitution and dishonor. At nearly thirty years, he had no future. Yet, he had not been cruel like his father. No, she thought, glancing at his bowed head, he had been her friend. Once, she had hoped for more. She felt her face flush with the embarrassing memory. Her girlish infatuation had died quickly under Hortense's guidance and with Walter's impeccable sense of propriety. Eternally grateful, she cherished their friendship and thanked her saints. Walter protected her and Marie from himself, his father, and any other man who would make his fortune by defiling highborn women.

As her skirts whispered softly over the rushes, Walter raised his head. She saw a flash of anguish, buried quickly beneath a welcoming smile as he stood to greet her. Arques' falconine eyes snapped from the documents to watch her.

"Ah, the Countess deigns to answer my summons."

"What is amiss?" Arques always used her title when trouble brewed. She inhaled, preparing herself.

Arques rose from his bench and kicked one of the dogs, its whimpers fading as it leaped away. He stepped around the table toward her. "You are to be married."

"T-to . . ." *Not to Arques. Please, God, not to him.* "To whom?"

He chuckled. "Despite my best efforts, you'll not be my bride." He reached out to stroke her cheek and laughed when she stepped back. She recognized the look in his eyes. It must be a curse to be attractive but old and dispossessed. There had been a time, she supposed, when the mere flicker of his desire would have brought women eagerly to his bed. She wished he would not look at her that way.

"This is your fourth betrothed. With your curse, this one will pass soon to Christ, too."

Elise did not rise to Arques' bait. The nuns claimed that all the men previously betrothed to her had died—suddenly, inexplicably, under strange, perhaps unnatural circumstances. She knew otherwise. The first, a youth of sixteen, died from a training wound. The second, a man older than Arques, had choked on his food, and the last, an infant barely three winters, drowned. She supposed that, despite her wealth, her *curse* was the reason Eustace had not yet arranged a marriage.

"Your groom is one of William's commanders," Arques said. "Eustace is in Bergues celebrating the release of his son held hostage by William during the invasion. He sent his retainer instead." He looked behind her.

Elise spun around, startled to see a figure emerging from the shadows near the screened alcove. She had not seen him when she'd searched the hall, a careless mistake.

Her tension eased upon recognizing Eustace's loyal and trusted captain, Brian *le Dogue* Dubec. She and her sister Marie had first met Brian when he had escorted them from Abbey Clarion to Paris, and afterward to Boulogne. She never understood why he'd sworn fealty to her tyrannical uncle. Everyone knew Brian would fight the saints if Eustace so ordered. Yet, she sensed he was his own man and that he chafed against his vassalage.

His face expressed his dislike of this mission. She imagined that Brian would rather slit someone's throat than dance around words knowing most of what happened in negotiations would be couched in flowery phrases and meaningless toasts. She watched him eyeing Arques, like a large and dangerous mastiff.

She guessed he was a few years older than Walter. He'd shaved his thick brown hair from the back of his head in the warrior's style. He had brown eyes accented by crow's feet, a result of squinting into bright sunlight rather than laughter, she suspected. Although the deep scars on his face did not make him hideous, they signaled his ferocity and implied battle wounds elsewhere.

"My lady," he said. "I will negotiate the betrothal particulars on your uncle's behalf."

"As her guardian for the last three years, *I* will dictate the terms!" Arques' plume, like hackles, flared.

"You have no legal authority." Brian turned to Elise. "Count Eustace never relinquished his responsibility for you and your sister. He intends, as always, to protect his interests."

Elise groaned inwardly, for this marked the beginning of a long and tedious battle. Tensions between Dubec and Arques had erupted on previous occasions. No friendship existed between them, only a long and smoldering animosity, which bound them together as closely as relatives. She believed their mutual dislike stemmed from Eustace, who dangled them both in dependency and often inflamed their loathing. She supposed their rivalry amused him.

"Will you protect *her* interests?" Walter said.

"This is not your concern," Arques, flicking his wrist in dismissal.

"Who is this commander?" Walter insisted. "How old is he?"

Brian studied Walter a moment before speaking to Elise. "Alaric the Norman of Ewyas is twenty-four, perhaps twenty-five. He is the legitimate issue of a marriage between the Archbishop's bastard, Simeon the Brave, and Julienne *the Fair*," he said to Arques.

Elise saw Arques' surprise and a slow smile. *What secret did they share?*

Brian continued to answer questions about Alaric's birth near the Welsh border and his contribution to William's venture. "He distinguished himself at Hastings."

"Whose life did he save?" Arques asked.

"Bishop Odo's," Brian answered without pause. "Your betrothed was enfeoffed—not by William the duke, but by William the *king*. A knight, he holds the insignia of the *corpus de royale* and attendant rights. He was granted the tenancy-in-chiefdom of Staffordshire. Lord Stafford is also *le Seigneur de Tutbierrie*, where his castle rises."

Rarely would a landless kinsman achieve such honor, Elise thought. As tenant-in-chief, he was nothing more than a military landlord, much like her own tenant-warriors who held land in exchange for protecting her estates. A knighthood merely distinguished him as a mounted warrior rather than a bowman or foot soldier. Yet, he was a member of the king's elite knights and had the rights and authority to act *on the king's behalf*. What had he done to win these privileges?

"The countess outranks him," Walter said.

"It matters little, you worm," Arques sneered. "This marriage is the wish of that bastard some fools call *the Conqueror*! Besides, she's too old to expect a better match."

Walter turned on his father. "Insults are unnecessary."

Elise appreciated Walter's defense, but in truth, she should have married at fourteen like most noblewomen. Her age of twenty-one would disappoint any man, and she might be too old to bear many children.

"My lady," Brian injected, obviously enjoying the discord between Walter and his father, "Eustace insisted, and William agreed, that you will retain your title despite your marriage."

"Why?" Arques asked, voicing her own question about the unusual arrangement.

"They believe your betrothed will match your rank very soon."

"Is he ambitious?" Walter asked.

"A former mercenary, he is brash, uncultured, and well suited to his destiny."

"As you are suited to your own?" Arques said.

Ignoring Arques' jibe, Brian turned to Elise. "Your uncle believes your betrothed has the makings of legend. They call him the Black Wolf. Some claim he changes into a wolf during battle, though I have not seen it myself."

Elise's heartbeat quickened. Only warriors of Odin were said to take the form of fiendish creatures. Such phantasms provoked Christ's Church, which sent the heretic and his entire family, from the eldest to the very youngest, to the stake.

"Take heart, Genevieve," Arques said. "Your wealth will buy you a seat next to God."

"Why does William want this marriage?" she asked Brian, infuriated at Arques' sacrilege.

He hesitated. "Black Wolf needs a Norman bride."

"A *rich* Norman bride," Arques said. "To buy soldiers and weapons and build castles to suppress the English."

Brian shrugged. "Philip approves."

She hid her alarm. Although the king of the Franks would be interested in this match, it was dangerous to attract the notice of a royal kinsman.

"Perhaps," Arques said, "he thinks you more useful in Englelond under William's nose."

"I wish to see the offers."

"The good nuns," Arques said, "should never have taught you to read."

As Elise read the documents, Walter watched Brian Dubec and his father circle each other. He and Brian had met shortly after his father's castle had fallen. Walter, sixteen, emaciated from the siege, had been wounded, blunting a mortal blow aimed at his father's bare head. The wound had given Arques his white plume, which afterward symbolized Arques' failure and his son's pathetic courage.

Arques surrendered and had sought refuge with Eustace in Boulogne. Walter vaguely remembered arriving at this very castle, a torch-lighted courtyard, Eustace and his father arguing. Walter fell from his horse, bleeding. Brian, a young soldier, ordered to situate Walter, carried him to the stables and left his fevered body on a rat-infested straw pallet to die.

Instead, his wounds healed. Afterward, Walter had followed

Brian around, fascinated by the cocky twenty-year-old soldier, by his violence, his rigor, and his endurance. Eager to earn a knighthood himself, Walter wanted to train with Brian, who spurned his requests. When Brian traveled with Eustace, he would return and describe his adventures, tantalizing Walter with a future he would never have. He realized the intensity of Brian's revulsion the day Walter overheard him speaking to a companion. *Although Arques demanded opportunity be given to him, Walter expected opportunities to arise for him. Without candle, coin, or sword, Walter has no future. I've no pity for him*, Brian had said. *He should find a life in the cracks. Like other snakes.*

Walter had recognized the truth of Brian's judgment, but even now, he felt intense shame for mistaking Brian as his friend.

"William," Arques said, "left his kingdom after two months on the throne, less than a year since his invasion. I wager most of the English still do not know William is king."

"You have no coins to wager," Brian taunted.

Arques scowled. "William cannot hold his throne long, especially now when he is in Rouen." Arques paced the room. "Someone . . . Someone *must* be gathering arms or making alliances. William's enemies could overthrow him in months."

Brian leaned his hip against the trestle table. His mocking gaze scalded Walter, promising a private encounter. Walter understood. He would face Brian's sword, his fist, or his men's thrashing, for Brian's chief entertainment had for some time been to humiliate Walter as often as he could.

Why did Eustace want this alliance? Elise wondered, searching the document for a clue among lists of her own lands and her betrothed's holdings, located in places with odd names. Did Philip have designs on her land in the Vexin? What did William gain? She studied her betrothed's signature mark. From the gouges in the parchment, she surmised he had been angry when he accepted the offer. *That*, she thought, was the single most important fact of her impending marriage.

She looked up from the document as Arques repeated his tired litany. "I am the *legitimate* son of Duke Richard, half-brother to the successor duke Robert. By line of descent, *I* should have inherited the duchy after Robert's death. Instead, the king and the Norman counts settled the duchy on my bastard nephew—a boy of seven."

Elise recalled the story of how young Duke William, a boy of fifteen, took sole reins of the duchy and gave the county of Arques, a rich fertile land, to his uncle. The benevolent gesture nettled Arques: *a bone when I deserve the carcass.*

As Duke William's power grew, Arques' hatred of his nephew grew like the bloated innards of a putrefying corpse until—nurtured by King Henri of the Franks—it exploded, coating everyone with his noxious bile. The old, ailing monarch feared William, his young, powerful vassal possessing the province along his northern border. Encouraged by the king to weaken William's duchy, Arques seized his fate. He built a gleaming stone castle, resolved to split the Norman duchy in half, thereby creating an independent province for himself. He renounced his vassalage to William and began seizing one Norman village after another, moving south toward Paris, fully confident that King Henri, who had instigated his revolt, the count of Anjou, and others would augment and provision Arques' forces.

Arques had wagered his future and lost.

Young William drove Arques back into his castle. After a yearlong siege and near starvation, Arques surrendered. Abandoned by the French king and his other princely allies, Arques lay bleeding on the altar of fickle fortunes.

His misadventure changed Elise's life forever. Infuriated by William's increasing strength, King Henri attacked Normandie, destroying village after village until William's forces faced him in battle near Mortemer. Fleeing in defeat, the French attacked Elise's home, and in the wake of the killings, she and Marie became Eustace's ward.

Duke William could have imprisoned Arques. But his leniency condemned Arques to fester with impotence and nearly servile dependency. Despite William's coins, despite his noble dress and bearing, Arques languished without land, titles, or soldiers: bored, frustrated, and despised by the nobility.

"All know," Arques said, "that I am the rightful duke of Nor—"

"—When is this marriage to occur?" Elise said, handing the documents to Brian.

"You will be betrothed by proxy this afternoon," Arques said brusquely. "King Philip's representative will arrive shortly as will Abbot Juhel from Clarion. You will be wed as soon as you join your betrothed."

The swiftness of these events astonished her. Usually, a betrothal among nobles lasted a year or more! "Has the Pope agreed?"

"Yes," Arques said. "Philip recalled Count Roland de Rennes from Rome. He arrived last night. Roland and Dubec will escort you to your husband's castle."

Elise felt as if she had been slapped. Roland went to Rome last year. King Philip would have had to summon him—months ago. They'd known of this betrothal for a long time. "Why was I not given more time to prepare?"

"You did not need to know," Arques said, "until I decided—"

"None of us needed to know," Walter said. "Father and I first learned of it last night when Brian arrived."

"It is the situation in Englelond, my lady," Dubec said. "Your marriage must be expedited."

"Does my betrothed come himself to negotiate?"

"No," Brian replied. "Dreux Marchand de Ville, Lord Norfolk, William's envoy will negotiate on his behalf and represent your husband by proxy. He arrives this afternoon."

"And for Philip?"

"Thierry de Châlons." Arques' smile curled into a nasty snarl.

Thierry! Elise thought, feeling a slight throbbing in the center of her forehead. With Thierry, King Philip's chief advisor, one took nothing for granted.

Chapter Twelve

Elise entered the solar and dismissed the servant who had accompanied her. As her eyes adjusted to the light flooding into the room, she sought out her younger sister and related the unfolding events. "Best behave, Marie," she grinned. "Abbot Juhel arrives this afternoon."

Marie crinkled her nose.

Elise felt the same. Juhel de Ponthieu, their kinsman, had been in and out of their lives often, and most constantly during their years at Abbey Clarion. Elise rushed to change the subject, to bury her dark, inexplicable dread of the abbey.

"I must leave in a month. Roland is back from Rome. He and Brian will deliver me to my husband."

Marie's eyes widened. "Roland is here? Will he stay for the entire month?" She put a hand to her breast and grabbed Elise's wrist, nearly swooning.

"Yes," Elise smiled. "He will stay until I am ready to leave."

"We haven't seen him since . . . ."

Elise remembered that day: fire, smoke, mutilated bodies, Roland, at fourteen, their last defender—disarmed, wounded, the point of a sword at his throat.

"A year ago!" Marie said. "He came just after he inherited his father's title, before going to Rome."

"Yes! Now, I remember." Elise and Marie had descended the stairs together and entered the great room to welcome Roland and his cousin Tristan de Vannes, *vicomte* de Brittany. The girls spotted Roland immediately. Despite his height, they would have recognized his dark brown hair and piercing blue eyes anywhere.

It took him a moment to notice them, but when he did, he started, for he had not seen them since the attack at Mortemer, when she was eight and Marie was six. His gaze acknowledged Elise warmly but riveted to Marie, who then, at seventeen, had become a radiant and poised woman. Marie herself seemed stunned into momentary inaction.

They greeted each other formally, their camaraderie of old lost temporarily. But Marie, rising to the occasion, looked up at Roland's immense height and said, "It is true, what they say."

"Is what true?" he asked.

"That the Bretons are short."

"Short-tempered, my lady," he responded. "I see the abbey did nothing to curb your sharp tongue!"

"The better to flay you with," she crooned, sweetly.

And from that moment until he left the next afternoon, they taunted each other mercilessly.

Now, Marie suddenly sobered. "We've never been apart before."

"We always knew this day would come." Elise squeezed Marie's hand, offering a smile to disguise her own disquiet. Without Elise as foil, Marie would face Arques' perversity alone. Eustace might marry her off to one of the Flemings. Or worse.

Hortense embraced the girls, her arms barely enfolding them. "Confine your fears, for there are many decisions to make."

Marie burst into a wicked chuckle, grabbed Elise's hands, and swung her around. "You're getting married, and soon you will have children and . . . " Marie flung herself onto a nearby bench. "You must write and tell me . . . *everything*!"

"Everything?" Elise asked, puzzled.

"Yes, you know." Marie raised her eyebrows. "Everything. I—"

"Now, Marie," Hortense interrupted.

"—I want to know how to capture Roland," Marie beamed at Elise and Hortense.

"Marie! It's sinful to speak so," Hortense said.

"I speak the truth! I want to know how to win my knight and keep him. You must do this one thing for me, Elise," she said, with a stubborn flip of her head. "Unless you want me to find out on my own."

"Absolutely not!" Elise said.

Hortense shook her head and snapped her skirts as if preparing to charge a gaggle of geese threatening to peck her legs. "I have known you since you were a wee babe. I do not know how you remained at Abbey Clarion lo these many years and came out untouched, with your irreverence, stubbornness, and brazen tongue intact!"

The tone of Hortense's voice was an ancient command Marie heeded immediately. She lowered her head, crinkled her brow in contrition. She looked sideways at Hortense. "I speak the words before I know they are mine. The nuns did not change me because Elise kept them from beating me," she said softly, glancing at Elise. "She snuck food into my cell when I was forbidden to eat. She stopped the lash before it hit my skin and instead was whipped for defiance. And sometimes she kicked me beneath the dining tables to silence my blasphemous giggles and pinched me awake when we knelt long in prayers."

Elise shook her head. "Marie, you embellish. The only time I took your beating was when we both disobeyed Sister Exencia. Remember?"

"Yes," Marie laughed but sobered at Hortense's glare.

"We refused to let her bathe Marie," Elise explained. To Marie, she continued, "That was the time she wanted to share your bed."

Hortense crossed herself and shook her head as her bluster waned.

"I confess, I am stubborn," Marie said. "But, is it sinful to choose my own husband?"

"No," Elise said. "But the choice is not yours. It's Eustace's."

"Unless," Marie said, with a mischievous sparkle in her eyes, "unless Roland asks for me himself. Perhaps I should—"

An embroidered pillow sailed across the room into Marie's face, and the girls broke into laughter.

"Agh, you two would have perplexed the Virgin Mother!" Hortense exploded with a huff. She picked up her sewing and sat on a bench where she jabbed her needle into the cloth. "I will instruct the servants about the betrothal feast. Decide your attire for the occasion."

Marie and Elise exchanged glances, for Hortense would remain cross until they changed her mood.

"I am to marry Alaric of Ewyas, son of Simeon d'Évreux," Elise said.

Hortense remained silent.

"Do you know his family?" Elise asked.

Hortense pinched the cloth with her needle. "Yes."

"Do you know them . . . well?" Elise encouraged.

Hortense took another stitch and scowled at the girls. "The family, as you know, are cousins to Duke William."

"Is that all?" Marie asked.

Hortense lifted her needle, tugging the thread up through the cloth. Elise and Marie moved restlessly about the room. "Instead of entering the Church as was expected, Simeon d'Évreux went to Englelond. That's all I know." She paused, her hand in mid-stitch. "I met him once when I was young." She squinted into the sunlight streaming through the windows as if lost in a long-ago memory. "He was . . . beautiful."

"Beautiful!" Marie looked at Elise, surprised Hortense would ever notice such a thing.

"Yes," Hortense said, taking another stitch. "There are men who are easy to look upon, and Simeon was one."

"And did you look upon him long?" Marie asked wickedly.

Hortense, with a blush rising on her cheeks, glared angrily at Marie and hissed, "May you be blessed with a daughter such as you." Still miffed, she said to Elise, "If your husband resembles his father, he will please your eyes."

"Oh," Marie said, pursing her lips. "Handsome means he will be easy to kiss, and if he is easy to kiss, he will be easy—"

"Marie," Hortense warned.

"— to bed! Elise, you will like kissing him. I just know it."

"Stop," Elise said, trying not to laugh. "This is an alliance, nothing more. I cannot think of such things."

"Well, you should give those things some thought!" Marie said insistently. "Methinks it would be an important consideration when waking up each morning and facing the day. Or, mayhap when going to bed and facing the . . . the knight!" With that, she burst into uncontrollable laughter, and so did Elise.

Hortense pressed her lips together, trying to hide her own smile, and sighed. "Handsomeness is less important than wisdom."

"Um," Marie said, still chuckling. "If your saints bless you, Elise, he will not beat you."

"Do not be foolish! He *will* beat you," Hortense said. "Pray he will not beat you often."

"I fear he will be as fierce in our chamber as he is in warfare. They say he is ruthless and changes into a wolf during battle."

"Do not fret, Elise," Hortense said. "It is proper to fear him. Rumors are important weapons in war, and although some truth may exist for this gossip, we do not know the man." Hortense's hands stitched rhythmically as she spoke. "You must go to him without expectations, and in the discovery, you will have to win his loyalty and respect. He could be just as surprised as you are about this betrothal and therefore, might be distant at first."

"He was angry," Elise said. "His mark tore the parchment."

Hortense appraised Elise. "Although most of your siblings died of the pox, God blessed you both with few scars."

Elise ran her fingers over the small scars at her left temple. She could only vaguely remember the chills, fevers, the pustules. But she clearly remembered the burials in an unending procession, her brothers and sisters, and her mother, who lashed a strand of leather thongs tied with beads across her naked back as punishment—for she had lost nearly all her children, and worse, because she had been spared.

"Your visage and physique will please him," Hortense said, "for a while. But you must learn quickly how to serve him best. In a few years, you and he might find solace in each other."

"Not so," Marie said. "He will cherish you, Elise. He will be enthralled. You'll see, he will not be able to resist you."

Hortense grunted. "Along with your estates, you give him the knowledge and ability to administer them. As chatelaine, you assist his seneschal, run his households, direct his servants, and see to his comforts. You will care for the villagers, represent him in his absences, even defend his holdings if you must. You will give him loyalty, virtue, and progeny. He, in turn, will protect you and give you a place of honor in his home. And since he is close to William, you will be close to the king as well. You must take care and be alert to all manner of intrigue."

"Speaking of intrigue, why did Eustace pursue this marriage?" Elise asked.

Hortense shook her head. "Eustace does nothing without purpose. He—" Hortense stopped. "No need to say more. My conjectures would be tainted by loathing."

"You cannot prejudice us," Elise said. "Eustace wears his ambition like a royal mantle. If you suspect his motives, you must tell me. Knowing his intrigues will help me."

Hortense shook her head. "Be wise, Elise. Never underestimate him."

"As did your husband?" Marie asked softly.

"It is time to plan for the festivities," Hortense said, setting her sewing aside.

"Marie's question," Elise said, chiding her sister, "though unwarranted by its rudeness, begs an answer. Eustace is dangerous. But surely, ignorance is more dangerous. In the days and weeks ahead, there may be no other time to prepare us for what may come."

Hortense studied both girls. Eustace would not have given so rich a bride and such important lands to someone who could not advance his ambitions or give him a port, a dukedom, a kingdom.

"I have known Eustace nearly all my life." Hortense paused, remembering when at nine she was sent to live with her first cousins, when her marriage three years later saved her from Eustace's attention. "I know him better than most. Be forewarned, not frightened. Knowing him may help you. Eustace will stop at nothing to attain his ends. He uses deceit and trickery. Through dense machinations, he makes others do his bidding. He will betray his liege lord if profitable to himself. He will do *anything* to ruin his opponents, even destroy a king in the process. He demands absolute loyalty, yet he can and will turn on his most loyal men. My husband, a Saxon, a lord in liege to Eustace, was one of Eustace's most loyal men, yet Eustace destroyed him. I tell you what little I know, so you may pause when dealing with him."

She began with Edward's unexpected rise to the English throne. "His mother, Englelond's Queen Emma of Normandie, had sent Edward and his siblings to Rouen for protection. They lived under the care of their uncle the duke for decades.

"When Eustace entered his eighteenth winter, his royal ambitions became clear. He married Godgifu, daughter of King Æthelred of the English, Edward's sister, a woman over thirty, newly widowed with two well-placed sons. One held the Vexin." Hortense looked pointedly at Elise. "Once Edward ascended the throne, Eustace, the king's brother-in-marriage, became exceedingly influential.

"Because King Edward had no heir, powerful families vied for the throne. Everyone knew a child of Eustace and Godgifu could inherit the throne. Only one daughter survived the marriage, and Eustace married her off when she was but twelve winters. Within a year, she had birthed a son.

"Shortly after his grandson's birth, Eustace and my husband traveled to London to ask King Edward to name the boy the king's heir."

"Heir to Englelond?" Elise asked.

Hortense explained the boy's pedigree: Edward's nephew, King Æthelred's great-grandson, a child in the direct line of the ancient heirs to the throne. "Edward favored the boy. The queen favored her brother, a Godwin. The king wavered. And that, according to my husband, is when Eustace set out to destroy the Godwins."

She shook her head and related what her husband had told her: "On their way back to Boulogne, Eustace and his men stopped in Dover, a Godwin stronghold. There, they provoked the villagers and killed a few men. Returning to London, Eustace claimed the villagers had attacked him and demanded the Godwins punish the village for disrespecting the king's own brother-in-marriage.

"The Godwins refused to punish villagers defending themselves against Eustace's aggression. The king recoiled at Godwin's insolence. Goaded by Eustace, he recalled Godwin's contempt when he haughtily denied murdering Edward's younger brother. Furious, Edward dispossessed and banished the entire family, including his queen.

"In the end," Hortense said, "the Godwins returned. They forced the king to outlaw all the French-speaking officials he had taken with him. Edward, humiliated and weakened by this event, blamed Eustace. Afterward, isolated without his Norman advisors, Edward became a virtual prisoner of Harold Godwinson, the strongest of Godwin's sons."

"And Eustace?" Marie asked.

"He returned to Boulogne."

"Where is the boy?" Elise asked.

"With our Maker," Hortense said, crossing herself. "It is said he died of the same pestilence that claimed most of your family."

"How, why did Eustace destroy you and your husband?" Marie asked.

"A few years after the Godwin's prevailed, Eustace sent my husband back across the Narrow Sea, on a secret mission to a monastery. After the Dover incident, it was dangerous for French-speaking travelers, especially someone from Boulogne to enter the kingdom. But my husband intended to speak only Saxon, told me not to fret, for when Eustace ruled, we would be well rewarded."

"Ruled what?" Elise asked.

"I never learned what he meant. Perhaps he failed. In my husband's absence, Eustace charged him with high crimes. When he landed in Boulogne, he was set upon and killed for bounty. Eustace seized all our lands and goods. Only your mother's pleas saved me from destitution."

"Eustace must regret the loss of his grandson," Elise said, "more now after William's venture."

"Yes. Had the boy survived, he could have ascended the throne, with Eustace as regent."

"William would have fought him," Elise said.

"Eustace would have checked him." Hortense picked up her sewing and resumed her work. "Your uncle has powerful allies. Through his second marriage, he is tied to the Dukes of Lorraine and to Emperor Henry. He vows that his sons will be kings. It is no jest that some people call him the *Kingmaker*. Even William did not pursue his English venture without Eustace's support."

"Thierry de Châlons negotiates for King Philip," Elise watched Hortense's hands stop in mid stitch before continuing.

"Your loyalties must be clear, Elise," Hortense said. "With this marriage, you will become a child of your new land. Eustace, or others, might try to use you or your husband to cripple William—or Philip. Be ever vigilant."

"And if Philip and William went to war?" Elise asked. "Am I to remain silent if my husband fights against the Franks, against my cousin Philip, even against Roland?"

Hortense put her sewing down and looked at Elise. "Your allegiance is to your husband. He is William's man. We can only hope such wars will not happen. Meanwhile, you will rise or fall with your husband. If he allows your council, you can advise him, perhaps steer him from manipulations. If he does not, you must honor his wishes, and if possible, lessen the damage of his errors."

"I will miss your counsel and wisdom, Hortense," Elise whispered.

"No need," Marie said. "She's going with you, aren't you, Hortense?"

"Marie!" Elise said. "Who would protect you from Arques and Eustace?"

"I will ask Thierry for Roland."

"You will do no such thing," Elise said.

"Then," Marie said with conviction, "I will invite Alys to visit. And Lesceline, and Judith, and . . . Anne. If Roland won't have me, I will live with Alys."

"What devilish motives you have," Elise laughed. "Tristan will never leave if Lesceline is here."

Marie smiled. "I know."

"Hortense?" Elise asked.

"We've talked it over, the two of us," Marie burst out. Hortense took another stitch without looking up. "Hortense knows about Saxons from her husband. She speaks their language and knows their ways. Besides, the journey will be treacherous but easier with someone you trust. Your husband will welcome Hortense, who will help you settle in. And I will keep the servants you do not take with you." Marie finished breathlessly.

Elise saw red blotches rising on Hortense's cheeks. "Marie! You planned this without talking to Hortense."

Marie pressed her lips together.

"It is the right decision," Hortense said. "One I had reached myself."

"But, what will happen to Marie?"

"Marie's plan is sound. If she marries Roland, she will be safe. If not, Thierry will find her another husband or a nunnery. Besides, we have a month to consider the details. Marie cannot stay here without you, and her friends will shield her for a while. You cannot go without me. The matter is settled. Now, what to wear for the betrothal ceremony?"

Seeing Hortense's determined glare, Elise withheld her opposition. Hortense's guidance would help her face a new life. And if Eustace planned to use her and this marriage for villainous purposes, Hortense would help her thwart him.

Chapter Thirteen

"W alter," Elise said with an irritated sigh, "this is not the time."

"Of course it is," he said, opening a beautifully burnished wooden casket inlaid with gold and silver designs. "It's the last chance I have to challenge you, and first time in years, I'll likely win." She frowned at him, and he continued. "We might as well play," he said, gesturing with his head toward the alcove. "This may take a while."

She followed his gaze to the white linen screens embroidered with red crosses shielding the betrothal negotiations. Hortense had banished Elise and Walter to the benches at the far end of the central hearth as she and Marie prepared the great room for celebration. From there, Elise could neither hear the negotiations nor participate in arranging the festivities. Dressed for ceremony in a soft green chemise beneath a white heavily embroidered wool cotte, a bejeweled belt at her hips, she sat quietly, her index finger tapping the wooden bench beside her knee.

Her gaze flitted over Walter sitting across from her. She wished he would go away so she could think. Instead, he arranged the checkered leather sheet on the stool situated between them.

Inside the casket, red silk covered the padded niches cradling the pieces. Walter's godfather, Henri, former king of the Franks, had given the game to him at his birth. Made in Persia, it was more refined than anything in Francia, and the only thing Walter had kept when exiled from Normandie—a beautiful yet painful reminder of a future lost to him forever.

He lifted out a small alabaster piece, simply carved with vertical lines rising to the jagged points of a crown. "I christen you, *William Rex*." He slid the throne across the leather. "Suppose we put him here . . . and beside him . . ." Walter removed a matching throne, as tall as the king but thinner, with the grooved shaft capped by a horizontal band. "His arch-chancellor, Matilda of Flanders."

Elise could not wholly suppress her smile, although she raised a hand to cover her lips. It was a wasted gesture, for her eyes gave her away. She caught Walter's infectious grin.

"You, Walter, are irreverent!"

"Yes, 'tis a sickness I have recently developed and . . . there is no cure."

He reached into the case again and pulled out two cubes, each topped, front and back, with points resembling a mitre. "Let's see now. This," he said, placing one piece next to Matilda, "is the archbishop of Rouen and this . . ." he balanced the other bishop in his hands as if testing its weight. He sighed, "I guess this has to be Stigand of Canterbury. We'll put him next to William—where he can be watched." Elise laughed, for everyone knew about Stigand, the scandalous archbishop excommunicated by five popes.

"Next, your favorite," Walter grinned and extracted a rectangular block with a horse's head and carved lines cleverly depicting its legs. "William has too many knights to choose from," Walter said. "I suppose we have to make one of these Guillaume fitz Osbern since he is the king's regent. Let's put him . . . here." He rubbed his hands together. "Now, we have Stigand cornered."

He tapped the second horse gently against the casket. "Now, at fourteen, William's son Robert is too young for knighthood. Instead, let us put Robert's guardian into play."

Watching him set the knight on a square, Elise felt none of the turmoil engulfing her years ago when Walter began teaching her this game. Once her infatuation eased, she'd learned quickly since chess was similar to *tafl*, a game she'd played often. Today, he had honored her by donning his finest, deep yellow tunic trimmed in black embroidery. He resembled his sire, she thought, gazing at his handsome, unblemished features, a brow furrowing in concentration, warm hazel eyes sometimes glowing like honey, and his full lips, which, unlike his father's, smiled often.

Arques went into frequent, vicious rampages and belittled his son as if Walter were to blame for his misery. Once at table, Arques said, "I often wondered what slathering coward your mother rutted with to bring you forth." Silence fell upon everyone, and she remembered the odd look on Walter's face. Calmly, Walter smiled at his father. "It is obvious to me," he said, raising his wine to toast his sire, who rose so quickly he nearly toppled the boards.

Now, absorbed by arranging the tall, slender towers, marked by long, deep clefts, he said, "Here is Westminster Palace, and this is the castle at Rouen."

"And the foot soldiers?" she grinned, shaking her head at him.

"In truth, that's the rest of William's lieutenants," he said, "but we should choose the best, don't you think, Elise?" He quickly arranged the squat, three-sided pieces on the row in front of the king.

"Now," he said, touching each pawn lightly with his middle finger as he ran down the row. "Here is Alain le Roux of Brittany, Dreux Marchand de Ville, and Guillaume Malet." Touching the two center pawns simultaneously with his index fingers, "William's brothers, Bishop Odo and Robert de Mortain." Moving to the other pawns, he continued. "Guillaume d'Évreux, Alaric of Ewyas, of course, and last but not least, *Uncle* Eustace. Do you want to tie a ribbon around your knight to give him your liege, my lady?"

"What?" she chuckled. "Encumber his charge with unfurled silks?"

"Ah," Walter said. "A sage wife."

She reached for the opposing throne, equally carved but with blue staining the carved grooves. "Who is this?"

Walter glanced at the alcove before whispering. "This is . . . *Philip*."

Elise grimaced. "Treasonous!" she chided in a conspiratorial whisper, placing the piece across from William.

"True." He wagged his eyebrows at her.

She set the matching blue chancellor beside Philip.

Walter frowned. "For shame, we cannot have the dowager Queen Mother." Elise cringed at Walter's innuendo, for he referred to the queen's affair with a married man.

"Instead, this is Thierry de Châlons, but he is no match for Matilda," he teased. "Soon, Philip will need his own queen." He looked up at her, his eyes twinkling. "You're already spoken for, but you would have made a wondrous queen."

She laughed and tipped her head, acknowledging the compliment. "The Church would bless that consanguineous marriage with excommunication and an interdiction against Francia."

"Mere trifles." He waved a hand over the board, chasing gnats away. "To whom shall we marry him?" he asked, adjusting the blue king on the board. "I know, let's give him a Danish princess. That ought to alarm William." He affected a tic and trembling hands.

Elise's mirth exploded, "Danish! It would alarm me, too. Especially if the Danes attack my new home in Englelond!"

She pulled out the rest of the pieces and set them on the board. Walter named them quickly: the dukes of Lorraine and Aquitaine, the counts of Anjou, Blois, Poitou, Berry, Bourbon. "And Flanders," he whispered.

Elise gasped. William's father-in-law, Baldwin of Flanders, was until recently Philip's regent and guardian. Of course, he would check William. In a moment, the board was ready. Elise played the white and Walter the blue.

"Ah," he said at her first move, "the lady advances her husband."

As they played, Elise realized how much she would miss Walter— the joy of talking with him, his refinements, and tastes, so like her own—and she wondered about her betrothed. *Brash and uncultured*, Brian had said. Alaric of Ewyas, born near Wales, far from Norman refinements, would be steeped in a coarse culture and exhibit crude, rough behaviors. Not only would their different ranks create a schism between them, but the smallest differences in their tastes would likely keep them strangers.

Remembering his angry mark on the betrothal documents, she feared calamity would come from this marriage. Could she stop the union, now, before it was too late? She glanced at the alcove where the negotiators conferred.

The nuns taught that consent was the first and most important step of marriage. If she did not consent, she could be sent back to the dreaded abbey or remain here with Arques. Neither Eustace nor

William would allow that. It was more likely she would be forced to marry involuntarily—occasioned by rape and abduction—a custom powerful men employed. No, she thought, she would consent.

Walter glanced up, "I'm thinking. I'm thinking."

"Take your time, Walter."

As he turned his attention to the board again, Elise stood up and paced before the hearth. She saw Marie placing greenery on the tables. Servants swept in from a side room with armloads of pitchers. Elise stopped walking and turned toward the alcove.

She could refuse to join her betrothed or speak the marriage vows. She immediately rejected that notion. Her presence was unnecessary, a proxy could speak her vows.

In the end, consummation made the marriage legal. Perhaps she and her betrothed could forge a quick alliance. In doing so, they might postpone consummation until they understood their positions better. This last recourse depended on her husband—his determination to have her land and wealth and his understanding of their situation. This match angered him. Perhaps, she could persuade him to delay the final act. If not, she must live with the consequences of her husband's alliances and the knowledge that he could thrust them into destitution. Her gaze moved to Walter, a daily reminder of how precarious her future could be, plunged as he had been from noble to pauper by his father's rash decisions.

Chapter Fourteen

Behind the screens shielding an alcove, the men deciding Elise's future spoke in hushed voices broken by an occasional chuckle or a muffled cough. Informal negotiations were in progress as they moved about the intimate room. A long narrow table draped in linen, surrounded by benches, was situated to one side. Blank parchments, ink, a quill and documents bearing ribbons and seals were scattered on the table. The room glowed from the light of tall candles placed in the triple-headed sconces of silver candelabrums flanking both ends of the table and from flaming oil in cressets mounted high on one wall. A side table, bearing a strip of red linen embroidered with blue thread, held a bowl of dried fruit, decanters of wine, and mazers.

The two most important men in the room were Thierry de Châlons, representing King Philip of the Franks, and Dreux Marchand de Ville, representing King William and the groom. Brian Dubec and Guillaume Arques both represented Elise's uncle. Juhel de Ponthieu, Abbot of Clarion, served as recorder.

Because Elise was a countess in her own right, a cousin of King Philip, and held land of importance to two kings, her betrothal had consisted of tentative offers. Without consent of the major parties, no marriage would ensue, so, as customary, they had semi-private talks with each other until the formal discussions began. Few of the real issues would be discussed candidly. These would be left to conjecture or deduced from what remained unspoken. Offers would be made and rejected like innocent swordplay—a parry here, a clash there—quickly withdrawn and thrust into play again beneath a ruse, all within the strict rules of decorum, rank, and protocol.

Dreux Marchand de Ville exemplified the robust Norsemen from whom the Normans descended. His alert body, poised for action, was clothed in a simple dark-green tunic, which barely concealed his bulging arms, and his hose emphasized thick, muscular legs.

Thierry de Châlons, nearly sixty, had silver hair, which fell over his high forehead, and a long, thin, humorless face with deep vertical grooves beside full lips. His pale, restless eyes glistened as they darted over everyone in the room. Simultaneously, he heard every conversation. His dress—unadorned black wool over gray—reflected his early monastic training.

Dreux and Thierry had greeted each other like old friends, having negotiated on behalf of Philip and William before. Thierry took no offense that William sent a mere knight to parley with King Philip's advisor. The balance was tipped in Thierry's favor—as always. Besides, Thierry enjoyed Dreux, the most able envoy he had met in years, except Roland de Rennes, of course. Although Thierry had tried to lure Dreux to King Philip's diplomatic corps, he had enormous respect for the young knight's refusal and his loyalty to William, a devotion Thierry himself had once embraced.

Dreux had a delicate mission: reaffirm Duke William's vassalage to his overlord King Philip while negotiating on behalf of *King* William to his peer *King* Philip. He also intended to capture rich Norman estates for Alaric, strengthening William's hold on the duchy without provoking Philip's aggression or distrust.

Thierry's mission was the opposite. On behalf of King Philip, he would negotiate only with Philip's *vassal*, the duke. He intended to weaken William's hold on the duchy by limiting the estates transferring to the groom. King Philip believed William wanted his crown and all of Francia. Philip would let William have Englelond, but William could not have both Englelond *and* Normandie.

Dreux and Thierry began with the traditional platitudes and moved on to their central tasks, neither openly discussing their intentions. To protect Normandie's border from attack, William wanted the eastern Aumale and Mortemer lands in Alaric's possession. Philip wanted the land to remain with Elise, thereby segmenting control of the border and pitting Elise against her husband.

Dreux offered a compromise: Divert the revenues. Both knew the move would render those lands virtually useless to the countess and her husband.

"The proposal has merit," Thierry said. He shifted the discussion to the Vexin, the more important of Elise's lands, the poisoned thorn prickling both Philip and William. With the formation of the Norman duchy, the Vexin province was divided along the River Epte. The northern Vexin belonged to the Normans, the southern part to the Franks. For years, the Norman dukes and the kings of Francia had fought over it.

A few years ago, William had seized the entire Vexin and captured its count and his wife, both of whom died in William's custody. Afterward, the Vexin went to Ralph de Crépi, William's loyal vassal, a man married to Philip's widowed mother, the dowager queen.

Elise held Fontenay, one of the last sovereign principalities remaining in the Vexin. Her land had immense strategic importance. Situated along the right bank of the Seine, where the river narrows and flows through a series of tight curves flanked by promontories—ideal for blocking invaders—it also hosted the road between Rouen and Paris.

Although the Vexin fell under Crépi's rule, Fontenay, Elise's independent principality within the Vexin, had passed from one generation to another since Charles le Magne. Following the tradition of his predecessors, King Philip had reaffirmed Elise's holding. As Thierry and Dreux discussed the Vexin, neither mentioned its strategic importance.

King Philip wanted the entire Vexin, not merely Elise's patrimony. At fifteen, Philip did not yet have the strength to seize the Vexin—or hold it once he got it. He was content to allow Elise her birthright. If her husband died, he would marry her quickly to a close ally. Philip had time on his side. William would be old when Philip reached his prime.

Thierry offered an attractive diversion: land in the province of Berry. "A marriage gift from King Philip, in exchange for an equal amount of land in the Vexin along the Seine." It was an interesting consideration, for it would plant a Norman seed in land not yet part of the Norman empire. Dreux graciously rejected the offer.

"King Phillip expects the countess to retain her title and the estates in her own right."

"Of course," Dreux smiled. It mattered little if the countess held the titles. Alaric would control the land. William would see to it. Although both knew William would determine how Alaric used the land, only Thierry knew what Philip planned for its future.

When their negotiations concluded, Thierry learned that Dreux and Alaric were close friends. "The groom is perhaps ambitious?"

Dreux laughed. "Aren't we all?"

Thierry nodded. His own investigations revealed how Eustace contrived the death of Alaric's family. He supposed Alaric was typically Norman: a common opportunist, wanting land, privilege, and tenure—at any cost. Useful qualities for Philip still learning how to control ambitious men. He could be generous when necessary, and he could always send Alaric to Jerusalem.

Thierry looked across the room and saw candlelight reflecting off Abbot Juhel's crucifix. For years, he had enjoyed reading Juhel's ecclesiastical doctrines challenging Rome's precepts. The abbot had recently scandalized the Church by arguing most succinctly against selling indulgences, relics, and benefices. Thierry had also enjoyed the controversy stirred when Juhel proposed prelates give up their wives and concubines.

In Thierry's estimation, Juhel de Ponthieu, Abbot of Clarion, one of the few ethical prelates left these days, deserved his high repute. Unlike William's brother, Bishop Odo, Juhel did not use his position to enrich himself and display ostentatious wealth comparable to the nobility's temporal estates. Juhel expressed his zeal through his ecclesiastical writings on the liturgy and apostolic traditions. His latest letter to the pope had warned of pagan rituals still occurring in Normandie today. The claim did not surprise Thierry, for even near Paris, pagans held secret ceremonies, although he thought they no longer sacrificed animals or humans.

Thierry knew that Rome was listening to Juhel's astonishing position on marriage. Traditionally, marriage began with a simple oral promise, private or public, between the parties. Juhel pressed the Church to consider the marriage ceremony a *sacrament*. It was an outrageous concept, of course. Marriage was profane, a carnal act, consigned to the laity, distinct from the sacred. Yet, Juhel argued that the Church must officiate unions among the nobility. He urged the

Church to decrease annulment requests based on incest by investigating the degrees of familial relationships between high-ranking couples *before* marriage. He also insisted the Church participate in these unions to record the accompanying land transfers. Of course, Juhel wrote, the Church must recognize its own wealth relied on endowments generated from these very unions, although prelates should take care not to confuse the secular and the sacred.

Both Thierry and King Philip understood the importance of the last point, and so it seemed did William. This marriage between Genevieve de Fontenay and Alaric of Ewyas commingled lands in Normandie and Englelond, and Juhel would document the agreement carefully.

"I'm getting old," Juhel said to Arques, reaching for a slice of dried apple. "My leg troubles me more and more, and I languish at Clarion." Juhel wore elegant white and blue robes of the finest Byzantine silk embroidered with bands of gold thread. Shorter than Arques, but equally commanding in his stance, he had large hands and a large, flat face, wide-spaced hazel eyes, and a pale complexion. At forty-eight, he felt the ravages of age. An old injury had left him with a throbbing pain that now, as he gained weight, bothered him more.

"You and William are still allies, I see," Arques said.

Arques meant the time when William revoked Juhel's lands and titles after the abbot incautiously speculated about the chastity of the duke's mother, a tanner's daughter. William restored all when he needed another vote on the ecclesiastical council.

"We understand the value of strong alliances." Juhel rocked on his feet. He had to make his move now. Pope Alexander was ill, and soon, a new pope would insist on ecclesiastical reforms. To implement those reforms, Juhel must obtain a high office in William's kingdom, where he could live out his last years amidst the greatest changes of his time.

"I am seeking appointment to the archbishopric of Canterbury," he said, running his fingers down the chain of his crucifix.

Arques understood immediately. In exchange for supporting Juhel's bid, the abbot would funnel rents from Genevieve's estates to Arques, who had augmented William's coins by skimming off her rents for years. But now, the rents would all go to her husband unless other arrangements were made. "Once," he reminded Juhel, "I contributed large endowments to your abbey and would do so again."

"Um." Juhel pursed his lips but did not dispute Arques' overstatement of the pittance he had given, which barely provided funds to roof the chapel.

"By keeping me in coin, I can . . . *influence* others on your behalf," Arques said.

Juhel nodded. Arques had little influence. Still, he had made a negligible request. "Perhaps Philip could be persuaded to reward your loyalty to his father."

"Thank you," Arques said. "I most humbly accept your intercession."

Brian Dubec had watched Juhel and Arques keenly, observing a pact in the making. He recalled Eustace's instructions: *make any concession necessary to seal this betrothal.* The count's reasons remained a mystery. With secret pleasure, Dubec remembered Alaric's knife at Eustace's throat. Perhaps the marriage intended to humiliate Alaric, to make him swallow the death of his family. Perhaps Eustace intended to use a man like the Black Wolf. Eustace took time assembling his puppets like a master player gathered his actors.

When Abbot Juhel joined the others, Dubec approached Arques. "At Eustace's command, you do not have a place at this table."

Arques glared at Dubec, Eustace's arse-tickler. He buried this insult in speechless anger, crossed the room to Thierry, and waited until the others left them alone before presenting his case for King Philip's support.

Thierry smiled, "Be assured, the king will hear of your suggestions."

At Juhel's request, the men took their seats. Since they'd resolved all issues informally, formal discussions began.

A s she waited for Walter's next move, Elise considered why Thierry de Châlons came to negotiate her betrothal. He had been her father's trusted friend, much like a beloved uncle. But that was not why he was here. After King Henri's death, Thierry had become and remained the most important advisor to the throne. Thierry's presence went beyond any friendship or familial ties. Her marriage was important to Francia.

Since leaving Abbey Clarion, she had taken more interest in the relationships among the provinces and kingdoms and the princely decisions affecting her villagers. Last year, with the movement of emis-saries, armies, and treasuries, she'd learned how alliances coalesced to support the invasion and how William tapped resources from near and far. The preparations had stirred her, although she never dreamed she would be enmeshed in the fortunes of the new Norman kingdom.

She counted the painted roses edging the whitewashed room. Her gaze drifted to the fading mural at the back wall portraying the Last Supper. She knew the disciples grouped around the table loosely rep-resented Normandie, Brittany, Flanders, and the Île de France. Each apostle stood for a powerful noble, surrounding the Pope as the Lord. Judas, the Germanic Holy Roman Emperor, sat alone.

She studied the Vexin, a painted wedge of cheese on a platter of fruit representing Francia. William needed strong warlords to protect the Vexin abutting Francia's border. Philip needed the Vexin to attack Normandie.

Her heart pounded. She and her husband would be called upon to defend Normandie for Duke William or to ensure its instability for King Philip. In either case, powerful forces would squeeze her and her husband, and any mistaken alliances would cost them, especially if Eustace tried to use the marriage for his purposes against either king—

"Pay attention, Elise," Walter yawned. "I've just taken one of your knights." He straightened his back and shifted on the bench. Walter watched the confusion on Elise's face as if trying to understand the effect of his move. He glanced toward the alcove and saw no move-ment. Behind him, he heard the preparations for the banquet still underway.

As Elise examined the board, his eyes followed the sweep of her shoulders down her arm to the hand resting in her lap. He longed to entwine his fingers in hers. Walter looked away. He knew there was no point, but his eyes drifted back to her hair, to an auburn wisp escaping one of her braids.

She had asked him once, last summer as they had walked in the garden, what he would most want to have if he could. He had not told her that *she* would have been the greatest prize. Instead, he had said he wanted King Philip to send him on a special mission. Whatever the task, left to his own devices, he would accomplish it with great success. Afterward, he would begin to regain the favor of the crown:

a few estates, perhaps, an heiress. She'd smiled at him. His heart had pounded. *I will pray for you to get another chance Walter*, she'd said softly, her dazzling eyes so deep, so blue, so guileless.

"Take that, you beast!" she glanced up at him, grinning, her eyes sparkling in that mischievous way she had that nearly sent him to his knees.

He looked down at the game and back at her. "Why you little . . . You think to check me. Not yet, my lady." He turned his attention to her pieces surrounding his king.

Watching Walter hover over the board, she became annoyed with herself. This morning, she let Marie lull her with visions of an enthralled husband. There was nothing carefree, innocent—nor amorous—about her marriage. It was an alliance. Like others among the nobility, it balanced titles, lands, and wealth, and assured military support. Uniting a duchy and a kingdom would become a complicated and dangerous life. She would need strength, all her wit, and vigilance to survive.

She gripped the bench tighter. Closing her eyes, she strove to calm her alarm by humming a chant the nuns had taught. *Oh, Holy Mother, in this place of darkness, guide and defend me against my enemies. Be my helper and . . . .* When she opened her eyes, she found Walter watching her, his dark, intense expression nearly frightening.

"Do not shrink from your new fortunes," he said softly. "As soon as you affix your seal, you will be free of your uncle and my father."

"Free?" she chuckled. "Free to be governed by a husband."

"A husband who battles for William, a husband likely to be killed very soon or perish from festering wounds. When widowed, you retain one-third of his estates, and you keep your own land. If you choose to marry again, you can, without interference from Eustace and my father, as long as Philip agrees."

"What of William?"

"You may have to forfeit your English lands. But unlike me, Elise, you have a chance. So, think carefully about your betrothal. Make sure you have something to bargain with, something that does not rely on your husband's life."

At that moment, Walter's father stepped out from behind the screen and motioned to Elise with a curt nod.

Chapter Fifteen

Elise had the distinct impression that she entered a den of lions. Five lions, to be exact. She nodded at the witnesses, silent and poised as if ready to attack.

These men had decided how to distribute her land and wealth. She knew all but the young, strikingly handsome man whose visage astonished her. She stared as Dreux Marchand de Ville was introduced and felt a flush rise on her cheeks before she snapped her gaze away.

"Countess de Fontenay?" Dreux asked incredulously.

Hearing astonishment, she looked at Dreux again. His lips twitched in amusement. His white-blond hair, pale blue eyes, and sculptured features disconcerted her. She frowned, seeing his gaze sweep from her hair to her figure, over her face, and stare too long at her eyes.

"I am . . . I am honored," he said, "to represent King William and to serve as your betrothed's proxy. I look forward to the blessed day Lord Stafford meets you himself."

"Thank you," she said, confused by Dreux's smile conveying both curiosity and mischief.

"Come," Abbot Juhel said.

The men circled her as she approached the table and the parchment arranged before her. Her presence, a mere formality, required her to attach her seal to the agreement. Regaining her composure and aware of the import of this moment, she refused the offered seat.

Abbot Juhel handed her a small bar of red wax and pointed out the silk ribbon. Holding the cool wax, she gazed at the white ribbons attached to the document, one bearing King William's seal, another her uncle's, and the others yet to be sealed.

She set the wax aside. "I would like to read the agreement."

"There is no need to do so," Arques said abruptly. "All is in order."

Abbot Juhel tapped his thick finger on the document at the place for her seal.

She smiled at the witnesses. "I invite you to have more wine or to take a stroll." She gestured toward the side table. "I will take but a moment." She raised the documents and began to read, turning toward the candlelight.

No one moved. They glared at her, their backs stiffened by disbelief.

Dreux's surprise that she could read quickly dissolved into outrage, a sentiment shared by the others, judging by their expressions. She trespassed into their domain as if she could alter the results. It was bluster. She had no option, and they all knew it. Despite his annoyance, he saluted her effort, wondering if she were reluctant to marry Alaric, who attracted women like woolen hose attracted stickers. He would enjoy telling Alaric that his bride hesitated.

As silent moments passed, Arques' fury became so ferocious he thought he might snap. He could not allow this *woman* to slight his authority in front of Thierry and the others. He must act. Glaring at Elise, he cleared his throat to get her attention. She continued to read.

Arques announced, "The Countess de Fontenay can read, but the words," his hand rocked in the air, "have little meaning to her." He shrugged and swept his gaze to Juhel.

"Yes," the abbot concurred. Leaning close to her ear, he urged softly, "Child, you cannot possibly understand the agreements. We, adept at such comprehension, have provided well for you."

She looked up at the abbot, startled by his hard eyes, which belied those gentle words.

"Abbot Juhel." Her gaze darted to the others in the room. "I mean no disrespect, but the nuns spent many years teaching me to read the scriptures. Surely, their endeavors were not wasted." She clutched the documents. "After all," she continued, "the scriptures have greater import than a mere listing of lands. Is that not so?" She smiled at him, hearing only the sputtering candle beside her in the heavy silence of the room.

"Yes." Juhel's eyes pierced hers, and his finger pointed in her face, nearly touching her nose. "Take care, Lady de Fontenay," his voice deepening. "Challenging your guardian may draw the devil's attention to your aspirations." He continued, his voice lower and more frightening, "I am sure you intend no insult to the agents of the kings of Francia and Englelond. My dear countess, you trust and obey your liege lords, do you not?"

Icy fear gripped her as she looked from Thierry to Dreux. Their expressions clearly demanded her acquiescence. Was her insistence treasonous? Could the Church excommunicate her for reading the documents? Had she crossed some invisible barrier marking her for life?

"My lords," she said, madly pressing her case, "I would like to read the documents. If you prefer," she paused, "I could affix my seal tomorrow after I have studied how the land and rents will be distributed." She tried to swallow, but her mouth was dry.

Her threat, delivered in a soft but determined voice, astonished them all. Before they could rail against her, Brian Dubec coughed. Everyone turned to him.

"The countess should read the documents now," he said, rubbing his chin and moving toward the side table. Looking at Thierry and Dreux, he asked, "will you join me in another wine?" After a brief hesitation, they did so, and Elise resumed reading.

She scanned her seneschal's inventory: the woods, meadows, pastures, manors, mills, and villages. Quickly, she glanced at the acres farmed, the timber cut, the crops sowed this year, and the estimated revenues from the spring, summer, and winter seed. She skipped over the tally of sheep, pigs, and other livestock, searching for the gold and silver.

In moments, she became aware of the men pacing the room. Occasionally one or another sighed loudly or yawned or rapped his rings on the table as he walked by. They urged her to hurry. They mentioned the feast awaiting them and that the hour grew late. She continued to read. Arques and Juhel hovered over her. Moments passed while she read, ignoring Arques' agitated, impatient grunts and

Juhel's growling stomach. Soon, all the men were standing around her again, waiting impatiently for her.

They all want this union too much. Although her betrothed held estates in places called Wessex and Mercia, they were small and unimportant. Consequently, her land would enrich him. He will gain legal authority and sole control over her wealth. He would not have to ask her about using the lands and rents, improvements, distribution, trades, or otherwise. She would have no say in which of her children, if any, inherited these lands. By law, he could distribute her wealth to anyone—a mistress, the Church. But he would not take everything.

Even after marriage, she would control Fontenay and retain her title, but it was unclear who would retain the Aumale and Mortemer rents. Her eyes raced across the pages, searching for their disposition, and stopped to reread a single clause.

Elise quickly read the disposition of her wealth if she outlived her husband and flushed, reading her betrothed's promise to maintain her according to God's law—a law requiring her absolute obedience. A law she had already broken by reading the documents. She could not now retreat. Betrothal documents superseded any other arrangement. They must be specific.

Raising her eyes to Arques, she asked, "Please clarify the provisional clause assigning the Aumale and Mortemer rents to you."

"The arrangement is quite customary," Arques insisted.

She turned to Juhel, who, in his anger at her effrontery, raised his arrogant nose and pointed at the documents. "It is all written clearly. You see, gentlemen," he chuckled, turning to the others, "she is a simpleton, unable to understand such matters." He tried to snatch the documents from her hand as someone snickered.

Anger heated her cheeks, and she trembled even as she clutched the parchment. She took a deep breath. Putting the documents down, she gripped the table's edge. In barely a whisper, she asked Thierry, "My lord, will you explain the provision?"

Thierry's silence condemned her. She counted slowly, commanding her breath to come easily. Very well, she thought. She stepped back from the table.

As if by silent agreement, all but Dubec moved in on her. Powerful men surrounded her. They glared at her with merciless eyes, with the snarling grimace and thin lips of predators. They blocked her exit, their faces towered above her. Trapped behind the table, she could not breathe. They erupted, speaking at once, their voices hurting her ears.

"This delay is not amusing," Thierry declared. "King Philip will find your insolence—"

"We have indulged your curiosity long enough," Arques boomed, pointing an accusing finger at her. "Your arrogance is intolerable, shameful!" He stabbed at the parchments. "As your guardian, I *command* you to approve these documents without further delay."

She did not move.

Juhel shook his head. "You have a wicked and sinful nature," he said, his voice rumbling deeply. "You have contradicted God's laws by disobeying us. We should spare your husband from such a wife! Eustace should send you back to the abbey."

The abbey! Inexplicable terror sparked down her spine. She tried to think as their anger throbbed in the room. Tilting up her face, she saw it—a slight gleam, a sparkle of excitement flickered among them, like beasts charging for the final kill. She recoiled. Her back flattened against the wall.

Dubec pushed through the men crowding her and planted both hands on the table directly in front of her. Leaning in, he caught her attention. "It was decided among us," his calm voice broke the tension, "the estates—"

"She has no need to know," Arques growled at Dubec and waved his arm in dismissal. "She—"

"We have already agreed," Thierry said, putting a thumb and forefinger against the bridge of his nose.

"She must obey her masters without question," Abbot Juhel said, snatching the parchments. "She must append her seal. Now!"

Dubec slammed his hand on the documents with a snarl and bared teeth. The abbot released them immediately. Straightening, Dubec said, "The countess still controls her dower." The other men turned on Dubec.

"You are pandering to this—this child," Juhel barked, flicking his hand toward Elise. "She cannot comprehend the divine will of kings."

Dubec looked solely at her and began to explain the disposition of the rents. The others backed away.

Able to breathe again, Elise felt too grateful for Brian's intercession to wonder at his motives. She listened intently to his explanation. Lifting her hand to her throat, she asked Dreux, "My betrothed gifts me estates near Wales. What are my rights?"

Despite his obvious annoyance, Dreux explained, "The English acknowledge a woman's ownership and control of her dower and all inherited land—even after her marriage."

Astonishing, Elise thought. With very few exceptions, Norman women lost those rights upon marriage.

Dreux continued. "Betrothal gifts are not inherited. Ordinarily, your husband would administer those estates. In this case, Alaric gives you the Leominster estates under Angle and Saxon laws, with the privilege to use and dispose of the land as you choose."

Elise picked up the documents again and stepped out from behind the table where she had been trapped a moment ago. "So, English laws govern English lands, and Norman laws govern Norman lands?"

"Precisely," Dreux answered.

"Will English laws change to Norman laws?" Elise moved away from the table. "Will they be applied to my betrothal gift?"

"We cannot know this now, my lady," Dreux answered as she slowly crossed the room toward the screen. "For now, King William intends to uphold English laws even if they do not conform to Norman laws."

She ignored his eyes crinkling as if he read her intention to bolt. A glance at the others milling about the room revealed they were too incensed to notice her movement.

"You have all been very diligent," she said. "However, there is one change I would like to make."

They stopped in mid-motion, their glances flashing to one another.

"Enough!" Arques shouted. "You trifle with our patience." He looked at the men. "A mere woman cannot dictate the matters of her betrothal."

Dubec turned to Arques, "Leave us, now."

"Underlings do not give orders," Arques snarled. "Go bark at your master!"

"Take care, Arques," Thierry warned. "Best not to offend your sole patron."

Elise gasped. Thierry's remark reminded everyone that only Eustace had given Arques sanctuary when he left Normandie in defeat. No one aided him now. All courteous pretense honoring his former rank and importance vanished. Arques' lips curled, exposing his thoughts: *Once, I would have crushed you all!*

After he brushed past Elise, she spoke. "My lords." She took a deep breath and felt behind her for the edge of the screen. "I . . ." her voice cracked. "I want the document to state specifically that the Aumale and Mortemer rents," she paused, "are solely mine to administer and distribute as I wish, even after my marriage."

Abbot Juhel turned toward Dreux, who shrugged and, in turn, glanced at Thierry. She understood. The decision belonged to Thierry alone.

Thierry looked at the young and very bold Countess Genevieve Elysia de Fontenay and recognized her cousin King Philip's tenacious mind. Thierry thought about Genevieve's mother, Eustace's sister, more clever than her husband. A woman could understand and manage her affairs or the affairs of a kingdom. Philip's own mother, Anna, handed him a solvent kingdom. During William's absence, the duchy thrived under Matilda's rule, and she had ensured no local conflict detracted from William's kingdom across the Narrow Sea.

He mentally reviewed the rents in question. Though substantial, the land produced revenues and wealth far beyond the rents. Aumale and Mortemer were vital for Francia's future. Of course, Philip would be pleased to have her keep the rents—until he needed them. But she could give them to her husband.

He measured the Countess de Fontenay. She had demonstrated an annoying courage today, he thought. An independent mind could endanger Philip if used against him. More importantly, the countess had known precisely when to act—an essential skill.

He raised an eyebrow. It was a gamble. He could not be sure, but he thought this countess understood the importance of her land, how precariously she balanced between Normandie and Francia. If so, she would be a formidable ally or a formidable opponent. In either case, she would tread carefully and check her husband.

Thierry's eyes flickered at her. "It shall be written so." Without further dissent, Abbot Juhel snatched the documents from her hand and began amending the final terms.

Elise stayed by the screen, allowing herself to breathe again. She closed her eyes, listened to the nib scraping against the parchment, and felt her body shaking. *It's too late to wonder what exactly I have done.* She started when her eyes opened. Dreux stood before her, offering a cup of wine.

"Please accept my esteem. Your betrothal has been far more interesting than I expected when first sent to represent Stafford." Though he smiled, she sensed resentment. "I had not foreseen a woman's . . . perplexity."

She warily took the wine. "Please forgive any discomfort I caused you." She sipped, realizing that Dreux would report everything to her husband before she ever met him.

"Apology accepted," he said soberly. He saluted her with his cup, yet his gesture warned against further offense.

When Juhel announced the documents ready, Elise returned to the table. She read the changes, and taking the wax bar, she paused. This betrothal would condemn her irrevocably to a life and all eternity as wife and chattel to a man she had never seen. Elise melted the wax and let it drip into something resembling a pool of blood on the ribbon beneath Alaric's angry, bold hand. She pressed her ring into it, leaving her distinctive seal: a standing woman within an oval, her name written around the edges. Dreux and Thierry added their seals.

Afterward, they all stood before Abbot Juhel. Excluded by custom from participating, Elise listened to the men flanking her. Dubec, on Eustace's behalf, gave her to Alaric of Ewyas. Dreux, as proxy, promised to wed her. Juhel ended his prayers, saying, "This betrothal, blessed in the year of our Lord's incarnation, 1067, is witnessed by God, and as long as both parties live, it may never be broken or set aside. The marriage will take place in all haste in Stafford province."

The finality chilled her.

Chapter Sixteen

Elise and Dreux entered the great hall, now illuminated with torches and candles. Hortense, Marie, and groups of knights in liege with those having interest in her marriage stood beside the central hearth and watched her approach. Elise's spirits rose when she saw Roland and his cousins.

Marie stepped into the center of the group. Her blue eyes widened in awe at Dreux.

"This is my sister, Marie," Elise said to Dreux.

"My!" she said breathlessly. "I would never have thought God made men like you!"

"Because she does not think at all," Roland teased.

Marie turned to Roland and smiled brightly. "True!" she said as if discovering the fact for the first time. "All my thoughts scatter when I see a man," she turned back to Dreux, "as tall, as strong, as deliciously—"

"Marie!" Hortense chided. Dreux chuckled.

Marie blinked as if coming out of a daze but kept her eyes on Dreux, ignoring Roland's frown as he whispered loudly, "You should find her a husband and quick!"

"Oh, we're looking," Marie said, smiling at Dreux and missing Roland's raised eyebrow.

Roland turned to greet Thierry de Châlons, to whom he reported. Hortense hugged Elise and greeted Dreux but returned at once to the banquet tables. As Marie gawked at Dreux, Roland took Elise's hands.

"My lady," he said, "God's blessings. May your husband worship your countenance, your wit, your virtue, your wealth."

"Ever my champion," she smiled before introducing Dreux and Roland.

Elise saw two hardened warriors beneath the comportment of skilled royal envoys measuring each other. Roland, slightly shorter than Dreux, had thick, dark wavy brown hair, and piercing blue eyes, which did not hide his fiery temper, no doubt aroused by Marie's flirtation.

"Does Stafford bear the Norse likeness as you do?" Roland asked.

"No. Dark as a Breton, I would say." He grinned at Roland.

Marie gestured to the group. "Come. The feast begins." She urged Elise and Dreux to the high table. "Coming, Roland? Tristan?" she asked, giving a sly side-glance.

Roland turned to Tristan. "They should unleash her in Englelond. She'd be William's greatest weapon. The English would drop their arms and fall to their knees."

Tristan, his eyes on the sway of Marie's hips, chuckled. "She'd be lethal to William's men, too," he said.

After Juhel's benediction, they all settled in for a luscious feast: beef, pork, swan and partridges, fish, bread, wine, and spirits. A round of toasts began, songs and jokes burst forth. Musicians performed, and all welcomed the entertainment and laughter after the somber days of Lent and Easter.

During a lull, Elise sliced into the moist, dark red swan's breast and asked Dreux, "You and my betrothed are acquainted?"

"Yes." He smiled. "We've known each other since our fostering days."

Elise saw him look at the faint scare on his palm. Ah, a blood oath. Brothers for life.

"He saved my life just days before I left for Boulogne. We are close."

"I have heard he is called the *Black Wolf.*"

"Yes," Dreux chuckled. "He often has the appearance of a wolf—a snarling, gaunt, hungry, black wolf." He laughed at her expression.

"No, my lady, he appears so because . . . ," he leaned over whispering, "he dislikes shaving, and his quick beard sinisters him."

She laughed. "Thank you. I'll not quake upon meeting him."

When the guests finished eating, Elise rose, signaling that all might move about the room. Immediately Thierry de Châlons approached her.

"You were disagreeable today, Genevieve," he said, escorting her toward the fire.

"I did not intend to be so, my lord." Elise felt like that small child he used to tease when visiting their home. "I am pleased to retain my ancestral land," she said, knowing the Vexin trapped her between Philip and William. "Please assure King Philip that I embrace my duty to preserve it."

"Of course. Philip remembers you and holds you dear, Genevieve. *Very* dear."

Elise understood: Philip's concern would follow her across the Narrow Sea. Despite sharing their lineage, his father, King Henri, had decimated Elise's home, destroyed her family, and sanctioned her people's rape and brutal murders. With hatred and fear of royal license, she had met King Philip for the first time at his coronation. She was fourteen, he was eight. Four years later, upon leaving the abbey, she paid homage to the young king. Despite their different ages, they experienced an easy camaraderie, as Philip loved riddles and puns, an interest Elise indulged. Even at twelve, Philip hid a keen, serious mind. Once, he had caught her watching him and chided—or warned—*Beloved cousin, best not be too observant!*

"Stay vigilant, Genevieve," Thierry said, banishing her memories. "You are like a daughter to me, and although I speak as a father, a friend, always remember I am Philip's advisor. Eustace has joined your land to a man rumored to have exceptional military abilities. The combination alone threatens Normandie *and* Francia, yet both William and Philip agreed to this union. We do not know Eustace's intent, but—"

"—he could use this marriage to pit William and Philip against each other. If so, there will be difficult times, difficult decisions."

"Astute as usual," Thierry nodded. "If you are ever in trouble with William, I will help you." Although spoken gently, his eyes held her with piercing intensity.

"In trouble?"

"I tutored William when he was a child and know him better than most. That alone inspires my pledge."

The gravity of this offer from Thierry de Châlons alarmed her. She had no idea what danger lie ahead, but Thierry clearly thought she would need him. "Would your assistance extend to my husband and children?" she asked.

"If you ask, Elise," his eyes sober, "such a request can only be met once."

She nodded.

They heard laughter, and both turned to see Marie talking with Roland. "Marie will be alone and in danger from Arques." Elise said. "She wishes to marry Roland de Rennes. Eustace may have other plans."

Thierry nodded. "I cannot promise such a favorable betrothal. The duchess of Brittany must agree. Rest assured, Marie will be safe until she is wed."

"Thank you, my lord. Please tell King Philip I am always his faithful servant."

"He depends on it." Thierry kissed her on the cheek before rejoining the festivities.

A sudden cacophony captured her attention. The dogs were all barking, leaping about, wagging their tails, and pointing their eager noses in the air. The celebrants jeered and laughed as a jongleur strutted down the center of a table, balancing beakers on his head and juggling wooden trenchers. Nobles bet how many trenchers he could juggle before dropping them. A Parisian knight tried to flip up the jongleur's short tunic, eliciting laughter from the Bretons, bawdy comments from Flemings, and censorious frowns from the Normans.

Hortense clapped her hands over both ears and tried to get up from a bench but was held in place by one of Thierry's men, a white-haired knight, who swept his arm around her and pulled her onto his lap, making her blush.

Searching the hall, Elise found Walter. The illustrious guests shunned him, for he had no standing among even the lowest soldiers, yet he laughed with the musicians and appeared interested in their instruments and clothing.

"I see Dubec has found entertainment," Roland said, joining her.

Following his gaze, she saw Brian ogling a couple of maidens whose side glances said they would entertain him later this night.

"Thank you for coming, Roland," she said. "I will appreciate your escort."

"Truly, it will be my pleasure." His demeanor stiffened when Dreux de Ville approached them. De Ville, the stunning Norseman, seemed intent to goad Roland by turning a lingering gaze on Marie.

"Will you stay long in Boulogne?" Elise asked to divert him.

"No," he said, facing her. "I must deliver your betrothal documents to Rouen. I will meet you at Lord Stafford's castle and witness your wedding."

He glanced again at Marie, then gave Roland a knowing smile and asked, "When you were in Rome, did you meet many Normans?"

"I did," Roland said curtly. "They infest the papal palace."

Dreux smiled. "My brothers in Sicily are establishing new markets and trade routes with the East. Normans supply William with exotic and rare goods."

"And choke the Pope with their avaricious appetites."

"And save him with their military acumen," Dreux parried.

The men stared at each other as if planning their next assault.

"Your *Duke* William," Roland said, "has inspired the Sicilian Normans to invade where Normans have no rights."

"As long as the Pope validates our rights, we shall extend them."

"To Brittany?"

Dreux shrugged. "No conflict exists between Normandie and Brittany—now. Not since your sister took the duchy's reins. We have among us many Bretons in league with my *King* William. Some, you may know. Some your kin, perhaps?"

"It has been my experience and perhaps yours, that kinship is a strong bond holding our provinces together, and the first sacrificed when rich spoils abound. Do you serve William from loyalty or for the promise of a fortune?"

"Like you, I have given my oath and serve my liege lord with my sword and my life. And rich English spoils will be a most welcome reward."

Elise asked, "Is it true Normans from Sicily showed William how they ship war horses on the Middle Sea?"

Both men turned to her as if stunned by her presence. Both relaxed their hackles and began to discuss the invasion. Others joined them as Dreux recalled the events: the nearly frenzied nighttime launch and the fog, which obscured William's lead ship. Someone asked about the vessels lost, the landing, and the first days.

Certain the discussion averted blows, Elise scanned the hall. Abbot Juhel caught her eye. Heeding his silent command, she wove through the room, passing Marie surrounded by several knights captivated by her wicked tales of the cloister. When the men roared with laughter, Elise glanced back and saw Roland's attention shift from Dreux to Marie.

"You have something to say to me, Genevieve," Juhel said when she reached him.

"Thank you, Abbe, for honoring me with your venerable presence."

"As your confessor, I admonish you to think carefully of your duty to your lord husband, a duty established by God's word and the apostle Paul." Juhel hard eyes blistered her. "Ambitious women displease God."

Abbot Juhel, a maternal relative, had protected Elise and Marie after Mortemer. She did not want their first meeting in three years to end with antagonism. She suspected his anger stemmed from a bruised pride. In front of royal emissaries, she had embarrassed him, a prelate highly respected by Rome and trusted by both kings.

"I shall endeavor to follow God's word," she said.

"As with all women, you carry within the seeds of great iniquity and malevolence. You must seek a pious life to correct these deficiencies."

"Is it true," she asked, attempting to shift his thoughts, "that William brought Archbishop Stigand of Canterbury with him to Rouen?"

"Adhere to your place, Genevieve. Matters of church and kingship are beyond your comprehension."

She watched his flaccid jaw, quivering with anger. We were so close once, she thought, looking at the bejeweled rings on his hands. After a pause, she pursued a different course. "When I was a child, you took me into your heart." He shuddered and looked away. "Despite your harsh discipline, Marie and I found peace. You helped us to heal the wounds of our disruption. I do not wish a corrosive reunion. Can you forgive me for seeking to preserve my lands for our king and duke as the scriptures guide us? I will travel to a land of upheaval, a land said to flounder under the weight of a weak and corrupt Church. My betrothed is reputed to be a crude knight of the lowest order. Should those lands be placed solely at his disposal, for him to use and protect when he knows little of their import? Would William be comforted to know that *you* and I allowed Arques, his enemy, to retain rents, which could be turned against him?"

Juhel looked at her sharply.

"Am I wrong to seek your forgiveness and blessings, my dear Abbe?"

Juhel's jaw relaxed. "No, my child. You are not wrong. I forgive you, Genevieve, again." He glanced about the room and back to her. "You have my blessings. I pray you obey your lord husband and the Church in all things. Protect your soul, my child. Care for the souls of your husband and his people. Curb your impudence."

"I shall," she said.

"I expect you to continue your beneficence to Abbey Clarion."

"You can be sure of it," Elise said.

After they parted, she recognized the tension slithering through the room. Drinking and gambling games had begun. Men circled each other, poised and ready to wrestle. Arques laughed wildly as his men recounted their cruel pleasures. The fire glowed a deep orange, dogs chewed bones, a minstrel sat on the floor, beat on a drum, and sang a rousing song about a monk and a goose.

"William surrounds himself with young and capable soldiers," Brian Dubec said, joining her.

Following his gaze, she saw Dreux laughing with his men. She found Roland across the room throwing dice with his. Elise turned to Brian. She would have liked him, but he always looked at her as if he expected her to know things she did not. "William needs strong, young soldiers, don't you agree?"

"Yes. He will need them for decades."

"In truth? I thought the English had been subdued. William is back in Rouen." She felt suddenly foolish. She'd heard about English berserkers and dreaded the thought of living among them.

"Perhaps you are right, my lady."

"Brian," she frowned. "Do not presume I am an empty-headed primrose though I may seem so at times."

He tilted his head as if acknowledging his thoughts precisely. "Yes, my lady."

"Do you know my betrothed?"

He hesitated. "Slightly."

"You do not like him!" The thought intrigued her.

Dubec shrugged. "He is a good soldier. I fight with many I neither like nor dislike. Stafford is one of those."

"I see," she said, glad for his candor. Although she had seldom seen Brian over the years, she felt they shared an unusually forthright relationship. She found his bluntness refreshing and reliable. "Will Eustace return to Wessex?"

Brian studied Elise before he spoke. "Not soon. He must turn his attention to Boulogne now."

"And you?"

"My fortunes are with Eustace, my lady," he said. "The more land Eustace receives, the more he will give to his vassals."

But not to you. Her uncle had never given Brian even a small piece of land. His loyalty puzzled her. She watched him signal to Arques across the room, and now his attention fell to her again. "Thank you for your assistance this afternoon."

"Your thanks are not required. I was sent to secure the match."

"Why did Eustace agree to this marriage?"

"Stafford is favored by the king. The marriage will strengthen Eustace's tie to William and to William's rich kingdom."

"My uncle is avaricious," she said. "This marriage gives land away, it does not enhance Eustace's coffers. What does he seek with this marriage?"

Brian shrugged. "Eustace believes Stafford will go far."

"Does he think to control Stafford's rise?"

Brian looked at her pointedly, and she realized, with this marriage, he already had.

"You are dangerously perceptive," he said—all semblance of casual chatter erased from his face. "You do not know Eustace or me well. Heed my words: He is revengeful and ambitious. I am neither your friend nor your enemy. I am his liege vassal. All I have done and will do has been at Eustace's bidding. These are uncertain times. Friend, enemy, relative, liege—none matters when the sword decides who is standing at the end of the day."

"Why are you telling me this, Brian?"

"If Stafford continues to soar in King William's estimation, Eustace will be showered in riches as well. If, however, Stafford flounders . . . well. Perhaps Eustace believes Stafford may benefit from the counsel of a clever ally—one who can demand and receive concessions from two royal envoys and a powerful abbot."

She winced at the reminder. "I saw Eustace a decade ago. He cannot possibly expect anything from me."

"Eustace knows a woman can be useful in shaping the course of events. He does not underestimate you. You are, after all, his niece." His gaze swept over the soldiers in the hall. "Alliances shift quickly. Victory grasped one moment will dissolve into defeat the next. This is the way of life."

He is telling me to be careful, she thought. "I hope we shall never be enemies, although I doubt we shall ever be friends."

He agreed with a tilt of his head.

She changed the subject. "Once we cross the Narrow Sea, will you stay with me long?"

"No. I will guide your entourage to your new demesne, and," he looked oddly at her, "I will witness the . . . wedding before joining Eustace."

She studied him a moment, unsure what she saw in his eyes. "Thank you, Brian," she whispered.

He nodded curtly to her and walked across the room to fill his beaker with wine.

Her mind swirled, and suddenly she felt exhausted. She turned to Marie, laughing with one of Roland's men. Catching her eye, Marie extricated herself from their guests and bid them all farewell before escorting Elise to their bedchamber.

"My saints! You look pale, Elise," she said. "What's wrong?"

Elise shook her head. "I'm tired." *And frightened.*

Chapter Seventeen

*E*vil lurks beneath your skin . . ."

Elise jolted upright, dripping with sweat. Her eyes flew open to the faint light of morning. Her heart pounded, and her body trembled. She sucked air past the terror lodged in her throat, past the bitter taste in her mouth. The dream was the same . . . no, different. She closed her eyes. Images washed over her.

Smoke—billowing, acrid. Shadowy figures, black hoods, circling, chanting. A shrill screech echoes in the cool meadow. Black-clothed figures drift to the writhing girl, younger than her. Strapped . . . naked. The girl shrieks, begs. Elise feels cool, damp grass. Freedom! Run! Angry shouts chase her. She jumps a creek, slips, falls into icy darkness. Satan comes. His shimmering mail and horns reflect the fire. Shadows obscure his face, yet his eyes glow, boring into her . . . his hands reach for her . . .

She blinked, reliving a terror as familiar and tangible as her own skin. Her sister slept soundly next to her, and Hortense snored in her adjacent bed. Elise forced herself to breathe, to calm the pounding in her chest, the cold, green terror prickling through her body. But, this time, as the torchlight in her dream flickered, she had seen the devil's full face. That infinitesimal memory vanished instantly. She wiped tears from her eyes and struggled to remember something about the devil. That, too, was gone.

She rose from her bed and dressed. Grabbing a candle, she slipped past the single torch at the top of the stairs, down to the main hall.

Picking her way between sleeping bodies, she stopped at the hearth to light her candle from the embers and went into the chapel.

Darkness surrounded her in this tomb-like, windowless room where she faced God's cold, dark silence. She held the candle high, so its light cast a halo on the floor. She walked toward the altar, listening to her fear, believing she stepped into the very battlefield between God and Satan. To her, each step was a trial by ordeal, as if she walked through a pack of snarling, howling demons that would test her resolve, make her flee, and prove she was unworthy of God's attention. And she feared God's attention, believing He would punish her for *annoying* Him.

Yet, her nightmare drove her here. Her heart drummed loudly in her ears, terrified more by the shadowy fragments of her dream than by the demons residing in the chapel.

At the altar, she dropped to her knees, fixing the candle in a pool of hot wax she spilled on the cold stone floor. She raised her gaze to the arches above, to the wooden cross, and spread her arms in supplication. Daunted by shadows across the vaulted ceiling, she silently repeated her special prayer once, twice, ten, twenty times. Tears dripped down her cheeks.

"Heavenly Father," she said aloud, her voice sounding belligerent to her ears. "Have pity on me," she whispered. Not wishing to offend God, she spoke silently through her heart. *Heavenly Father, power of eternity, who have ordered all things in your heart, by whose word all things are created, have pity on me.*

She paused, struggling for words. *This vision haunts me. Release me from this visitation. If there be evil in my soul, cast it from me. Forgive my sins.* She looked up at the shadowed arches, the dream still flickering across her memory. Shaking her head to clear the dream, she took a deep breath and remembered: she was betrothed to an angry stranger, she would leave her sister. Brian's caution and Thierry's promise warned her. She was a pawn in a dangerous game between Eustace and William and Philip.

Please . . . please guide me.

Suddenly, it felt arrogant to ask anything of God. She dropped her arms to her sides, distressed that so simple a movement echoed loudly in the chapel. She waited, hoping to hear God's answer, imagining the devil behind her, reaching for her. She watched the narrow flame of her candle rise steadily in the still chamber. Her stomach growled, her knees ached. She crossed herself, rose, and slowly, cautiously turned to find no demons. She left the chapel, feeling . . . abandoned.

I f it had been me," Brian Dubec said, his sword poised to thrust. "I would have taken her to my bed the moment she arrived."

Walter, already staggering from the beating Brian's men had given him, held his sword in his sweating palm. "A man without honor."

"Honor!" Brian said, slashing his sword against Walter's. "I call it stupidity. But . . . you've . . . always," he emphasized each blow, "been slow . . ."

With a rapid exchange of clashing swords, Brian forced Walter to back up step by step until one of Brian's men tripped him from behind. Walter went down hard, and they all laughed. He rolled to his side to defend himself as Brian charged and swung his sword again, knocking Walter's weapon out of his hand and into the air. It landed nearby, and one of Brian's men retrieved it.

"Behold, Walter Arquesson, a high-born maggot!" Brian said. His men laughed.

They'd been careless, Walter thought, wiping the blood dripping down his face. Brian had left a trace of the beating this time.

Three years ago, without land, income, sword, or priestly garb, Walter had decided to seek his fortune with the Normans in Sicily— and then Elise and Marie had arrived. He could not leave these two innocents at the mercy of his degenerate father and cursed Eustace for dangling his nieces before such a lascivious and cruel creature.

But last spring, when preparations were underway for the invasion, Walter had tried to join Eustace's forces, hoping to prove himself worthy and gain some minor subsistence. Neither Eustace nor any other noble would take him as squire, page, or even as a mere groom. Brian delivered Eustace's rejection with gleeful contempt. "You have no future. Change your name, Walter son of Arques, and tend the land—if you dare. I doubt you'd last a week behind a plow."

Stripped of everything that had at one time distinguished him from the rabble, Walter now possessed only two things he valued: his chess set and the glorious past his noble name had once evoked. He would relinquish neither.

But with Elise's betrothal, the world intruded upon this small crumbling sanctuary. In the presence of men united by oaths, Walter felt his stinging isolation. The doors of privilege had been slammed, bolted, and barred against him. He was breathless at the totality of his loss.

Now, Walter rolled to his feet. "Are we finished today?"

Brian's sneer faded behind a deadly glare.

Walter refused to cower, refused to run. He would not break. His noble bearing infuriated Brian the most, and Walter wielded his composure like a weapon despite nearly daily thrashings. As Brian raised his blade again, Walter looked forward to his next lesson, for these encounters taught him how to duck, feint, thrust, fall—and survive.

A servant ran up to Brian but stopped abruptly, sensing danger. Brian lowered his weapon and glowered at the servant.

"The Countess requests a word, sir," the boy said quickly.

$\mathcal{T}$he English have plows." Tristan looked at her as if she were a dullard.

"I'm sure they do," she said, calmly annoyed at Brian's smirking grin as he let Tristan lead the challenge. She had summoned Brian to hear his views on transporting the heavier items, such as the heavy-wheeled plow.

"My seneschal," she said, "uses the new heavy plow to till virgin, arable land beside the woods. The plow has increased crop production."

"Fine," Tristan retorted. "Let your seneschal drag it to your new home!"

For days, Elise had been packing for her journey. Nearly all her tangible wealth would travel with her or be sent in subsequent shipments. Daily trunks and crates arrived from Fontenay, filled with plate, jewels, gold and silver coins, braziers for interior heating, furnishings, and hangings. At Boulogne's market, she had purchased dyestuff imported from the East, the finest Persian wool dyed expensively in deep blues, reds, and greens, and the best ermine, sable, and mink she could find to make winter clothing for her husband and herself. She found silks sent north from the Normans who controlled the Sicilian silk works and bought finely woven flax and linen cloth, a new upright loom, spindles, needles, and precious scissors.

Anticipating the coming winter, she had packed beeswax, molds and new dipping racks, seeds, cooking and forging implements, and now she had turned to the tanning vats and the heavy plow.

"Brian says my husband builds a new castle, that his demesne is isolated and located on the frontier near the Danelaw." She reminded Tristan of the need to plant a kitchen garden or expand the winter crops. "I do not intend to starve my first winter," she said. "And neither will the villagers."

Roland reluctantly agreed to take the heavy plow. Brian suggested they take a couple of two-wheeled carts to carry the larger items, which would be reassembled when they reached their destination. "We'll buy packhorses, oxen, and more carts when we arrive," he assured Roland.

Pleased, Elise decided to take new horse collars and harnesses, and other items likely absent in a crude, primitive land.

As the days passed, Roland prepared his ships for the journey. Dubec and his men grew restless. They hunted and traveled to coastal villages, seeking manly pleasures elsewhere. The women raced through their preparations.

The bulk of Elise's richly embroidered clothing and jewels were packed away, except for a single chest that would house her wedding attire. Her travel attire, chosen for simplicity and durability, consisted of linen and wool tunics with little or no embroidery and thick woolen mantles. She selected hooded leather cloaks lined in wool and fur, and several pairs of sturdy shoes for winter comfort. And every evening, Hortense made sachets of wormwood and mint to place between the furs to keep them free from moths, while Elise and Marie sewed coins and jewels into her clothing. A precaution.

One day, a servant carrying a tooled-leather case followed Marie to the solar. "It is our tradition, Elise," she said. "The eldest always keeps the family book." Marie unfastened the straps and carefully pulled back the skins. This rare book—equivalent in value to an entire manor: fields, meadows, woods—was about the size of a saddle and a foot thick. It had been in the family for generations. Salvaged from their destroyed home, they had taken it with them to Abbey Clarion, and with them again to Boulogne.

Elise traced her fingers across the thin wooden covers chiseled with crosses at each corner and hinged with leather straps. A rectangular groove had been carved on its face, framing the picture painted in the carved depression. On a thin coat of plaster, God sat on a throne surrounded by angels, the saints, and Jesus at His feet. As if the Scriptures were imbued with the Holy Spirit itself, Marie blew softly across the maple brown background, once representing the golden glow of heaven.

"It's darker than I remembered," whispered Marie in awe. She slid her hand across the still-visible green and red robes now nearly black.

Elise stared at one face, so like her mother's, faintly glowing, despite the spiderweb cracks and dark paint, as if she peered out through the veil of memory. Elise caressed the gentle face softly with her finger, feeling the plaster crumble. "Woodworms," she said, indicating the needle-sized holes, squiggled tracks, and powdery residue.

Marie and Elise lifted the cover from the folios.

"Here." Marie pointed to the names of their parents written on the thin vellum. "The priest will enter your names after the ceremony."

They turned the sheets arranged in quires, flesh side to flesh side, hair side to hair side. The tiny script had faded in places to a pale brown or faint gray. Free from mold, the book smelled faintly of crushed pine needles. The gold leaf and richly colored illustrations were still crisp and vibrant as if newly assembled. They closed and rewrapped the book, setting it carefully inside Elise's most prized possession: a large wooden chest hewn from a solid tree trunk and handsomely carved.

Another day, Elise looked over a few gifts she would take to her betrothed. She knew so little of the man who now ruled her life. Perhaps her gifts would ease his fury at the marriage. Perhaps he would accept her as an ally. She felt confident that the wooden serving platters, bowls, trenchers, and mazers all richly carved and trimmed with a matching narrow band of silver would enhance her husband's stature.

Picking up the brooch, she felt almost afraid. She'd asked the silversmith to create a clasp for her husband's cloak, imagining a wolf engraved on silver. Instead, he gave her an odd piece of amber, not yellow like her necklaces, but black, the size of her palm with streaks of red in its fiery depths. Her fingers slid over the cool surface where the smith had etched a leaping wolf so perfect it startled her, even now. As she moved the piece against the light, she felt the power of enchantment, for the wolf seemed alive. Blazing red eyes glowed. Sharp teeth snarled at her, a lean, skeletal body twisted in attack as his long tail curled low near clawed hind feet.

Edged in a tooled silver band, the wolf could be worn as a brooch or a pendant. Deciding to give it to her husband when she knew him better, she attached the silver chain to the brooch and slipped it over her head, tucking it beneath her clothing. She hoped this gift would enchant him as it had charmed her. Immediately, she crossed herself begging God's forgiveness for her heathen thoughts.

Chapter Eighteen

In the dim chapel beside the old castle's ruins, Alaric leaned against the crumbling plaster, its gray coldness seeping into his shoulder. He stood because he could no longer kneel, the cloak he had used for a cushion hung over his arm. As he had daily since Easter, he had come to the chapel at dawn this mid-April morning. Here, he kept a solitary vigil, bearing the agony of knees on hard earth until he finally stood, asking forgiveness for his weak body.

He listened, glad for the simple space of this small room and the thick walls shutting out the world beyond. Wind whistled through the thatching above the timbered beams, the candle flame quivered, making the painted figures on the wall appear to dance. *I hear God*, he thought of the wind. *He hisses in the rafters. His fingers brush against my chin. I give Him my heart, an offering for my family, for their salvation.*

Divine presence, he knew, gave him the stamina to pray. He sacrificed his body, ignoring hunger and thirst from his self-imposed fast so his family would be released from eternal sufferings, for they had died without benefit of confession and divine forgiveness.

When he had first learned of their deaths five months ago, he had tried to rein in his emotions as he went from one village to another. Yet, every day, his family traveled with him in his heart, in his mind. They saw what he saw. They spoke to him in remembered words, a gesture, a scent of days past, and every remembrance renewed his anguish.

Shifting his weight, his boots scraped against the floor. He remembered last Easter here in this very chapel. He had not known how to tell his father he would join Duke William. Alaric tipped his head and looked up at the notched trusses. He would never again carry the cross with his brother, kneel beside his father in vigil, or share his mother's awe. He had not known their solemn feast would be their last meal together.

One year. So much had changed. He lived, a victor. They died, the vanquished. He had relinquished his mercenary sword with a vow putting him in liege to the king. A commander of the king's forces, he carried a royal banner. Now he had land, titles, and a castle in Staffordshire. Yet all these honors and riches were tainted by his family's death, and a marriage forced on him as reparations.

Alaric looked at the burning candles that accompanied his prayers for the souls of his family. He pushed away from the wall and, wanting to take God's grace within, he inhaled the resinous scent.

Leaving the chapel, he thought about Johan, who had nearly lost his leg, and Father Pierre, whose concubine had another child. The only thing that had not changed was Marguerite, he thought, approaching the hall. At the beginning of their liaison, he had told Marguerite he would not marry her. He'd never loved her, and more often than not, he found her tedious. But since resuming their affair, she'd eased his body's hunger, and Marguerite would plague Eustace's niece until Alaric had time to deal with the woman. He felt entirely absolved from the sin of fornication. Rumored to mirror her uncle in all things, his bride was likely as unchaste as Eustace—a man known for his sins.

Marguerite d'Hesdins, nineteen years old and terrified, stood beside the fire pit in Hereford Hall, warming herself. The door opened, and the wet, cold, blustery day followed Alaric inside. Without a glance at her, he gathered his men around a table. One of them pulled a handful of dry sand from a bag and scattered it onto the boards, and, as a servant took his wet cloak, Alaric began sketching a map. She turned her face away from the smoke swirling up to the louvers and looked over the crowded room. Merchants stroking their beards, monks with hands hidden in their habits no doubt rubbing their members, and smug soldiers—all measured her with furtive glances.

Merchants like these had left her to die, bloodied, discarded like chicken innards beside a road. Monks had revealed their evil, disguised as piety, and soldiers had given her safe passage—for a price. She knew what these men thought, what they wanted. Today, at least, Alaric shielded her.

Watching him, she recalled his surprise at finding her still in Hereford, where he had abandoned her to join William. She had remained here, near the border, close enough to flee if necessary. In desperation, she had sought refuge in a cloister to await the results of William's invasion. A mistake, for amid the familiar prayers and fasts, the false devotion and hushed manners, she relived the torment of the last time she'd sought refuge—when the nuns who should have helped her in childbirth mutilated her womb.

Beside her, now, a burning log broke into pieces and crumbled. Marguerite stared as the sanguine embers pulsed like her grieving heart. Finding Johan among the wounded had saved her from despair. When Alaric had returned to Hereford a few days ago to take Johan away, she could hardly breathe until, as an afterthought, he collected her, too. As chatelaine of Alaric's castle, Marguerite would govern the domestic affairs of his demesne. She had not embraced this position with all the humility and gratitude of one receiving a great *honor*, as Alaric no doubt thought of his generosity.

As before, she traded her body for safety, her soul for food.

She would not let her improved fortune seduce her, she thought, glancing at servants weaving throughout the room. From the age of eleven, her life had been precarious. She had two assets: her beauty and her youth, both fading quickly. She must tread carefully. At all costs, she must survive and solidify her position. She must never again be left without a protector, vulnerable to the tyranny of strangers.

And she must never reveal that she loved Johan.

When the hall door opened, she spotted him immediately. *Short Shank*, she mentally called him as he limped across the room. He fawned over the girl beside him. With arrested attention, Marguerite studied the newcomer and recognized the colors worn by soldiers accompanying her.

Ah, the long-awaited Clare of Wolenbroth. About fifteen winters, Marguerite guessed, plain, brownish hair, a smallish figure. She walked with her head bowed, her humility draped around her like a veil—or a spider's web. Marguerite had heard that Clare was the daughter of a thegn who had died fighting King William at Hastings. Her family's lands and titles had been confiscated. Now, the girl, Dreux de Ville's captive, was merely his thrall. Marguerite, herself once the beloved daughter of a count, felt no affiliation to another woman who had likewise fallen from her family's pedestal.

Instead, her Norman blood—the blood of conquerors—outranked the girl and most English nobles, especially now as Alaric's mistress. Yet, she would relinquish everything to marry Johan. She quashed that thought. She had nowhere else to go.

As Alaric turned from Hereford's castellan to observe Clare's approach, Marguerite's heart quickened. *Please don't desire her*, she thought, knowing how easily he could replace her. She saw the girl's eyes flicker up to him and downward submissively, and when Alaric told Johan to put the girl in one of the upper chambers, Marguerite stepped forward and caught his eye.

"Servants do not sleep above, my lord," she smiled sweetly. "She must remain here," she swept her hand around the hall, "with others of her position."

Alaric looked at Marguerite a moment before nodding his head at Johan, who took the girl to the stairs. "Come," he gestured, inviting Marguerite to sit on the bench beside him.

Hiding her resentment, she sat. Alaric remained standing and resumed his discussion. She could smell his sex, she thought, and imagined slipping her hands under his knee-length tunic, over the thick leggings to his crotch. Already she could feel heat building between them as his hand caressed her shoulder. She leaned her breast against his thigh, intending to stir his memory of her body and knew by his strengthened grip she had succeeded.

Looking about the room, she saw that none, save an old, toothless servant, had noticed her ploy. *How dare that filthy crone grin at me*, thought Marguerite. *A few lashes would curb that smirk.* She flashed the hag a withering glance. When the woman fled, Marguerite realized that she could demand a whipping for any servant who displeased her at Alaric's castle.

On a crisp morning, Alaric left Hereford's chapel for the last time and met Johan limping toward him.

"All are ready," Johan said. "Marguerite is chiding the girl again."

Alaric nodded and strode through the courtyard where he found Marguerite, astride her horse, glaring down at Clare of Wolenbroth. Alaric was struck again by the composure of this girl-child. She stood humbly, her head slightly bowed, yet she retained the air of her English nobility.

"You shall clean my boots with your very own hands, you sluggard," Marguerite ordered, "else feel the lash—"

"What is amiss?" Alaric asked.

"This servant soiled my boot." Marguerite stretched out her small booted foot from beneath her long tunic.

Alaric saw the smear of horse dung along one edge of the leather and motioned to his groom, who rushed forward with a rag.

"She did it. She should clean it," Marguerite said. "I demand it!"

Alaric watched the girl raise her head and look up at Marguerite. Her clear, hazel eyes held no resentment. Dreux had picked well, thought Alaric, surveying the delicate lines of the girl's face—proud and strong. As Dreux had hoped, she was with child. Alaric would transport her carefully. "Johan," he said. "Put the girl in Father Pierre's cart." He turned to Marguerite. "We shall not tarry, lady."

As the groom cleaned Marguerite's boot, Alaric mounted his horse. He shouted a command, and the rest of his soldiers took to their horses. Alaric glanced at Johan, who nodded his readiness, and at his groom, who now scrambled to take his place. Alaric waved at the captain-at-arms who would remain at Hereford. His eyes flickered to Marguerite's still angry scowl, and he signaled his soldiers to move into formation.

They began a five-day trek north to Tutbury. Alaric and Johan rode behind the scouts, then came the standard bearer and three rows of soldiers, six abreast. Next came Marguerite, escorted by a pair of soldiers. Behind her rolled several carts and packhorses. Forty or so foot soldiers guarded the flanks, interspersed with footmen carrying red and black pennons jostling into position. Grooms and squires led a string of horses, which nipped at one another, and one reared as they moved out, followed by the armorers and farrier. An assortment of pages and servants walked, and thirty mounted soldiers brought up the rear.

In the sun's heat, a steamy vapor rose from the muddy roads. Alaric expected the first day to go slowly. As the roads dried, they would travel more quickly. He glanced at Johan riding beside him. Along with Edo, Roderick, and Gilbert, Johan had followed Alaric to fight with the Normans. Alaric thought he had died at Hastings with Edo and the others.

"Does it pain you to ride?" Alaric asked.

"A little." Johan rubbed his fist along the deep wound that had gouged most of his outer thigh away.

Alaric turned in his saddle and faced Johan. "I do not favor you from charity. I need a seneschal at the seat of my holdings. You have good judgment and are cautious. Besides, you learned counting. In the Ewyas days, when you and Roddy played with spotted tiles, you always knew exactly how many spots carried the game. I need a good man, Johan. You're the only one I can trust with the authority to oversee the land and wealth at all my estates here and abroad."

"You left Roddy to build Tutbury." Johan could not hide his envy.

"Yes. And Gilbert to keep Roddy out of trouble. Roddy is my second-in-command. Gilbert, as castellan, will be yours."

"What?" Johan asked in surprise, turning to look at Alaric.

"You hold the senior position to steward the settlement and growth of the castle and village. Monkman will build Tutbury's defenses, oversee the garrisons, and administer the constabulary responsibilities. He has authority to defend the castle and hold the area in my absence. He will also keep our forces trained and deploy them when needed."

Alaric glanced at the clouds, gauging the wind. "I have granted demesnes to you, Gilbert, and Roddy," he said. "You have enough land to support a knight's obligation now that you cannot fight—woodland, pastureland, a couple villages and many tenants."

Johan grinned. "Thank you," then as an afterthought, "*my lord.*"

Johan saw Alaric wince and supposed the title still sounded

awkward to him, too. Remembering their childhood at Ewyas, he should not be surprised Alaric was his liege lord. Even as boys, Alaric had been their leader, and Roddy their boisterous giant. He missed Roddy as much as he missed Rannulf, Alaric's now-deceased brother. Gilbert, despite his quiet piety, was a strong, capable warrior, and a trustworthy friend. Together, they would all serve Alaric well. All except Edo, who had run across the beach in woman's garb and met the axe at Hastings.

Johan had thought he, too, would die there. Pinned by his dead horse, he could not move. He could see only the bloodied hand of the dying knight beneath him. As the battle raged, as the soldier's moans ceased, Johan watched the ants trail across the bloodied fingers that twitched and hardened into a claw-like shape, pressing close to Johan's eye.

He barely remembered them sawing through his horse to reach him or the trip to Hereford and the pig-faced woman whose hands had tended him. He had fevered nightmares and saw monstrous apparitions. He even imagined hearing Marguerite's voice urging him to drink.

Glad to be alive, he felt honored and grateful to serve the king's favorite. He glanced at Alaric's angular features and shook his head. Reunited for only days, he and Alaric had little time to talk. But Johan had heard the drunken remarks of highborn Normans. They resented Alaric's command and spoke their pleasure that the king had commanded Alaric to marry Eustace's niece, an old shrew, with a mannish temperament and a face disfigured by pustules.

No wonder Alaric took up with Marguerite again, Johan thought.

As Alaric rode beside Johan, he wondered if Dreux had finalized the betrothal agreement. All the land in the world would not erase his bitterness that the marriage would bind him through eternity to Eustace. He knew Dreux would race to Tutbury to see his Clare and bring with him the wedding pact sealed, blessed, and cursed.

Still, it would be good to see Dreux again. He remembered their first day at York, a village fermenting with resistance and rebellion. Amid hostile eyes, they had trudged toward the church when Dreux suddenly lunged at him. A bolt hurtled past Alaric's head and drove into the thick oak door as, together, they tumbled into a pit of clammy mud.

He sobered, reliving their last day together. They'd ridden away from York to the gills. At one small, narrow valley, Deux's horse broke through an ice bridge above the gorge. He scrambled up and balanced on his saddle as the horse's belly rested on the ice, its legs flailing. Alaric threw him a rope. A sudden wrench pulled him to the ground. Twisting onto his back, he skidded toward the cliff's edge and braced his feet against an outcropping. Alaric heard the horse scream when it fell, the thuds and silence. He clung to the rope as Dreux pulled himself up to the ledge. Grabbing Alaric's hand, he climbed over the top, collapsing beside him. Again, he felt his heart pounding, his body drenched in sweat, his muscles trembling and the tears stinging his eyes. Again, he heard Dreux's rasping voice. "You know that . . . that horse you won?"

Alaric's memory broke abruptly in response to Johan's question, which, judging by a familiar scowl, had been asked more than once.

"What's it like, this Tutbury?"

"Bleak," Alaric said.

"Will you take Marguerite with you when you leave?"

"She will stay with you and the countess," Alaric said. "I'll send for her on occasion."

Johan frowned.

Alaric laughed. "It will not be dull."

Chapter Nineteen

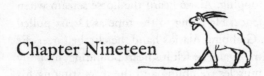

Elise's goods had been packed, carted down to the dock, and loaded onto three ships. Each ship had enough food and wine for the travelers and crews, including extra nuts, dried fruits and meats, and hard bread. The journey required more than one hundred people, including the principles, the men-at-arms, and the crews.

Elise and Marie knew they might not see each other for years—if ever again. The night before Elise left, they said their goodbyes alone, with tears and laughter, with reminiscence and silence, and finally with tight hugs and whispered vows never to forget each other. Elise gave Marie her best arm bracelet.

"You may need this," Marie said, clutching her baptismal ring to her bosom.

"Keep it safe, and send it to me when you marry Roland."

They laughed at their shared hope for Marie's future.

The morning after May Day, Walter watched Elise and Hortense descend the stone steps for the last time. He and his father waited in the hall beside the fire. Elise dropped to an elegant curtsey before his father, a salute to his former rank. Arques, in a rare expression of grandeur, took her hand in his, held it silently, and bowed before leaving the room without a word.

Walter took her hands and smiled down at her, his eyes warm.

"If there is ever anything I can do for you, Elise . . . " He hesitated, embarrassed. He shook his head, knowing he could do nothing for her. He caught Dubec watching him intensely, ready to spear him with a final insult.

"Thank you," she said and squeezed his hands. She hoped he would never discover the arrangements she'd made to help him. She had intended to give him a small estate or an innocuous position among her garrisons. Hortense reminded her that she could not support someone Duke William had disinherited, for doing so would violate her own duty to her lord. Instead, at Christmas next, Walter would receive an anonymous packet she'd left for him. The coins and a patent would allow him to travel and help him find a place somewhere. "Watch over Marie until she weds?"

"Indeed I shall," he smiled broadly, glancing at Roland talking to one of his soldiers in the courtyard. "Good journey, Elise, and to you, Brian." He released her hands, dipping his head to them both. Ignoring Dubec's speculative eyes, Walter grabbed Hortense around the waist, lifted, and whirled her about. She demanded to be set down as all laughed.

"Behave yourself, Walter!" she hissed, slapping his arm.

"You, too!" he teased, kissing her on the cheek.

As Elise rode out of the bailey and beyond the castle gates, Walter watched with a despair he'd never felt before. He balled one fist into his other hand and cracked his knuckles. The future stretched ahead of him dark, dismal . . . empty.

The very mention of your name sends roses to her cheeks," Elise said, glancing at Tristan sideways from her horse as they entered Boulogne.

His startled eyes pinned her.

She nodded. "Lesceline is waiting for you to pledge for her."

"Shush! Elise," Hortense scolded. "You've no privilege to speak so, even if it's true."

"He's shy," Giles chuckled. He won a scathing glance from Tristan.

"The fair Lesceline," Yves teased, "the most beautiful woman in Rennes, pines away for this simpleton. Still, he says nothing! And worse, he *does* nothing."

"You did not ask for Emmaline," growled Tristan, turning on Yves.

"Think you not?" Yves challenged.

"Well, well," Giles said. He sniffed at his Lady Anne's scarf just enough for Tristan to see it. Tristan's brow furrowed, and they laughed.

Ahead of them, Roland and Brian led the way through the crowded streets to the docks. Elise neared the piers with growing excitement. Dozens of large open boats sat ashore on timber rollers ready to be hauled into the water. Hundreds of sailing vessels bobbed and rolled, waiting for a favorable wind. She looked out at the sea beyond and saw colorful sails coming into the port. Further out, other ships lay at anchor in the broad mouth of the river. At the dock, ships were being loaded and unloaded. Men, bent from huge bundles on their backs, trailed like ants crisscrossing through and among carts. Seamen shouted, and priests moved up and down the piers offering prayers and blessings for the journey. Roland pointed out their ships lashed together at one end of the pier. None was fitted for oars, and all would rely solely on the wind.

She and Hortense boarded their ship and placed their personal bags beneath a canopy sheltering their pallet and personal items. Afterward, they leaned against the bulwarks and watched the activity on the dock. Elise spotted a partially built ship across the wharf. The ribs had been hewn from timbers and its skeletal frame tilted at an odd angle upon wooden blocking. A shipwright wielded an adze over a long, squared timber of pine. As she watched, he hacked away at this log with such speed wood chips seemed to fly about like brown moths fluttering around his head. A group of ragged little children tried to collect the chips, for kindling, no doubt. They scattered and swirled like autumn leaves around a tree when the shipwright chased them away.

Again, the shipwright bent over his timber and swung his adze. Before her very eyes, he drew out a perfectly round, smooth tapered pole—a mast. He ran his hands over the wood and chipped another piece away. Finally, he bent down and, closing one eye, he sighted down the pole, turning it ever so slightly, and chipping a little here and a little there until he was satisfied. He called to another worker. Together, each took one end of the mast, hoisted it up onto their shoulders and walked it through their building yard. Her gaze traveled over the stockpile of uncut logs, some nearly the diameter of a man with outstretched arms.

She recalled asking Brian about the number and size of the ships built for William's invasion. Now she thought about those six hundred vessels, and, with her abacus packed away, she made a rough mental calculation. Ten thousand trees, she thought, aghast, understanding for the first time, why the monks decried the patches of decimated forests in the Brotonne.

A shout from Roland grabbed her attention. Suddenly, the entire dock erupted in a charged frenzy. Elise looked at the rippling pennons. Hortense noticed the shifting wind. Brian ran across the deck, jumping over bundles and skirting barrels and down the plank to join Roland on the beach, which suddenly seemed more crowded as word of the wind spread.

Hortense bumped up against Elise and began chattering: "My, these ships heave in the water. Look! The little ones are already heading toward the channel. Roland must be excited. Look, a blue sail! Oh, the sun feels good against this wind. Cover your face, Elise. My, that is a huge sailing ship! Oh . . . this ship is certainly rocking! Are you sure we brought everything, Elise?"

Soon the priest arrived to bless the ship and travelers. After a final flourish of holy water sprayed over bowed heads, the passengers and crew crossed themselves and rose. The priest ran down the plank, his robes a flurry as he rushed to the next ship. The crew pulled up the plank, cast off the ropes, and poled the vessel from its mooring. Square sails began to rise, flapping and snapping, as pulleys squealed and gulls squawked overhead. Slowly, the ship drifted with the tide away from the pier toward the river mouth. Elise and her companions watched the large, rust-colored sail fill and billow.

"How long will the crossing take?" Hortense asked Tristan, her voice unsteady as she clutched the rail.

"It depends on the wind," he said.

"Days? Weeks!" Hortense quivered, paling.

Seeing her expression, he quickly reminded her that William had made the crossing in one night, and their crossing would be quick if the wind held.

"I'll go to our quarters, Elise. No, no need to follow me," she said, waving her hand. She wobbled along the planks and might have fallen if Giles had not grabbed her arm and escorted her to their shelter. Hortense stopped there, turned, and fluttered her hand weakly just before dipping down under the awning flaps and easing herself onto the straw pallet.

Elise smiled to herself and pulled her thick cloak tighter against the cool breeze, colder now they were moving. She watched their ship quickly slip down the mouth of the river and to the sea. Within a short time, they felt the first surge of the Narrow Sea.

A couple of hours later, Elise shielded her eyes from the sun and looked back toward the port. She offered a silent prayer for Marie, and let her gaze drift to her companions. It pleased her to see Roland and Dubec's men working in small groups together without the usual tension among soldiers eager to prove their manly strengths. Instead, they tended their armor, sharpened their swords, teased the crew, or traded jokes. Well, she thought, their journey is young. Plenty of time for boasts, taunts, contests, and bitter rivalries to emerge.

Turning away, she squinted at the sunlight reflecting off the water and peered into the gilded distance toward her new life.

Chapter Twenty

The edges of a small storm caught them just after dawn, and, as the crew scrambled to control the vessel, Elise stood near the bow, holding firmly to the stem rail. The ship rode large, rolling waves. Terrified, she watched the sea, a gigantic, amorphous beast changing shape and color as it swelled. Terrified, she watched the cold, dark, angry sea split and heard it roar as it rammed them, tipping their vessel precariously. Yet she relished the taste of salty spray and the biting wind. She laughed aloud when a wave grabbed the ship and raised it so high it balanced on the sharp tip of a crest a moment before rolling under them, easing them back into the water and up again as if cradled in God's embrace.

Green, gray, blue. Swirling and powerful. With a strong wooden vessel beneath her, she felt powerful and . . . and free! Joining the wind and sea in this dance, she screamed out her joy, knowing only the storm could hear her. Exhilarated, she thought it incongruous that a woman with such feral thoughts had been sent to tame the wild English.

The gusts calmed to a brisk, steady wind, and the sea gentled. Mesmerized and lulled now by the ship's mild rocking, Elise watched the tips of the waves curl atop one another, the white caps hurrying in a ceaseless motion, stretching toward the white cliffs, as the wind sent her closer to the unknown.

It disquieted her to think a marriage between two people who had never even met would last a lifetime, a span of years she could not imagine. She had been raised to expect nothing more—or less—than a contract between families exchanging land, wealth, duties, alliances, and obligations, like her own parents. Yet, she had not expected to live so far away from Fontenay. She glanced at Brian, now playing a dicing game with others, and remembered his warning and Thierry's promise. Francia, Englelond. Philip, William. Here in the sea between two kings, she felt content and safe.

Letting her thoughts drift, she wondered why her betrothed had accepted the marriage offers with such fury? Her lands should have pleased him. Transforming the image of a frightening, ferocious beast, she thought of the "Black Wolf" as a large, friendly hound. Then again, she thought, he could be diseased, a sniveling, weak, or stupid man. He might be maliciously cruel, like her uncle. She felt for the wolf brooch she wore as a pendant beneath her tunic. As her mind calmed, she recognized her greatest fear: violence on her person. Husbands beat their wives. Her mother had borne the marks of her husband's rods. A beating was one thing, but Elise did not want to be disfigured. Oh, vanity!

Of course, she knew her husband's alliances were more important than her vain concerns; and he would require her to accommodate those alliances in every way. Her responsibilities could take a bizarre twist if he were so inclined. Some husbands gave their wives, or daughters, to their overlords and allies to bed as symbolic acts of trust, to seal treaties and such. Or, from her own mother's experience, to humiliate her for being outspoken or to punish her disobedience. Elise watched the shimmering light on the waves. She must keep her temper in check and not raise her voice to him, she thought, believing herself capable of such a feat.

Obedience. Obedience, she chanted to herself as the ship rose and fell over the swells. At the abbey, she had struggled with obedience, and now she recalled the monks discussing a count who'd had his wife's head chopped off because she had "an ungrateful tongue." The Church and courts pardoned the count for his deed because she'd driven him to it. The monks of Clarion agreed. Still, they argued there should be a law, so husbands should not have to seek pardon. Instead, they agreed that any husband should be granted the legal right to remove shrewish wives as the count did. Elise supposed a shrewish wife was one who disagreed with her husband about anything.

She glanced at Tristan. He would relish Lesceline's disagreements. Looking back at the sea, she remembered how Marie sparred with Roland. Her wit charmed him even as she infuriated him. Elise would never feel what Marie felt for Roland or what was palpable between Tristan and Lesceline. Her parents had not *loved* each other. She did not expect love. She hoped for respect, but she wished, with all her heart, for something special, something she could not name.

May 1067, London

(M)erchant ships of all sizes traveled up and down the River Thames. Sails fluttered and bobbed, rowers propelled fast, narrow ships throughout the waterway, transporting cargo. As they rounded a bend, they encountered more vessels, and Elise got her first full view of London and thought it under attack for the thick smoke. In moments, she recognized a large, sprawling town sweeping along the north bank. Larger than any place she'd ever seen, the town frightened her at first.

"Are we going to dock?" Elise asked.

"No," Roland said. He checked the tide and the sail, and signaled to the other ships following his lead. "We'll avoid the tolls and go up river."

As they approached the town's edge, the crew kept away from jetties and steps. Dubec pointed out the crumbling stones of a Roman fort surrounding a scattered group of timbered buildings. "Few people go into the old city," he said. "Wights live there."

"Ghosts?" Elise said. "Do you jest, Brian?"

"No." He said, staring at the walls.

The sounds of hammers and mallets clunked out over the water and drew her attention to a half-built tower. Men climbed over the timber structure, bellowing to one another. Ropes hung from each of the walls hoisting planks and tools to the top. Beside the tower, carpenters notched timbers, others split and hewed boards, some grooved the planks for a slotted fit. Elise looked down the waterway and back. The tower would dominate the river.

"Days after his coronation, William started repairing the old fort," Dubec said. "He charged his builders to strengthen the stone curtain walls, the ramparts, and battlements to protect the tower."

"Will he build a stone fortress, like the ducal palace at Rouen?" Elise asked.

"Perhaps."

Elise watched what she thought were hundreds of men digging a trench and shoring up the old walls. Oxen pulled carts laden with dirt, masons chipped and set large blocks of stones. An anchored barge held logs for the palisade, laborers rolled them onto the land, and hitched oxen dragged the timbers to the building site.

As they passed the tower, she saw a few stone structures. Timbered buildings were rising everywhere she looked, dominating the smaller mud and thatched buildings peppering the smoky town. At the docking posts, toll takers wearing symbols of their rank, carried ledgers and counted goods, and aides held the treasury chests beside armed Norman guards. On the river, rowboats and sailing vessels traveled from side to side, weaving through or towing the larger, slower merchant ships and barges.

Approaching the bridge, Elise feasted on the sights. Fishers scooped their catch into barrels as squawking gulls circled above. Men unloaded salt barrels and sacks, pushed carts filled with ale, flax, thatching reeds, and wool, and crisscrossed over the docks and toward the streets. Next to a tannery, bright orange mud oozed into the river, accompanied by a stench so pungent it made her eyes water. She looked up at the bridge filled with carts and people carrying bundles traveling in both directions and saw a company of knights gallop across, scattering everyone out of the way. Watching them, she remembered her betrothed, forgotten in her wonder.

As their vessel passed under the bridge, she asked Brian, "How many people live here?"

"Twelve, perhaps fifteen thousand."

"Fifteen thousand?" she said incredulously, trying to imagine so many people in one place. Elise had heard Paris had fifteen thousand people, but thinking back three years ago, she realized she had not seen much of Paris beyond the royal quarter of the citadel island. All she remembered now of Philip's palace were the moldy, decaying tower and the dim passageways filled with seeping slime.

Beyond the bridge, muck wagons lined up at the quay where swarms of men dumped their cargo into the river. Roland's ship bobbed through the murky water filled with foamy human waste, carcasses of dogs and cats, raw vegetation, and large rats, alive and clinging to debris.

"Is Rome this big?" she asked.

Roland and his men laughed. "Much bigger," Tristan said, as the wind filled the sail with a slap and a shudder. "We counted forty-six fortresses."

"Forty-six!" Elise looked back at William's single castle, trying to imagine more than one.

"And another two hundred watchtowers," Roland said. "Thousands and thousands live there."

"London," Giles said, "is a pigsty. In Rome, nearly all the streets are paved, and most buildings are made of stone."

Eagerly they told her about water flowing into houses, marble buildings, a circular altar with an open eye in the ceiling, gleaming churches, colored tiles, and festivals.

"Ah, Rome," Yves sighed. "The winter is warm, the fruits are succulent, and—"

"And angels," Tristan smiled, "fly about the ceilings."

"And I suppose," Elise said, "Roman carts never bounce on cobble streets, and Roman fires never smoke."

They all laughed.

"Bertrand," Elise said, turning to the man on her left. "Do they jest, or tell me true?"

Bertrand turned a bright red and squirmed. "T-t-true, m-m-my lad-d-dy."

"Really?"

He nodded.

"Then it must be so." She turned toward London unperturbed by descriptions of a place she was likely never to see. This town was the center of her husband's world, and now hers, too.

They sailed beyond the clustered buildings, past a church, a small river draining into the Thames, burned out cottages, and several stationary water mills. Some time ago, a floating mill had broken away from its mooring and crashed into a barge, leaving a wreckage of splintered timbers. Rotting piers jutted into the river alongside partially submerged sunken ships. Along the shore, sparsely planted huts gave way to green fields or marshes. Merchants and soldiers traveling in groups for safety, she supposed, used the river trail, dogs barked at passing vessels. They rounded another broad bend.

"St. Peter's Church and the new abbey," Dubec said. "William was crowned there last Christmas."

She looked at the arches and towers behind the other buildings rising nearby. Brian pointed out the walled compound, the king's palace and hall, sharing the island with the abbey, the bridges and watchtowers. Seeing the ships bearing William's colors, she asked, "When will William return from Rouen?"

"Perhaps never. The people are subdued."

That night, Hortense, making her first appearance since they had left Boulogne, joined the others. Buried in a fur cloak, she ate dried cheese and bread and drank a little wine. Elise asked her about the English, for Hortense had once lived among them with her English husband. Hortense repeated tales told in English halls and recited several Saxon lines of poetry. Elise frowned, Yves and Giles laughed at her expression.

"You'll become accustomed to it," Yves said. "The Saxon tongue sounds harsh to our ears, and their coarse words nearly always sound a challenge to fight."

"I will remember to not take offense," Elise said, lifting her hood as it began to rain.

Chapter Twenty-One

May 1067, Tutbury, Staffordshire

"Conan!" Alaric shouted as he mounted his horse. Wheeling the beast in Tutbury's bailey, he ordered, "Get the slaves and villagers up here. No one leaves the hilltop. No one!"

While Alaric's captain gave orders, Johan limped hurriedly toward the inner palisades circling the tower's earthen mound.

"What happened?" Marguerite asked, running up to Johan, pulling Clare along with her.

"Armed men, possibly rebels, are moving through the woods."

"Again? Can they breach the castle?"

"Only if they learn how few walls we have. Take Clare and go to Alaric's quarters. You'll be safe there."

"But—"

"Go! Alaric will clear them from the woods." He turned and ran to the tower.

When Johan reached the ramparts, he braced himself against the chilly, gusting wind. He followed the arm of a sentry pointing out the trail Alaric and his knights had taken into the woods. In the village, he saw Conan's men herding villagers away from their huts hugging the base of the crag and up Castle Road.

A few soldiers searched the huts for stragglers or rebels—or weapons. Some kicked over pots cooking on open fires. Others circled the plowed fields. Johan stayed atop, even after everyone returned to the castle. Leaning into the wind, he watched the trees swaying wildly, the flames of still burning cook fires whipping furiously.

He had been watching the woods for signs of Alaric's return when shouts drew his gaze to a woman racing down Castle Road. A few villagers followed, and soldiers afoot chased after the group. Startled, he recognized Clare of Wolenbroth in the lead. With one hand bracing her pregnant belly, another holding her skirts high, she ran awkwardly through the village. Her gait staggered as other villagers heading toward the woods passed her. Beside Johan, archers shot at the runners. An arrow hit the ground before her. A villager, a pace ahead of her, screamed and dropped, tripping her. She fell and rolled against one of the carts, out of sight. Simultaneously, a ragged band of armed men ran into the village from the woods. They cut down the villagers fleeing toward the woods and hacked at the foot soldiers pursuing the villagers. Archers released a cloud of arrows. A shed burst into flames. From the castle, knights galloped into the village, trampling downed villagers and driving attackers into the thickets. Leaving the dead, they gathered the wounded and marched those unhurt back to the castle.

Johan ran down from High Tower and met Conan and the others entering the compound. A roar of fury arose from those gathered in the bailey. Conan, clutching Clare's arm, pulled her toward the tower, through the enraged throng.

"Maim the slut! Blind her! Chop off her feet!" Normans chanted.

"Slay the traitor!" English voices shouted.

Another horn blasted, signaling Alaric's return. The mob surged and demanded Alaric punish Clare. Soldiers pushed them back, and Alaric took Clare and Johan to his quarters.

Johan turned on Marguerite. "Why didn't you keep her here?"

"I'm not—"

"—Why, Clare?" Alaric asked. "Why did you leave the castle?"

"I thought . . . ," she glanced at Marguerite and away. "I thought my sisters were with the rebels. I went to find them."

"Why did you think they were here? Did they send you a message?"

"It does not matter now."

Alaric stared at Clare a moment before turning to Johan. "Have Marguerite escorted safely to the tower and wait for me outside."

When Alaric later emerged from the longhouse, Johan recognized his contained fury. Scanning the courtyard, seeing the curious and resentful English, the contemptuous gaze of his Norman soldiers— some many years his senior, holding higher ranks in Normandie, Alaric's cheek throbbed.

As *Seigneur de Tutbierrie*, Alaric administered justice. As William's agent, he upheld the king's laws. As Dreux's friend, he had promised to keep Clare safe. But Clare *had* disobeyed orders. She *had* endangered others. She was English, and her action caused Norman soldiers to die. Johan watched Alaric look over the angry crowd awaiting his decision.

"Shackle Clare to the tower so all can see her atop the motte," Alaric ordered Conan, "but do not let anyone get to her! I will deal with her when I return. In the meantime, secure the periphery as best you can. We've found an encampment. Roddy and Gilbert are destroying it, but there may be other bands in the denser woods. Go!"

He explained to Johan. "Clare told me that her sisters had fled with soldiers escaping Hastings. In London, she'd learned from an English noble that they traveled with Mercians, that they knew Dreux kept her, and that they would come for her. But someone here told her they had come for her today. Find the *fiz a putain* and cut out his tongue. If we find Clare's sisters, we'll bring them in."

Buffeted by fierce winds, Dreux Marchand de Ville and six of his soldiers rode toward Tutbury. Alaric's betrothal documents, and his own, were rolled tightly and stuffed into a leather satchel belted at his waist. He also carried William's orders that immediately after Alaric's wedding, he and Alaric were to leave on another joint mission.

Impatient to see Clare again, Dreux had not minded crossing the rough sea or the cold days riding through rainstorms and mud. He would ask Alaric's priest, Father Pierre, to marry them right away rather than wait a few weeks for Alaric's bride to arrive.

If Clare would have him.

He had not told her of his intent when he'd seen her in March, and now nearing Tutbury, the more apprehensive he became. She might not want him.

During the two weeks he'd spent with her last Christmas, she had become as essential to him as breath. It seemed the more they coupled, the more fascinating she became. At first, he thought her merely grateful for keeping her to himself, for, despite the king's admonition against fornication, other captives were traded and shared like group property, abused, and demeaned for amusement. Clare's innocence and curiosity convinced him her attention was more than gratitude.

As she grew more comfortable with him, she delighted him with her stories, accurately describing everyone in the household, imitating their lisps, the tilt of their noses, the swagger of their steps. She exaggerated his broken Saxon and teased him in broken French about his men, who scurried when he gave them orders. She made him laugh.

"My lord, your . . . form," she said in French, "is as graceful as . . . *le*," she paused for the French word. "*Le* . . . shovel."

"*Cheval*," he laughed. "A horse?"

"*Oies*." she nodded, meaning to agree but using the French word for geese instead.

Now, with the recollection, he smiled at the joy she had brought into his life. And he felt grateful that, unlike his peers' mistresses, she did not exploit her new status or demand special privileges. More importantly, she did not blame him for her family's destruction, for the condition of her life, or for the complete loss of all she had once known.

He had seen her two months ago, in March, after subduing York with Alaric. As he had hoped, Clare was pregnant. They had two days together before he sailed to negotiate Alaric's betrothal. He had restored the jewelry he had taken from her that first day, along with the jewels found in her family's home before it was fired, and a torc made especially for her. She ran a finger over the twelve gold circles, each depicting a month marked by intricate nielloed designs, and linked together with twisted silver bands.

"I will wear this every day until you return, Dreux."

He remembered holding her and breathing as if for the first time in months. He was glad he had sent Clare to Hereford to meet Alaric. He had wanted to remove her from other English captives who derided her or called her a traitor for being a Norman's whore.

Now, as he rode to her under the weak sun he wondered uneasily if he should have mentioned marriage when he saw Clare last. No. Better to have waited until he had permission to marry her and the covenants to her family's estates. With their marriage, she would become the noblewoman of her ancestral lands. She should be about five months along now, he surmised. His castle at Thetford would not be ready yet. But Dreux had time to rebuild the hall where their child would be born.

At the top of a ridge, he and his soldiers reined in their horses. Chaos met them across the basin. Tutbury's tower was aflame. Dreux spurred his horse forward and raced across the valley.

Galloping through the main gates, he scattered screaming people running through the bailey in every direction. Instinctively, he rode toward the blazing inner palisade surrounding the mound and tower. He saw Clare chained to the timber tower beyond the acrid black smoke.

He fought his horse to leap through the fiery inner gates. His horse's frightened cries were lost in the hissing and crackling sounds as beams burned overhead. Black smoke and crimson flame made day into hellish night, and the shifting wind hid Clare from his view.

His horse reared. At Dreux's vicious kick, his steed lunged past the gate and up the planked steps of the tower's mound. The fire roared and licked up the tower walls. He heard Clare's inhuman scream, undulating low to its grating depths, then screeching higher and higher. His mount threw him, and he lost his helmet. He crawled toward her through whirling flames and saw her completely ablaze, like a torch's well-soaked rushes. Her eyes, roasted in their sockets, glared at him.

Standing, he raised his arm to block his face from the heat, and watched in horror as the skin of her face bubbled, then split and peeled in curls, exposing the raw flesh, which shrank from the bone. Yet still, she lived. Dreux heard his name upon her lipless mouth, the teeth exposed in a skeletal grin. Her howl above the din silenced only when his thrown dagger pierced her heart. She fell against her chains. He staggered toward her until his men tackled him and dragged him from the burning ruins.

Afterward, beside a shaded bank of the River Dove, Dreux leaned on the burr plate forming the pommel of his wooden saddle, staring. His man kept guard nearby. Dreux stared into a soft green, clear pool of water as it slipped ever so quietly over a broad, flat stone and whirled into a foamy funnel. The eddy should have calmed him, but instead, each swirl felt like a rope around his neck, pulling tighter and tighter until there was no breath.

He closed his eyes and saw her again as she had been only a few hours ago. The vision twisted inside his hollow soul as the sound of water seeped back into his mind. From the moment he first saw the blazing tower, he knew she was trapped within. Now he sat here beside the tranquil river, alive. And Clare was dead.

Dead.

Merciful God, he pleaded as the vision began again, and he shut his eyes to force it away and groaned aloud when the images sharpened in his mind's eye. God has no mercy!

He dismounted and stumbled to the creek. As his knees fell into the soft, damp bank, he gagged. The smoke of her burning flesh and the stench lingered within him—a bittersweet taste infused with the bile of his hatred. He spat and nearly vomited. He was covered in soot. His hair and eyebrows were singed, the skin of his hands and face were blistered.

He plunged his red hands into the cold water and sluiced water over his head.

As if a spell were broken, the vision fled. Dreux raised his dripping head and looked beyond the river to the valley at the base of Tutbury, from horizon to horizon through dark green woods and pale fields, to blooming hillsides. The blustery wind had ceased. He watched the soft white clouds, swans gliding upon a blue lake, listened to the birds atop the nearby tree, and the water gurgling gently before him. A breeze, as gentle as Clare's touch, lifted a forelock and fluttered his scorched cape. His eyes swept to Alaric's castle and his gaze hardened like tempered iron into a cold black void, more dangerous in intent than even the fire that took Clare from him. Nothing ever happened without the knowledge and consent of a castle's lord. Alaric had her chained like an animal and left her to die like that.

I shall avenge you, he whispered to her in his heart. I shall destroy him that destroyed you and our child. I shall kill him slowly—slowly, he vowed, envisioning Alaric's bloody heart in his hand, the hand bearing the scar of their blood bond.

Chapter Twenty-Two

May 1067, Cricklade, Wiltshire

Elise stood at the prow shivering. It had rained every day since leaving London, and despite an overcast sky, it seemed to have finally stopped. Absent the midday sun, the damp, chilled air enveloped her and her companions in grim silence.

The River Thames had narrowed. A cool breeze rippled the water, lapping against their hull. Roland had told her they would dock at the next village within the hour. Now, watching merchants through the trees, traveling in groups, pulling their packhorses on a trail following the banks, she realized that leaving the ship was another step farther from Marie, from her home in Fontenay. To combat her trepidation, she helped Hortense prepare for their departure.

After packing their belongings, Elise and Hortense left their shelter. An astonishing sight greeted them. Brilliant purple and white mottled flowers skipped across the green meadows, nestled against stones and swept over low hills, rippling like waves. The blossoms reminded her of guinea fowl as they bounced on tall thin stalks, and she wondered if they had curative uses. Closer to shore, mixed among the reeds, she watched them bob and dip in response to the ship's wake. Her embroiderer's eye studied the petals as delicate as butterfly wings, and a single long greenish-blue leaf, poised like a sword above the bell-shaped flower.

As they rounded a bend, Elise spotted a walled village. One manor house was situated outside the village along with a mill and a few store-houses. Every other structure sat within a peripheral stone wall. Beyond a few rowboats, no other ships were moored, and she could not see any people on the dock, no watchtower or sign of a Norman garrison.

"Tristan," Roland called. "Take a handful of men and reconnoiter the village before we disembark."

"Are you worried?" Elise asked.

"I am a careful man," he said, scanning the riverbanks. "I like to make sure things are the way they seem before finding out they are not." He turned to Brian, whose frown mirrored his and to Tristan, who had joined them.

"We'll wait for you to tell us what you've found." Roland sent him off with a cuff on his back. Tristan strode quickly across the ship and called for Bertrand. Roland shouted an order to his soldiers on the second ship. A message spread to the third vessel as well. In response, the soldiers donned their helmets and readied their swords.

Elise wondered what they would do if English warriors pounced on them, and before fear gripped her, she heard horns from ashore and saw colorful banners and pennons. In moments, a contingent of Normans appeared on the landing. Roland ordered his flags raised and received a welcome banner tilted before them. Tristan grinned broadly at Roland.

Relieved, Roland turned to Brian, her uncle's man. "Will Lord Stafford be here to meet his bride?"

"Perhaps," Dubec said, his expression sliding into a scowl.

On the wharf, a group of villagers watched, warily, silently, daring to snicker when, seduced by those purple flowers, Elise plucked a bouquet and found they released a foul smell. They sobered quickly when the captain-of-arms shouted at them, and they shrank from the whip. Still, those English eyes glistened with hostility, and their lips curled in insolent snarls until soldiers pushed or knocked them aside where they lay like submissive dogs. Elise shuddered, seeing the murderous stare of one young woman who had watched her. With her head high, Elise walked past her, sure a knife would plunge into her back. In that instant, Elise understood that these people had not yet been conquered and doubted they ever would be. Furthermore, they despised her because she was—Norman.

That afternoon, the captain of Cricklade's garrison entertained her, Hortense, Brian, and Roland. He occupied the largest house in the village from which he had a commanding view of the river and thus had no need for a tower. After nearly nine months away from Normandie, he was hungry for news. Roland answered all his questions and gave him a keg of French wine. He opened it immediately, telling them how much more he preferred wine to mead.

"Is it safe to travel now?" Elise asked.

"No route is safer than others," the captain told them, launching into colorful tales of rebels seeking shelter in the woods, of bands of robbers, and of his own forays to suppress the brigands. He embellished his tales with such lively heroic detail that Elise wondered if he exaggerated.

At the captain's query, Roland answered. "We are taking Lady de Fontenay to her husband, Alaric of Ewyas, lord of Staffordshire, awaiting us at Tutbury."

Elise caught a sudden flash in his eyes and the nearly imperceptible rise of his eyebrows.

"Blackwolf," he said. His eyes glanced warily to her, to Roland, and Brian.

"You know him?" Elise asked, smiling softly.

"Not personally. He is well known among us." In a subdued, formal manner, he returned to their journey, explaining that recent flooding had destroyed the Roman Road near Tewkesbury. He suggested an alternative well-traveled road, which would take them through the woods and open fields, onto Watling Street.

"You will travel faster. It is a main route, filled with travelers now after Easter. Although it is unlikely your party would be ambushed, my lady, I suggest you travel on ahead and let your goods follow."

"Why?" Elise asked the now guarded captain.

"From the size of your ships, you are transporting a great deal of cargo. It will take your wagons weeks to get to Tutbury, prolonging your journey," he said. "A smaller party with a few packhorses and carts could travel more quickly. I would be honored to augment your retinue with fifty men and deliver your goods safely."

With Roland and Brian's advice, she accepted the captain's offer. Elise left her heavy wagons with Brian's men and began the overland journey. She and her retinue traveled quickly. On Fosse Way, she saw few merchants, but many small groups of men, women, and children with hopeless faces, walking dazed, some hostile, others injured. With bundles on their heads or strapped to their backs, they traveled in wary silence, moving off the road when Elise's party appeared. Some groups were accompanied by soldiers using whips to move them forward.

They passed several burned out villages and hamlets with cowering people. Although they could appropriate food along the way by right-of-might, Elise insisted on purchasing food instead, thinking her largess would be appreciated. But one villager sneered at the silver dropped into his palm. Offended, she turned away, assuming him ignorant that Norman coins were superior to English coins. When one of the soldiers joked that the man would give his children equal portions of the silver penny for their meal, she remembered seeing dirty children barely peeking out from behind the thatched hut. She wondered if they had anything else to eat before dismissing the uneasy thought. It was not her concern. God had made them English, and if it were his will, they would be hungry. She glanced at Hortense and found her staring ahead, her lips pressed together.

Afterward, Elise no longer sought food from local inhabitants and felt relieved when they entered the woodland, avoided by unarmed travelers. With plentiful game and water for the horses, she no longer saw the villagers' silent, accusing stares nor heard their guttural phrases uttered softly—curses, she supposed, or worse.

May 1067, Staffordshire

Nearly a week later, Elise sat on her white mare, praying for patience. Small groups of Roland's soldiers stood beside the road talking, some relieved themselves on the grasses or nearby trees. Many more pushed and shoved and lifted the carts stuck in deep mud. She clenched her teeth at every sound Hortense made: her cajoling, her grunts, her impatient sighs, her shouts intending to aid the soldiers in their task. Her constant chatter—like the sound of cawing, belligerent ravens roosting at dusk—accompanied every move they made.

They had left Burton Abbey this morning, expecting to reach her new home today. Shortly after leaving the main road, they took the narrow, rutted track. Watching the struggling men, she thought it might take another day or more to go even a short distance.

An unbearable tension crept up Elise's spine. She hated being between things. She wanted to get settled. Yet, each step pulled her farther from home, from Marie, and closer to the unknown. After her wedding, everyone but Hortense and she would leave. Alone in this strange land. And as much as she loved Hortense, at this very moment, Elise wished she had not come. She winced at her wicked thought, for she could see the toll this trip had taken on her aunt.

Regaining her composure, Elise looked at the land this glorious mid-May morning. Her gaze traveled across the expanse of bluebells sweeping far into the woodland beneath the dappled canopy on one side of the track. Eased by the spectacular color, she saw pink-blossomed plants she did not know, nestling in the wooded shade. They'd passed hazel trees with mossy trunks, oak, ash, birch, brambles, and wild berries. Green rolling hills flanked the other side of the road and stretched for miles into the distance. *Dent-de-lion* raced across the fields. She spotted the cowslip, whose sweet nectar helped her sleep, and another plant used for snakebites. Here in this somewhat familiar place, she would live among the most foreign creatures: the Mercians, Angles, and Saxon peoples.

At Cricklade, she had found them crude, primitive, brutes. Their language, a jumble of harsh, grunting sounds, had grated and clashed in her ears. Their dirty, coarse tunics and rough tools bespoke their backward ways. Glancing back at her entourage, she hoped the Mercian monk from Burton Abbey would be less so. Sitting awkwardly on his palfrey, Brother Derrick talked to Bertrand. Rather appropriate, she thought, for when she greeted him, he sputtered and blushed and seemed as shy as Bertrand, *sans* stutter. The monk would serve as Tutbury's clerk and scribe for years. There was time to befriend him.

Brian Dubec hollered from atop his mount, and the soldiers began to move into a crude, irregular formation.

"We are ready to continue, my lady," he said, reining in beside her. He had removed his helmet and thrown his mail back from his head where it hung like a monk's cowl. She watched him gaze down the track and over the landscape surrounding them and felt again that he hid something from her. Perhaps about her husband. Often during their journey, she'd caught him watching her. She could not be sure, but she sensed . . . sorrow? Reluctance? She hoped she did not discern compassion seeping from his iron soul. That would truly frighten her.

The white mare she had bought at Cricklade seemed as anxious as she to resume the journey. She pranced sideways, dipped and raised her head, pulling on the reins. "How much further?" Elise asked, biting her tongue, having sworn to herself she would not ask that question.

Brian wheeled his horse and waved at Roland, seeing to the last cart before turning back to her. "We should reach Tutbury well before dark, my lady. The road leads through open fields, and it should be dry after we leave the woodlands." He looked toward the sun, shading his eyes. Curling his lower lip inward, he whistled. A rider spurred his horse, passed them, and headed down the track. "A messenger to tell Stafford we're near."

Roland joined them and, at his signal, all began to move again. Elise's irritation vanished instantly. Perhaps it was the breeze, she thought, as welcome gusts rippled through the grasses and unfurled their banners.

A little after nones, Roland stopped the party with a raised arm. "Riders coming," he said tensely.

Dubec quickly rode back among the soldiers giving orders. Elise steadied her horse as Tristan, Giles, Yves, and Bertrand surrounded her. She looked over the fields and saw something flickering in the distance.

Soldiers pulled the carts and packhorses together and formed a defensive wall around them. Although Dubec had expected sporadic attacks, they had traveled without ambush. Clad in armor, the soldiers settled into an alert calm. Roland and the others put on their helmets and fingered the hilt of their swords. Dubec returned, leading

Hortense's horse and Brother Derrick's mount to Elise. They waited for what seemed like a long time before the riders neared.

The men approaching them were also dressed for war. Beneath the spring sun, they shimmered and glittered, and the pounding of their horses' hooves on the hard-packed earth was threatening. Brian said to Elise, "Stafford's banners. He comes to meet us."

Her heart fluttered, and she glanced at Hortense, who smiled encouragingly. Suddenly she felt hot, dirty, and sticky. A thin line of perspiration snaked its way down between her breasts, reminding her that the wolf pendant hung there. She swallowed thickly and watched the riders come nearer as she sat taller and straighter upon her mount.

A young man rode at the lead, rocking in a smooth canter. She looked at him carefully, vexed that the nose guard of his helmet hid the planes of his face. She felt herself tremble and held her reins tightly so her hands would not shake. The lead rider raised his hand, and the ten men behind him reined in. Roland moved forward. The leader removed his helmet. The two men exchanged greetings. The stranger's eyes swept to her.

She saw a handsome man with sandy hair, warm brown eyes, and an easy smile. The Black Wolf? Elise wondered, trying to reconcile the tales of a ferocious, ruthless warrior with this seemingly friendly young man, not much older than her own twenty-one winters.

He urged his horse forward to greet her. "Countess de Fontenay?" he asked incredulously, reminding her of Dreux who asked the same at her betrothal, with the same voice. She saw his quick glance at Dubec, and Brian's mocking smile.

"Welcome, welcome," the stranger said, nearly stammering. "I am your servant, Johan de Vaux, seneschal to my liege, Lord Stafford. He . . . he is unable to greet you personally. I have come in his stead."

Elise felt Roland's sudden anger. One did not entrust this initial greeting to an underling. She knew it, but she also knew this was a time of war. Her fiancé had not attended the betrothal negotiations because the king had sent him elsewhere. He held the king's confidence and might find it necessary to have a proxy for the wedding as well. This was not the beginning she had hoped for. Nevertheless, it was her beginning to make of it what she would.

Elise gave Johan a radiant smile. "Your welcome is most appreciated for it means we near our destination."

"Yes," he said, clearing his throat, "it is only another hour's ride." His gaze flitted over the *fleur-de-lis* on her green and blue pennons, her cavalcade. Anticipating his question, she told him that the rest of her chattel would arrive in a few weeks.

He looked at the monk, "Are you the scribe sent to me from Abbey Burton?"

"Yes, my lord. I am Brother Derrick."

"Good." Johan turned his horse and rode beside Elise. Asking her about the journey and the weather, he glanced at her frequently, almost surreptitiously. She learned that Johan and the men with him had all been mercenaries a few months ago. Now, liegemen to her betrothed, they served him loyally. To ease Johan's awkward attempts to converse with her, she asked about the area. His answers sparked a series of questions from Tristan and Giles, which diverted Johan's attention from her.

As the travelers reached the crest of a hill, they paused.

"Tutbury," Johan said.

A lush narrow valley spread out before them. In the distance, Elise saw a natural crag that seemed to rise abruptly from the vale. A timber tower crowned the top. On the left, a woodland spread from north to south, hugged the hill, and extended west as far as she could see. Beyond the escarpment, a river meandered and arched to the right, curving east through the valley, disappearing from her view as it entered more woods spreading eastward.

"River Dove," Johan said, "flooded this last spring, and the marshes are still boggy."

At her questions, she learned the area was sparsely populated, that although the land appeared rich in red marl, there were few crops. Johan told her the river's fish should sustain them until they could plant more, and the woodland was full of berries and game. She smiled. At the very least, she and her husband might enjoy hunting and hawking together.

He pointed out the sheep. "We brought those with us to settle the land."

"In Cricklade, I purchased long, wooly ringlets," she said.

"I've seen such sheep. It was a good purchase," Johan said. "Lord

Stafford's sheep have coarse, tight fleece, and we do not yet have enough to supply the castle."

"Tell me about the woods and the woodland dwellers."

"It is very thick, dense, with a heavy canopy. We've found some huts tucked among the trees, and the people scatter and hide when approached. Their language is Welsh."

"Are we close to the border?" She'd heard blood-chilling stories of Welsh raiders, especially how they steal women.

As if he had forgotten what they were talking about, Johan blinked and looked away. Clearing his throat, he said, "Not too close, my lady. But the Welsh have hunted here for years, and over time, some have settled the land."

"Who chose this site for a castle? The king?" she asked.

"Lord Stafford."

"He chose well, did he not?" She was too far away to see the details but knew the tower would have an unobstructed view of the surrounding land for miles. Since it was difficult to move an army through dense trees, the castle would not fall easily to surprise attack from any challenger. Her husband's sensible decision impressed her. If the castle were attacked in his absence, she, like any lord's wife, must defend it, and the advantageous position would help.

They descended into the valley, and when they reached a small stream in the valley's center, they stopped to water their horses.

"My lady," Johan said, "I beg leave to return to the castle ahead of you. I have matters to attend, and if it gives you no offense, Castellan Gilbert fitz Gilbert will remain with you." Johan glanced quickly at Gilbert and away. "He will answer any other questions you may have."

Elise glanced at Roland's still-angry eyes and said, "No offense taken. Your men," her smile encompassed them all, "will guide us to the castle directly."

Seeing Gilbert's jaw clench as Johan galloped away, Elise sought to divert his irritation. She asked Roland what he could tell about the two large groups of soldiers occupying the fields beside the woods.

"Both are large armies, each with several companies," Roland said. "They are preparing to march." Nodding at the red and black pennons, he continued, "Stafford is a rigorous commander."

"How do you know?" Elise asked.

"Only a well-disciplined army will safeguard their armor and weapons as these have." Roland and Gilbert seemed to assess each other before Gilbert nodded.

Looking the troops over, she hoped the size of Stafford's force was as much a testament to the king's trust as to her betrothed's ability to command. Elise gestured at the green and brown pennons, marking the other troops. "They belong to Dreux Marchand de Ville?"

Gilbert nodded.

"We met Lord Norfolk," she said to Roland, "at the betrothal."

"So we did," he said, coolly, reminding her of the tension between the two men.

"Will you leave with the others?" she asked Gilbert. Unlike Johan, who had removed his helmet, Gilbert wore his. Despite the nose guard, she saw hard greenish eyes measuring her and lips thinned with resentment. She knew men disliked the changes a wife brought to their world. Each member of her betrothed's household, all his servants, his liegemen, and his friends would pass judgment on her. It was an important moment. She did not shrink from his gaze.

"No. I will remain to command the garrison and oversee our defenses," Gilbert said.

"A great honor. I am sure Lord Stafford would entrust Tutbury to only his most worthy and capable men. Perhaps he will grant you estates as well," she suggested.

"He has."

"Excellent," she said, pleased her betrothed understood that good relations between a lord and his vassals demanded mutual rewards, a factor often disregarded by those new to the nobility.

When they resumed their journey, Hortense, though visibly exhausted, smiled cheerfully at her. Elise looked for the pleasures she would share with her husband despite feeling a sudden, hollow foreboding. This new place, she thought, might one day become a large village, with a church, a market, a mill, or a mint. The possibilities stirred her confidence.

As they neared the village, her gaze traveled to the timbered tower rising above, nearly oppressive in its size. She wondered if her betrothed were there, looking down at the valley watching her party, thinking about her.

Chapter Twenty-Three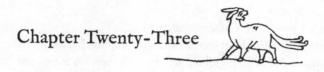

Johan found Alaric in the common room of High Tower. After the steep climb, he leaned against the timbered wall, short of breath, his leg aching as Alaric and two of his builders discussed the castle's fortifications. Unarmed, wearing a faded wadmal tunic, Alaric looked as he had the night Malet had told them of William's claim to the throne.

At the time, Johan never thought Alaric would have a castle of his own, much less that he would have built and garrisoned seven of the thirteen border castles erected during the last three months. Soon, Alaric and Dreux would survey the interior, establish garrisons at key inland towns, rivers, and crossroads. Before leaving, Alaric had turned his full attention to securing Tutbury—especially after the recent fire, which had consumed the first tower and inner palisade.

As Alaric leaned over the trestle table marking a section of defense walls on a cloth, Johan approached the table. He looked over the drawing and assumed the half-circle represented the main body of the castle grounds. A straight line ran north to south along the western edge, arrows indicated the steep slope which fell more than two-hundred feet to the marsh. At the southern corner of this line, a spiral represented the tower. Crosses showed the ditch, which would arc the edge of castle rock on three sides. Ovals marked where to deposit soil from the trench to build flats north and south and an earthwork ramparts for the palisades.

"Watchtowers and gates here, here, a barbican at the bottom of Castle Road," Alaric said, placing charcoal x's on the cloth. "Timber walls." He added double lines and looked up at his builders, who nodded. He rolled up the map, handed it to one of the men. "Gilbert will answer your questions should they arise."

"We must talk," Johan said, glancing at the men leaving the chamber.

"Your journey was quick." Alaric tossed his charcoal into the brazier. "Where is she?"

"Still in the valley. I left Gilbert to escort her."

"So repulsive you could not stand another moment, I venture."

"Let's go up to the gallery," Johan invited, although his leg would scream at the climb. Alaric frowned, and as if recognizing Johan's sacrifice, nodded. He blew out the oil lamp, pitching the chamber into gloom.

They climbed from the hollow room and stepped out into bright afternoon sunlight. Alaric circled the walkway behind the parapet and spoke a few words to each man.

Through a notch built into the battlement, Johan looked at the approaching cavalcade and scanned the troops where Roderick prepared the men, regretting again that he would not join them. Alaric came over, leaned against the timber, and also gazed at the encampment.

Reunited with Alaric for less than a month, Johan had been too preoccupied with the trip from Hereford and recent events to ask him about his impending marriage. The moment he met the Countess de Fontenay, Johan wondered why rumor painted her as an ugly, ancient shrew with a pockmarked face, and why some claimed she was masculine or diabolically tempered.

About to tread on dangerous ground, Johan braced himself. He knew Alaric well. Usually calm and controlled, Alaric, when enraged, became violent and lashed out viciously. And Alaric was stubborn. Once he made his mind up, rarely could anyone change it.

Johan ran his fingers over slashes carved into the wood by bored soldiers. "We have been friends a long time, you and I," he began carefully. "We are more than lord and vassal."

Alaric turned toward Johan as if bemused by this solemn preface.

"I have fought at your back many times, even took a sword for you once," Johan continued, seeing Alaric's eyes spark at the reminder. "You have honored me with land and position. I will serve you as diligently as you serve the king. In your stead, I will manage your lands and honor your wife."

"Honor my wife?"

"Yes," Johan said. "As custom dictates."

"Not if you serve me." Alaric spoke the words slowly, deliberately.

"Then explain to me why I must not." Johan shifted his weight from his bad leg.

"You need no explanation. You need only obey my orders," Alaric said.

"Yes, *my lord*," Johan said, teasingly, hoping to remind Alaric of their childhood friendship and that their formal allegiance and responsibilities were new to them both. Alaric stared at him, clearly unimpressed with his attempted humor.

Johan scratched his eyebrow with his thumbnail, giving himself time to arrange his thoughts. "I intend to obey you fully, my lord. But now I've met the countess—" Johan raised his hands to prevent Alaric from interrupting. "I must understand why you intend to subject her to Marguerite's authority, to set her beneath we who are her inferiors."

"One meeting," Alaric said sardonically. He leaned back against the parapet, a condescending stance Johan recognized. "A few words passed between you. How long did you ride with her, Johan?" He glanced at the woman's retinue. "An hour?" His voice hardened as he straightened from his relaxed pose. "And in all that time, you have come to know her well enough to champion her cause." He shook his head. "She must be a witch to have turned your head so quickly. I wonder what spell the old hag used to influence you so."

"She is not old," Johan said. "She is gracious and comely. She—"

"Comely!" Alaric said. "Appearance has little to do with a pure heart, Johan, and is a great weapon for villainy—as you, of all men, must know."

"That was four years ago." Johan resented the reminder of his disastrous marriage, begun when he was nineteen. His black-haired, wild and vicious beauty, a Welshwoman, had stirred his lust. When she died within months of their wedding, he felt intense relief, not sorrow.

"A low blow to raise the flag of my folly," Johan said. "But your attack will not divert my question. Why do you detest her?"

"It matters not if I detest her. Whether she's beautiful, wrathful, foolish, proud, or deformed, it's too late. We must wed." He glared at the travelers. "We try out a horse, our clothes and armaments before we accept them. But a wife we take unseen, unmet, at the command of our overlords. This marriage exceeds anything previously within my grasp. I question the motives behind it."

"You question a marriage that enriches you?" Johan asked incredulously.

Alaric looked through the notch. "I am not privy to my king's intensions. But William is shrewd. This marriage has import to him. It ties me to the duchy and assures my loyalty."

"He distrusts you?" Johan asked.

Alaric turned back to Johan. "One can never be sure, can one? Born in Ewyas, I am an outlander. William's advisors believe English water taints my loyalty. They claim my allegiance remains with the English and that I would turn the king's army and my local knowledge to aid Harold's pups."

"And when you marry the countess," Johan said, "you accept Eustace's wergeld, the blood price paid for the death of your family. The marriage forestalls a feud."

"So it would appear," Alaric said, giving Johan pause. "The king needs unity among his followers and obedience from his kin—despite my family's death. Disregarding William's ban against private wars would have challenged his authority, days after his coronation. William gave me a choice: death or marriage."

Johan started.

A bitter smile twisted Alaric's lips. "Nothing less than death would have made me take Eustace's niece."

"He paid far beyond the customary guerdon," Johan said. "Her carts bring coins, gold plate, and jewels."

"And every coin is an insult to my family, to my honor. By accepting her, I profit from their death. I pardon Eustace and dismiss his crime as a mishap—not the deliberate murder of his foes."

"Her wealth will extract riches from this land and build Tutbury."

"And provoke William's enemies," Alaric said. "Think, Johan!"

At a loss, Johan frowned and shook his head.

"Kingdoms throughout Christendom have suffered famines nearly every other year. But here, the last famine was long before our time. English grain will strengthen William. Normans hold Apulia and control Sicily. Under William, we belong to a Norman empire with markets extending now from York to the Middle Sea, from Gibraltar to Byzantium. We are despised. Even Rome seeks our military might. And William's enemies will strike to cut him down."

"Who would dare?" Johan said.

"King Philip. His dukes and counts, Brittany, Anjou, and Maine." Alaric shook his head. "The countess is King Philip's kin. Her wealth could support any challenger to William—here or in Normandie. And if Eustace ever plots against William, she will surely join her uncle."

"Would he? Would she?" Johan asked.

"Would they not?" Alaric said. "A few months ago, William and Eustace quarreled bitterly, and Eustace left abruptly for Boulogne. What if Eustace turned against William? What if she stood with her uncle?"

"That would be treason," Johan said.

"Yes. You and I, Roderick and Gilbert, would be caught in the middle of it by mere association."

Johan studied Alaric, a nameless soldier less than a year ago, now raised by this marriage to the highest levels where power and intrigue ruled. "But—"

"—Suppose the king anticipates a future plot?" Alaric looked expectantly at Johan.

"Then, this marriage is meant to check Eustace," Johan said.

Alaric smiled. "I think he gave me her wealth and borderlands to nullify such threats. If she were kept here, a hostage of sorts, guarded, isolated near the center of the kingdom, it would be impossible for Eustace to reach her or for her advance his cause. This castle could easily imprison anyone who displeases the crown."

Johan nodded. He accepted Alaric's suspicion of Eustace and the king's possible motives, but that did not explain why Alaric vehemently despised the woman herself and why he intended a bleak existence for her. "It is completely possible she is innocent of all plots."

"Not likely. Noblemen knowing her family and history claim she shares affinity with Eustace and is uniquely attuned to kingcraft. If she has only one sliver of Eustace's character, she's dangerous, and even if she were the most beautiful woman in the world, her charm would be deadly."

"I don't believe she schemes."

"You might not, but Dreux," Alaric said softly, "reported how she twisted the betrothal negotiations to her advantage."

Johan cringed. Tension between Alaric and Dreux had been unbearable since Clare's death. Johan followed Alaric's gaze to the charred huts and remembered the rebel attack. No one was sure how the fire began, but everyone saw flames roaring swiftly through more than half of the cottages nestled at the foot of the scarp, up the wooded slope to the tower. And Johan remembered Alaric's return from his foray, his discovery of Clare's death, and Dreux in a stupor—soot-streaked, burns on his face and hands—delivering Alaric's betrothal documents.

"Dreux," Johan said, "may have wronged the countess in his anguish. Besides, she will be your wife for eternity."

"We won't be married long," Alaric said, scratching his stubble.

Alarmed, Johan said, "Murdering her will betray God's sacrament and condemn your soul!"

Alaric barked a bitter laugh. "Think you I won't roast for all those I have killed for William's cause? Papal banner or not, my soul will feed Lucifer's fire. One more will not matter."

"You need sons."

"I will beget sons, but not on her. Although I will consummate this marriage, beyond the barest legal requirement, I shall have no wife."

Johan recalled how the countess had greeted him, her warmth, and suddenly he was angry. "You must give her a chance! She's—"

"Johan! The woman carries the blood of the man who murdered my family, who bragged about raping my mother. He even ridiculed her memory when he learned of her death. How could I ever let my sons bear the blood of such a man?"

Johan watched the throbbing along Alaric's jaw. "You want to exact vengeance on her, whether innocent or guilty."

"Ease your concern. I will not strangle her in the wedding bed."

"And if you are wrong about her?" Johan said.

"If?" Alaric said. "I cannot stop this marriage. All I can do is use all the rights accorded me by law. It is my *duty* to thwart treason, even if only suspected. I am required by my oath to protect the king and his realm. No law prohibits me from prudently limiting the woman's freedom, from revoking her authority to rule my home and vassals or restricting access to her wealth. Until we confirm she is innocent, subjugating her to the rule of my vassals and my mistress is a fitting compromise. And in the meantime, if Eustace plans to use her as his pawn, I will use her as mine."

Before Johan could respond, Alaric spoke. "Enough! I am about to leave you with all my possessions, with the power to protect or destroy me. You can return to Hereford and administer my estates from there, without penalty. But if you stay here, at the seat of my tenancy and with the countess, you must be my agent and imprison her, have her beaten or shackled as I wish. Decide now. Do you serve me?"

"You doubt me?" Johan asked.

Alaric looked at Johan for a long, measured moment. "Yes. Once, you jeopardized an entire garrison by trusting a beautiful woman."

Johan nodded and looked away from Alaric's intense eyes. He could not deny the past. Upon meeting the countess, her smile, her sapphire eyes sparkling without guile had struck him nearly speechless. He would have been far less trusting if she looked like the village goose girl. Recalling the countess's questions and observations, he realized she saw all with an intelligent eye. Beauty and intelligence *were* dangerous. With a sweet smile, a soft word, a flirtatious eye, she could extract information from obedient servants and careless, lonely soldiers.

Suppose she *were* adept at intrigue and subterfuge, he thought, recalling Brian Dubec's mocking grin. Dubec, Eustace's man. Suppose, like Dubec, she obeyed Eustace without question. Johan knew nothing about her, whether she would beat her servants, how long she would haggle over the price of onions, whether she would whine and complain, talk incessantly, or if she would drink the blood of her enemies.

"Don't look so forlorn," Alaric said. "Few men are immune to a comely face."

Johan winced. Though not very courageous, he was his own man. "I grant you that I do not know what kind of woman she is. But neither do you. Until there is proof of her culpability, you will not harm her person—else you face my sword."

Alaric grabbed Johan by his tunic and pulled him against his chest. "You betray your oath!"

"I swore fealty to you before witnesses and will do so again," Johan babbled quickly to forestall Alaric's fist. "I will do as you command, even if it displeases me. I will remain cautious and suspicious, alert for any schemes the countess may pursue, and if you wish to imprison her, I shall. But I will not be senselessly cruel to her, and until there is evidence she is the duplicitous woman you believe her to be, I will protect her against your violence."

Alaric released Johan abruptly, nearly shoving him into the wall. "So easily she drove a wedge between us." Alaric turned to look out at the distant horizon, and after a long silent moment, he said, "I've not seen you so spirited since you insisted we wait for Edo." The memory broke the tension between them. He turned to Johan, "Know this: I hold you responsible for the countess—as Conan was held responsible for Clare."

"Yes, my lord," Conan's misjudgment and quick execution were fresh reminders of one's responsibility to his liege lord.

They walked around the ramparts and stood together, watching the countess's traveling party, her banners fluttering in the light breeze.

"She wears blue and rides the white horse," Johan said.

"I will send orders from the field," Alaric said. "Greet her in my stead, Johan. No civilities. I have no desire to exchange pleasantries. The wedding is a mere formality accepting Eustace's reparations. It will take place tomorrow night. If she objects to a night ceremony, proceed with the wedding immediately, you as my proxy."

Chapter Twenty-Four

May 1067, Tutbury, Staffordshire

"A recent fire?" Elise asked Gilbert. She and Hortense exchanged uneasy glances. Fire always reminded them of Mortemer, the attack both had survived. As they approached the village, her gaze traveled slowly from the burnt structures and brambles at the base of the escarpment up over the charred trees sweeping up to the crest where the tower stood.

"Yes," Gilbert said. A dark look flitted across his face, and she doubted he would elaborate without a prompt.

"The cause?"

He paused as if deciding what to tell her. "Rebels."

She had seen the murderous, hostile English in Cricklade, and could well imagine their violence. Again, she felt exposed but knew her taciturn guide would give no comfort.

"Was the attack serious?"

"Soldiers and villagers died," he said. "The first tower and inner palisade burned down. Those responsible were punished. All will soon learn to obey their masters."

Elise looked from Gilbert to the tower. He knew more than he said, she thought. "How long ago was the fire?"

"A fortnight."

"Two weeks!" she said, "A testament to the builder's efficiency."

She looked up at the new tower. She supposed it possible. The captain at Cricklade had told her William had kept his several thousand troops busy building towers. One rose in only eight days. Lord Stafford must have had hundreds of workers unless . . . "Was any fort here when Lord Stafford took possession of the land?"

"No," he said.

No doubt her betrothed's troops were adept at digging trenches, building castles and bridges quickly. In a hostile land, no warrior would balk at building a strong defense behind which he could sleep easier than in an open field. But they would need many hands to build this castle and troops were preparing to march. She wondered if they had slaves, but refrained from asking an underling. He seemed to resent her inquiries, and there was no need to impose her authority or censure his surly manners at their first meeting.

Gilbert would defend this place and, despite his hostility, he would protect her as well. Accustomed to the defense of her own lands, she studied the scarp and castle. A sentry atop the parapets could see enemy troops long before they reached the valley. Besides the High Tower, she knew each gate would have watchtowers as well. The fewer gates, the better, she thought, hoping builders could complete the barest defenses before winter. Once atop the rise, she would know how well the castle's defenses had been planned.

Gilbert reigned in and spoke to Roland. "My lord, there is limited space above on the castle grounds. Your retinue must remain here." He pointed to an edge of the valley far from the two armies. "We have tents above for only a few of you," he said, including Brian Dubec. "Your wagons and carts will take up much room."

Roland and Brian agreed. Tristan took command of their company remaining in the field.

Elise turned to her companions during the journey. "Thank you all for escorting me." She proceeded to give each a separate farewell, asking Giles to give her regards to Anne, commenting to Yves on his future nuptials, and expressing her desire to see Bertrand again. To Tristan, she said, "Tell Lesceline I would like her to visit me. It would please me very much if you bring her yourself." He frowned before blowing her a kiss.

Turning toward the tower, she felt a piercing sadness. She would miss her jovial, teasing friends dreadfully. In a few moments, she would enter a world of strangers. Her betrothed's world.

"Come along, Brother Derrick," Hortense said, drawing Elise's attention from the past and future to the present. "Soon, you can get off that horse. No doubt your . . . you are sore." Everyone laughed, including Brother Derrick.

As soon as they crossed the last creek straddling the valley, they entered an area filled with activity. Workers felled trees, hammered, sawed, chipped, and hewed timbers, cross-stacked logs dried for future buildings. Next to the log yard, workers stripped, lashed, and notched trunks together into sections for the palisade. Others stacked these sets into wagons and loaded wagons headed toward the main road.

A few old huts with gaping holes and rotted thatching reminded Elise of toothless old men with hairy tufts protruding from balding heads. Elsewhere, workers crawled all over a half dozen newer dwellings, three of sod, one with a full thatched roof, all planted randomly along a narrow, jagged road. She could discern the pattern of an emerging village, and even recognized an alehouse, distinguished by the stacked barrels. Bubbling cauldrons sat on open fires, and the stench of tallow filled the air. Women carried baskets or water buckets, and some worked beside the men. Dogs ran in packs, barking and yapping at their horse's heels. Children of all ages worked, ran twisting and turning through the settlement, or stared in wary curiosity at the approaching riders. Excluding the children, she estimated only about three-dozen villagers, not enough to farm the area and provision the castle without slaves.

Looking back at the narrow valley, she saw a few strips of sown land. It was mid-May, too late to plant for the fall harvest. She considered the need to gather enough food and provisions before winter and the tilling that must be done for next year's crops.

Gilbert turned in his saddle toward Brother Derrick and pointed out the cleared area on the right, marked by half timbers lying on the ground. "Lord Stafford has set aside this land for a church."

As they began their ascent up Castle Road, she saw men pulling down huts, whole and charred, tucked against the hill, and workers digging a wide, deep ditch at the base of the scarp. A moat or ring-work, she supposed, seeing the newly exposed orange-red earth, naked as flayed meat. Wagons filled with freshly dug soil and rocks traveled up the road, slowing their progress.

Near the top, they paused where the road forked. Gilbert explained that the right fork continued around the castle toward Northgate, unseen from their perspective, for wagons, carts and most of the foot traffic. After sending Elise's carts onward, he led Elise and her party to the left fork.

"Southgate," Gilbert said, signaling the guards who watched their approach. A horn bellowed. The Southgate Road narrowed and curved sharply to the left precipitously, a defense mechanism to prevent amassed forces from overrunning the gate. Workers had dug out both sides of the road, and one day a deep fosse would cut through, leaving only platforms for a drawbridge. Until then, this road was the primary defense, as it required them to ride single file across wood planks laid as much to protect the bare ground from erosion as to announce their approach. Elise recognized the danger immediately. One wrong move could send a horse down into the ditch. She glanced at Hortense, who lifted her chin, unfazed by the challenge.

Two small towers flanked the timber gate, which opened with a wail. A sharp, loud snap startled Elise. Above her, a large red banner with a snarling, ferocious black wolf greeted her. The flag whipped and slapped in the wind, and the wolf's red eyes seemed to track her. Suddenly feeling awkward and wary, she reached for the wolf pendant and ducked her head to ride through the low gate, catching the scent of recently hewn timbers.

She entered a world of deafening chaos: clanging metal, sawing, shouting, screeching. Whips whistled and cracked in the air. They rode along a street traversing the bailey. Piles of goods, stacked timbers, crates, bundles of wares lined both sides. Unlike the lush, green valley below, every piece of ground was trampled, leaving barren dirt. They trod over deep ruts and caked mud. Dozens of people swirled around them: men bent forward carrying bundled faggots on their backs, others rolled barrels marked with the salt symbol, women lugged baskets of fish. They passed a string of packhorses, muck carts, wagons hauling tubs of water, and pushcarts heavily laden with sacks of grain.

Disappointment filled her. She had left Boulogne, a place she had never considered her home, and traveled for nearly twenty days to an alien and hostile place. Although she'd shared a deteriorating, crumbling hovel with Arques, on reflection, it seemed a palace compared with this place, barely more than a rough training ground.

Despite everything she had been told, she had envisioned her new home as resembling her chateau at Fontenay, or even the quiet cleanliness of the dreaded abbey. At the very least, she had imagined rows of whitewashed houses, crowned with thatched roofs, like those she had seen in Cricklade. Instead, a single timber tower rose atop the large earthwork mound. Stark, dark, forbidding, the fortress, a malevolent presence, overshadowed the courtyard and made her shiver.

Beside the tower, she spotted a thatched longhouse, built low to the ground with a single pitched roof positioned on a small rise to look out over the yard.

"Lord Stafford's lodging," Gilbert said in answer to her question. "It houses his treasures and charters and is guarded day and night."

On her right, in a random, haphazard order, canvas tents dotted the field. A dog scattered a flock of chickens, leaving dust and feathers floating in the wake of their flapping wings and incensed squawks. Piglets and children ran about the castle grounds, a couple of dogs fought with one another, snarling and snapping until a large man pushed his way through the crowds and kicked them until they separated and skulked away.

Soon they passed a large dining tent, its flaps rolled up, shaded rows of trestle tables beside baking ovens, smokehouses, and long fire pits. Workers stacked thin, day-old bread trenchers. Cooks stirred cauldrons bubbling with stew or soup, and one slammed her long-handled spoon into the head of a boy she chased away. Butchers filleted a carcass, spit turners roasted others. With the smell of meat, Elise's stomach growled, but her hunger died quickly with the odor of burnt feathers and the blood draining from hung poultry.

She searched for, but did not see, a kitchen garden, and made a mental note to have one planted as soon as possible, for they would need fruits, herbs, and vegetables.

She smelled the stables before she saw them and was surprised her party drew up beside them. A group of four tents had been raised along the northern side of the bailey beside the unfenced edge, which sloped steeply to the marsh. She dismounted, feeling her legs wobble as she touched solid ground. Roland and Brian helped Hortense dismount, and Hortense pointed to a tent with an unspoken question to Elise.

"Lady de Fontenay," Johan de Vaux called out.

She turned to see him threading his way through the crowds gathered to observe her party. As he neared, she noticed a distinct rocking gait and his painful expression as he limped toward her. She resisted looking at his legs, smiling instead.

"I apologize, my lady, for the disorder you find," Johan said. "We are trying to finish the defenses before winter sets in."

"Yes," she glanced around and back to Johan. "There is much to do."

"We are unable to put you into the High Tower until tomorrow. I hope these accommodations will be satisfactory for now." There was an awkward pause. Roland and Brian glared at Johan. She understood their fury at these odious tents unbefitting persons of their rank and status.

"Lord Stafford sends his regrets," Johan said to Elise and the men beside her. "He is not able to meet you now as he prepares to march in two days. He requests the wedding occur tomorrow night, for the king expects his departure soon afterward."

Her betrothed's failure to greet them himself was a serious breach of decorum—an insult really—and she felt it, as did everyone else in her party. Roland tensed, taking immediate offense. Even Brian bristled and narrowed his eyes at Johan but said nothing.

"If you wish the wedding to proceed earlier, Lord Stafford has offered . . . He has offered me for proxy, my lady." Johan bowed before her.

Elise glanced at a tired and cranky Hortense and knew her entire party was likely to erupt in a volatile explosion. She smiled at everyone, including Brian, and placed her hand on Roland's arm as he gripped the hilt of his sword. Perhaps, with preparing his soldiers to march, her betrothed was unable to meet her. To wed a soldier meant sacrifice, as she well knew.

"There may be rebels nearby, Roland," she said. "You understand how inconvenient a wedding could be at a time like this."

To Johan, she said, "I had hoped for more time to become

acquainted with Lord Stafford before the wedding, but since he must leave so soon, one day will do. The vows may be spoken tomorrow night as his lordship wishes. Would it be possible for all of us to have meals and washing water this afternoon?"

"Of course, my lady," Johan said, his relief obvious.

She thanked him and Gilbert, who had remained mounted. She gave Brother Derrick a pointed look. He seemed momentarily confused, and then ran after Johan for whom he would scribe. She entered the large tent she would share with Hortense, hoping her acceptance of the circumstances would keep Roland and Brian calm.

The next day, Elise struggled to control an unusual spurt of anger. She had assumed her betrothed would meet her before the wedding. He had not approached her the previous evening, nor had he come to her today. His rudeness was evident, and his absence, like the cool, cloudy day, cast a pall over her and her companions. She imagined a brooding, ill-tempered man like Guillaume Arques, and the thought of marrying such a man made her want to flee.

She chided herself. If she had been cleverer, she might have quipped to Johan that the wedding could be postponed indefinitely! Instead of letting her annoyance fester, she met with Johan to discuss storing the possessions brought with her and preparations for the wagons arriving in the next few weeks. With the men assigned to assist her, Elise had the carts unloaded and stored the chattels in a tent hastily erected beside her betrothed's longhouse or taken up to the High Tower where she would reside after the wedding. The task kept her spirits up.

Hortense, meanwhile, surveyed the living quarters in the tower and prepared the bedding chamber.

Near day's end, Elise and Hortense strolled the castle grounds with Johan as their escort. Hortense, unusually quiet, appeared haggard, yet she trudged forth, lifting her skirts and stepping over puddles. Elise glanced nervously at her aunt, whose clenched jaw and thin lips betrayed her silent rage.

At the bailey's northern edge, Johan pointed out the distant mountains. Looking west, where the sun had just touched the horizon, Elise felt hollow. They were isolated. An enemy would have difficulty fighting his way up to this castle, and once the palisade was completed, a prisoner would find it difficult to escape.

Johan led them across the courtyard and pointed out the tent erected for the wedding feast.

"Ah," he said as they passed the canopy, "Lady Marguerite d'Hesdins."

"God grant you peace," Elise said, smiling at the lovely woman, who stared at her with a raised chin and cold blue eyes before walking away. Surprised by the woman's discourtesy, she asked Johan, "A knight's wife?"

"A knight's widow."

The woman's petite figure and blond hair, uncovered in the custom of unmarried women, reminded Elise of her sister Marie. To Hortense she said, "A noblewoman, perhaps a friend and compeer. We'll gift her some fine cloth or furs."

Johan coughed under Hortense's scrutiny.

"A widow?" Hortense asked mockingly.

Before Elise could ask her meaning, a horn blew. She turned toward the gate towers. A single rider rode into the bailey and up to the timber dwelling where he dismounted. A squire took his horse's reins and led it away as he turned and ducked into the longhouse.

"Lord Stafford has arrived, my lady," Johan said. "I beg your leave. The wedding will commence within the hour."

Chapter Twenty-Five

In a few moments, Alaric would have more land and wealth than he had ever imagined, and a treacherous bride to go with them. He found the situation ironic. It satisfied the fiend in him.

As he waited, anticipation, like molten iron, rose up his spine just as it did before a battle. He stood with the witnesses and Father Pierre beside the crude altar, which had been erected hastily outside Northgate on the unfinished outer baileys. He stared into one of the fires flanking the priest.

Night encased the blazing logs. Watching sparks rise into the blackness, Alaric recalled the smoldering bodies, the skeletal grimace, and charred flesh of his family's bodies, so like Clare's found in the rubble.

He looked across at Dreux and felt a stab to his heart. *Dreux*, he called silently, to a face rigid as sculpted stone, to eyes staring past Alaric. He understood. Dreux had lost Clare and his unborn child. But Alaric could not fathom the horror, the agony of seeing Clare writhing in the flames. He could not have lived with such a memory. How could Dreux?

Alaric did not know how to ease Dreux's pain or what he could say if Dreux would let him speak. He must try again, even if he could not breach the wall between them. Alaric thought of sweet Clare, how she had begged him to make a world for her child who would be both English and Norman, and keep her safe from the Normans who wanted to tear her to shreds and safe from her people who believed her a traitor to her English blood. Safe.

One day Dreux would avenge his Clare. Just as, one day, Alaric would kill Eustace, or his sons—or his niece.

Alaric's gaze met Eustace's man, Brian Dubec, whose mocking expression failed to goad him. The Mastiff had bragged about the death of Alaric's family. Had he fired the church himself? Dubec would witness Alaric's submission to Eustace's design. The thought chaffed, but the marriage was a prerequisite for Alaric's own design.

Marguerite, standing beside Dubec, caught Alaric's eye. She raised an eyebrow and swept her tongue against her upper lip in that slow, sensuous way of hers. Alaric had never told Marguerite about Eustace or the reason for this marriage. He intended she remain ignorant.

A gust whipped the flames and made the firelight dance wildly about the platform. When the priest looked up, Alaric followed his gaze to the double row of small fires marching from the planked floor where he waited, along the road up to the castle.

The bride appeared, escorted by Count Roland de Rennes. Alaric measured the Breton a moment, wondering if King Philip's envoy would again express his anger about the countess's treatment. No doubt, the countess had many champions, he thought, shifting his gaze to the woman.

Coldly, his eyes flickered over the veil obscuring her face. Eustace's description of his niece matched Alaric's last memory of Goda, the crone who had pointed out where his family died. He could not shake this vision now, despite Johan's words to the contrary.

She stepped carefully from the rough planks, over stones and piles of dirt down the crude path toward him. Beauty or the lack of it mattered little to him. He had no doubts that she would use her wiles and wealth and her position to advance Eustace's aims. The betrothal documents ensured she would outrank him. And as his wife, she would expect to rule his castle and people, govern his estates and wealth in his absence—rights Eustace presumed. Rights Alaric would revoke.

When she came within a few steps of him, Alaric turned his back on her, intending to offend. He heard her pause before stepping beside him and felt her escort bristle in militant tension. At Alaric's nod, the priest began.

As Father Pierre droned the ancient words, Alaric looked beyond the altar and into the flat, black night mirroring his feelings. He prayed for his father, Simeon, who had lived honorably and died hideously. He prayed for his mother, Julienne the Fair, who had stood beside Simeon to the end. He prayed for his brother and Rannulf's wife Leota and their newborn babe, and begged God to assist him in avenging his family. He prayed for his men and his cousin, the king. Then, drawing a deep breath, he prayed for Clare and for Dreux, who must endure a wedding, not his own.

Finally, the priest repeated the words Alaric had asked of him.

"I wish to remind you, Genevieve Elysia de Fontenay," he said in French, "it is the husband's duty to train a wife as he would train a horse, to chastise her as he would his vassals or any that serve him, for she belongs to him, as do the others. Thus, if he beats you for discipline's sake, he incurs no punishment nor the stigma of excommunication."

Marguerite grunted softly. The countess stiffened and nodded her understanding.

Good, thought Alaric, the training has begun. He felt her intense gaze through her veil. He took her icy hand and slipped a thin, flat, cross-hatched iron band onto her finger. After the final vows, instead of raising her veil and kissing her cheek, he brushed his lips across her hand. Taking her arm, he led the priest and witnesses back along the fire-dotted path up to the castle gates, listening for Dreux following behind. Noticing that she nearly ran to keep up with him, he slowed his pace as they walked toward the gates and into the inner bailey to the large feasting tent aglow with candles. As evidenced by the sounds of laughter and singing coming from within, the wedding feast had already begun. Alaric brought her to an abrupt stop and released her so quickly she nearly staggered into Johan, who grabbed her arm and steadied her. Johan glared at Alaric.

"See to the lady's . . . comforts," Alaric said, ignoring Johan's anger and trudging away before she could say a word to him.

Elise stared after Alaric as he wove through the bailey and as he shouted to soldiers nearby. She lost sight of him when people and horses blocked her view.

"Lady Stafford?" Johan said, drawing her attention. He gave her a weak smile. "He has much on his mind this night," he offered by way of excuse.

She nodded, "I—"

"—Where did our esteemed *host* go?" Roland said, joining her.

Elise raised her silk veil over her head so Roland could see her unperturbed expression. With a smile, she put a hand on his arm, hoping to calm his explosive temper. "Come, Roland, a feast awaits us," Looking at Johan, "I believe my lord husband will not join us this eve."

Johan nodded, "He. . . ."

"Yes," she said, lowering her voice in feigned gravity. "He has much to do before leaving tomorrow." She laughed. "Come, Johan. Will you join us?" She smiled as much for herself as to ease his discomfort and gestured to the priest and Brian Dubec. "I would be honored to have your fine company." Spotting Lady Marguerite watching her, she began to invite her, but the woman swept right through the center of the group and into the tent.

Elise motioned to the others, only pausing to talk to the priest a moment. In her fluent Latin, she thanked him and gave him a small pouch. He seemed leery but took the coins. Placing his hand upon her head, he muttered a blessing. Unexpected tears suddenly stung her eyes. She took a deep breath and turned toward the tent.

When Johan opened the flap for them to enter, screams and shouts erupted. People began pouring out of the canvas structure.

"Get back! Back!" Johan ordered.

Marguerite ran from the tent, shrieking, as it leaped into flames. A burning flap brushed across Elise's veil setting it instantly aflame and singeing her loose hair. Johan whipped the silk from her head and swept Elise behind him with a protective arm. People ran to surround the burning cloth and put out the fire that raced up the side and spread instantly up the pitched canopy roof.

Terrified of fire, Elise moved quickly away from the men who pulled at the ropes and canvas to collapse the tent before its embers could ignite others. A loud voice roared orders behind her. Startled, she spun around to see Alaric leap onto a wagon situated atop a dirt mound.

The fire behind her cast a bright yellow light on him, and she got a clear look at the man she had married. He appeared taller than she had thought, having just moments ago stood beside him. He balanced with agility and grace on the uneven bundles. Unusually long black hair blew about his shoulders. His clean-shaven face and angular, sharp features drew her, and she walked slowly toward him. He had light eyes, but she could not tell their color, for they flashed, reflecting the fire. In his hard face, she saw forcefulness, the potential for seductive carnality, stained perhaps by brutality. He looked courageous and passionate, ferocious and shrewd, and savagely wondrous. *Is he a godlike creature? Or a demon,* she thought, when the fading firelight created shadows across his now ominous features.

She looked back to see the downed tent, a few leaping flames beneath the thick smoke swirling in the courtyard. Returning her gaze to Alaric, she saw only his back as he ran from the wagon toward a group of knights preparing to depart.

Elise moved into the shadows of the castle grounds and, unseen by distracted guards, she slipped beside her husband's longhouse. From there, she watched him approach Dreux, cautiously, it seemed. These two warriors, nearly equally matched in size, looked at one another without speaking. Alaric reached out to Dreux, who looked down at the extended arm slowly, contemptuously. Alaric's arm fell to his side, and still, they did not speak. Dreux turned, his mantle flaring as he swung onto his horse. Alaric grabbed Dreux's reins near the bit and spoke words she could not hear. He clasped Dreux's arm. Dreux shook off Alaric's hand and reared his horse, forcing Alaric to jump aside. He wheeled his mount and spurred away. Alaric stood alone, one arm stretched across his body, kneading his left shoulder, long after the gates had closed.

The incident confused her. Dreux had negotiated the betrothal for Alaric and had been his proxy. Less than two months ago, Dreux had told her he would trust his life to Alaric and said he would become her friend as well. Today, when she greeted him, he stalked past her without a spark of recognition, his eyes dark and deathly cold, his jaw taut, his body rigid. She remembered his beguiling smile at the betrothal feast, but today he had not once shared a glimmer of levity.

Alaric slowly walked toward his quarters, beside which she stood unseen in the shadows. *What had happened between these two friends?* Alaric reached his lodge and dismissed the guards. He turned to look over the bailey. Standing perhaps six steps away, she saw his tense, confused expression and a deep sorrow as he turned and went inside.

Elise picked her way along the rutted path to the earthwork mound at the base of the High Tower. Climbing the wooden planks, she counted silently, *forty-four, forty-five, forty-six.*

At the top, she paused and looked out over the castle grounds, her new home. Tents glowed with oil lamps, torches marked passageways, the armory, and gates. The remains of her wedding celebration smoldered near the kitchens, leaving the sour smell of burnt canvas and charred meat. Lady Marguerite strolled through the bailey with Brian Dubec. Roland laughed with Johan, relieving her worry, for she knew Roland would brawl if he thought her distressed.

Elise peered over the precipice into a void. Neither maiden nor wife, apprehension echoed within—deep, low. Tonight, she had become the possession of a complete stranger. She felt unbalanced, lost, an outsider among these Normans, in a strange land, among people speaking a strange language.

In the moonless sky, four bright stars marched in line northward. She imagined them dancing maidens and yearned to join them. She glanced at the fires dotting the valley floor marking the two armies and climbed the stairs on the tower's exterior.

Stepping into the common room for the first time, she paused. A few oil lanterns created sparse pools of light in the large dark room. On her right, stairs spiraled to the upper floors, the back stairs went down to the strongroom.

This room would serve as the lord's hall, with a dais on one end to delineate the lord's high table. No tapestries or banners graced the rough wooden walls. Nothing indicated that this tower would house her immediate family one day or host important guests, possibly the king.

Barely a couple of weeks old, the room contained trestle tables, benches and arms for the sentries. By its appearance, she assumed her husband had not used the tower for his quarters.

The large brazier had been lit, warming the room. Beside the fire, Hortense slept on a bench. Elise put a hand gently on Hortense's shoulder, which awakened her instantly.

"Elise, are you here already?" she croaked.

"Yes," Elise said quietly. "You did not come to the wedding. Are you ill?"

"No, just tired." Hortense edged her legs to the floor, trying to stand. "I did not feel up to the festivities. Are you offended I did not come?"

"Not at all," Elise said, helping Hortense to stand. "It was a short ceremony and the feasting tent caught fire."

"I am more tired than I've ever been," Hortense said through a yawn as she rubbed her back. "I am just glad we do not have to travel tomorrow."

"We journeyed further and longer than we expected."

"Let me help you." The weariness cracked in Hortense's voice. "Oh! Your cloak! Your hair!"

Elise looked at her shoulder, seeing the burnt cloth and felt the strands of her crinkled, singed hair. "No need to help me," Elise said. "Try to get a good night's sleep. I expect we will all rise early tomorrow." She hugged Hortense.

"Yes." Hortense began to leave but hesitated a moment. She looked back. "You are uneasy?"

"I hope there will be no bedding ceremony."

"I do not think his lordship's men will witness the consummation—even if they are drunk. But I will stay if you wish."

"No. No, I . . . ," Elise shook her head and smiled.

Hortense took Elise's hands and squeezed. "Consummation is required by the Church, yet some men relish the pleasure they bring to a woman."

"From his behavior so far, this marriage has greatly displeased my husband. I doubt he will desire my pleasure. I hope he will not . . . desire my pain."

"Oh, my dear," Hortense said. "Your fears are sound. But remember that Eustace bartered you for this alliance. Although we have yet to discern his reasons, both kings approved. Your husband accepted it. Together you and he will protect the kingdom and the duchy—even if Eustace tries to use you and your husband for villainous purposes."

"I understand," Elise said.

"Understand also that within this tapestry of royal intrigue, a pleasurable marriage bed is unimportant. Your husband may or may not please you. Your pleasure will not be required. Although you might feel some pain, if you submit completely, it will be over quickly. If God smiles on you, you will bear a son. Although you may not, at first, enjoy your marriage duty, many women come to enjoy coupling."

"Did you?" Elise asked.

Hortense lowered her head as if the question perplexed her. She nodded and looked up. "I did, in time."

Elise gave her a thin smile and nodded. Afterward, Elise climbed the stairs to the highest floor before the fighting platform. She found several large rooms, a block of empty chambers, and one Hortense suggested for a solar as it had shuttered windows. The bedding chamber was situated next to the guards' stairs and had a stiff, oxhide curtain across the entrance.

Lighted by a single thick candle seated in a wall sconce, the windowless room seemed quite small, more fit for storage. The narrow box bed, little more than a raised pallet, sat in a corner, its length against an exterior wall. The head and footboards rose from floor to ceiling, Hortense had had a feather mattress unpacked and placed on the planked platform, knee-high above the floor. The room smelled of still-fresh-cut oak. Pulling the mattress away from the wall, Elise saw that black, sticky resin had oozed onto the linen.

She took off her fine woolen cloak, scorched by the flaming tent, and removed her cotte stained by smoke and ash. She shed the rest of her clothing and packed them into her coffer. After a brief hesitation, she removed the wolf pendant and placed it beneath her clothes. Running her fingers through her loose hair, she felt singed tresses break off and then climbed naked into the narrow bed, beneath the gossamer sheets and the sable blanket brought with her. They seemed fragile luxuries here in this crude place. She clutched her hands together, whispered a prayer and waited, her body tense, alert for any sound.

Sentries changing the guard clambered up and down the stairs. The curtain swayed as they passed. On the deck above, she heard low, soft voices, a few chuckles, a sword clank against the wall. She longed for sleep to take her worries away. The candle sputtered and died, leaving her in absolute darkness. She drifted to sleep.

Elise woke instantly when something banged into a wall on the floor below. Startled, she sat up in the dark room and heard someone climbing the stairs. The curtain flared open. She shielded her face against the blinding candlelight before the curtain's draught extinguished the flame. She heard Alaric's curse, the sound of the iron candleholder fall to the floor and crash against the far wall. She cried out and shrank into a corner of the bed.

Alaric stood silently for a moment, orienting himself to the room. He listened for more whimpers but heard only feather-soft breathing, strained as if she tried to inhale quietly. A bird caught in a trap, he thought.

Trapped as he was. Every aspect of his being revolted against taking this woman to wife.

"I did not mean to startle you, Madam," surprised his voice sounded so loud in this small room. He had also not meant to kick the candleholder across the room, annoyed that he had no flint to relight the candle. He considered going back down to the get another but rejected the notion. It did not matter. He cared not to inspect the woman, nor to remain long.

"We are wed at the command of our kings," he said, moving toward the bed. He did not remove his tunic, leggings or boots, but fumbled with his linen braies, pulling at the thongs that held the loose-fitting breeches around his waist. Approaching the bed, he tugged the bed covers from her grip and reached for her in the dark, finding her pressed against the wall. She trembled as he eased her away from the wall and stretched out beside her.

As soon as he pressed his head down, he smelled her singed hair, and immediately the memory of his family's charred bodies came to him, along with a rush of nausea.

God, help me, he pleaded, swallowing the bile, his revulsion, and memories. He shifted atop her, his entire weight holding her down.

He could feel her breath on his neck. "It will be more painful if you resist. I will be quick."

She nodded, her head hitting his jaw in the dark. For a moment, he did not move. He had never taken a woman by force. He thought it would be easy to drive hard into this woman to make her suffer for the sins of her uncle. Instead, easing himself to her side, his hand urged her to spread her legs. Despite trembling, she opened to him. Her fear inexplicably angered him. He checked his ire and put his palm against her triangle, stopping when her body froze. He stroked his hand over her thigh and belly, back to her mons, and stopped. He heard heavy boots scraping on the stairs below.

"Damn his Saints! Dubec comes to witness," Alaric said. "Do you wish a public bedding?"

Beside him, her head shook vigorously, hitting his jaw again.

"God's will!" he swore, mounting her with little ceremony, causing her to cry out as he burst through her maidenhead. He withdrew immediately, his seed unspilled. He rolled off her and rose from the bed.

In the dimness, he saw only the vague line of her jaw turned away from him. "We have done our duty to our kings," he said, adjusting his clothing. "No more, no less. Your duty is to obey me and my agents in all things. Disobedience is dealt with swiftly. I am ruthlessly creative in my punishments."

As he tied the thongs, he continued. "My duty is to see you are protected from the English at all times. That is my only duty to you." He turned and left the room.

Elise, stunned by this bleak, perfunctory consummation, listened to Alaric's boots pound down the steps, to the sound of him arguing with Brian. She had been unable to move or feel anything. That man had lain heavily atop her, her legs spread beneath him, her body bound by his grip. She felt exposed and violated. She turned on her side, curling into a protective ball. Women *like* the marriage duty? She nearly laughed but choked back tears. She had expected something else, not sure what exactly, having heard servants whispering about mysterious desires and her own foolish dreams for something . . . special.

She began to breathe again, the throbbing in her heart began to ease. The curtain ripped open, and she cried out, squinting her eyes against the bright candlelight.

Brian Dubec, accompanied by a servant holding a candelabrum, entered the room. Seeing his rigid jaw and hard black eyes, she recoiled.

"I am to verify the bedding for your uncle, my lady. Pardon my intrusion. This must be done." He quickly moved to the bed and pulled her legs apart to see the smear of blood she knew would be there.

"No," she sobbed, scratching at his hand and twisting away from him. A drop of hot wax fell on her naked thigh as the servant turned quickly away. The men left without another word.

She welcomed the darkness as she heard Alaric and Brian descending the outer stairs, their angry voices rising as they left the tower. The men above her in the galleries shouted their bawdy remarks applauding Alaric's prowess. Silent tears dropped to the feather mattress she had so carefully packed and brought with her along with all of her hopes.

Chapter Twenty-Six

arguerite stood on the parapet beside High Tower just as the sun winked over the horizon. Dread accompanied the familiar sight of knights riding into the distance, as when her father and brothers rode out to fight and die for Duke William, the day her husband rode toward his last skirmish, the first time Alaric abandoned her in Hereford.

Unspeakable horrors had followed each departure.

The wind flared her mantle and she wrapped it tightly around her body, encasing her distress. What new brutality would beset her now?

Widowed, without family to arrange a marriage, she had pursued Alaric—a man who could protect her from others, for whom tender feelings were unnecessary. After he deserted her to join William, she had not once wondered if he'd lived or died. Her thoughts then, as now, had been only for Johan.

No one, least of all Alaric, knew that she had discovered Johan among the wounded and bedraggled soldiers arriving at Hereford. She'd spent weeks cleaning his mangled flesh and tending his mindless, shivering body. And one terrible night when his fever had risen again, she had bathed him with cool water until he'd regained his senses and rasped, *Marguerite? I should have known. Either I am dead and in hell, or I am alive, and you have come to torment me. In either case, get your scut away from me.* And no one knew she had gone to the chapel and prayed tearfully for his life.

A cawing raven drew her attention up to High Tower's thatching where it perched. At the tower's ramparts, she saw Alaric's bride looking toward the valley. When the raven flapped its wings, Marguerite crossed herself and spit on the back of her fingers. *Death begone!* She watched it glide over the people and carts, horses and pigs filling the yard below, now her domain.

She tried to feel grateful. A mistress rarely had the privilege of sub-jugating her protector's wife, of usurping a wife's domestic authority. But Marguerite knew little about ruling a lord's manor and she could not risk failure. Suddenly she despised Alaric for leaving her in this tenuous position, isolated at this bleak, primitive place, cut off from the royal court—with Johan.

Elise also watched Alaric leaving the valley and did not know what she felt. Wedded and bedded by a complete stranger who clearly loathed her, she thought anger would be more appropriate than dejection. She had believed that any man would, if not cherish her, welcome her usefulness. Her mistaken conviction appalled her, and shame heated her cheeks. As the sun sprang fully into the sky, she heard Hortense coming to join her and composed her features to present an untroubled countenance.

"Did he hurt you?" Hortense asked, glancing over the ramparts at troops.

"No." The consummation had merely frightened her. But her husband's threats and Brian Dubec's intrusion into her bed had seared her heart.

"Well and good," Hortense said. "Here, allow me the honor."

Elise dipped her head for the ritual dressing of her hair. As Hortense adjusted the wimple distinguishing a married woman, she said, "I saw Roland off. He and your husband nearly crossed swords this morning."

"What?" The prospect of her husband killing her dear friend—and King Philip's envoy—horrified Elise. "Why?"

"He accused Stafford of abusing you. Your husband refused to fight. Instead, he mocked Roland's interest in his marriage and ordered Gilbert to see Roland to the main gates with all respect due to a high-ranking courtier. I assured Roland that you are well and gave him a message for your sister."

"Thank you for diverting his thoughts to Marie. I will miss him. Is Brian . . . still here?"

"He left last night. Come," Hortense said. "The seneschal and castellan await you. It is time to take charge of your new home and your people."

As they descended the stairs, Elise pushed her gloom aside. She had much to do, and with God's will and her husband's liegemen, she intended to establish a castle worthy of any nobleman.

The benches and tables crowding the tower's common room last night were moved aside, leaving a large hollow space. Elise approached Johan and Gilbert standing beside the brazier, providing the only light in the dark room.

"Good morrow," she said, smiling.

"Lady Stafford," Johan began as Marguerite stepped out from the shadows. "His lordship left instructions that he did not want you . . . burdened by the rigors of overseeing the castle in his absence."

Elise frowned, and before she could speak, Marguerite said, "Lord Stafford has revoked your rights to govern his demesne and his *feudum*. He gave those rights to Johan, Gilbert, and to me. I—not you—will decide where hearth servants work and what personal services you need. You are forbidden to administer his estates, which are now entirely under Johan's authority. If you wish to leave High Tower, you must request of Gilbert armed guards to accompany you. Do you understand, lady? Anything, and everything, you seek will come through us."

"As I thought," Hortense said, assessing Marguerite. "Lord Stafford has raised his whore from the dung heap!"

Marguerite gasped. "Why you old—"

"Desist!" Johan grabbed Marguerite's raised arm.

Alaric's mistress! Elise thought, and Hortense knew it when they'd met her yesterday! Although mistresses were common, husbands never set them above their wives.

"So, he has revoked Lady Stafford's rights!" Hortense said to Johan. "The reason for this uncommon arrangement?"

"These are his lordship's orders," he said. "We do not question. We obey."

"Clarify his lordship's orders, Johan!" Hortense demanded.

As Johan revealed the details, Elise studied his flushed cheeks and felt the full weight of her marriage descend upon her. Numb as a worm in winter, she met Gilbert's cool, distant gaze and ignored Marguerite's impertinent smile.

"I understand," Hortense said, "that your authority supersedes the authority of all others. Is this so?"

"It is."

"Good. Let us be clear," Hortense said. "Lord Stafford's restrictions apply to his wife only. They do not apply to me."

Johan and Gilbert exchanged glances, and, after a brief hesitation, Johan answered, "Yes."

"Very well," Hortense said. "In accordance with Norman practice, you will ensure that all honor, privileges, and courtesies are extended to me as the kin of your lord and lady, including unlimited access throughout the castle and to the village."

"Yes."

"I intend to serve my niece and convey her needs to you directly, without appealing to underlings, who have no authority over me."

"What?" Marguerite said. "I am chatelaine, here!"

"Do you, Johan de Vaux, sworn in fealty to your lord, take orders from this woman?"

"I rule the castle and all those within these walls," he answered with a slight smile.

"Excellent," Hortense said. "I will assist my niece, *your* ladyship, to become accustomed to her constraints and allow you to oblige his lordship without contention. Do you agree to this arrangement?"

"I do," Johan said. "Until I deem it necessary to change this arrangement, you alone are exempt from anyone's interference. And you may bring your requests directly to me."

Chapter Twenty-Seven

May 1067, Lichfield, Staffordshire

P riest!" bellowed Alaric from his tent, his annoyance at Father Pierre, his malingering personal confessor, increasing by the moment. Thanks to his mother's relentless cajoling, Alaric could read and write French—barely. But he could not read or write Latin, the language of the court, the church, and commerce. Like most nobles, Alaric relied on priests and monks for all written communications, which he preferred over oral messages easily forgotten by couriers.

Father Pierre ducked beneath the flaps and scurried into the tent.

"A letter to Johan," Alaric said as his squire loosened his quilted aketon.

"So soon? You left him just yester morning." At Alaric's scowl, Father Pierre quickly crossed the tent and sat on the stool. There he pulled the writing board and accoutrements from his satchel.

Pierre had served Alaric's father for years in Hereford. Simeon's move to Eashing and the disruption after Hastings had left Pierre an itinerant priest until Alaric returned to Herefordshire and found him. To honor his father, Alaric took on the priest and his family, who all traveled with him.

Impatiently, Alaric watched Father Pierre assemble his reeds and ink and unroll a quarter sheet of parchment.

"One moment, my son," Pierre said. He wrote the date and salutation.

Six days before Whit Sunday, May 21, 1067, in the first year of our King William's reign. To Johan de Vaux, my loyal friend and honored seneschal, from Alaric, Seigneur de Tutbierrie.

Father Pierre nodded.

Alaric began. "I trust that you will rule my wife as diligently as you rule my estates."

With God's blessings, I have entrusted to you the honor of governing my land and riches and my bride, in confidence that you would do so with care and in accordance with my wishes.

Pierre looked up.

"Your oath must prevail over sentiment. If she opposes my restrictions or disobeys in any way, you must punish her on my behalf as you would punish anyone who disobeys my orders."

Your liege duty to me, wrote Pierre, *supersedes any pity you may engender toward the lady. If she disobeys you, she disobeys her husband, who, by God's law, is her master. I charge you with full authority and responsibility to punish her as you see fit. Deny her food, beat her with rod, or lock her in the tower or pillory if it must be done.*

As the priest tapped his freshly inked pen against the pot, Alaric continued.

"This marriage exceeds my reach. Eustace de Boulogne, not known for generosity—"

—gave me riches far beyond the customary blood price, which means this marriage serves him alone. We can only conjecture his intent, but all know that he relishes power and aspires to influence the realms surrounding his county. He boasts that he gave William the throne, despite God's hand placed upon our holy king's humble head, and, with brazen arrogance, he proclaims his sons will be kings. Ambition might drive him to one day revoke his sworn alliance to William and seek greater rewards through armed challenge. What better accomplice than a niece tucked within the nest of William's most trustworthy lieutenant?

Whether the countess were innocent or not, you know why I loath her and her uncle. Although William forced this marriage to preserve the kingdom's unity, I intend to null the marriage.

Severance of a divinely endowed union must, of necessity, win the king's support. Only proof of treason will suffice, for William's piety will accept no lesser plea. I must present evidence of such deceit to him.

As my agent, you shall succor this burden and provide my eyes and ears so I may end this virulent wedlock. I shall seek in your letters precise information concerning the countess and her conduct. Report her manner upon receiving my dictates and her behavior henceforth. Determine whether the countess speaks any languages but French and whether she can speak or understand Saxon. All missives sent to her are to be intercepted, deciphered, and preserved for court council. Your scribe may read them to her, but they must be withheld lest there be secret symbols known only to her. She may send no letters unless dictated in your presence. These documents may help me gain William's support for my annulment.

Seek counsel with Monkman for any matters of conscience these orders cause you. Remember, the Church warns us about the odious burden of grievous wives. Cloister your sympathies and guard your loyalty to me, for a traitor may well hide beneath a guileless smile or a gentle word.

May 1067, Tutbury, Staffordshire

Three days after the wedding, Brother Derrick finished translating Alaric's letter aloud to Johan and Gilbert and looked up to see them staring at him. He rolled the scroll and handed it to Johan with a slight bow.

"Get to your task," Johan said.

Dismissed, the nineteen-year-old monk crossed the loud, crowded bailey, so different from Burton Abbey where he'd lived since childhood. A few days ago, his prior had sent him to serve Johan because he was proficient in secular and ecclesiastical law—and in Norman French. And now he was headed down Castle Road to count slaves.

As he neared the trench, a whip cracked. An old man screamed and crumbled to his knees. A soldier dragged the bleeding villager to his feet and shoved him into a group of workers lifting stones onto a wagon. Derrick's anger boiled. He wondered if he could have helped his people better as a warrior like his namesake, Saint Theodoric, who died a martyr fighting the pagan Norse, ancestors of these Normans.

Derrick, known by the Saxon form of his ordained name, found the Normans impious, avaricious, and malevolent, for they, like Father Pierre's pompous letter, expressed *Norman* assumptions of superiority. They had stolen the English crown and defiled this place once belonging to the ancient Mercian kings who had ruled before Alfred. Though a distant relative of those great families, he tasted the bitter ale of his people brushed aside and trampled by Normans, who took for themselves all his people had built.

A traitor may well hide beneath a guileless smile or a gentle word, or beneath a monk's habit, thought Derrick.

He had not met the Black Wolf, rumored to favor brutal pleasures. His letter did not inspire a desire to do so, although it aroused his sympathy for Lady Stafford. Prepared to dislike this Norman countess who'd come to rule over his people, her kindness had disarmed him. Now, he found it ironic that, like his own people, she had fallen from a once glorious past in Blackwolf's wake.

Lord on high, guide me, he prayed, gazing at the overcast sky. He believed that God did not care if people were English or Norman. Derrick himself cared deeply, and in this, he sinned. His duty to God was to minister to all: Saxon, Angles, or Mercians. His duty to the Normans was unclear, for he possessed all the skills to aid the Normans oppress his people. He hid the sting of Judas beneath his robes and reached for his waxed tally board.

As the days marched into June, Hortense's companionship kept Elise from total isolation. Elise rarely saw Marguerite or Johan. Gilbert kept his distance, acknowledging her presence with a cool gaze. She assumed he rotated the two guards accompanying her daily walks so that she would not befriend them. Servants coming to the tower seldom spoke. Likewise, she heard Brother Derrick's voice only when he ministered the sacraments.

Elise's outings were limited to the stables to visit her mare and the adjacent smith works where she watched in fascination the forging and shaping of iron. Occasionally she spun yarn in the shadow of an outlying tent on the edge of the bailey, which swarmed with hundreds of soldiers overcrowding the castle, training, moving carts or carrying building materials.

In these moments, as she twirled and dropped the spindle, she resisted thinking about her sister which might bring dismal tears. Instead, she conjugated verbs, first in Latin, then in Greek. She missed playing chess with Walter and their long talks. She even missed Guillaume Arques. But despite her husband, she vowed to find a place for herself at Tutbury.

Frequently, she climbed to High Tower's ramparts above her quarters to see how the village and castle fared. From a young age she had learned the skills necessary for the wife of a great lord. In addition to reading and writing, the nuns, her seneschal, and castellans had taught her how to manage and defend her land.

Accustomed to looking after her Norman estates, she observed—and dreaded—the coming months. The harvest would not feed the castle's soldiers, much less the villagers pressed into hard labor or the slaves. No one plowed new fields to support the inhabitants. Few people were hunting, gathering, or drying food. Although sawyers cut and stacked timber for defense walls, no one was preparing enough wood for winter fires.

She understood why Johan and Gilbert rushed to build the castle. Work gangs, including soldiers, dug the wide, deep defense ditch. Oxen hauled wagonloads of dirt and rocks from the excavation to the top, where more gangs built raised banks bordering the castle's periphery. These would support the timber palisades encircling the castle, but the earthwork created a basin, which flooded during rainstorms and made passage within the courtyard difficult. Worse still, the latrine—a trench unwisely situated to drain down to the marshes—also flooded, leaving a pervasive stench. She ached to order the privy moved and lined with tight-fitting wood or baked clay as Tristan described the Roman works. Foolishly, she had Hortense speak to Johan, who replied that her duty was to look after her niece and not challenge his authority.

Neither of them would again jeopardize Hortense's position, for, unlike Elise, Hortense had full access about the castle and village and spoke Saxon. When they were alone, she reported the deficiencies of Marguerite's rule over the domestic affairs.

"The kitchens are in disarray," she said, stabbing a needle into her linen. "Bakers use too much yeast or bad grain. Meat left untended on fire pits chars to a crisp. Pigs run amuck through the tents, hounds roam in packs, devouring precious chickens and eggs, and killing tethered goats."

Elise turned another seam as Hortense confirmed what she feared. "Do English tongues wag freely in your presence?"

"For now."

"What do servants say?"

"Ah! The maids assigned to you are the concubine's spies, serving you in fear of Marguerite's whip. She is delighted that you did not conceive from the consummation bedding."

Elise nodded, annoyed at the woman's interest.

"Servants boast about pilfering joints or cheese from under her nose, and claim they follow Marguerite's thieving ways. They say she stole a gold and silver torc of cunning workmanship from an English noblewoman, now dead, and wears it hidden beneath her clothes."

"No doubt the villagers resent being forced into hard labor."

"They grumble that their fields lie fallow. A few women, those not digging the ring ditch, scurry to find food, fearing hunger will take their children. Today, a group went to the river to wash Marguerite's clothes. One scolded another for hoarding food. They tore each other's hair, biting and slapping. Meanwhile, some of Marguerite's clothes were lost in the current, and she had the washerwomen whipped."

Elise put her sewing down and paced the small chamber. She understood that obedience could and often must be obtained through the whip, yet Norman survival required villagers to provide sustenance, and few would labor hard to feed Marguerite.

Hortense set her own sewing aside. "Never forget that you are the highest ranking member of your husband's household, King Philip's cousin, a countess in your own right. I chafe at the grace with which you bear your diminished authority and especially Marguerite d'Hesdins. By my faith, that woman enjoys her elevated position far too much. I long to see you smite her down."

"Like an avenging angel?"

"Like a wild boar in armor."

Elise laughed and shook her head. "God bless you, Aunt, but my purpose is fixed. My husband is master. He ruled me from the moment I sealed the betrothal documents. I must obey, as Church and law require, and will serve him as he and God see fit. I only wish to learn why he imprisons me."

"His reason may stem from Eustace. I've learned that Eustace and your husband are foes although I have not yet discovered the cause."

"If they are enemies, this marriage is an alliance pursued by William himself. Even so, it must benefit Eustace, for he would not have given my estates to a lowly knight who could not further his ambitions or to a man he could not control."

"The Vexin has always been Eustace's foremost interest. He sought to control the county by marrying his first wife. Your Fontenay controls the road from Rouen to Paris, which alone could threaten either William or Philip. I cannot yet see how Eustace would use it or your husband. Or why. But I am certain he intends to create havoc."

Chapter Twenty-Eight

The rest of Elise's wagons arrived at Tutbury in mid-June. Hortense obtained Johan's permission for Brother Derrick and a few servants to assist them in recounting the chattel brought to the marriage—without Marguerite's presence or interference. The task took them several days. At Elise's suggestion, conveyed to Johan via Hortense, precious pots, pans, and utensils went to the kitchens, tools to craftsmen, the rest to the treasury beneath High Tower rather than in Lord Stafford's longhouse, occupied by Marguerite.

Hortense used the opportunity to establish Elise's rightful place, in trappings if not by direct interaction. With Johan's consent she furnished the tower rooms allotted to them. She left the ornate beds and thick mattresses stored with the gold and silver but covered the box beds built into their small chambers with embroidered linens and fur blankets. Sheepskin curtains replaced the ox hides and gave them privacy and warmth. An etched silver candelabra, wooden trenchers and mazers with silver bands graced an elaborately burnished table, and Elise once again had her carved chests.

The day after concluding their task, soldiers accompanied Elise and Hortense as they looked surreptitiously for a place to situate the kitchen garden.

"More tents have been cleared from the bailey," Elise said softly in French.

"Yes," Hortense said. "The sooner the soldiers are all moved to the garrisons, the more space we'll have for other uses."

"G'day, milady," a man said to Hortense as they approached him.

"Doff your hat to her ladyship, Frith!" she answered in Saxon.

"Aye, milady," he said, obeying immediately.

Elise nodded, accepting the respect shown her only in Hortense's presence. Determined to undermine her jailers, Hortense demanded that everyone treat her niece with customary honor.

"What are those stakes?" Hortense asked, "And why you are churning up the mud?"

"'Tis the foundation for a hall. Them be markers, fifty paces long and thirty a breadth."

"And that?" she asked, pointing to a roped off area nearby.

"Ah, a well. At last!"

Elise answered Hortense's translation in French, "It is ill placed." She pointedly glanced back the way they had come.

Hortense nodded. "Tell the jackdaw who picked this spot that a well, located two hundred paces south would better serve both the kitchens and the hall."

"Aye, milady, aye."

"Well, lift your toes, man."

Following on his heels, the women walked along the markers and out from under the afternoon shadow of High Tower along the steep edge.

"Here?" Hortense asked.

"No," Elise said. "The tower and the hall when built would block the sun."

They paused to look out toward the river. Behind them, Marguerite called out, "Lady Stafford!"

Elise and Hortense exchanged glances before turning to see the woman and her maidservants approaching them.

"It has come to my attention that you have furnished your rooms with his lordship's goods. You overstep your privileges. I have not authorized the distribution of his property."

"Curb your voice," Hortense said. "And bow to those greater than you."

Marguerite's eyes flashed. "Such reverence is unnecessary. My lineage is far older than any here."

"It may be old, but it lies beneath her ladyship's feet. Honor her or leave us."

"Lady Stafford," Marguerite said. "I intend to reclaim those items taken from his lordship's goods."

"Your intentions are arrows without fletch. Come." Hortense took Elise's arm and turned her away.

"Take care when you turn your back to me, Lady Stafford. Your aunt takes you down a dangerous path and I assure you, once there, none will help you escape his lordship's wrath."

"The land of the Welsh, I am told," Hortense said, pointing out the distant mountains to her niece.

Elise heard Marguerite's retreating footsteps and glanced at Hortense. "You provoke her."

"I do. She is easily incited, and it brings me cruel pleasure to mock her."

They skirted the stable muckers wastefully shoveling dung over the edge. Leaving the smithies, they cut to the interior of the bailey, around sheds and stacked timbers and again toward Northgate where a storehouse was rising. They took a side street that divided the remaining tents and the hastily erected longhouses.

"Gilbert needs at least two more to house the last of the soldiers," Elise said, as they passed the thatched structures. Glancing around the bailey, she imagined where she would move the kitchens, where she would locate drying huts, a weaver and candle works, and shook her head. "The garden should be situated where the armory was," Elise said. "Close enough to the well, and far enough from the stables."

"Yes," Hortense said as they turned down a narrow lane. "A few servants can plow—" she gasped suddenly and stumbled.

Elise cried out as Hortense broke her fall by clamping a merciless grip on Elise's arm.

"What is amiss? Are you ill?" Elise asked, bracing against Hortense's weight as her guards rushed in to assist. Once righted, Hortense appeared struck dumb and deaf, and unable to move. Elise scanned Hortense's pale face, terrified by her aunt's panting breath, by her blue eyes now black and staring at the main gatehouse.

"Dear God," Elise said, following the line of Hortense's gaze and seeing nothing more than Gilbert speaking to one of his men.

"Come!" Hortense croaked roughly, pulling at Elise's arm. She staggered into the crowds flooding the main street and pulled Elise with her.

"What?" Elise asked, feeling Hortense tremble as she led Elise deeper into the busy street. At Hortense's silence, Elise glanced back at the gate. She caught a brief glimpse of Gilbert before people obscured her view. But when the crowd parted again, she saw a lanky, aged soldier speaking to Gilbert.

After a few more steps, Hortense turned again off the main street and headed to High Tower. She slowed her pace to an easy stroll and took a deep breath. Smiling weakly at Elise, she said. "No worries, my dear. I had a fright. I . . . I thought I saw a . . . a ghost."

"Ghost?"

Hortense tipped her head toward the baking ovens, indicating Johan's proximity. "You brought many items to help his lordship expand the castle and the village," she said too loud.

"I did," Elise said, confused by how quickly Hortense regained her composure.

"I remember when Tristan argued against bringing the heavy-wheeled plow."

Suddenly understanding Hortense's intent, Elise spoke loud enough for Johan's hearing. "Yes. My seneschal uses the plow to bring new land into cultivation quickly, for it easily removes stumps and rocks. He also insisted that I bring the shoulder harnesses we use at home. The collars, stuffed with straw, let horses breathe so they can pull the plow and work the fields longer than oxen."

"How many did you bring?" Hortense asked, as Johan nodded to them.

"Only three. The bridlers here could copy them, he supposed."

After morning prayers and breaking fast, Hortense followed Elise down the tower steps and into the bailey. Elise met her guards and went one way, Hortense, an empty basket in tow, joined the daily procession of people leaving the castle. She had much on her mind this morning and carefully scanned the soldiers coming and going, hoping to avoid another surprise. As usual, the watchtower guards did not notice her walking through Southgate and down to the village.

There she exchanged greetings with the village elder and purchased a jug of ale from her favorite brewer, a woman who told her the village gossip. Today, she learned nothing more than who had beaten his wife and who was pregnant or ill.

She reentered the main gates and went to the kitchens, passing the butchers slicing and chopping and several kitchen maids hauling buckets. She glared at the lazy fire tenders until their bellows whooshed vigorously, and at the sauce makers gossiping as their juices scorched. After catching the attention of the master cook, she conferred with him about Elise's meals. Afterward, she filled her basket with a half round of bread, an onion, two roasted partridge legs, and two wooden mazers. Thus armed, she headed toward the garrisons to find her quarry.

Hortense approached the newest longhouse, spotting the two knights she sought. She discovered recently that they had lived and fought in Ewyas with Lord Stafford and had joined him to support William. She hoped they could tell her about Marguerite. Like other soldiers who were neither training nor digging, they sat in the shade repairing their kit.

They put their shields and tongs aside and took the empty cups Hortense offered. "My lady, we most gratefully accept your ale. Join us," one said brushing off the bench for her. He looked nervously around before settling on an adjacent bench.

"Does my presence alarm you, Drago?" she asked.

"No, my lady. You are most welcome. Our commander is quick to misjudge our pleasure for inattention to our weapons."

"Is Gilbert a harsh commander?"

"No, no," said the other knight, shaking his head. "Drago is wary of Jeoffroi d'Ardain, captain of the knights. He is Gilbert's second-in-command and rides us hard."

Hortense poured each man a mazer of ale, surprised her hands did not shake. *Do not ask about him!* "Have some bread and tell me about your Ewyas days."

While eating they shared their recollections. From her skillful questions, Hortense learned that Marguerite had indeed come from nobility, the daughter of a count who had died serving a young Duke William. She had been married to a man many years her senior, an obscure knight with a fiefdom in Lisieux.

Drago paused and lifted his cup to Hortense with a knowing grin. "As you are curious about Marguerite, we shall quench your thirst as you quench ours."

"I thought you would," Hortense said, pouring more ale into his cup.

"At fifteen winters," Drago said, "she was a childless widow, and had lost her husband's fiefdom. Afterward she traveled to Hereford to join a cousin serving with the Norman garrison, perhaps to reclaim her lands with his help or find a new husband. Rumor says she attached herself to a Flemish knight who escorted her safely across Wessex."

"What happened to him?"

"Died in a dispute along the road. Afterward, they say, she traveled with the Danish lord who had killed her Fleming."

Hortense watched both men laugh. Did they speak from ale or from envy?

"Her cousin," Drago said, "died in a skirmish before she arrived. Lord Stafford's father gave her protection. She is a feisty beauty. Jealous of any woman who might compete with her. She hated Johan de Vaux's wife."

"Yes," the other knight said. "Some claimed the woman died after drinking Marguerite's potion."

"What kind of potion?" Hortense asked sharply.

"It was a tale to pass the winter nights, nothing more," Drago said.

"A mere tale," chuckled his companion, winking at Hortense. "But ye'll not catch me drinking from any bowl Marguerite offers."

"What else do people say about her?"

"The usual. That bewitchments snared his lordship. An archer claims he bedded her. The infantry captain vows he will."

"We don't believe the archer. He says she murdered the English noblewoman, but the girl died in a fire, and Marguerite did not cause that blaze."

"Who was this noblewoman?" Hortense asked.

Neither knew much. "We heard that she was a favorite among the servants and villagers. A captive belonging to a Norman commander and pitied for carrying his child. We were on patrol when she died, and when we returned, everyone worked to rebuild the tower. Rebels in the vicinity, you see."

"Did she belong to Lord Stafford?" Hortense asked carefully, wondering if he hated his wife because he'd loved the English woman.

They looked at one another and shrugged. "We never heard that."

"Who is the archer enamored of Marguerite?" Hortense asked.

"A fool," Drago said. "A foot soldier whose vanity is inflated because he's mastered the crossbow. Like other infantry he is good only for guarding the stores or whipping villagers."

The knights laughed in disdain at the lower ranks.

"The captain?" Hortense asked.

Drago shook his head. "An able commander, though infantry. He'll kill the archer one day. Or his lordship will hear that some among his men want to drink from his cup."

That, Hortense knew, would be dangerous for both men. "Does Marguerite entertain their attentions?"

"Hah! Her tongue slashes any who casts a wandering gaze her way. She rules by the grace of her lord, and she knows it."

"Know you why his lordship subjects his wife to Marguerite?"

"No, but it is an admirable practice. One I would follow," Drago said, "were I given leave to wed."

Chapter Twenty-Nine

The sound of chainmail jingling beyond the thick door signaled the soldier's arrival. The two men seated at the table exchanged quick glances. The younger of the two rose abruptly, wrapped his cloak about him and pulled his hood low over his face. He faded into the deep shadows of the vaulted alcove. The other remained seated, facing the door, and continued to write upon a sheet of vellum.

When the deeply carved oak door opened, Brian Dubec slipped inside. His breath came in gasps as if he had run a long distance. He strode toward the table and paused, waiting until he was addressed, aware of the faint scent of freshly shaved cedar.

He knew he would be made to wait. His keen eyes assessed Thierry de Châlons, advisor to King Philip, who had negotiated Lady Stafford's betrothal for Francia. Thierry continued to write with a reed pen encased in a silver holder. He wore a large emerald ring on his index finger and a bejeweled chain around his neck, which sparkled against the finely woven, black wool of his robes. A distinctive gold and silver brooch, two lions with entwined tails, clasped his gray mantle at the shoulder.

Dubec looked about the plush, small room, a sufficiently discreet chamber buried in the *Palais*. His gaze swept over the ornate raised brazier and the rock-crystal torch sconces elaborately carved with fishes; at pools of bright light reflecting off polished marble walls. He admired the thick, woven rushes, an expensive and rare luxury; the gold candelabra, noting they were unmarked by identifying seals; and his eyes lingered on the sumptuous burgundy drapery hanging from ceiling to floor. Peering into the shadows, he concluded they were alone, a condition he'd required when switching masters.

"You bring word of the marriage?" Thierry asked without looking up.

"The deed is done."

Thierry nodded and, taking another sheet of vellum, continued to write. "Eustace?"

"His liaison meets in secret with Edric 'the Wild.'"

"The . . . *Wild*?" Thierry smiled, amused.

"A former thegn of Shropshire. He and his band live in a great woods, like beasts, they say."

"Ah," the seated man nodded. "Tell me about L'Enfant. Who is he? What is his pedigree, and why is Eustace interested in him?"

"I know only that he is young, perhaps fifteen winters. He studies at Sithiu monastery in Flanders. I don't know the reason for Eustace's interest."

Thierry put down his pen, rotated the emerald ring on his finger and studied the soldier. Dubec waited for a challenge.

"Guillaume Arques?"

Disappointed by the question, Dubec answered, "In Boulogne, awaiting your summons."

The king's advisor slid a packet of missives across the table toward Dubec. He then took one of the banded scrolls stacked on the table beside him and stood, tapping the scroll across his palm as if measuring the messenger.

Dubec did not flinch under the scrutiny.

"This land is yours," Thierry said, his bejeweled hand passing the document to Dubec. "And these coins." He gazed at a leather pouch sitting on the table. "Deliver the missives as instructed. We will contact you again." With a flick of his head, he dismissed the soldier.

Dubec took the scroll, tucked the missives into his belt and lifted the pouch resisting an urge to weigh the coins. "Thank you, my lord." He bowed and departed.

When the door closed, Thierry stepped around the table, went to the door and dropped the latch. He leaned his back against the portal and listened to the fading echo of boots on the stone floor and nodded at the shadows.

King Philip emerged. He threw his hood back and folded his hands into the large sleeves of his gold-embroidered tunic. A slow, satisfied smile spread across his face.

Chapter Thirty

St. John's Day, June 24, 1067. To Alaric, my
friend and liege, from Johan de Vaux.

*Y*our lady wife has been informed of her position and the rights you
revoked. Although surprised, she did not challenge your orders as
did her aunt and companion Hortense de Tourny. They reside in High
Tower. The countess will occasionally stroll about the upper ramparts.
Accompanied by guards, she walks through the inner bailey, speaking to
no one save her aunt. She speaks, reads, and writes French and Latin.
Her aunt, and only companion, is versed in Saxon and translates for her
niece.

Her chattel goods have arrived. By God's grace, Alaric, she brought
unimaginable riches. The heavy plow, blessed by Brother Derrick and
pulled by horses in new chest bridles, has tilled ten furrows and clears the
tree stumps and field stones with ease.

Seeding has begun, although it is too late to expect much this year.
We continue to dig the fosse. The perimeter earthworks and timber walls
rise. We have completed the storehouse, staked out the hall, and begun
digging the well. Three monks have joined Brother Derrick. We call his
unsponsored cell a priory and Derrick the prior. With my permission, they
are building a temporary structure on the outer south bailey.

Marguerite continues to occupy your longhouse. She has sufficiently
usurped the countess's authority. Without a hall, there is little for her to

do, save meddle with Gilbert and me as we administer your estates and build the castle's defenses.

I shall remain vigilant.

Elise had looked forward to Midsummer, hoping the bonfires and dancing would bring levity to her dull days. Instead, the Normans had not stopped the work crews to celebrate, and solstice had passed with little more than a few drunken soldiers throwing lighted torches into the river.

Later that week, she and Hortense retreated to their top-floor rooms in High Tower to escape the stench of the camp privy overflowing again in the heavy rain. Elise ran her hands over the fine Persian wool that had arrived with her goods. The deep red pleased her. She'd begun making a cloak for her husband, which she would line with the sable packed into her chests. She did not intend to send it to him, supposing he might assume it a plea to ease her imprisonment. She merely needed something to do.

"Dear Aunt," Elise said, stitching the edge of a double seam, "I fear I would go mad without you. I have no people, no church or Abbey to serve. I dwindle day to day."

"Pluck your own feathers if you must," Hortense said, curtly. "Languor will not defeat you. Your mind is merely lacking a worthy challenge. I will teach you the Saxon tongue. As you learn, we will plan how to boot the concubine from her pillar. For now," she lifted the tunic in her hands, "the English call this *cotte* a *kirtle*."

Suddenly recognizing the sound of Johan's hobbling footsteps on the stairs, Elise and Hortense exchanged a glance and put their sewing aside.

Entering the chamber, he pushed back his wet hood and nodded a greeting to Hortense. "Lady Stafford," he bowed. Gaining his breath, he glanced around the interior.

Would he punish her for taking liberties? Elise wondered. Most of High Tower remained as built—raw, timbered, and unfinished but she and Hortense had transformed this chamber. They had plastered and whitewashed the walls. The rough floor, scrubbed clean, now hosted an octagonal design of alternating crimson stripes and azure diamond shapes. The open shutters were green and edged with decorative blue vines. She watched him notice the stuffed cushions, the embroidered table covering, the wall hangings, and fresh-cut flowers. He seemed captivated by the decorative brazier: a hammered-copper bucket, with an open basket-weave bottom set upon a three-legged stand, its ash pan ringed with gleaming pewter.

"I am sorry to disturb you, my lady," he said. "I am puzzled by this device found among your chattels." He handed her a rectangular piece of wood.

He had not spoken to her directly in weeks. Elise supposed he condescended to do so from curiosity. She offered him a seat on a cushioned bench and Hortense poured him a bowl of wine.

Tilting the instrument, Elise recalled that she had brought this and other items she thought might be new to William's kingdom. Light reflected off the horizontal band of inlaid, iridescent shells, which ran lengthwise across the center of the polished cherrywood. Vertical grooves ran from the center to the outer edge of the frame. She turned the article so that the shorter slots were on top, the longer ones on the bottom, and as she did so, oval green beads of polished lion stone slid and clinked softly within the carved tracks. She ran her index finger over the cool inlay, remembering how her cousin King Philip had dazzled her with a similar device. He did not think she could learn how to use such an ingenious contrivance, but after giving her a little instruction, she surprised him, though she took care not to appear more agile in its use than he.

"The Greeks call this an *abákos*," she explained. "The Romans call these small pebbles *calculi*. It is used to count numbers." She told him it had recently come to Francia through commerce with the Normans who had settled near Rome. She showed him how it worked, enjoying the sound as she slid the green beads away from the pearly axis. Johan learned quickly, and she saw his amazement as he clustered and slid the beads back and forth.

"The Church condemns its use, for it comes from infidels. Still, my seneschal uses one," Elise said. "Have you written to him?" she asked. Seeing his suspicious frown, she continued haltingly, "He usually sends accounts of the planting, harvests, and stores at solstice and equinox. You might wish to know about his lordship's estates in Normandie." Johan thanked her stiffly before leaving.

Elise shrugged at Hortense and climbed up to the galleries. Sheltered from the rain beneath the eaves, she watched the storm clouds sail slowly across the sky, recalling her husband's orders to obey his agents in all things. Despite her knowledge and capabilities, her wealth and chattel goods, she was a wife—nothing more—a singular stitch in the tapestry that held the new Norman kingdom together. These were the first few months of the rest of her life. Resistance would not free her. The appearance of acceptance might win her small concessions.

The following week, Hortense descended the stairs to the common room. But before taking the last three steps, she paused and looked over the heads of the soldiers milling about, and spotted Johan and Gilbert with the builders. She lowered her head in determination and stepped down. Short and squat, she waded with difficulty through the men standing in groups, some adjusting their armor, others drinking, laughing or arguing. As she neared the table, her breath caught when she saw Gilbert's second-in-command.

With a slight bow, the aged knight moved aside.

Her heart pounding, she glided by without a word and approached the table to wait for Johan or Gilbert to notice her. The men leaned over a table, studying a cloth. She recognized a map of the castle as Johan, using a piece of burnt wood, drew several lines. Gilbert pointed to another mark, and the builders spoke of their progress. Behind her, she heard the old warrior clear his throat.

"My lord." His deep, clear voice sent familiar shivers up her spine.

Gilbert looked up, and seeing Hortense, he directed Johan's attention to her.

"Good morning, gentle men," Hortense said. "A word when you are able."

"Excellent timing as usual, Lady Hortense. We are finished here." Johan said.

As the builders rolled up the cloth and departed, Hortense began. "Although her ladyship has obeyed his lordship's requests in all things, her sequestration is tedious. Her limitations would be more tolerable if she were allowed to ride daily."

"Her ladyship would not be safe beyond the castle's walls," Johan said.

"Even with an armed guard? Enough men to ensure her safety?"

Johan and Gilbert exchanged glances before Gilbert looked beyond Hortense to his second-in-command standing behind her. Although she felt the soldier's gaze, she kept her eyes on the castellan.

"Led by an *experienced* captain," Hortense said to Gilbert as her cheeks heated, "her ladyship could ride with the knights who daily course the castle's immediate domain, all within view of the soldiers on the ramparts. And I shall remain here, a hostage, if you will, to assure you of her timely return."

"We will give this matter consideration, Lady Hortense," Johan said. "Have you other requests?"

"I do. There is much to do before winter, and her ladyship detests idleness. Perhaps she could undertake a few tasks."

"Such as?" Johan said, suspicion in his voice.

"Tasks deemed useful by any wise seneschal, Johan." She turned, and with her head high, walked back toward the stairs.

July 1067, Tutbury, Staffordshire

The looming tower behind taunted Elise with the depth of her imprisonment. Holding herself rigid in the saddle, she rode beside Jeoffroi d'Ardain ahead of the others, past watchtowers, gatehouses, and sentries posted along Castle Road. Impressive barriers should she ever try to leave on her own.

Her attempt to converse with him met silence, and upon leaving the village, he charged ahead as his fifty knights moved forward, placing her at the center. They rode hard and fast and blocked her mare from dropping back as they traveled around the valley and over the moors.

She understood immediately. They would try to dissuade her from riding with them, hoping that after a hard, miserable day in the saddle, she would never wish to ride again. Knowing she would be stiff and sore, she disguised her discomfort and endured without complaint the mud from lead horses splattering her. When they stopped to rest, she dismounted without stumbling, stood straight as a pine tree without quaking, and, when ready walked her mare to the creek. Afterward, without the aid normally extended to a lady in their midst, she checked her mount's hooves, tightened the girth and, with the aid of an outcropping, she remounted—and even managed to stay aright.

At the end of another stop, as she prepared to remount, two men began to argue. A push received an answering shove, and within moments nearly half the knights were engaged in a full-fledged rough and tumble brawl. Sensing the exhibit intended to frighten her, she stepped calmly out of the way and waited. When the men finished, as they wiped blood from their fists and faces, she turned to d'Ardain standing nearby who no doubt expected her to squawk like a wing-flapping hen. "Shall we proceed?"

Within a week, the knights became accustomed to her presence. They rode a little slower, which she assumed was their usual pace, knowing it would be difficult otherwise for them and their horses to respond to a sudden threat. She took care to appear uninterested in them and in the immediate vicinity, though she began to recognize several knights and how they split up, some riding the perimeter, others entering the woodlands. Soon, a separate retinue of ten knights, led by d'Ardain, accompanied her about the immediate vicinity, as the larger company ranged through the countryside.

Despite the rain and the increasingly hot days, her daily rides continued. As her outings took on a regular pattern, her guards began to relax their vigilance. She intensified hers, noting the terrain, proximity to the roads, and trails leading to the river and into the woods.

The charred structures hugging the escarpment she'd seen when she first arrived were gone. The ditch had taken their place. More cottages existed now. Merchants traveled Burton Road, troops marched through the village, small units of knights arrived and departed.

Studying High Tower from afar, she supposed it signaled that the Normans had conquered the English and all would be well, but she'd put hoardings over the open ramparts and shore up the gate towers at the base of the Castle Road. She'd build a timber wall around the village as well, keeping it small and compact against attack.

One day, d'Ardain hesitated before giving her a small bow and quiver. She nearly laughed, reading his caution as concern she might use them against her guards. The weapon, useful for small game, would not injure armored men. Still, it was a welcome privilege, she thought, as they rode into the woods for the first time.

It appeared that the villagers had encroached only the fringes of the woods. A coppice separated the marshes from the thicket, and almost immediately, a deeply rutted road wound around massive trees, whose size humbled her. All of them indicated a wood far older than any she'd seen in Normandie. She felt a sudden chill. Did moss folk watch from the shadows? The nuns had proclaimed that demons and devils, elves and witches inhabited the wilds, and she looked for the poisonous mist slithering in the underbrush until they moved into a single file to pass a wagon and pairs of oxen dragging felled logs to the village. She wondered where the road went, if there were others, for neither a company of knights nor soldiers afoot could easily get through the tangled wilderness flanking them.

They took a barely visible trail leading off the road and into the deep woods. Awe settled over her when they walked their horses past an ancient elm with a trunk wider than two horses, nose to tail. Her gaze traveled up the branches, which seemed to her the thickness of any common tree and which spanned more than forty paces from one end to the other. Elise ached to climb this majestic tree and disappear among the fairies fluttering the leaves. She glanced at her guards, appalled by her pagan thought, and found d'Ardain studying her. His unguarded gaze shifted quickly, but not before she saw a glint of resentment. It sobered her. No doubt, he had more important duties than guarding her.

Chapter Thirty-One

St Benedict's Day, July 11, 1067, in the first year of our
King William's reign. To Johan de Vaux, my loyal friend and
honored seneschal, from Alaric, Seigneur de Tutbierrie.

King William gave the castle at Dover and all of Kent to his
brother Bishop Odo of Bayeux, and the western shire of Hereford
to Guillaume fitz Osbern, who is rebuilding the old castle at Ewyas.
Both rule in William's absence. Dreux serves Bishop Odo and oversees
the garrisons at Dover and I serve fitz Osbern along the southern shires.

Archbishop Stigand, the earls of Mercia and Northumbria, and
others who might stir trouble are in Rouen with William—in gilded
captivity. William has yet to distribute the southern lands and titles once
belonging to the Godwins. The deposed English lords of lesser standing
may not endure the new charters and settlements. Gilbert must expect
resistance. Finish the fosse.

Lose not your heart to a wealth-bearing countess. The avaricious
believe all others to be thus and use riches to bribe the innocent and
seduce the unwary. Guard your sympathies. Remember that Eustace could
send someone to contact her.

Send Marguerite to me.

Hortense did not tell Elise what she'd learned about Marguerite. Instead, she looked beneath Marguerite's incessant anger, saw how she stirred discord between Johan and Gilbert, and noticed that cats, thunderstorms, and ravens frightened her as much as did the English. *Saxon speech is filled with incantations,* Marguerite once told Johan, crossing herself.

One morning, Hortense braced her back against a wagon to make room for the foot soldiers heading toward Northgate, her arms ladened with clean, folded linen. Across the road, she spotted Marguerite and Johan arguing. As he limped away, Marguerite's gaze followed him until two maidservants approached her. She chided them and pushed one ahead as all three crossed the bailey.

Hortense followed at a distance, pondering the look in Marguerite's unguarded face. Skirting the rigging and ropes for the well-diggers, she saw Marguerite and the maidservants enter High Tower. Since Elise's marriage, Marguerite had never been to the tower. Assured by a quick glance that Elise and her guards were at the stable, Hortense hurried after Marguerite.

She found her crouched before one of Elise's coffers, reaching to open it as the servants looked on.

"I'm surprised you have come to see us," Hortense said.

Startled, Marguerite turned. The maidservants jumped back.

"I'm here," Marguerite said coolly, rising slowly to her feet, "to ensure that you and your niece have not stolen from his lordship." She gestured to Elise's chests.

Hortense walked over to the table beside Marguerite, making the servants step aside, and set down the linens. "Does his lordship claim for his own Lady Stafford's undergarments? Her chemises and blood rags?"

The maidservants giggled but sobered at Marguerite's glance.

"Everything belongs to his lordship," she said. "Even this." Marguerite gestured at an open chest and reached for the blue samite, a rare silk interwoven with gold thread.

Hortense slammed the chest lid shut, nearly catching Marguerite's hand. The servants gasped.

"Everything in our possession has been approved by Johan, despite your attempts to remove them," Hortense said. "These chests are for Lady Stafford's *exclusive* use. If you want to join his lordship with new gowns, there is no need to take cloth and furs from her ladyship. Ask Johan for access to his lordship's treasures—if you dare."

"What do you mean?"

Hortense smiled, tempted to reveal her suspicion that Marguerite harbored a private love for Johan. "What do you think I mean?"

Marguerite frowned at Hortense. Looking around the room, her gaze settled on the rare book. "I doubt Johan meant to leave this with your niece. Lord Stafford—not Johan—will determine who reads them." Marguerite lifted the large tome and turned to leave.

"A quean with talons steeped in fornication should take care when touching sacred texts," Hortense said. "Be warned, Marguerite d'Hesdins. God sees your soul. Think you will remain unscorched by His judgment? Flames already surround you."

The maidservants recoiled from Marguerite and hurriedly crossed themselves.

"The Scriptures," Hortense said, reaching for the book, "stay with her ladyship until her husband or Johan request them."

"Hortense?" Elise asked, entering the chamber.

Marguerite suddenly released the book to Hortense. "You foam," she said to Hortense. "A snail wallowing in salt. I have remedies to cap your spume."

"Is there anything else you wish to . . . see?"

Marguerite looked again around the chamber, and without another word, she brushed past Elise, her servants following.

Hortense held a finger before her lips, signaling Elise to silence. She put the book on the table and followed the women until they had left the tower.

"Take care, Aunt," Elise said, placing the book in its tooled leather case. "She may be more dangerous than she appears."

"*Nought vera harmish.*" Hortense said in Saxon.

"*Eyo hopan ye spake troth,*" Elise answered.

Hortense smiled. Elise was learning the language quickly. Knowing Saxon and keeping her knowledge secret would help her niece either ascend to her rightful place or help her escape. Preferring the latter,

Hortense had assessed the prospects. Escape would be difficult. It could be done, although she had yet to propose it to Elise. But for now, speaking in Saxon, Hortense told Elise the village gossip.

A few days later, Marguerite climbed into her cart, gloating that Alaric had sent for her, not his wife. Watching her departure, Hortense prayed that a rash would fester on Alaric's privates and make large pustules ooze between Marguerite's legs. Elise, on the other hand, hoped her husband would forget his wife entirely.

August 1067, Tutbury, Staffordshire

On Lammas Day, Elise and Hortense observed their first English festival: the annual Blessing of the Well, completed more quickly than Elise had imagined possible. With grand ceremony, servants dressed the well house with bouquets of colorful flowers, leaves, and moss. Elise understood enough Saxon now to hear a few servants grumbling: freed from hauling water up from the river, they complained about hauling buckets up from the well.

As Brother Derrick prepared to bless the well for continued water, Norman soldiers, believing it a pagan ritual, chided him for denigrating the Feast of Saint Peter's Chains. To Elise's surprise, Gilbert calmed his soldiers by asking Derrick to bless and dedicate bread from the new wheat for Saint Peter and allowed the English to bathe in the river. After the bathing and blessings, some villagers grumbled about being forced into hard labor. Soldiers whipped them and made them sing praises to their Norman masters. Afterward, nearly everyone descended to the village to feast and dance, while Elise and Hortense returned to High Tower.

There, they found Jeoffroi d'Ardain in the common room. Elise greeted him and introduced him to Hortense before climbing to the ramparts to enjoy the festivities, leaving Hortense and Jeoffroi alone.

"You old goat! I *did* recognize you," Hortense said gruffly. "Don't you dare put your filthy boot on that table," she warned.

Jeoffroi d'Ardain, sitting on one of the benches, suspended his leg in the air for a moment before lowering it back to the floor.

"Then, why did you never deign to acknowledge me? It was only . . . what? Thirteen, fourteen years ago?"

"I've been busy." Hortense did not want to remember those chaotic days. Besides if Johan or Gilbert knew about their past, they might remove him from Elise's retinue. "It was a long time ago."

He chuckled. "It's a mark of true nobility: the lower one falls the higher the airs they adopt."

Hortense leveled her eyes on Jeoffroi, choosing carefully the exact words she would use to slice him into shreds. As she remembered, his eyes were hazel, and they twinkled now, anticipating her attack. Her anger vanished. She took a deep breath and shrugged. Well, he had been her great lover once, and their liaison had healed her heart. He had taught her the pleasure of coupling and how to laugh again after Eustace had her husband murdered and confiscated her fortune.

"We never saw each other again after Mortemer," she said softly, remembering his wife and all his children had been killed.

"No," he answered, looking away from her to the past. He turned again to her. "But, I was glad to see you alive and well when you came to Tutbury with Lady Stafford."

She grunted.

"Have you missed me, Tensa?" he asked, using the name he had given her one night as she lay in his arms. He reached across the table to take her hand.

She looked at his dark brown hair, his gray sideburns, and his lips, still sensual after all these years. He must be in his mid-sixties, she thought, looking at the lines in his face accentuating his lean, rugged features. Hortense did not want to talk about the past they had shared.

"His lordship," she hissed, pulling her hand away, "has given us great pleasure by sending for his mistress."

Jeoffroi smiled and cautiously raised his boot to the table. She watched his impudence with a twittering heart. "My niece tells me you are kind, Jeoffroi. I thank you for that."

"She loves you dearly," he said, patting the bench beside him in invitation and leaning lazily against a timbered wall.

"I have yet to discover," Hortense said, sitting down across from him, "why Lord Stafford keeps his wife a prisoner. Do you know the reason?"

"No. Lord Stafford is a fair man, and once he has time for his wife, things will change. Her beauty reminds me of you."

Hortense glanced at his relaxed body. "Still the Thief of Hearts, Jeoffroi?"

He shrugged. "Truce?"

"Friends and nothing more," Hortense said firmly.

"*Nothing* more?" he teased with a smile.

"Psssh! I am old, and fat, and gray. You are—"

"—Old, and brittle, and gray. We suit."

She laughed and shook her head. "No, Jeoffroi. And I mean no," she said, with a smile twitching at the edges of her lips. He's doing it again, she thought, her heart tripping.

Chapter Thirty-Two

As Elise's daily rides continued into mid-August, the number of her guards had steadily decreased. With only five guards, Elise rode at an easy walk along a rutted track edging the woods, glad for the shade that cooled this hot day. Encouraged that a reticent Jeoffroi d'Ardain had answered her morning greeting with one of his own, she ventured to converse.

"My aunt tells me you hail from Mortemer."

"Yes. I served in the garrisons."

"What?" She turned in her saddle, startled. "Why did you not tell me?"

"There was no reason, my lady. When the land passed to another, I had leave to join the duke's men."

"Were you there . . . during the attack?"

"I witnessed the attack from a hill. I was one of your guards on the hunting expedition. Do you not remember me?"

Elise studied Jeoffroi, remembering that cold February day when she was eight years old. She and Marie, six, were hunting with their brother when they saw the village burning. She vaguely recalled someone trying to restrain her. But she followed her brother and fled toward blood and death, and the terror that had bound Roland and Marie, Elise and Hortense together.

"No, I do not remember you, Jeoffroi."

"A long, bloody time ago, my lady," Jeoffroi said. "When we failed to keep you from danger, my companions and I rode toward Rouen to alert the duke. We intercepted his forces coming to Mortemer. By the time we returned, it was too late." He shook his head. "Young Roland, who fostered with your family, protected you. I still remember his ferocious yell when we found you. He charged us. The duke snatched the boy by his tunic and dangled him at arm's length until Roland realized we were friend, not foe."

She nodded, missing Roland, and recalling her mother's lifeless body, her brother's final shriek. "Did you lose family in the attack?"

"My wife, all my sons and their families."

"I am truly sorry, Jeoffroi." She reined in her horse and pulled an arrow from her quiver. With great solemnity, she placed the arrow across her palms and offered it to him. "I thank you for your vigilance then, and now, Jeoffroi d'Ardain. I am privileged to have such an escort."

From his smile, she knew he had recognized the gesture, a simple imitation of the ritual honoring a brave knight with a new sword. As his soldiers watched curiously, Jeoffroi took the arrow with equal solemnity, accepting her tribute.

"How did you come to serve Black Wolf?" she asked when they resumed their journey.

"The invasion gave many of us a chance to find new lords who could support us. I was among the first group of soldiers assigned to your husband at Hastings. I have been with him to this day, and if God grants me, I shall continue to serve him."

During the last days of the meager harvest, Jeoffroi became her sole escort. He allowed her to hunt small game with her bow or explore the river ford, the marshes, and the narrow valley along Burton Road. Often they began their ride as usual, but when they left the small coppice beside the village, Jeoffroi abandoned the well-used tracks, each time taking a circuitous route leading her a little deeper into the thickets than before.

Just after dawn near August's end, they rode single-file, following a narrow path into the tangled woods. Elise cherished the expectant hush among the oak, alder, hazel, and ash as giant trees faded into the cool damp mist and the glorious scents: damp bark, moss, mulching leaves, the wondrous aromas of peppery smoke and resin.

Mesmerized by the sound of hooves thumping a hollow rhythm on the thick woodland carpet and the occasional snap of brittle twigs, she listened to the soft jingles of the harnesses, the swish and rustle when dry leaves brushed against her linen veil. The dappled light and the air soothed something within her, and yet Jeoffroi's silence and their slow movement farther into the dense, ancient trees unsettled her. He stopped at the edge of a creek and tilted his head as if to listen.

"Are we far from the castle?" she whispered, sensing his caution.

"Not far," he said softly, motioning her with his hand to silence. Giving his horse a nudge, he jumped the creek. Elise followed. They entered a small meadow. He reigned in, whistled, and waited.

An old woman stepped out from behind a tree. "So, this Norman pup brings you to see his sweetheart!" she said, in French.

"Now, Frigga," Jeoffroi said as he dismounted. "You need not insult Lady Stafford."

"Lady Stafford? Of the castle?" she asked, looking startled at Jeoffroi. He nodded. "You're more fool than I thought," she chided. She studied Elise a long moment before speaking to Jeoffroi. "Scat, old man. Her ladyship and I have business."

Jeoffroi helped Elise dismount. Then, with an impudent grin, he remounted and slowly rode away, taking Elise's horse with him.

Frigga tipped her head, a silent invitation, turned, and walked around the base of an oak tree the size of six men abreast.

Elise followed through a grove of wych elms, slipping around one, around another, and another until they reached a clearing, where she found the woman standing beside the entrance of a dwelling built into the hollowed base of a tree. Beyond a drawn curtain of wolfskins, Elise saw an ingenious shelter, about the size of a wagon. A carved ledge covered with sheepskins served as a bed. She saw folded blankets of animal fur, several baskets, a large closed chest, a small brazier, a bench, and clothing rod.

Turning from the shelter, she walked slowly around the clearing. She had never seen anything like this place. Three concentric rings of ancient elms, obviously tended through the years, shielded the clearing from all sight beyond, and the overhead branches provided a sheltering canopy. Faces, animals, and peculiar markings were carved into each tree's trunk. A small circular fire pit had been dug deep into the center. A ledge made of flat stones ringed the pit, providing low seats so one could sit in the circle sheltered from the wind. Four red posts carved with strange symbols from their base to the pointed tops, stood like sentries beside the pit. A little taller than she, each bore an odd-shaped crown. One, a crescent moon, like worshiping arms raised to the sky. Another held a diamond-shaped plate balanced on one point. An oval ring with a dagger angled through sat atop the third post, and the fourth pillar had three rusty spikes splayed horizontally like a flag.

Elise turned to study Frigga, who looked decades older than Jeoffroi. Her sun-bronzed face was completely wrinkled, and laugh lines accentuated her eyes: tiny black beads gazing speculatively at Elise. Her uncovered brilliant-white hair, the color of spring clouds, fell to her waist in thick waves, uncovered like a maiden. Despite shaking, gnarled hands and an ancient body, she stood with a straight, proud back. She stepped down into the seating area of the fire pit and sat—deliberately—as if testing Elise somehow.

"*Thaer beon a flor*," Frigga said, in Saxon, "that grows in the woods. It is rare, and few people have ever seen it, but the memory of its aroma sends men to endless years of hunting for it. The small flower, white with a pale red center, grows in the soft, thick moss of tree hollows. It is lonely. Sometimes, you can hear the flower singing. It raises its head and looks through the tree branches and leaves for the blue sky. Mostly, the flower cries silently. It is shaped like a bowl and gathers its tears in the base of its blossom. They say the man who drinks this nectar will have wealth beyond gold, health beyond a sound body, and love beyond the passion of the bed. They say the man who worships the flower will know laughter."

"*Es no a . . . synn?*" Elise asked, her Saxon, thickly clouded with a French accent, "*to worthscipe othur than Gott?*"

"*Ye spacan the Anglisc toung. Do ye synn agan yer Franc-spacan kyng?* Do not be afraid," she cautioned in French at Elise's stiffening. "You are safe here, my lady."

Safe? Hardly, Elise thought, looking around the small clearing with its crude shelter. It was all so odd: things hung from the tree branches, drying strips of meat, clay masks, herbs and such. And it was almost too quiet. She wondered if Frigga lived alone here in the woods.

"I do," Frigga said in French, startling Elise.

"Are you a witch?" Elise asked, watching Frigga's eyes widen in surprise.

"No. I am a squatter. 'Twill be but a matter of time before I am found out and my home destroyed."

"Why do you stay? Why do you not come to the village?"

Frigga laughed. "Death lives where there are people. Have you not found this so?" she asked.

Elise thought about it and nodded.

Silence fell between them as Frigga studied Elise, who listened to the tinkling sounds of the wind brushing bits of hardened clay, strung together and hanging in the trees.

"They say you are imprisoned upon the great stone rock."

Elise looked directly into Frigga's eyes. Perhaps this woman was one of her husband's spies. She answered carefully. "Do they?"

Frigga laughed. "They will never imprison your spirit, my lady."

"What else do they say?"

Frigga lowered her head, rubbed the knuckles of one hand, and as if deciding something, she lifted bold eyes to Elise.

"They say the usurper Norman king does not speak our language, that he cares nothing of our court, our laws, or our customs. They say he gave Totta Burh, as we call it, to a vicious warrior. Our new master and his Frankish men are said to believe nothing existed here before they came. They desecrate the seat of our Mercian kings, ignore our village *gerefa*, our rights, our markets, mill, and quarry. They say whether their Frankish master is good, bad, indifferent, kind, cruel or demonic, he rules over the people greedily. He takes the best land, forces the people to build his castle, to pay geld to keep what they always had. Worse, they say, is that his men gloat when they invade the humblest huts, making the people quake in fear and the children believe they were born enslaved."

Elise saw no hostility in Frigga's eyes, merely an honest response to her question. "I suppose it does not matter that Lord Stafford was born in this land, speaks Saxon, and knows something of English ways."

"No," Frigga said. "He is not from the blood of Angles, neither Saxon nor Mercian nor from among the tribes that held the land through *mutual* consent. That matters."

Elise turned her head when the priory bell, a muted, distant sound, announced the third hour of the day.

"Terce," Frigga said. She placed her palms on her knees and pushed herself up. "It is decided." With her fingers in her mouth, she blew a shrill whistle. "You shall come to me at least once a week, and more when the weather allows it. I will send my granddaughter Serilda to you."

Elise heard the sound of hoofbeats and followed Frigga as she slipped between the trees. Jeoffroi rode toward them. She was confused. What was decided? Why would she come here again? Why did Jeoffroi bring her to begin with?

Frigga shook her head. "You will know everything soon enough, my lady."

Chapter Thirty-Three

In the first week of September, Johan summoned Elise.

"God's blessings, Johan. Brother Derrick," she said, entering her husband's longhouse, used by Johan in Marguerite's absence.

Johan stood behind a table, and beside him, Brother Derrick held a small scroll in his hand, looking very young and very uncomfortable. She had never been in her husband's quarters and made a quick note of the scattered documents, charters and writs, strewn across Johan's table.

"My lady," Johan said. "You have received a letter from abroad."

She raised her eyebrows in surprise and looked from Derrick to Johan's puzzling gaze.

"Is something amiss?" she whispered, suddenly frightened that the letter held dire news. *Marie!* she thought. "May I see the letter?" She held out her hand.

"I'm sorry, my lady. I cannot give it to you, but Brother Derrick will read it." He motioned to the monk.

Annoyed and anxious, she looked at the monk.

"It is from Brittany," Brother Derrick said. "My Dearest Sister. Roland and I married as our blessed Lord willed on the Feast of St. Christopher, July 25th. We reside in Rennes. Roland's vassals have sworn the customary oaths of fealty and obedience to me, his countess."

Elise clasped her hands together. Closing her eyes, she shielded the joyful tears welling behind her lids. *Marie is safe! She is loved! She is free from Eustace and Arques!* When she opened her eyes again, she saw Johan's unfettered curiosity and sadly remembered that none of Alaric's men had sworn fealty and obedience to her as was their duty and her honor.

Brother Derrick continued. "I have found, as I trust you have, that . . . that marriage is all I had hoped for and more. We humbly request of your husband permission to visit you in the spring, unless . . .." The monk hesitated and continued falteringly. "Unless . . . I am . . . with child."

Elise laughed with delight. Her sister could be carrying a child even now, as they stood here in the longhouse. Brother Derrick and Johan exchanged glances.

"That is all, my lady," Brother Derrick said, rolling the parchment again. Her eyes watched it greedily, knowing Marie would have said something about their lands, King Philip, perhaps Arques and Walter.

"Most gentle of men, I could demand to see the letter in my own right as your lord's wife and lady." She paused, knowing any show of irritation would be reported to her husband. To Johan, she said, "Please ask his lordship's permission for my sister and her husband to visit."

She left the longhouse abruptly, scattering chickens as she fled across the bailey to the edge of the escarpment most hidden from the courtyard. Shadowed by the tower, she looked out at the river.

Marie, dear, sweet Marie is safe! Elise blinked back the tears and whispered a prayer of thanks to the God who had abandoned her. For a brief and painful moment, she remembered the bantering and laughter shared between Marie and dear Roland.

"My lady," Johan said softly behind her.

"Johan," she said without facing him.

"You are distressed."

"No." She could barely say the word and shook her head. "I . . . I wish to be alone," she said, aware of the irony, for she had been nearly isolated these last months.

"The news troubles you."

"The news gladdens me."

"But, you shed tears."

She turned to him, tears brimming in her eyes. "You hold all rights over me as given you by my husband. Please give me the right to be alone when I so choose."

"As you wish." He nodded respectfully and departed. She watched him limp away, regretting her sharp words. Turning toward the river, she let her tears fall freely.

Are we too dangerous to leave behind?" Hortense wondered aloud, settling into her saddle.

Amused by the thought of a dangerous Hortense, Elise supposed her very near the truth. Given the breadth of her husband's restrictions, Johan and Gilbert would not trust another to watch them in their absence. Then again, taking them on this much-needed market excursion might be Johan's apology for inquiring about her tears a week ago.

As the wagons and knights took their positions, Johan and Gilbert rode up to flank the women. Elise toggled her quiver to her saddle, and the journey began. Skirting the marshes, she caught Hortense's eye and said, "Do you remember how marshlands near Mortemer were drained to expose rich soil for crops?"

"Yes," Hortense said loud enough for the men to hear. "The channels stopped some of the flooding. And your father built a flume for the watermill. I thought you found an old millstone nearby, half-buried in the mud."

"I did," Elise said as they approached the ford, "I wonder if William would encourage his lords to build mills as he did in Normandie."

"No doubt," Hortense said. "Mills produce revenue." Later, Hortense asked how many beehives would be needed to provide honey, and, more importantly, a decent supply of wax. Together they discussed how many dovecotes would supply a castle the size of Tutbury, whether Norman deer could live in English woods, the reasons for establishing a fishpond, the need for a kitchen garden, and many other things to be considered when administering the castle.

It took more than half a day to reach the intersection of several roads, where Derby sat, like two villages divided by a river. The carved plaques beside the gates told Elise that the village had a hundred burgesses, a priory which would likely shelter them this night, a dozen mills, a mint, and the king's license to host a market, held this week, as evidenced by the blue and yellow banners rippling in the wind.

Their party followed the people carrying large, deep baskets of goods strapped over their shoulders and those wheeling handcarts piled with wares. Elise marveled at the dwellings lining High Street and the two churches flanking the river. As the crowds thickened, Gilbert's knights closed ranks, surrounding her and Hortense until they reached the open market. They dismounted and walked with Johan and Gilbert among the wagons and booths, smelling fresh-baked bread and a whiff of the swine stalls.

For the first time in months, Elise's spirits rose as they passed poultrymen, cheesemakers, and fishers calling out their dry and live catch, and wondered if the village could host a smaller market.

"You will not interfere, my lady," Johan warned her.

"Of course." Johan's comment irked but did not dampen her aim. Johan, a former mercenary, a seneschal for only three months, knew nothing about feeding the castle's inhabitants this coming winter. But if she tried to guide him openly, he might send her to the priory where she could not help him at all. Ignoring the temptation of the spice merchants and tinkers, she tempered her irritation that she must try to influence Johan by feigning disinterest. Elise took Hortense's arm, and they stayed close to him, commenting about the vegetables and fruits that would last through the winter. Together they speculated on the quantity of grain needed for Tutbury, and Elise explained how her seneschal bargained good prices. Soon, Elise noticed that Johan heeded their words. Once, he sent her an inquiring glance before scowling as if regretting he'd sought her opinion.

Two days later, Gilbert led them and their heavily ladened wagons back by way of the woods on a route said to be shorter. Unlike Needwood beside Tutbury, this woodland had been well tended by the villagers. The broad tracks, the open meadows and stumps left a verdant and sunny grassland between well-spaced trees, which allowed them to hunt small game easily.

Hours later, they traveled in untended, tangled woods, and hunting became more difficult. By the time they entered a particularly dense thicket, she had detected rain in the muted, wooded scents and realized it had not rained for a week. The horses became uncommonly edgy when the track narrowed and the trees closed in on them. Alarmed, Elise searched but could not see beyond the leafy walls. When the trail curved, they entered a clearing dimmed by a dense canopy. Demons, she thought, feeling the hair on her nape rise. The horses snorted, threw back their heads, and reared or tried to turn.

The sky exploded with a loud, crackling boom. Blue lightning shimmered down the mighty oak before them. The tree burst apart and flames shot up through the branches.

A sign! She struggled to keep her horse from bolting as the tree blazed. The echoing blast vibrated within and her heart pounded. Beside her, Johan helped Hortense control her mount. Elise felt the prickly sensation of being watched, of all-seeing eyes. Swallowing the acrid smoke, she imagined the metallic taste of Satan's gaze.

As her horse calmed, she relaxed her grip, surprised to find one hand still clasping her bow and a single nocked arrow. Gilbert dismounted and fell to his knees. Other knights followed. He prayed aloud, crossing himself several times.

Slowly, as if the shadow of a giant hand descended over them, the clearing became dark as dusk, and they heard the sound of large drops hitting the leafy canopy as the tree burned. Elise scanned the ferns, the thick bushes and heavy vines obscuring the tree trunks encircling them. She breathed in the hot, heavy air—the amber wolf pendant hidden beneath her clothes sparked between her breasts.

A soft rustling beside Gilbert's bowed head drew her attention to the tangled, dense foliage where a brownish pelt bobbed between the leaves. She released her arrow before seeing a hairy face, the glint of an axe. A scream followed.

Bandits! It was over in moments, though it seemed like hours. Elise had wounded the first: a brigand about to cleave Gilbert's skull. Nearly a dozen raiders, intent on stealing their horses and wagons, had attacked. Outmaneuvered by Gilbert's experienced warriors, most slipped quickly back into the woods, leaving their wounded and dead behind. The rain, now falling heavily through the leaves, began to extinguish the fire. As Gilbert's men roped their captives together, he approached Elise.

"You shot true, my lady. Clean and quick. My life was delivered by your dispatch. I thank you." He bowed.

"No need, Gilbert," she said. "I merely thought it was our dinner."

Chapter Thirty-Four

Sennight before Equinox, September 1067, Tutbury. To my lord Alaric, from Johan de Vaux, your friend.

*T*he fosse is nearly completed. The palisade surrounding the outer baileys continues to rise, the curtain wall for the inner bailey is finished. We have yet to rebuild the inner palisades circling High Tower. The drawbridge has been installed, and both the North and South Gate barbicans are fortified.

Only seven fires have erupted in the bailey since removing the tents. When completed, the hall will house the sleeping chambers you requested, a chapel, the treasury, dry stores, and a great room. We will move in before Christmas.

We are banking the river and building channels to capture the marshes for crops. Would the king grant you a charter for a mill? We will need one next year, and it would add coins to your coffers. I have written to the countess's seneschal requesting his reports.

On your behalf, I have given the monks a bronze bell. The first knells jarred us, but now we are accustomed to the tolling, which can be heard throughout the valley. If necessary, we will use it to warn villagers of danger.

Your lady wife rides daily about the castle, accompanied by Jeoffroi d'Ardain, an officer in command of the knights. At sixty-four winters, he

*has experience and has served well in your ranks. He will not be lured
from his duty. When she leaves, her aunt remains in the castle.*

*I have allowed her ladyship to tend the kitchen garden. She also makes
rushlights and candles for the winter using the wax, wicks, and molds she
brought with her. Under guard, she and her aunt gather tanning bark
to prepare for the arrival of the freeman tanner you requested. I will, on
occasion, allow her to pursue other small tasks. Perchance busy hands
will prevent idle schemes if she is so inclined, although I cannot yet see
vile intentions.*

*The countess received a missive from her sister who married recently
and requests permission to visit Tutbury in the spring, with her husband
Count de Rennes of Brittany.*

September 1067, Tutbury, Staffordshire

"First, the truth," Frigga said in Norman French, after Jeoffroi left
them alone. She motioned Elise to sit beside the fire.

"I am old. I am dying. I was blessed with a mother who taught me
ancient arts . . . arts which the Church would call witchcraft."

Elise felt the color drain from her face.

"It is time to pass my knowledge on. I have but one granddaughter,
the girl Serilda. She can no longer dwell with me. Besides, she is too
young.

"I believe," Frigga said, observing Elise carefully, "you are not
only capable of learning these arts, but you are capable of using them
wisely. I would like to pass my knowledge on to you." She held up her
hand to prevent Elise from interrupting and continued.

"I am no witch as you once thought," Frigga continued softly. "I
don't know about talismans, or curses, or charms against the evil eye.
I don't know how to make someone love you, how to cause warts or
how to protect you from elves. I don't know how to bring someone
back to life."

Elise gasped at the words spoken so boldly.

"There are five things I can teach you: the art of coloring cloth,
the art of savory cooking, the art of beauty, the art of healing, and . . .
the art of killing."

"Holy Mother, preserve us," Elise whispered, crossing herself.

Frigga caught and held Elise's eyes with her own. "Yes, I know how to kill with a potion—so I can cure a poison if caught in time. I know how to help women bear children and how to seal a gaping wound. The healing arts have been passed down from generation to generation from my people, and when I was young, I studied in Salerno among the great healers.

"But all these arts challenge Church doctrines. Prelates teach that affliction is proof of the devil's possession or evidence of a godless soul, and the cure must rely on driving out the demons, on miracles or physical punishment. The Church deems it sinful to use certain plants to color, or flavor, or enhance one's appearance, condemning these efforts as blasphemous insults to God's perfection. Priests say doing so is the sin of arrogance committed by presumptuous, impious people discontent with God's natural gifts.

"The Church falls hard on those who diverge from its teachings. And many people are quick to condemn those who practice these arts."

Elise's heart pounded, and she glanced around the circle, expecting someone to step forward and accuse them of heresy.

"You must tell me which of these five arts you wish to learn, for I will only teach you those and not the others. Take care in your choice, my lady, for there may come a time when your knowledge of any one of these arts will stand as proof against you.

"If you agree, it will be hard work. What took me years to learn, you must learn in months. It will take concentration, diligence and . . . secrecy." Frigga paused. "Do you understand, my lady? Once this chest of knowledge is open to you, it can never be closed."

Elise nodded. "And if I choose to learn none of these arts?"

"Then," Frigga smiled, "we shall make music!" She walked to her treehouse and ducked inside. When she emerged, she held three instruments—a partially strung lyre, a flute, and a small drum.

Elise laughed, but when she stood up and walked around the circle, she sobered. She looked at the trees sheltering this place, and at the odd figures hung in the branches. Her eyes lingered on a white mask carved of wood that sat within the hollow of a tree, resembling an ass, with a red snout, long blue ears, and acorn eyes. Not the face of a saint, she thought.

Medicaments and dyes were familiar to her. The abbey grew herbs. With the nuns, Elise had foraged for curative plants. The nuns used walnuts to dye wool for the monk's robes and to make ink for the scribes.

She glanced at Frigga, who held the lyre upright between her knees as she restrung it. What if she were to learn these arts? Surely not all priests thought dyeing cloth was against God's will, for they often wore many-colored cloths. She could hardly complain about the boiled gruel and vegetables they ate during this year of scarce food. But one day they might have plenty of food, and a savory dish would be pleasing. Was it truly a sin to have flavorful food?

As Frigga strummed the instrument, Elise's fingers stroked the sharp, elongated features of a man's face, etched in the bark. "Who is this?" she asked.

Frigga looked up from her instrument and shrugged. "It was the way the bark grew. I merely deepened the lines with my knife many years ago."

Witchcraft? Elise wondered. Was it devil's work to ease a woman's birth pangs? She shuddered. Someday she might face childbirth herself. She remembered her mother's ordeal with one child, where her servants repeatedly lifted and dropped her onto the bed to hasten her labor. To the Church, childbirth pain is God's punishment for Eve's sin. Yet, the Church faults obstinate, devilish infants for prolonged labor and instructs cutting these demonic creatures from the womb—in pieces.

"Why does the Church condemn these arts?"

"The Church proclaims itself the arbiter of all Christendom. It praises war, wealth, and power. At various times, it has condemned music, women, marriage, and hunting. The Church determines what things are godly and what things belong to Satan, and no king or villager will disagree. I have traveled to far lands and seen many things." Frigga strummed the lyre, stopped to tune a string before continuing.

"I have seen the Church sanction an herb in one place, forbid it in another and there, burn to death any who merely possess it. Many priests cannot read scripture, much less the texts of wise people who lived long ago. My own people have forgotten the ancient arts, and from fear, they cleave to inexplicable mysteries."

"You speak as though the Church was corrupt." Elise sat down across from Frigga.

"The Church is corrupt, and I do not fear the saying of it." She paused, leveling her gaze at Elise. "I know the Church better than most. I was, once, an abbess."

Elise inhaled sharply, fighting an involuntary impulse to kneel as she did before her abbess at Clarion. She studied Frigga. Only those who stem from the highest nobility could ever hold such a position: a king's daughter, the emperor's niece.

"Look around you," Frigga said. "Although the Church preaches against fornication and adultery, many an archbishop or priest has both wife and concubine, or illegitimate child, like your husband's father, the illegitimate son of an Archbishop. Yes, I know much about the men who rule the Church," she said. "Even monks have women to service them in the priories. Have you ever known a fat priest who did not take a meal from the poor? Demand coins for a burial or seize a farmer's tools? Or a priest who wears silks and furs when his flock wears rags?" Frigga shook her head.

It was dangerous, Elise thought, to speak so of the Church. The pope had blessed William's invasion. Yet, if not corrupt, the Church was easily corrupted. King Philip, Eustace, and many others swore to uphold God's laws and gave rich endowments. Yet, they often pursued corrupt ends and received sanctions from clergy who understood the advantages of having important and wealthy friends.

She studied the four red posts. What secrets did these carvings hold? Elise wondered, feeling the powerful lure of forbidden knowledge. She could bring harm to Hortense. She had already harmed Hortense by bringing her, for she, too, was imprisoned at the castle. Elise faced a bleak future. How long could she live in forced idleness and boredom, subject to the whims of Johan or Marguerite? She watched Frigga tilt the lyre upright on one knee and strum a few notes.

"I . . . I wish to learn . . . all the arts," Elise said. "And especially the art of music."

Alaric fought a brooding desolation. A year ago, he had discovered his family murdered here in Eashing. He stepped outside his tent and gazed at the gray sky, feeling the crisp mid-November wind. He scanned the ruins of what had once been a hill fort and village. His eyes slid to the ruins of the church.

Would I have followed William had I known the cost would be so great?

His men prepared for another march, and Roderick hovered nearby as if his presence could ease the bitter memory. "Get Father Pierre," Alaric said softly, as much to send Roderick away as to summon the priest.

Father Pierre had presided over Martinmas and, in a private service with Alaric, prayed for the souls of his family. Afterward, they talked quietly, stirring memories of good times past. His irritation with the priest eased with Pierre's tender blessings and the priest's own confession that he sorely missed Alaric's father. With his soldiers and entourage, they had shared a rare feast: fresh meat, dried fruits, ale and grain from the recent harvest, a celebration before fasting in advance of Christmastide.

Waiting for the priest, Alaric thought how quickly everything changed. Last month, he had shared a rare camaraderie with William's regents, Bishop Odo and Guillaume fitz Osbern, as their combined forces chased Edric through the Herefordshire borderlands. They'd appreciated Alaric leading them along the old trails, mountains, and ravines he knew so well—until he mentioned William's prohibition on rape. Now, with news of Eustace's exploits, the regents challenged Alaric's loyalty anew. He expected William would do the same when he returned from Rouen. And no matter how many castles he had built and garrisoned to protect William's kingdom, nothing would protect Alaric from William's violence.

Father Pierre lumbered toward Alaric's tent and ducked inside. Alaric followed and said to Marguerite, "Go to the baggage train."

"Must I go again? It's so cold!"

"For a short time. Here, take the furs. Roddy!" he called. When Roderick appeared, Alaric told him to escort Marguerite to her destination. Grabbing her fox-trimmed mantle, she barely glanced at Alaric as she left the tent to await his summons.

"My son?" Father Pierre said his writing implements readied.

To Johan de Vaux:

Roddy and I celebrated last year's victory near Hastings. Long may our holy King William live! Praise the glory of God's will.

You might have heard that the Welsh princes, rarely aligned with the English, have joined one Edric of the Wilds, a Shropshire thane, said to be living in the great woods abutting Staffordshire. In September they attacked Hereford, inspiring rebellion throughout the shire. With well-armed forces, strong, unmarred horses, and ample supplies, Edric delivered the most severe blow to William's reign since Hastings. The frequent and well-planned strikes took place over three weeks and kept the regents' forces on the western border. We routed them, only to discover that these assaults diverted us from the eastern coast, where Eustace de Boulogne invaded Dover. Dreux countered the attack. His garrisons retook the village and captured members of the invading party, which he now holds hostage until the king returns. Eustace abandoned his followers and escaped.

The king and his regents are enraged by Eustace's treason. No one knows how far William will go to assuage his anger. Any and all involved with Eustace, especially the clerics and villagers said to have invited him, are deemed traitors. Joined to Eustace by unholy matrimony, I, too, am suspect.

Interrogate the countess. Discover if she had foreknowledge of her uncle's exploits. Had her sister's correspondence revealed this plot? Had she intended to aid Eustace—or Edric?

Father Pierre has prepared my annulment petition. I will take it to William's Christmas court. After Eustace's treason, he may see the wisdom of severing this marriage. Keep my annulment in confidence, for such knowledge might spur the countess to reckless enterprise, and Marguerite might expect me to wed her when this marriage is nulled.

When you move the countess to Tutbury Hall, note the state of her rooms, her habits, where she dines, and her manner about the castle grounds. Mark and know well her stature and the features of her person, for evidence of debauchery, excessive drink, dissipation, and cuckoldry will be useful. Marguerite tells me she is querulous. Record her tempests, for any vitriolic outburst is proof of her treasonous disposition and shall aid my petition.

The woman's request for visitors is denied. I need not further jeopardize my position with William by hosting the powerful count of Rennes—especially now when Brittany is restive.

William gave me a new holding near Monmouth. Add this charter to my estates. My builders are erecting a small fortress above a woodland said to be full of fairies.

With this missive, I return Marguerite to your care.

Chapter Thirty-Five

Why does she get the west wing?" Marguerite demanded loudly. "Because you have the room adjacent to Alaric's," Johan said, exasperated by Marguerite's complaints.

"She should remain in High Tower."

"Alaric wishes her to reside here."

Elise ignored Marguerite and Johan arguing beside the central hearth and followed a servant through the cold, hollow room that smelled faintly of limewash. Her gaze traveled up one of the columns, a thick bark-stripped tree trunk, to the rafters, to the familiar pattern of the trusses and crossbeams, and to the arched wind braces. Though pleased to see the finished hall, she knew that like all the other structures, it was built quickly to secure the castle. None of the longhouses, the tower, or the timber walls surrounding the castle had the strength or longevity of wood aged a year or more. The unseasoned oak would soon begin to split.

Elise slipped between the double rows of columns and into her new bedchamber. She had been given a southwest room. Despite the cold day, the shutters were open. Bright light filtered through the waxed linen covering the single window.

Hortense had been busy. A fire in the brazier warmed the chamber. The bed Elise had brought with her from Boulogne had been unpacked, assembled, and made up with fresh, rose-scented linens and furs, a welcome relief from the pallets they'd used in the tower. Thick curtains hung from the canopy to give warmth. Her beautifully carved chest sat in one corner.

Elise put her bundles on a table and walked to the window wall. She raised her hand to the seams between the planks where the wattle and daub had been set, seeking the source of the slight whistle she heard from the constant wind blowing across the escarpment. She felt the breeze and made a mental note to save her wood ash to seal the cracks.

It was far more primitive than the room she had shared with her sister in Boulogne, but far more spacious than the storeroom in the High Tower she and Hortense had shared since May. Yes, she thought, this would do.

Hortense, given a room in the same wing, entered Elise's chamber through the wardrobe they shared for storage and bathing. "You have been invited to the inaugural feast," she said, placing candles in the holders driven into the wall. "Brother Derrick will bless the hall and consecrate the chapel."

"Will you join us?" Elise asked.

"No," Hortense said. "I would prefer the company of a braying jackass to that she-devil."

Marguerite stood at the center of the high table between Gilbert on her left and Johan on her right, waiting for Brother Derrick to give the benediction. Recently returned to Tutbury, she missed the privilege and courtesy shown her as mistress of the king's lieutenant. Still, after months of travel, baggage wagons, and tents, she relished sleeping in a real bed on a real stuffed pad, and she looked forward to ruling over Alaric's wife.

Excruciatingly aware of Johan beside her, Marguerite glanced over the hall within which she would preside. She turned her gaze to the chapel. The countess, accompanied by Brother Derrick and his monks, crossed the room, not to the high table where Marguerite sat, but to the side tables flanking the central hearth used by *lower* personages, among twenty or so hearth knights. Brother Derrick gave a quick benediction, and everyone took their seats.

"Brother Derrick," Marguerite called out. "Are you aware that Judas pollutes our table?"

Derrick put down his trencher and looked around as the chatter in the room quieted.

"Don't start," Johan warned beneath his breath.

Ignoring Johan, Marguerite smiled at the countess, who set her drinking bowl aside and met her gaze with calm eyes.

"In this hall sits the Countess Genevieve de Fontenay, the niece of Eustace de Boulogne—the same count who in September betrayed our most blessed king."

Soldiers murmured in astonishment at this news, glancing and commenting to one another. Brother Derrick looked at Johan expectantly before gazing across the room at the countess.

Marguerite quickly told everyone the details of Eustace's failed invasion and treason. "William vows to crush Eustace," she said. "He will be tried and condemned for treason. By custom, those who joined in his betrayal and those associated by kinship or foreknowledge, are also deemed traitors. The Norman penalty for treason is perpetual imprisonment, is it not, Johan?"

Johan remained silent.

Marguerite hoped to see the countess flush in disgrace—or squirm in fear, but the woman gazed at her with guileless eyes. Dullard! Marguerite thought, very nearly purring.

Warned and armed," Elise smiled at Hortense upon returning to her chamber. "Thank you."

Yesterday, Hortense, invisible as a flea in the rushes, sat in a dim corner of the hall embroidering and listening to Johan tell Gilbert all about the Dover invasion, which she had repeated to Elise.

Hortense grunted now, carding wool energetically in her ire. "Have no fear. If William intended to arrest you, the regents would have summoned you months ago, shortly after Eustace fled."

"Yes," Elise said, picking up her distaff and spindle. "But why betray William? Why invade Dover?"

Hortense locked the carders and looked up. "I've been thinking of that all day. Years ago, Eustace provoked a violent encounter in Dover, a ploy he used to have his foes the Godwins exiled. Eustace may have expected Dover as his reward for financing William's invasion. With his ports in Calais and Boulogne, he would control the shortest shipping route across the Narrow Sea."

"William would never let him have it," Elise said, spinning yarn.

"That may be why he invaded."

"Why would he sever his alliance now?"

"Eustace seizes opportunity," Hortense said, carding again. "William has been away since February or March. He might never return."

Drawing forth wisps of wool, Elise recalled Brian Dubec's warning about shifting loyalties. She did not think that William's brothers and the men, like her husband, raised from obscurity, would abandon William—yet. Nor would the border lords in Normandie, especially when William was there, especially if long-standing conflicts with Flanders, Brittany, and Francia resumed. She knew little of the kingdoms surrounding this island but had no doubt avaricious eyes would gaze warmly on English land, and William's absence left it assailable.

"Eustace thinks William is weak," Elise said. "That he cannot hold his kingdom."

Hortense looked intently at Elise. "He may have reason to believe so. If William loses his crown, we would be trapped among hostile peoples."

"My husband may protect us," Elise said sardonically.

"He might," Hortense said. "He, too, is related to Eustace now by marriage, a point Marguerite ignores in her zeal. If Stafford falters or withdraws his alliance, we would all go down with him. That is why you must prepare to act, no matter what happens."

The following morning, Johan summoned Elise to his antechamber, a private room in the new hall he now used to administer Alaric's estates. There she found Brother Derrick, Gilbert, and Johan waiting for her.

"God's day," she said to them.

"Lady Stafford," Johan began. "In light of the events revealed last night, I must ask if you had any foreknowledge of your uncle's intention toward Dover."

"And how would I have known my uncle's plan, Johan?" she asked.

"Has he sent me any letters? If so, I have not received them, for you withhold all my correspondence." She looked slowly from one man to the other. Derrick's eyes turned away, Gilbert's usual cool gaze did not flicker. Johan's impassive expression held.

"No, Johan," she said firmly, "I did not know what Eustace planned."

"Did your sister's letter reveal this plot?"

"I did not see my sister's letter. You could show it to me now." *If you dare*, she thought. "As I recall," she said, "Marie's letter told me of her marriage and requested permission to visit me next spring. Has my husband granted this request?"

"He denied your request." Johan's fingers drummed nervously on his table.

"I see. What else do you wish to ask?"

"Would you . . . did you have plans to assist your uncle with his treason?"

Her heart pounded. "Do you, Johan de Vaux, before these witnesses now charge me with treason? If so, I demand an immediate escort to London where I may be formally charged, arraigned, and where I may present my defense to the king's court in accordance with my position, rank, and the king's law."

"That will not be necessary," Johan said. She and Johan stared at each other for a long moment. Finally, he nodded, "Thank you."

She left the antechamber, and, without stopping to grab a mantle, she fled from the hall out to the bailey searching for Jeoffroi. The wind had ceased, leaving an eerie, muffled silence. Thick clouds had settled low, a few snowflakes drifted down. Despite shivering in the icy air, she wanted desperately to ride out, away from accusing, speculative eyes.

"My lady," Johan called after her.

She spun to him, unable to contain her fury. He hurriedly approached her, his limp more conspicuous in his urgency. Huffing breathlessly, he stopped and offered her a cloak he had brought with him. She stared disdainfully at him. He glanced away, as if suddenly embarrassed, and back to her. "It grieves me to have caused you uneasiness. I—"

"Apology accepted. Do not speak of it again," Elise said sharply. Johan visibly recoiled. She turned to walk away.

"I . . . I feel obliged to ease the burden of your life here."

She whirled back toward him. "It is neither necessary nor wise," she said tersely. "I am enmeshed in a prison defined by my husband. The limits of that world are clear: you have your duties and responsibilities. You *execute* your duties and responsibilities."

"Yet, within my purview, I may provide you with reasonable comforts. Is there nothing, some small indulgence, a material change you desire?"

An escort to Fontenay! Did he think a bribe would make me forgive his accusation? She struggled against taking her anger out on him. Johan was merely her husband's vassal.

She looked at the thatched roofs, the palisades surrounding her. Johan had authority to grant or withdraw privileges. Over the last few months, he had allowed her to ride. He let Jeoffroi be her sole escort. She had met Frigga. She would not now jeopardize those precious gifts. Turning back to him, she said softly, "I will think on it, Johan."

First Monday of December 1067, Tutbury. Lord Stafford:

*T*he Countess denies having foreknowledge of Eustace's deceit. Her sister's missive contained no mention of their uncle. We have no evidence she intended to participate in Eustace's venture, had she known of it.

Perhaps you will deign to accept the gifts she made for you: woolen leggings and a magnificent cloak of black sable and scarlet Persian wool, materials provided by our Sicilian Normans that she brought with her to enrich you.

Chapter Thirty-Six

Elise accepted Johan's offer, and, with Hortense as intermediary, he gave them a few servants to assist in spinning, weaving, and other tasks they pursued. She continued to ride daily, a privilege she treasured dearly, especially since she felt more confined living at Tutbury Hall close to her jailers. Elise and Jeoffroi had gone to Frigga's Circle as often as weather permitted, and as often as they could without causing undue notice. Every time she entered the deep woods, her tension eased, and her excitement grew with every breath as if inhaling a precious, exotic perfume: freedom.

Cool December days muted the color of land and sky. A light snowfall softened the landscape, muffled sounds, and stirred everyone with wonder at the crisp, white cover until it melted. She had overcome all the fears about possessing forbidden knowledge. But to protect Hortense, she did not tell her about Frigga or what she did during her daily outings.

Today, as she and Jeoffroi returned to the castle, Elise saw the woods differently. She mentally repeated part of Frigga's song. *Hart's tongue nods among the moss, aside the lea cowslips cross. Neath oak and elm, beech and ash, Dog ears hide their deadly rash.* Now she could read the bark and recognize the markings of small animals. Once again, Jeoffroi had taken a slightly different route, a deer trail, and she appreciated his flawless sense of direction in these dense woods, especially when they emerged onto a familiar track and circled the village.

On Castle Road, they found an elderly monk struggling with a mule that had ceased to go further. He pulled on the animal's rope, but the beast planted his forelegs firmly in resistance. A young girl, carrying a basket of fish on her head, joined him. Using one hand to hold the basket steady, with her other she gestured to the monk who nodded vigorously. The girl took the rope and snapped the harness twice. The mule began moving, following the girl and the monk.

Elise watched curiously as the pair exchanged gestures. His hands and arms made grand movements, and with exaggerated facial expressions, the monk told the girl of his journey. Surprisingly, Elise understood his tale, though not a sound came from his lips. When she and Jeoffroi, still mounted, came abreast the couple, Elise asked slowly in French, "Do you understand him?" The girl blushed and looked down at her feet.

"Answer her ladyship!" Jeoffroi ordered.

The girl looked up and quickly dropped her eyes. She nodded, and in broken French, she said, "He . . . he quests . . . priory. I not know . . . is . . . where."

Elise studied the monk, a large, robust man, with slightly stooped shoulders, wearing brown, faded robes. He had a shiny bald head, a cherubic face that appeared to be missing eyebrows, pale, small eyes sunk into deep sockets, and red lips, which smiled broadly, revealing a gap between his front teeth.

"You, girl," Jeoffroi said. "Where are you going?"

She gestured up to the castle. "I . . . to work," she struggled in French. "Cookhouse."

Elise's gaze flickered over the girl, barely fourteen winters, she guessed. With a lowered face, the girl clutched the top of her tunic and trembled more from fear than from cold. Elise noticed the single black design on the back of the girl's hand, a mark identical to one of the figures atop a red post in Frigga's circle. "What is your name?"

"Serilda." She did not look up.

Ah. Elise recognized the name of Frigga's granddaughter. From Jeoffroi's impatience, she gathered he knew nothing about the girl.

"Come, Jeoffroi. Let us take the monk to Brother Derrick and the girl to the kitchens."

Elise told Hortense that the new kitchenmaid, young enough to train, could serve them exclusively as their personal servant. Hortense agreed. Johan granted her request and made a surprising request of his own: Elise's help in situating the tannery, which she fulfilled graciously.

Soon afterward, Johan noticed Serilda and the new monk, Brother Herluin, making Christmas wreaths in the great room. Arrested by her excited smile and accompanying dimples, he watched her hands wave and poke the air as she "spoke" with the mute.

"How did you learn his language?" Johan asked, approaching her.

She stiffened and her liveliness vanished immediately.

"Speak girl!" He ordered, annoyed that her bowed head and trembling body expressed such terror at his attention.

"It . . . *cumen*," she said in Saxon, her eyes down, her cheeks reddening.

"What comes?" Her diffidence frustrated him.

"Pictures with . . . hands." She blushed. "I did . . . wrong, my lord?"

"You certainly did!" Marguerite said, joining them. She glanced warily at Brother Herluin before pouncing on the girl. "Why are you in the hall? You belong outside in the kitchens with the others."

"Actually," Johan intervened, "the girl now serves Lady Stafford and her aunt."

"Why was I not consulted about this matter?"

"Because," Hortense said, emerging from her chamber, "the matter did not concern you." She joined Marguerite and Johan hovering over a terrified Serilda. "Go to her ladyship," she said to the girl.

Serilda hesitated in confusion. "Go on, girl." Hortense tipped her head.

"Stop!" Marguerite said.

Hortense turned to Johan. "Will you please inform your lordship's concubine that the girl belongs to me and her ladyship, or shall I do so. You can be sure I will not mince words."

"Why you—"

"Marguerite!" Johan grabbed her arm, blunting her strike.

Hortense nodded as Johan pulled Marguerite across the room to her chamber.

"You have no right to treat me so." Marguerite rubbed her arm where Johan's hand had held her. "And you certainly have no right determining where the servants work. That is my right as Alaric's chatelaine."

"There are exceptions to your rule. It was my decision to make. The girl serves the countess and her aunt, and that is final."

"What about that harridan? Are you going to let her insult me?"

"What insult?" Johan said, his voice rising along with his rage. "You are Alaric's concubine. Would you prefer whore or mistress instead? Neither word changes what you are, and Hortense will not be punished for speaking the truth."

Marguerite gave Johan a slow, easy smile and raised a single eyebrow.

"You disgust me." He turned and limped away. Annoyed and angry, he did not know why Marguerite's laughter irked him.

January 1068, Tutbury, Staffordshire

In January, the ceaseless wind atop the escarpment pierced even the thickest furs. Restless soldiers trained in the north outer bailey, servants struggled to work in frozen mud. Deadly accidents occurred all over the castle: a ladder broke, horses became lame, heavy icicles crashed onto skulls, a cook nearly severed his hand. Servants clashed with each other, soldiers brawled, and Gilbert's men thrashed people who had hoarded food. Tension within the hall became unbearable.

Elise had noticed a change in Marguerite. Despite the dozens of people always flowing in and out of the hall, Marguerite often sat alone near the fire, isolated in plain view, perhaps in a prison of her own making. These last days, she had been quieter, pensive, watching the activities in the hall as if distracted. Pregnant? Elise wondered, knowing Marguerite had been with Alaric less than three months ago.

Today, despite a crowded hall, Marguerite huddled beside the smoking fire, staring as if dazed. Lonely, thought Elise, recognizing the feeling. Marguerite closed her eyes, squeezing them tight as if trying to expunge a spiral of unwanted memories, and a slight shudder crossed her shoulders. Elise thought Marguerite looked like a frightened, vulnerable child. She suddenly remembered that Marguerite was near the age of Marie. A flush of compassion washed over her and dissolved quickly when Marguerite opened her eyes and caught Elise watching her. Instantly, Marguerite's eyes glistened in rage, and before she could speak, Elise slipped into her own chamber.

January 16, 1068, in the second year of King William's reign, Thorney Island. To Johan de Vaux:

I will ignore the pebble slung in your last letter and dismiss your scorn as the result of a painful leg, foul weather, or the strains of mediating between two hissing cats. Do not provoke me again.

Father Pierre died suddenly. I sent his wife and children to Herefordshire. Arrange for their support. A Norman monk scribes in his stead.

After King William returned to London, Eustace was tried in absentia and found guilty. The Norman penalty is perpetual imprisonment, death by English law if he ever returns. His English lands are forfeited. Through marriage, I am now related to a convicted traitor. My annulment petition will be submitted to the ecclesiastical council after Pentecost but, for now, William will not support it unless I can sway him to my cause. Your letters must provide details about the countess's activities, and despite your unease, search for evidence of a treasonous alliance with her uncle.

We marched to Exeter when the villagers withheld their oaths, but after more than two weeks, we could not breach the walls. The village surrendered when William confirmed Exeter's ancient privileges and accepted the customary crown fee in place of swearing fealty. We left a castle and garrison behind. William forbade pillaging under the surrender terms to constrain the zeal of his well-paid Mercian, Saxon, and Angle mercenaries.

Your responsibilities increase with my wealth. I received a manor

outside London's walls and one near Winchester. Both need attention.
Spare no expense. Along with these and other estates, more people depend
on me for their lives. See to it that good tenants are found for my new
lands. Discuss with Gilbert the protection of these holdings and how to
meet my knight's service obligations.

The king has granted a charter restoring Tutbury's mill. Build it to the
design sent with this missive. Roderick sends a wagon of goods plundered
before the king's ban, and deeds and twigs in lieu of livery, granting you
and Gilbert lands. These estates should provide you each with additional
resources to fulfill your military obligations to me.

January 1068, Tutbury, Staffordsire

Marguerite invited the monks to dine with them during this winter of scarcity. After one sparse meal, Elise, Hortense, and Serilda had together moved to the edge of the room. Hortense squinted as she taught Serilda Norman embroidery. Elise spun wool, aware maidservants scurried to avoid the pawing, grasping men or to refill beakers. Men gathered in small groups to gamble, some took carnal pleasures in dark corners. Others told bold stories, wrestled or engaged in contests.

Elise recognized a scathing laugh and looked for the source. Dogs were growling and drunk men spun Herluin around. Someone dumped a grease-soaked trencher on his bald head. A couple of soldiers held him fast, and another squeezed his jaw and used a piece of charred wood to mark eyebrows, a mustache, and beard on his face. One soldier grabbed a female slave, shoved her into Herluin's arms, and tripped them, so the monk fell atop the squirming girl.

Elise rose from her bench to intervene when Hortense grabbed her arm and pulled her back.

Stepping to the forefront herself, Hortense called out, "Gilbert fitz Gilbert!" Her commanding voice carried all the way across the hall.

Gilbert, talking with Brother Derrick, turned to Hortense as she moved toward him, her head lowered like a charging bull.

"I did not think you a cruel man, Lord Castellan. Yet, cruelty allows your men to denigrate a man of the cloth. Stop them immediately!" Hortense demanded.

Gilbert looked around, and with Brother Derrick following, he cut through the crowd, issuing soft orders. The soldiers disbursed. Derrick helped Herluin to rise, freeing him from his tormentors.

Marguerite watched from the high table. "That crone and her niece," she said to Johan sitting next to her, "by Alaric's order, have no say in his demesne." Marguerite turned to him as if expecting his concurrence.

"All are aware you are chatelaine here."

"All but you, it seems."

Johan studied her as she glared at him. She had lost none of her Nordic beauty: wide-set blue eyes, golden hair, wide, red lips. *Ah, Marguerite, what makes you so mean?* At his silent question, she looked away.

Alaric did not love this woman and would not care if someone else had her. Once, Johan had been tempted to test Marguerite's crusty temperament but, after his wife died, he no longer wanted a fiery beauty in his bed. He wanted a gentle woman, someone he did not have to fight all the time.

Johan's gaze slipped to Lady Stafford and quickly away.

"That monk is evil!" Marguerite gestured toward Herluin.

Johan looked at Herluin, who had slipped easily into the castle's life. He collected tithes and wove rushes. Herluin moved about the castle as if walking on the tips of his toes, appearing aimless, yet he could be found everywhere. He guessed Herluin to be near Hortense's age, late fifties, yet his cherubic face remained unlined, his expression as vacant, as bland as a feeble-minded child. Except for the tiny hisses slipping through his teeth like steam from a kettle, and an occasional grunt, he communicated only with gestures. Seeing him, some people burst out laughing, others—like Marguerite—crossed themselves in fear and scattered quickly out of his sight.

Tonight's incident was not unique. People often ridiculed Herluin, mimicked his bobbing head and gestures, and received applause for their perversions. Children tugged his belt, lifted his robes, played tricks on him. Johan frequently found him asleep sitting up in the hall, rocking to and fro. The poor monk would awaken to find thistles hung on his robe, weed brush tucked into his belt or eyebright sprinkled on him—charms against the evil eye. Through it all, as now, Herluin smiled innocently to everyone.

To Marguerite, he said, "We are all trapped here. Try to endure. If you cannot, shall I ask Alaric to send you to his London manor?"

She lowered her head and then looked up at him, her eyes brimming. "I am Alaric's servant as you are, Johan. Unlike you, I will be discarded when no longer needed. He placed me here to usurp her ladyship's authority. I must remain here to serve him."

Johan frowned, confused by the hurt in her eyes. She shook her head suddenly and gave him a hard smile before looking away.

Chapter Thirty-Seven

Sennight after the Feast of St. Valentinus.
To Alaric, Seigneur de Tutbierrie:

Ki**ing** William's couriers delivered a royal summons to your lady wife, commanding her attendance at the queen's coronation. Although William has invited his nobles and their ladies, this summons may signify the end of your marriage. The coronation and feast days of Pentecost will occur in May. Couriers informed us that you will remain in York over the festivities.

If William does not send Royal Guards to take the countess into custody, Gilbert, Marguerite, and I will deliver her to Westminster. Jeoffroi d'Ardain will maintain the castle's security in our absence. Unless William imprisons her, we will attend the countess at all times and see that she comports herself with the obedience and reverence worthy of your position. Anticipating your wishes, I will send you a report of her conduct, especially her meeting with the king and queen.

Here are the particulars I failed to include previously. The countess and her aunt share a small solar between their quarters. Lady Stafford wears a large mantle of thick cloth over her long tunics, thus, it is not easy to perceive either her visage or the features of her form. She appears to be thin as she slips easily between the farthermost back column and the wall in the great room. She comports herself with discretion, is deliberate

*in her speech, answering with few words. Not knowing Saxon, she turns
to her aunt for understanding. Servants have reported hearing laughter
between the countess and her aunt. This I cannot verify, for when their
solitude is breached, she presents a demure countenance, speaking few
words, eyes lowered, and with reverence, honor, and obedience to all.*

*She and her aunt are inseparable except when she rides with Jeoffroi
d'Ardain as weather permits. The villagers, though suspicious of her, seem
to enjoy her passing. She often purchases items such as ale, bread, or a ball
of cheese. With assistance from a few servants, she is making gifts for the
king and queen and spring gowns from the wool and linens she brought
with her. She selects modest hues, unlike those sewn for Marguerite, made
from the rich cloth and furs you have sent her. Your wife does not seek to
compete with Marguerite.*

*The winter on this stony rise is bleak. Daily, we send out hunters,
for we had a meager harvest, and strive to conserve the grain purchased
at Derby. The icy wind blows across our flat plane, gusting against our
shelters, howling like women finding their dead on the killing field.
We sit in the clouds. The valley is rarely visible from our precipice, and
when the clouds lift it appears gray or white, dusted in new snow. The
path winding around the castle is so deeply rutted we must walk our
horses. The villagers toiled to fortify their huts before true winter arrived.
Methinks the village, shielded by the woods, fares better than us atop this
barren flat.*

*After losing some sheep and villagers to wolves, we moved your flock.
Unlike Ewyas, the sheep have yet to begin shedding. I partitioned the
fields and established your lordship's boundaries, leaving the inferior land
for villagers. Last fall, livestock grazed on your fields to crop the weeds
and dung the land for the spring planting, which began when villagers
broke the soil after Plow Monday with Brother Derrick's blessings. Your
fields are furrowed. The fishers will build two fishponds and set traps, and
drying sheds will preserve food for winter months.*

*The new tanner and his family are pleased by the tanning implements
the countess provided. Derrick's monastic cell has grown to nine. The
newest, a Norman, Herluin de Lessay, neither speaks nor hears. I have
allowed the monks to charge the villagers fees for using the village well,
and have arranged support for Father Pierre's family.*

Gilbert sends small companies out to harass the villages to the West.

*His agents surveyed your new holdings and will situate garrisons as
needed. I have found reliable tenants to secure your knights service.*

Gilbert and I thank you for your endowments. I serve you as always.

February 1068, Tutbury, Staffordshire

Alone in her chamber, Elise teased out another pinch of fibers and
twirled the spindle, letting the whorl draw the fleece into yarn.
She played out more wool and gave the spindle another twist, though
her sticky fingers felt clumsy. Steam accompanied each breath, and she
shivered, despite wearing three woolen tunics and a fur-lined mantle.
An icicle hung in her chamber, where the plaster had cracked beneath
the window, shuttered since Christmas. Without a hint of the weak
midday sun, the burning wick beside her gave little light. It seemed a
precious gift, even when a draught quivered the delicate flame of her
last candle this winter.

Everyone else huddled around the central hearth in the great
room, wallowing in the lethargy of Lent. Servants and soldiers slept
on pallets, ignoring the smell of sheep occupying the pens. The more
people and animals in the room, the warmer, but they foolishly burned
green logs and she had fled the thick, black smoke.

She wound the yarn on the spindle and notched the thread.
Setting her work aside, she paced the room trying to release the talons
clutching her heart. How would the king punish her for Eustace's
deed? Imprisonment? Worse? She had time to prepare, and used it
well. But today, she felt neither the calm she presented to Hortense
nor the courage to face the king. Too late, she regretted the letter she'd
sent secretly via Frigga to her sister. Knowledge of such correspondence would surely condemn her. Ah, well, that was before the king's
summons. Now, her primary concern was Hortense.

She had to trust that Johan would keep his vow. Although he had
been kind to her from the beginning, last December, he had ques-
tioned her harshly about Eustace's treason, accusing her of collusion
and foreknowledge. Although they had not spoken to each other since
their angry exchange, she'd sensed that his regret had turned to affec-
tion. He'd buried it well—until the Royal couriers arrived.

In the privacy of his antechamber, he gave her the king's summons. She read it. Suddenly, Johan grabbed her arm, perhaps to steady her when she felt the ground beneath her vanish.

He stammered, "Let . . . let me hold—"

"—No need, good sir," she said curtly, forcing her trembling legs to hold her upright.

He released her immediately and stepped back.

"This summons may have lasting consequences," she said, gathering strength. "I beg you now, Johan, to use all the resources you have as seneschal to see Hortense returned safely to Normandie if . . . if I am detained."

"It may not—"

"Your word, Sir! Nothing more." She pinioned him with her gaze. Spurned by his silence, she turned toward the door.

"You have my word, Lady."

Her back to him, she nodded and left the room.

She had been very careful since. For she had longed to crawl into someone's arms to feel safe for just a moment. One word from her, one look, would be misunderstood. In these close confines, with their lives interwoven atop this barren rock, everyone knew all that transpired. Gossip bred of boredom spread like the wind. Innuendo twisted the most innocent encounters into salacious rendezvous. And Marguerite waited, like a vulture, for Elise to stumble.

If Elise survived William's court, if William lost his kingdom, or if Alaric betrayed him, Johan would help her and Hortense flee—but only if he remained seneschal, only if he retained access to Alaric's treasury. She must do nothing to jeopardize his position, yet she understood him.

Like most knights, men without women of their own, Johan was quickly enamored by one woman after another, believing each love truer than the one before. He does not know his own heart, she thought. To turn his attentions away from her, Johan needed his own woman. A wife.

Marguerite came to mind. Elise hoped nothing but rivalry lit the spark that crackled between them.

Perhaps, Elise thought, she could shift his attention to Serilda.

April 1068, Tutbury, Staffordshire

Do you think to frighten me?" Hortense asked Marguerite amid a tumultuous hall filled with servants preparing for the journey. Guards opened the doors to let a trio of servants carry a large bundle out to the wagons. An icy April wind swirled into the great room, billowing Hortense's fur mantle.

"You have something to fear," Marguerite said, burying her hands in her cloak. "Your niece may soon feel William's lash, and *you* will no longer dwell here."

"If so, his lordship will have no more use for you."

Marguerite smiled. "His lordship will keep me for a long time."

"Even when he learns of your involvement in the English girl's death?"

"Clare disobeyed orders and jeopardized the castle. She was duly punished."

"Truly?" Hortense said. "I wonder who told the girl her sisters were with the rebels?"

"I've wondered myself," Marguerite said.

"And who killed Johan's wife? Did you hope he would turn to you for comfort?"

Marguerite knew better than to deny these charges. "Johan's wife was known for witchery. Perchance she died by her own spell. Hardly a concern after all these years."

"Witnesses say otherwise," Hortense said.

"Witnesses? Lecherous soldiers? Aggrieved servants? Perhaps you repeat the drunken charge of a man I refused to bed. Lord Stafford will slice off his tongue. See to your niece, old woman, and disassociate yourself from idle whisperings."

"Ah, Marguerite," Hortense said, "your devilish deeds condemn you, and your fickle heart will hasten your ruin."

"Curb your reckless speech!" Marguerite said, her heart pounding. "All know the devil accuses the just. The finger that points belongs to Satan. The Pope has said so."

"Tell that to the bishops," Hortense said, turning toward her chamber.

"Oh," Marguerite said, causing Hortense to pause and turn back. "I believe some items were stolen from Lord Stafford's treasury. As you know, the penalty for such a crime is—severe. It would be easy to search everyone's quarters. I wonder why someone would hide stolen goods in their rooms where they could be so easily found."

Hortense smiled. "I and her ladyship would welcome a search. I've been told a torc belonging to the girl, Clare, was stolen. An attentive search would reveal the thief and recover the item."

"If a torc exists, it could be found anywhere." Marguerite parried. "You know how servants are. They misplace things and spread tales. The truth is so hard to discover, is it not?" She laughed and swept out of the great room and into the chapel.

In the dim small room lighted by a single candle, Marguerite walked toward the altar inhaling a faint, resinous aroma. She cursed that spiteful archer again. She would not sleep with him, even if he continued to spread rumors.

Long ago, she had learned that moral fortitude would not keep her safe—or alive. It was no surprise people believed the worst of her. People could not abide the truth. They would certainly never believe that Clare gave her the torc for safekeeping.

Marguerite was angry at herself for being careless, for letting her past surface the other morning when she had cradled a servant's newborn. The tiny infant, warm and soft, had provoked uncontrollable anguish and tears for the loss of her own murdered babe. Now, Marguerite recalled Hortense's sudden appearance. She'd dispersed the hostile, jeering crowd and took Marguerite to her quarters. Had Hortense followed her that day? Marguerite bristled, baffled and infuriated by Hortense, who had witnessed her unguarded moment, who hinted that she knew Marguerite's heart.

She knelt before the crucifix, clasping her trembling hands together, too frightened to pray, listening for sounds behind her. She hoped the old screeching bat would follow her into the chapel. She imagined it would be easy to dispose of Hortense here. *I heard a sound, I was frightened, I thought I was being attacked.* She envisioned her tearful plea to Johan and Gilbert as she stood over Hortense's fallen body, holding a bloody dagger in her hand. No, she thought, poison was more expedient.

Chapter Thirty-Eight

Before passing out of the castle's view, Elise glanced back up Burton Road to the tower. Despite her unease, she knew that Serilda would properly care for Hortense, too ill in recent days to travel. Now facing the road ahead, Elise reasoned that her aunt would be safer at Tutbury than at the king's court, especially if Elise were held hostage or worse.

Although she did not look forward to this trip, she could not suppress her joy at leaving the castle. Her retinue consisted of a long line of mounted soldiers, carts, packhorses, and baggage wagons. Johan and Gilbert led the way. Elise, refusing the dubious comfort of sharing a covered cart with Marguerite, rode instead upon her own white mare, which seemed as happy as she to get out of Tutbury.

Since Derrick remained behind with Jeoffroi, two young monks attended Johan. Despite Marguerite's objections, Johan had allowed Brother Herluin to accompany Elise. She relished his presence, for his odd grunts, grins, and twitches kept people away and gave her solace when considering the threat William's summons implied.

Still, she savored each day: the sudden hard rains, the cold winds, the dappled sun, and brilliant clouds as they traveled through woodlands, meadows, valleys, beside planted fields, into villages. Along the busy, crowded road, she discovered a peaceful, verdant land, unlike last year's encounters with hostile villagers. The people seemed to have accepted their Norman masters, stopping their work to watch their procession, made festive with flags and pennons.

During the journey, she recalled her cousin's coronation, the grandeur and solemnity, the intrigue and danger. Like Philip had done then, William would use Matilda's coronation to form new alliances, make trade agreements, bestow his largesse among his followers, grant privileges, land, and titles, and adjudicate legal cases. He would flatter and enrich his ecclesiastical partners, and assess the loyalty of his followers. There would be no room for ambivalence, no time to discern how the winds of William's fortune blew before casting lots. Allegiance would be demanded and reaffirmed. William would penalize those whose loyalty had cracked, as had Eustace's.

Eustace's treason would affect her. Suspicion always bubbled beneath the surface of elegant surroundings and gracious courtly rituals. Until the king moved against her, he and the court would treat her according to *her* rank and status, not Alaric's. Her every action and reaction, every word, sigh, expression would be observed, evaluated, and discussed, for she linked Alaric—the king's trusted commander—to Eustace and treachery. Likewise, the court would judge Alaric through his wife and followers.

It seemed that her jailers recognized this as well, even when the discomforts of weather and travel tended to spark bad tempers. The closer they got to London, the more courteous Johan and Gilbert became. Marguerite no longer shrieked at servants. Instead, she asked after Elise's comfort as if she were her personal handmaiden. A ploy, Elise thought, for gaining access to the greater nobles. Still, Marguerite had handpicked the women attending Elise. Marguerite's spies, she knew.

After nearly two weeks, they spotted Westminster's towers. Her tension swelled, especially when Royal Guards met her at the crossing.

"Greetings, Lady Stafford," the captain said, recognizing Stafford's pennons. He'd spoken directly to her, ignoring Johan and Gilbert.

"God's peace," she replied.

"Lodgings have been arranged for you and your party."

When they entered the palace gates, the royal bailiff himself greeted her. "Lady Stafford," he said, ordering servants to help her dismount. "The king and queen will be delighted you have graced them with your presence."

As he ushered Elise to her chambers, she introduced Johan and Gilbert before dispatching them to have servants unpack the baggage and garrison their soldiers. Marguerite followed along and held her tongue when Elise requested separate quarters for her. Even when the bailiff augmented Marguerite's handpicked servants with Norman noblewomen. William's spies, Elise knew.

She received the first clue of her husband's position at court when she entered the plush, comfortable quarters assigned to her: clean, gilded, colorful, draped, warm, and safe. She felt immediate relief to find herself a guest rather than a prisoner—for now.

May 1068, Westminster

On the eve of Pentecost, her jailers, accustomed to seeing her in drab clothing, gawked when she emerged from her chamber. Over a long azure shift, she wore a close-fitting emerald green cotte trimmed at the hem and sleeves in gold embroidery. Her crimson cloak bore an embroidered outline of a black wolf. The shoulder clasps, bejeweled with emeralds and rubies, matched the *filet* holding her silk veil in place and the studded chain girding her hips.

Accompanied by Marguerite, Johan, Gilbert, and four hand-maidens, Elise joined the noblemen and women gathered in King's Hall. Opulent in carved crystal hanging lights, gold and silver sconces, rich tapestries, and wall paintings, the room seemed a pale stage for the people dressed in brilliant colors, silks, samite, furs, and covered in glittering jewels.

Elise saw Abbot Juhel across the room, speaking with a bishop. She had not seen her kinsman since her betrothal, and when he noticed her, he smiled broadly and nodded a greeting. Knowing they would become reacquainted over these next days, she returned his greeting from afar.

Norman and English nobles mingled with emissaries from Francia, Rome, Germania, Scotia, Catalonia and elsewhere. People recognized her as Blackwolf's wife, and whispers preceded her. Some speculated

aloud about her lovers since all knew Alaric had left her alone for
months. Some smirked at Johan and Gilbert with knowing smiles.
Her glance prevented them from reacting. Johan and Gilbert, recent
mercenaries, were unacquainted with courtly traditions. She would
caution them to ignore these inferences, for these speculations, as well
as seduction and dalliance, were customary diversions at court.

Nearby, a group of young knights wagered as to whom among
them could bed her before week's end. One leered at her as she passed.
Another said bluntly, "I would never bed Eustace's niece. Why toss
away the king's confidence for the petals beneath a skirt?"

The comment sobered the knights and told Elise how deeply
Eustace's betrayal had affected the king and his court.

She caught a glimpse of Dreux Marchand de Ville, and . . . Roland!
She took a step toward her sister's husband but a tall, elegantly dressed
man stepped in front of her.

"Lady Stafford," he said.

She recognized this man. Moments before, she had seen him
laughing with the king and his brothers.

"Allow me to present myself. I am Count Guillaume d'Évreux.
Your cousin-in-marriage."

Unsure of her response, she studied the tall young man, seeing his
reddish-blond hair, thin facial features, and blue eyes.

"Ah," he said. "Clearly, Alaric never told you about me. I terrorized
him and his younger brother when they fostered with us. We are first
cousins."

"I see," she smiled. "Our lands flank the Seine, do they not?"

"Yes! You hold Fontenay in the Vexin," he said. "Have you been
to court before?"

"I've attended Philip's court, but this is my first time at William's."

"Well, perhaps you will find it tedious, although I think the ladies
tolerate it better than do we." He offered his arm and said, "Allow me
to exercise a familial privilege by escorting you."

As they began to walk, Johan, Gilbert, and Marguerite followed.
Guillaume stopped and gave them a condescending stare. Elise
dismissed all but two of William's spies. Immediately, her jailers
withdrew.

"Have you met the king?" Guillaume asked.

"Not yet." She said. "I will meet William and Matilda after the coronation."

"Ah, Matilda. It is good to have her here. She brings peace to the king."

At that extraordinary statement, Elise looked at Count d'Évreux as he watched the crowds and gestured silent greetings to his peers. He turned to her and said, "Perhaps you also bring peace to my cousin? With you, God and the king favored Alaric."

"My lord?"

He laughed. "It was a compliment, my lady. Alaric has grown in stature and esteem since he joined William. He has worked hard and fights hard. He is intelligent and an exacting commander. His troops are the most disciplined I have ever seen, even surpassing my own. Therefore, it surprised only a few that the king granted him favors. What surprised us all, however, is that even sight unseen my cousin was blessed by the selection of his bride."

"It was a match made in a dark room among men of great power."

"Yes," he said, "as was my own recent marriage to Countess Hewisa, daughter of William de Nevers."

"Is your wife here, my lord?"

"Yes, I shall introduce you tomorrow, for she is resting in our chamber this night. We are newly wed, and I would be honored if you befriended her. She is unused to Englelond, and the rebellions frighten her."

"Rebellions? It seemed peaceful traveling here."

"If Watling Street seemed peaceful, Alaric has made it so. Since Exeter last December, there have been no more uprisings and all is quiet throughout the kingdom."

"Even Dover?" she asked quietly.

His eyes twinkled in amusement. He steered her to a quiet corner of King's Hall where no one could hear them.

"Dover is safe for William," Guillaume said. "Eustace displeased him, as you well know. It was a raw betrayal and continues to irk the king. He will remember such deceit for a long time."

She nodded. "Has the betrayal tainted my husband?"

Count d'Évreux looked deeply into her eyes as if measuring the motive behind her question. "Your kinship to Eustace and to Philip causes envious lords to wonder if Alaric has ambitions of his own. We have not always been friends, he and I, but I respect him. Alaric paid a severe price to follow William. He left his family, who supported Harold Godwinson, and when they died, his choice tormented him. Our peers remember he was born in a border hamlet near Wales. They consider him an outlander, nothing more than a richly paid mercenary, and knowing his family's allegiance, they question his loyalty to William. They think Alaric loves his birthplace more than he loves the king, and they speculate what he would do if he had to choose between the two."

"What do *you* think, my lord?"

"Alaric is a man of fearsome loyalty. He stands with William because, without him, the kingdom would disintegrate into scattered provinces ruled by competing warlords."

"And what does the king think?"

"He knows Alaric to be true. But, if the rumors continue, the king may listen."

She nodded. Her husband's position was precarious. "Is the duchy well, my lord?"

"For now. William will try to unite Englelond and Normandie under one rule."

"An arduous task."

"Yes," he said. "He has named his eldest son Robert, now sixteen winters, heir to the duchy, but holds the reins tightly. In William's absence, the boy rules only through his mother."

"He is young."

"At sixteen, William was a formidable duke. Robert is called *le Courte-Heuse*. He is a weak shadow of his father, yet when the time comes, I will give him my fealty."

"What of King Philip. And the Vexin?" she asked, hiding her surprise that people had already judged Robert unable to fill his father's hose.

"Young Philip has been quiet," Guillaume said. "My soldiers patrol the borderlands of Francia along the River Epte. Count Ralph de Crépi of the Vexin and I conduct joint maneuvers. Every month I send a company of men across the Seine to train with his men. Perhaps your own soldiers can join our maneuvers as well?"

A test, she knew. Demonstrate loyalty to William by joining Évreux and Crépi to threaten Philip? Join with Crépi, now married to Philip's mother, the dowager queen, to threaten William?

"A worthwhile proposal," she said, deciding not to convey the request to Gilbert. It would alarm him as it should. In a proper alliance with Alaric, they would together explore the implications of these maneuvers. Excluded by his orders from estate matters, she would not interfere with Gilbert's constabulary responsibility.

Guillaume continued. "William believes Philip will seek alliances with Flanders and Maine."

She nearly groaned. Eustace, living beyond William's reach in Boulogne, would be right in the middle of any plan to flank the duchy with enemies. "And Brittany?"

"Tense but not likely to erupt soon. You have a new brother-in-marriage, Count Roland de Rennes?"

"Yes. I hope to speak to him about my sister."

"I think," Guillaume said, "Roland is not easily drawn to capricious plots, and although he is himself close to King Philip, he seeks an independent Brittany."

At his urging, they resumed walking along the edges of the vast room, nodding to men and women on the way, although lost in their own thoughts for a moment. She wondered why he had told her so much. Had he spoken truth? Had he a sinister purpose?

"Tell me, do you stand with your husband, my lady?"

"Do you doubt my allegiance to William?"

"Yes. For the same reasons you suspect mine." He laughed. "You need not look surprised, my lady. We have only just met, and you cannot know my intentions. William knows well *my* support."

"I stand with my husband and with his liege lord, King William," she said. She watched him assess her response.

He nodded as if he had decided to believe her. "I'm glad. Alaric needs an ally here at court. Come, let me introduce you to one of Alaric's enemies."

She met several members of King William's inner circle. The king's brothers eyed her cautiously. His seneschal Guillaume fitz Osbern's initial surprise shifted to speculation. Alain le Roux's glaring disfavor gave her pause and she surmised that he, the king's chief advisor, was her husband's principal adversary. A man whose enmity she must try to contain.

With skillful diplomacy, Guillaume extracted her quickly, and once away from the inner circle, he summarized each man's ties to the king, the kingdom and the duchy. He told her which men supported, resented, or were impartial to her husband. His lessons were insightful.

"Alaric is new to our world," he said. "My father stole his brother's birthright and left Alaric's father without title or land, an outcast from his noble roots. Alaric will need someone to caution him against possible intrigue, someone to teach him the subtler arts." He turned to her. "I trust you will guide him."

"I don't know how," she said, poignantly aware of the role denied her. "We do not see each other . . . often."

Guillaume smiled softly and shook his head. "It must torture him to leave you at all."

Chapter Thirty-Nine

She is running, running from the hideous screams, from Satan. He trips her, she falls. Torchlight exposes a person's face when the mask slips. She knows that face! It's not the devil. It's the face of . . .

Her eyes flew open, and she clutched at the linens of her bedding. Elise struggled for breath. Her heart pounded and sweat drenched her. The vision faded, leaving a hint of familiarity. She'd known that face, yet the memory had vanished now. She trembled, chilled from fear. She tried to swallow. A fleeting image came to her: a symbol on the devil's bare chest.

Her old, recurring dream was back.

May 1068, Westminster

Elise took her place in St. Peter's Church, with others of her rank. She studied the crossbeams and the golden candelabras flanking the royal box where William sat. Close enough to see his expressions, her gaze drifted over his russet hair and his resplendent white tunic and cloak of crimson samite woven with the golden lions of Normandie. He appeared to study the empty throne until his comportment shifted. He turned toward the chanting monks approaching the entrance. She knew the moment Matilda appeared, for his expression remained nearly unreadable, save his narrowing eyes. His gaze did not waver even when Matilda neared the altar.

Elise thought it odd that Matilda of Flanders wore white when brilliant colors expressed royal prerogative. Her cotte shimmered as she moved, and instead of colorful jewels, a wide band of pearls caught the light subtly, revealing a row of *fleur-de-lys* along the hem and at the cuffs of her close-fitting sleeves. Unconventionally, her two braids fell down her back and remained uncovered.

Matilda, who had already borne William several children, was now visibly pregnant. Five months, Elise guessed. She wondered if it were true that Matilda frequently opposed her formidable husband and if William had kept his fidelity all these years, even when apart.

Archbishop Ealdred of York anointed Matilda and, to Elise's astonishment, said that God had divinely placed her as queen, that she shared with the king all royal powers, and that her people were blessed by her power and her virtue. Watching William's unperturbed expression as comprehension flowed to those present, she searched her memory. She'd never heard of any king sharing his royal powers *equally* with his queen! Breathtaking, thought Elise, as the archbishop draped Matilda in a stunning golden robe, gave her the scepter and sword, and placed the heavily jeweled crown on her head.

After the mass, Elise joined the solemn procession to Westminster Palace. By the time she entered King's Hall, she found William and Matilda climbing the steps toward the royal table situated above the others. Near the top, they paused, side by side, and looked over the assemblage.

William's long arms and legs, his broad chest, and the sheer power emanating from his stance should have but, oddly, did not eclipse his delicate wife. Together, adorned with their sumptuous robes and crowns, they presented an extraordinary vision. Alone, Matilda climbed the last step to the dais. When she turned back to William, they were at eye level. He clasped her hands, and their gazes locked to each other. Elise held her breath. It was an astonishingly *personal* moment.

Trumpets broke the moment, and collective shouts arose in unison to acclaim Matilda. Moved by what she had seen, Elise quietly joined the festivities. Tomorrow, she would pay homage and come face to face with the king her uncle had betrayed.

T hey say he was thrown from his horse and had to walk through the woods that night." Three days later, in a pavilion beside the field, a noblewoman sitting beside Elise waved a fan as she spoke. "He passed a meadow. Saw the fairies dancing beneath the moonlight."

"Were they naked?" one of the men asked.

"Shh!" the matron hissed, and the others laughed.

Elise pressed her twitching lips together and glanced at her blushing new cousin-in-marriage, Hewisa de Nevers, Countess d'Évreux, one of the tallest women she had ever met.

"They say the Queen of the Fairies danced in the center, her long blond hair reached to her hips, it swayed as her bare feet . . ."

"They *were* naked—"

"And he fell to his knees, struck dumb by her beauty."

The women twittered, the men snickered. Surrounded by her peers, Elise sat beneath a multicolored canopy, eating fruit and listening to the gossip before the next game. Hewisa, a light-haired girl of fifteen years, glanced shyly at her husband, Count Guillaume d'Évreux. He smiled at her and patted her hand once. The gesture embarrassed Elise, though she knew not why. She looked across the field where Marguerite, Johan, and Gilbert were situated far from the king and queen.

"He married her, you know," a loud man bellowed. He sat on the bench behind them.

Another countess turned. "Who?"

"Edric!" He shouted. "Imagine the rebel, Edric the Wild, marrying the Queen of the Fairies! It's disgusting."

"It may be," another man said in a deep voice. "But the king sent for her."

"No!" They all laughed. "He didn't!"

"He did. He sent the Royal Guard to bring her to court." They sobered, shocked by the king's summons. Elise glanced at the king and queen sitting under the adjacent canopy, imagining a meeting between William and the fairy queen.

When they heard the short blasts of a horn, the men in their pavilion all took their leave, scurrying down to participate in the next event.

It was a warm, bright day, and Elise smiled, relishing the company of the women, their stories, and their laughter. These last days, she had learned a great deal about the situation across the Narrow Sea, throughout the kingdom, and which nobles revered her husband. And those who despised him. Trumpets blared, and all leaned forward to watch a small group of men ride about the field displaying their horsemanship.

"Shh! Look!" one of the women hissed. "*The Butcher.*" A hush fell over the women, and Elise saw their hard looks. Some, like Hewisa, seemed to shrink into their seats. Another woman with a pale face suddenly had bright red blotches on her cheeks. Her large black eyes glared at the figure on the field. Elise followed the woman's gaze and saw a man of medium build upon a tan horse, wearing a pale blue tunic. His blond hair seemed to glisten in the sun. From a distance, he looked neither handsome nor ugly. In silence, the women watched him race his horse with another around the obstacles placed in the field. He rode well, precisely, his horse well trained to dip and turn, to leap and rear.

"Who is this knight?" Elise said.

"A wife killer," one said.

"Silence, lest you be overheard," the matron said.

"It's true," another woman said.

"He is protected."

Elise noticed that as he completed turns and jumped one hurdle after another, the men in the pavilions and along the side of the field cheered, but few women uttered a sound.

"Who was his wife?" Elise asked, turning her iron wedding ring, already worn thin.

"A girl of nearly fourteen winters," the matron said. "Young despite her years. She argued with him, he beat her, she went home to her parents."

"Poor girl," one woman said.

"Foolish girl," another said.

"The Church," said the matron, "vindicated him."

"His *brother* vindicated him—"

"His brother, the bishop of Amiens," said another.

"He went to her parents' home," the matron explained, "and fetched her back. He tied her to the bed and quartered her. He sent the pieces to her relatives because they had sheltered her and hung the bloodied linens, like a flag, above his castle walls. The bishop said it was just punishment for leaving her husband."

"The Church concurred," said another woman. "They decreed that God gave him the right to punish his wife. Now, any of our husbands can do the same."

"Any man," the matron said, her voice hard and bitter, "who wants to remove a wife can merely claim she disobeyed or abandoned him. These days, the Church will burn her—so he need not stain his linens."

The women around Elise held their lips in tight, thin lines. Hewisa trembled.

In King's Hall that evening an elderly noble approached Elise and greeted Johan and Gilbert. She saw his gray hair and curious eyes as he smiled at her and introduced himself.

"I am Guillaume Malet, *vicomte* of Yorkshire," he said. "Your husband and I have been friends for many years as Johan and Gilbert, here, can attest."

She acknowledged him with a slight nod, making a deliberate effort to hide her alarm.

"Alaric protects York in my stead, allowing me to enjoy the festivities."

"How is my lord husband?"

"Stubborn," Malet said.

Startled, she laughed, noting that Johan and Gilbert exchanged glances. "Forgive me, my lord. I am not as well acquainted with Lord Stafford as you are."

"I know. Be patient. He—"

"Malet," Bishop Odo stepped beside Elise. "Pardon, Lady Stafford," he said urgently, "the king summons Malet to his private chamber."

"Of course," she said to the king's brother.

"I hope we will have another chance to talk," Malet said to Elise.

"I would like that," she responded. "If not, please give Lord Stafford my regards."

Malet smiled. He cuffed Johan's arm and nodded at Gilbert before he and the bishop departed. A curious encounter, she thought, watching them walk quickly toward the arched corridor at the end of the hall. She glanced at Johan and Gilbert, knowing neither would tell her about this man, his relationship to her husband, and to them, but did not fret. She had her own sources now and would ask them. She began to turn away when Abbot Juhel joined her.

"Genevieve," he smiled, panting slightly from exertion. "Forgive me. I was unable to meet with you until now. I'm glad to see you here."

"And I you, my lord Abbot. You were not so glad to see me at my betrothal," she teased, seeing Johan's surprise at her remark.

"Indeed, I was not." Juhel frowned, remembering, and smiled brightly again. "I hope marriage has tamed your willful spirit and that you have since found your husband suitable."

"My husband is quite satisfactory," she said, omitting he would continue to be so—as long as he stayed away.

"Excellent. Adhere to his wishes in all things, Genevieve," he said. "He has risen quickly. The king's brothers praise his military acumen, and he is likely to enrich your future. Come, my child, let us walk."

In all the years she had known the abbot, she had never seen him so buoyant. His smile glowed. Over the last few days, she had seen Juhel engage with many of William's prelates and magnates holding powerful positions in William's duchy and his kingdom. Even now, walking together, nearly everyone they passed acknowledged him.

"You have been busy these last days, my lord Abbot."

"Very. I still have much to do, but I have a few moments to become reacquainted with you. How do you find your new home, Genevieve?" Juhel asked.

"It is similar yet different from Francia. I miss Marie."

"Of course. No doubt your sister misses you, too."

"You traveled with the queen's entourage?" Elise asked.

"Yes, at William's request. He wants to reform the English Church."

It did not surprise her that King William would consult Juhel.

Besides one prominent bishop in Rome, Juhel was the preeminent voice of reform and the most passionate advocate for the movement. "Does Archbishop Stigand agree with the king's view?" she asked.

"He does not. To set the Church on a new course William will need a strong Archbishop in Canterbury."

She knew that Stigand held the office despite his multiple excommunications. That's why William had the fully ordained, consecrated Archbishop Eldred of York perform both coronations—to ensure that the king and his queen were sanction by an ordained priest.

"Will the king replace Stigand?"

"The pope supported William's invasion solely because he promised to remove Stigand, who had crowned the oath-breaker and usurper Harold," Juhel said. "I can only hope King William finds my devotion to the Church worthy of his service."

"Archbishop of Canterbury?"

"A strong church will make a strong kingdom. Whoever ascends to the position must find honor only in saving the Church."

Juhel's interest in the archbishopric should not have surprised her. Although prominently placed for the position, she at once realized the great benefit and the great risk such a blood tie would pose to herself and her husband.

"Are other Normans interested in reforms as well?" she asked.

"Indeed. Hugh de Lisieux and Lanfranc de Bec."

Both, she knew, had strong disadvantages, making Juhel's appointment more likely. "How fares Abbey Clarion?" she asked.

"It is well. The Abbess is aging." Juhel acknowledged another prelate and turned to her again. "Tell me, has your husband provided for your spiritual sustenance and that of your people?"

"The village is very small. We have a monastic cell."

"Um," he said, hardly listening, perhaps uninterested in the details of such an obscure place.

"We do not yet have a priest," she said, "but someday, when the village grows, there will be a church."

Mention of a priest renewed his attention. "Without a priest, you must return to Abbey Clarion for spiritual refreshment."

"No." She shook her head. "I will never go back to Clarion."

"Never, Genevieve?" He pressed his bottom lip between his thumb and forefinger in thought. "Clarion is a Godly house, a place of solitude and peace. Many a soul has rested in the embrace of the good sisters. And the abbess would give you a deep welcome."

"I will continue to support the abbey, of course, but I will not return."

"Forgive me, Genevieve," Juhel said, seeing a page cutting through the crowd towards him. "Perhaps we will meet again before I leave. May God's peace be with you, my child." He turned, and before she could wish him farewell, he quickly departed, greeting others along the way.

Chapter Forty

"Come with me to Rennes," Roland said the next day as they dined together in King's Hall. Amid all the council meetings, diplomatic engagements, and festivities, she and her brother-in-marriage finally had a chance to talk. Jongleurs and minstrels entertained the guests, and as others around them laughed and clapped, she and Roland continued their private talk.

"I cannot leave Hortense at Tutbury to face them alone," she said. "Besides, it would be misconstrued. You are Philip's envoy."

"You cannot stay in that *beast's* lair. Besides, you are in danger."

At Roland's fury, she remembered he had nearly crossed swords with Alaric once. "I am in no *immediate* danger." She glanced toward the king and queen before turning to Roland. "Please, you know I cannot."

She watched him wrestle with his urge to protect her, and the consequences they knew would follow her escape. Her assumed alliance with Eustace and Philip would be confirmed the moment she left Englelond with him. Roland would not care how her departure would affect her husband's place in William's court. But he and Elise both knew that although Eustace had little use for her once she crossed the Narrow Sea, Philip would use her against William. In response, William could march his troops into Brittany, quite possibly under Alaric's command.

Exasperated, Roland expelled his breath. "Very well," he said to her. "If you ever find you *must* leave, I will send Tristan to you. After leaving you at Tutbury last year, we took a nearly deserted track eastward across the land. Unencumbered with wagons and packhorses, we reached the coast in a few days. Though the route is dangerous, Tristan can reach you quickly."

"Thank you, Roland." His acquiescence relieved her, for Roland would defend her and Marie ferociously. Although she longed to see her sister again, such joys were minor these days.

"Are secret communiqués necessary?" He asked, referring to the letter she'd sent to Marie through Frigga. Beneath the table, he passed her Marie's answering letter, pulled from his sleeve.

She tucked the treasure into a hidden seam sewn into her cloak.

"Do they prevent you from sending and receiving letters? Even from your sister?"

"Yes," she said. "You would do the same if you thought Marie conspired against Philip."

Reluctantly, he agreed. She told him a little about Frigga and that the woman would help get her letters to Marie.

"Can you trust her?" he asked.

"Strangely enough, I can," she said. "And a monk may also help."

"Be careful. These are dangerous times. It would be easy to spring the trap of another's making."

She glanced out over the assemblage and saw Johan and Gilbert at a distance watching her carefully. She lifted her drinking bowl, saluted their vigilance, and drank.

Elise, Johan, and Gilbert rode the next morning with the king's hunting party into a nearby wood. The sky was not yet blue when the party came to a large clearing. The king held his falcon as the falconer removed the bird's straps. Elise and her escorts dismounted. Carrying her bow and quiver, she wandered to the edge of the clearing, and stood beneath a large oak tree. Johan and Gilbert followed. The king spoke gently to his bird, and all watched as he flung it to the sky. It circled up and up, higher, higher and shrieked from above. They all watched in awe the bird's graceful movement and felt its tension when it seemed to hover an instant before diving hard and fast from view. They waited and collectively sighed when the falcon reappeared. The party clapped as the king extended his arm and the falcon landed, his sharp talons clutching the thick leather arm brace.

"Do you know falconry?" Johan said.

"No." She had once hoped her husband would teach her, and through this diversion, they would learn to be together. Dismissing her thought, she turned to them.

"As the wife of your lord, I bid you hear me well." She had not meant to startle them with the authority in her voice. When they recovered, she continued, more softly.

"All rights accorded to me as Lord Stafford's wife have been severed by my husband. This I accept and have striven to obey his wishes. Things are different here, where I serve the king and queen on Lord Stafford's behalf, are they not?" She waited. Gilbert stared at her coldly. Johan gave her a reluctant nod.

"I assure you, after leaving the court, all things shall resume as they were. But until we leave, I shall exercise my lawful rights. In this regard, I bring one concern to your attention and ask only that you take action consistent with Lord Stafford's wishes.

"Marguerite d'Hesdins," she continued. Gilbert and Johan exchanged knowing, almost smirking glances.

"Do not misunderstand me!" Her voice commanded their immediate attention. "Marguerite attempts to dishonor me here at court. My debasement will smear Lord Stafford. Many of his peers, especially those envious of his sudden rise, would use scandal to demote him and lessen the king's regard. I seek no personal redress, only caution you such plots are in the making."

"Lady Stafford," Hewisa called. "Come, we will break our fast in the meadow."

Elise waved at Hewisa and left Johan and Gilbert to watch her.

*S*he is running, running. The girl's shrieks stop suddenly. She feels Satan's claws as he grabs her . . . His horns and hood fall away. His face blurs, but the mark on his chest . . . the mark nears her face.

*E*lise walked through King's Hall with her entourage, troubled by the persistent effects of her last dream. Despite the festivities, the dream had come to her every night, and had become more explicit.

Again last night, she jolted awake, sweating from the lingering horror, from the sights, smells, and sounds, especially the sound of her own screams. She knew the girl had been murdered.

She had made a dangerous decision and sent Abbot Juhel a message. Now, as she greeted her peers, she sought him out. Simultaneously, she and Juhel spotted each other and exchanged a mutual acknowledgement. He said something to his party and left them to join her, greeting others as he pressed through the crowd to her.

"Abbot Juhel," Elise said, her heart pounding.

"Genevieve," he smiled. "We meet again. I must soon record the council's meeting. What is this urgent matter you want to discuss?"

"Walk with me in the King's Garden?" she invited.

"Will this take long? I have people waiting for me."

"No." At her gesture, her entourage followed at a discreet distance. She and Juhel entered the garden.

Elise had carefully considered the risks of approaching Juhel. He had been her confessor and protector for years. But despite their kinship and once genuine affections, in recent years she and Juhel had had an unsettling, sometimes hostile relationship. Perhaps it stemmed from the lashings she had received that day he found her outside the cloister in her tree where she had taken refuge to escape the tedium of the abbey. Perhaps it stemmed from the time a young monk had spoken to her. She had scoured her memory to understand Juhel's murderous rage, for he had nearly killed the monk, so severe was his punishment. But encouraged by the warmth of their recent meeting, and now, with the mere hint of an archbishopric, she thought he had a powerful reason to help her.

"Have you finished your *Historia Ecclesiastica de Normandie*," she asked.

Juhel stopped walking and studied her. Immediately, she realized her error. His book was a sensitive topic. For decades, he had struggled with it, with the controversial, dangerously unpopular ecclesiastical thoughts, some verging on heresy. "You did not request a meeting to discuss my work, Genevieve."

She nodded, and they resumed their walk. "In recent days, I have experienced something that frightens me. I hope you will help me to dispel this . . . this fear."

"I am not your wet nurse, Genevieve. Unless it concerns the well being of your soul, you can find others to indulge you."

"Forgive me. I do not wish to offend you, Abbe," she said. "I only hope you will guide me to take the right course."

He motioned to a nearby bench at the edge of the garden. Before sitting, he glanced around to assure their privacy. "Speak."

"Over the years, I have been plagued by a peculiar nightmare. Please, do not judge my words as childish nonsense. The dream takes place in the Abbey's forest. There is a ritual, a fire. Men, perhaps demons, wear hooded cloaks, a stone slab, perhaps an altar. There is a girl. I know her. She was a year younger than I, a novice.

"The devil, Satan, robed, with horns protruding from his temples, leads the ceremony. He, and the others . . . *do* things to her." She looked pointedly at Juhel.

He stared at her in horror, which changed to disbelief.

"Her shrieks terrify me. I scream and run away. They chase me. Satan himself catches me, his claws . . ."

Juhel shook his head back and forth. "Genevieve—"

"Please, my Lord Abbot, Hear me." She glanced at Johan, watching them intently from a distance. Assured of their privacy, she continued. "In more recent dreams, Satan opens his cloak and presses me against his . . . his bare chest. He is branded. A strange symbol . . . a cross, I think."

"No!" he said, jumping to his feet. "No. You did not see this!"

She touched his sleeve, a plea. Juhel whipped his sleeve from her fingers. "This nightmare," she continued, "began at Abbey Clarion when I was not yet ten winters. The girl died in truth, but not from fever, as the Abbess said. She was murdered. I'm sure of it now. I saw it."

Juhel gazed about the garden. As if suddenly embarrassed at his public display, he sat back down. "*Saw* it?" he asked, his voice low and furious. "These visions, these dreams stem from you, from your own weak nature. Your sinful heart, your *carnal* desires. Oh, Genevieve, your soul is in great peril with these phantasms."

"And if my dream, my vision, is real," she said, "the villagers still practice ancient rituals, that—"

"Silence!" Juhel grabbed her arm and squeezed so hard she nearly cried out. He released her abruptly.

"You do not know what you imply with your reckless words!" he said. "I have served Abbey Clarion for years, working with the Abbess to build the two houses side by side. If pagan worship or *murder*, as you say, occurred there, the blame would rest on my shoulders. Even the hint of such evil would destroy me. Why? Why are you telling these . . . these lies? What do you want of me, Genevieve?"

"Your guidance."

"Guidance! You must repent for your wicked, evil thoughts. Confession, prayers, and penance."

"To whom should I speak, if not to you, my kinsman? My confessor? Who else should I ask to discover the truth?"

Juhel turned his face away.

"Dear Abbe," she said softly. "If this girl died a dozen years ago from pagan worship—"

"Blasphemy!" Juhel said.

"Or if evil resides near Abbey Clarion, someone must know of it. Who would *you* trust to seek the truth carefully, with discretion? Is there anyone who could discover the truth without destroying either your reputation or the Abbey's?"

"And if the truth is nothing more than your wicked heart?"

"Are there no prayers to dispel these visions?" she asked.

"You frighten me, Genevieve."

"I, too, am frightened," she whispered. "What priest will hear me? Who can perform a discreet mass without speaking or writing an incautious word that would harm you?"

She watched the implications of her words seep into Juhel's mind. He clasped the cross dangling on the chain at his chest and stared out at the garden. She saw the side of his cheek throbbing. He bowed his head, and his lips moved as if in deep thought or prayer. She waited, trembling inside.

"Have you told others of these manifestations?"

"Only Hortense, who resides with me at Tutbury."

"Your sister?"

"No."

He nodded. "I will arrange a private mass for you tonight in the small east chapel immediately after Matins. Go alone if you can. Do not interrupt me!" he said harshly. "There is no truth in your suspicions. As with all women, your weak mind is easily swayed by wicked imaginings. But you balance on the precipice of great danger. Anyone hearing you speak about these visions might think you a handmaiden of the devil. You well know the penalty for serving the devil."

She knew. The Church preferred a public burning.

He rubbed his forehead before putting his palm on her hand. "They do not know you as I do, Genevieve. They might assume you cavort with Lucifer, but *I* know you merely lack piety and devotion. You are far less reverent than your queen, far less virtuous than your impish and stubborn sister. Daily devotion will make you less susceptible to these incubi."

"And the girl? Pagans?"

"Yes, yes," he said, rising from the bench. "I will look into it myself when I return. I will purge you of these visions, and you need never again mention pagan worship at Abbey Clarion."

Chapter Forty-One

The next morning, Elise and her watchful servants, Marguerite's spies, walked about the King's Garden keeping their skirts from the wet verges along the paths. Rains had freshened the mid-May morning, releasing spicy scents, prompting her intense longing for Fontenay. She watched gray clouds gathering in the pale sky, floating lethargically to gloom, and adjusted her cloak against the cool breeze.

Last night, Brother Herluin had accompanied her to the small chapel. Waiting for Abbot Juhel, she had studied the royal arms marking Edward's tomb, the king before the usurper Harold, before William. She had thought the device too humble for a king: a golden crown topped a golden cross, surrounded by five golden doves on a dark blue background. But as her candle flickered, she saw that against the blue, the gold glistened, and the shimmering doves seemed to fly. The illusion took her breath away.

When Abbot Juhel arrived, he expressed fury at Herluin's presence, until Elise explained that the monk could neither hear nor speak. He stared at Herluin before beginning. She had expected hours of kneeling, or harsh penances. Instead, Juhel hurried through a series of simple prayers. As if distracted, he quickly dabbed oil on her forehead, and sprinkled her face with holy water, and ended by putting his hand heavily on her head. "You are purged of incautious dreams."

Her attempt to thank him received a brusque gesture of dismissal. "Go now, with God in your heart and *silence* on your lips."

Although she'd slept without dreams, now, bathed in morning sunlight, she reflected back to Juhel's parting glance at Herluin. An odd gaze, one she had not been able to read. Turning to inspect the King's Garden, she noticed a tall, blond man walking toward her. Raising her hand to shield her eyes, she recognized Dreux Marchand de Ville.

He smiled broadly as he approached. "My lady, what a pleasure to see you again. I trust you are well and that you find Englelond to your liking?"

She had seen him last almost exactly a year before, the night of her wedding, as he left the castle, nearly trampling her husband with his horse. *Had the rift between the two healed?* She smiled and answered. "I have seen little since I arrived, but the trip this spring was wonderful. You fare well yourself, my lord?"

"Yes." He rubbed his right elbow. "A bit sore from the sword, but all is well. May I walk with you?"

She glanced around the garden and saw Johan and Gilbert watching from an arched portico, and from across the garden Roland de Rennes, her brother-in-marriage, seemed interested in this meeting as well.

"My pleasure," she said as they turned and strolled down a path. "Have you been back to Normandie at all, my lord?"

"No, not since your betrothal," he said. "William has given me land near the eastern coast, and although I have a smallholding at Fécamp, my home is here now. And you, my lady?"

"I do not plan to return for many years. I reside at Tutbury, though it is still a crude settlement."

"Ah." Dreux glanced away and back to her with a slightly forced smile. "I had forgotten how barren Staffordshire is. Well, it will grow. Will you stay here long?"

"Only until the end of the festivities. I had not met either William or Matilda before the coronation."

"You made a deep impression, my lady."

"I had not intended to do so," she said.

"Didn't you?"

"I was more surprised at the appearance of William and Matilda together," she said, recalling William's large frame beside his petite queen. "It is . . . incongruous."

Dreux agreed. "Despite her size, Matilda rules the duchy with an iron staff when she must. As any good wife should."

"What of you, my lord? Have you taken a wife yet?"

At the question, Dreux looked away. His gaze moved over the tower and ramparts to the clouds for a moment before he turned pained eyes back to Elise. He stared at her as if expecting her to know something.

She frowned, about to apologize for her intrusive question when he answered.

"No, my lady. I chose a bride once but she died before we could speak the vows." He studied her a moment and shook his head. "In truth, when I think of the women I have met, you stand above them all." She felt the heat rise on her cheeks. "I have disturbed you, my lady," he said quickly.

"Forgive me or not," he continued, "but I have never forgotten you. You stir something deep in me. I wish I could have wed you myself."

Shocked by his bold statement, she looked into his eyes. "My lord, you jest with me. Perhaps you shall find a lady here at court." She gestured toward the King's Hall, turning from his intense scrutiny, painfully aware that Marguerite's spies had overheard this encounter and would repeat every word.

"Perhaps," Dreux said, watching her. "Perhaps I have already found her."

Startled, Elise looked at him again. He raised his eyebrows in speculation.

She broke away from his mesmerizing eyes, confused, feeling threatened somehow. As if reading her discomfort, Roland strode quickly across the garden to join her. He looked at Dreux as if expecting an explanation for giving offense.

"No need for introductions," Dreux said to Elise. "Count de Rennes and I met the night of your betrothal. You had just returned from Rome."

"I had," Roland said, measuring Dreux. "We discussed how William transported horses across the Narrow Sea for the invasion."

"Yes. As King Philip's envoy," Dreux said, "you no doubt brought his greetings to William and Matilda. And Philip's greetings to Lady Stafford?"

Roland stiffened at the implication that Philip would send a secret message to Elise or anyone else in William's kingdom. "Lady Stafford and I are now related through my marriage to her sister."

"Of course. I expected you would be," Dreux chuckled dryly. "Sooner than later. Please give my regards to your *bewitching* wife."

Elise nearly gasped. Dreux's comment skimmed the edge of insult.

"I will gladly convey your regards to my wife, the Countess de Rennes," said Roland. Marie's title set her far above Dreux's rank.

Elise heard the challenge in each man's voice, mystified by the swiftness and reason behind this volatile encounter. She watched Roland stroke one side of his dark mustache with a knuckle as his piercing blue eyes studied Dreux, who raised a single, amused pale yellow eyebrow in response.

As if sensing a brawl and eager to join the fray, Johan and Gilbert arrived and flanked Elise. Dreux's amusement faded, and he gave Johan and Gilbert icy glances.

"Have you a castle, my lord?" Elise asked Dreux quickly, diverting the conversation.

"Yes," he said to Elise. "My castle is located at a place called Thetford."

At the sound of bells marking the end of Morning Prayer, Dreux bowed. "I beg your leave, my lady. I must meet with the king. I hope we will have a chance to speak again." He nodded curtly at Roland, ignored Johan and Gilbert, and departed.

She hoped she would not see him again, aware her guardians seemed wrapped in pensive contemplation as everyone watched Dreux enter the hall.

From within a sheltered portico, Marguerite had seen Lady Stafford and Dreux in the garden. Experienced at seduction, Marguerite understood Dreux's intentions. Dreux, a powerful lieutenant very much like Alaric, was not married. Perhaps she could attract his interest.

As Dreux headed back to King's Hall, she threaded her way

through the crowds to intercept him. Feigning a trip, she bumped into him. Hands on her arms, he righted her.

"Forgive me," she said. "Thank you for your kind assistance, my lord. Have we met?"

He gave her a distracted nod, glancing in the direction of his errand. "I believe not." He turned to her. "Lady . . . ?"

"Marguerite d'Hesdins."

He nodded curtly. "Forgive me. I am summoned." He bowed quickly and left without introducing himself.

She watched his lithe body move quickly through the crowd. Intrigued by his haste, she followed him. He entered a small alcove, and letting the door nearly hide him, he glanced back. His searching gaze brushed over her as if she were invisible. Moving closer, she watched him slip inside. And just before the oak door closed, she saw Abbot Juhel pacing impatiently.

Marguerite stepped into a nearby recess intending to wait for Dreux to return, wondering what he and the abbot had to talk about in secret, for this assignation was clearly in secret. Did this meeting have to do with Lady Stafford? Marguerite's spies had told her Brother Herluin had accompanied her to a chapel last night, where she prayed with Juhel. Nothing strange in that, she supposed. But this morning, Dreux had approached the countess, and now Dreux and Juhel met.

Although she had not formally made Dreux's acquaintance, she knew he and Alaric had been close as brothers once. She'd discovered that one night in Alaric's arms as she stroked the scar on his palm and heard tales of their adventures and their blood bond. After witnessing the events following Clare's death, she had no doubt their friendship had ended. She doubted Dreux knew she was Alaric's mistress. Men rarely talked about such things, trading their women like slave girls between them.

"Well, well," a man said beside her.

Marguerite froze, recognizing the voice of her sister's husband. She slowly turned toward Raoul de Vere, realizing she was nearly trapped in this recess. Trying to swallow her alarm, she looked at this large, lavishly dressed man beside her.

"I had no idea you would grow into such a beauty, Marguerite. Have you no greeting for me after all these years?"

"Does my sister . . . live?" Marguerite asked, terrified to know the answer.

"Our Holy Father took my young wife to his bosom years ago, I'm afraid," he said, a grin on his face.

She had not thought her ten-year old sister would live long in his hands, yet she had prayed for her every day, begging God to give her the strength and courage to endure.

"You have traveled far to attend the coronation." She kept her voice calm.

"I have," he said, studying her. "William and Matilda are generous to me." He looked about the room. "You should come back to Normandie, dear sister. Your husband's brothers would *gladly* embrace you."

"God's day, my lord," she said, pushing her way past him. Walking away on shaking legs, she heard him chuckle behind her. *If I were a man, I would kill him right here, right now.* At a glance, her maid-servants appeared, giving her a temporary shield.

Reaching her quarters, Marguerite dismissed her servants and sat staring at the fire in the brazier. She folded her icy hands together, bracing herself as her long-buried memories returned in full: her rich ancestral home, her brave father and brothers who had died fighting for a young Duke William. Her widowed mother, alone, with two daughters the last of her dozen children.

At eleven, Marguerite had only a scant understanding of the events. She knew her mother had petitioned Duke William for per-mission to remarry a knight of his choosing, a man strong enough to defend their castle and fiefdom from raiding nobles. The duke granted permission for a marriage and gave the estate charters to de Vere, a knight of considerable substance. He and his retinue arrived one day amid trumpets, his flags whipping in the wind as her mother scurried to present a great feast.

Marguerite remembered her mother's relief, her eagerness to greet her new husband, to tell him of the defenses, the attacks being planned on the demesne. She'd expected to use her knowledge and experience to share, as she had with her first husband, the governance of her land. Instead, de Vere told all standing in the hall that he had come to marry her youngest daughter—a girl of ten winters.

Immediately after the wedding, hastily conducted that day, her mother left, under armed guard, for the nunnery. Marguerite never saw her again. One year later, when she had just turned twelve, de Vere stripped Marguerite of her large dowry and married her off to his vassal, a fifty-two-year-old knight.

She squeezed her eyes tight to shut out the vision of her little sister screaming as they dragged Marguerite away. Very quickly her memories spun to the day her own husband died. His brothers and their wives threw her from his holding. Foolishly, she'd sought help from merchants who raped her instead, although she was near her birthing time. Now, weeping softly, she recalled the stabbing labor pains, the nuns who cut her infant—piece by piece—out of her womb, the abbess clucking that they'd made her barren, for her sin of fornicating with the merchants, and the *pious* monk who used her butchered body that night.

Suddenly hearing herself sob, Marguerite stood up abruptly. Wiping her eyes, she shook her skirts and the memories away.

Her mother, her sister, and all the women she knew, perished at the whim of the men in their lives. But she would not. The brothers had tried. She'd fought them off. But now, preparing to return to the hall, she vowed: *They will never make me their whore. Never.*

It's true!" Hewisa said. "He is mad with love for you. He walks through King's Hall, making it obvious to everyone. His eyes glisten whenever he looks at you, and when asked, he does not deny it. He stutters and stares as if he is bewitched, and . . ."

"Hewisa! Please do not say such things. You know how quickly such rumors could reach my husband, and he might think I urged de Ville along." Elise ran her fingers through her unbraided hair. *What must the king think, and Matilda?*

Why is Dreux doing this, she wondered. Certainly, he flirted with her yesterday morning, but she gave him no encouragement. Marguerite! It's Marguerite's doing. Elise imagined the joy with which Marguerite must be spreading the gossip that sprang up within hours of that meeting.

"What will you do?" Hewisa asked. "You have to do *something*. The court is hissing with speculation. My husband is furious. He says knights wager how long it will take de Ville to have you, and he made Count Roland de Rennes leave early before he challenged de Ville for besmirching your reputation. Can you imagine what would happen if King Philip's envoy challenged one of King William's lieutenants?"

Elise squeezed her eyes shut. *Merciful God in Heaven. Roland!* There was an enormous difference between the casual gossip of the knights she encountered her first night and the gossip tied to a specific man. These rumors must stop immediately, she thought. Denial would only fan the talk. She could not expect anything but her husband's presence to quash the rumors. Unless . . . she thought. There must be a public rejection of Dreux. It was risky. A rejection confirmed an offer had been made. A delayed rejection meant an offer had been thought about—before being declined—as damning as acceptance. A desperate plan began to formulate in Elise's mind.

She turned to Hewisa. "I need your help. Promise me you will do as I say."

"Gladly," Hewisa nodded.

"My servants are in Marguerite d'Hesdins' purse. Let your servants overhear you telling your husband you heard that a mysterious noble-woman plans to meet Dreux tonight in the tent next to the King's pavilion. Tell him you suspect that I am the woman."

"You cannot, you . . ."

"Just tell him in front of your servants. They will tell my servants, who will tell Marguerite. If I am right, Marguerite will tell Dreux, and as many others as she can."

"But . . . ."

"Trust me, Hewisa, I will bring no shame to your husband or to mine. We shall leave tomorrow, and when we do, all thoughts of a tryst will cease."

"Oh, Genevieve. Be careful. If your husband believes you unfaithful, he could have you beaten or, or worse!"

Chapter Forty-Two

near the end of May, Alaric welcomed Malet back to York and received the king's instructions to build a castle at Warwick. Before leaving, he spent a few days showing Malet improvements he'd made to the town's fortifications and potential sites for a castle. After concluding their practical business, they decided to spend Alaric's last afternoon gaming, drinking, and talking of times past.

On their way to the brewer's, they hopped from one thatched eave to another, dodging torrential rains. Lightning flashed, nearly blinding them. Immediately thunder cracked, rumbled, and shook the timbered huts. Laughing at the terror evoked by the blast, with pounding hearts they ducked into the alehouse and settled down for a long afternoon near the fire.

Alaric watched Malet take off his cloak and noted the travel-weary lines about his face and that his hair was all gray now. He'd first brought news of King Edward's death to Ewyas. The two had fought together at Hastings. They'd buried Harold's body, and when Alaric discovered his family's corpses, Malet had seen to their burial and remained Alaric's steadfast ally. Alaric trusted him, as he would have trusted his own father.

Malet drank from his mazer and said, "I met your wife at the coronation."

Despite the closed shutters, lightning lit up the entire room for a moment, followed by another explosion. Alaric scanned the thatched roof, seeing no leaks but hearing the sizzling whisper of rain. By habit, the mention of his wife conjured up the memory of Goda's pock-marked face cackling as she pointed to the burned church.

"Some would say you are blessed," Malet said.

"Blessed? Hardly. She's a festering pustule I hope to squeeze from my life."

Malet nodded and began to describe the new armor worn by one of the Germanic princes who participated in the tournaments.

Alaric ignored Malet's diversion. "You heard Dubec repeating Eustace's boast about *raping* my mother and his tale about my family's death. After betraying the king, Eustace faces lifelong prison should William apprehend him. *The Kingmaker*, as his minions call him, and his niece, are known for their greed, ambition, and machinations. Together they erode my reputation."

He ran his hand through his damp hair. "At court, you must have heard the men of William's inner circle challenge my loyalty or spec-ulate that I would join Eustace in another treason."

"Yes. And some say you conspire with Edgar."

"Edgar Atheling of Wessex?"

Malet nodded.

Alaric flushed with impotent rage and let it go. He could not defend himself away from court.

"Few give those whispers credence," Malet said. "You have allies. Your wi—, your . . . cousins: King William and Guillaume d'Évreux."

Alaric nodded. "Is it true that Guillaume's father seized my father's lands and titles when Simeon won my mother?"

"Yes. And it is likely that Eustace took her in revenge."

Alaric touched his chest where the cross she gave him hung. "She is . . . was still beautiful."

"Beauty was the *least* of her virtues! Julienne was extremely intelli-gent and . . . No need to go into details, now," Malet said. "At the coronation, I was reminded that a good woman could be a great asset. William has Matilda. Your father had Julienne. You have Genevieve de Fontenay."

Alaric shook his head. "Tell me, do you *truly* think me blessed to have a possible traitor in my bed? A woman bearing the blood of my mother's rapist, my family's murderer?"

"You will judge that for yourself, Alaric. Repudiate her or not, no matter what you do to secure William's kingdom, some will always distrust you or work against you. Learn to recognize your true enemies."

June 1068, Alrehede, Warwickshire

Johan's letter finally caught up with Alaric in Alrehede where his men were building another castle for one of William's followers. As a monk read the letter aloud, Alaric turned his gaze from the tower rising on the new mound and looked out over the River Avon.

My lord, we have returned to Tutbury, which fared well under d'Ardain's command.

A large assemblage of lay and ecclesiastical magnates attended Matilda's coronation and festivities, resplendent with William's gold and silver. Embroidery, richly dressed servants, and magnificent feasts made deep impressions, as did the king's esteem for your service.

The countess comported herself with stately dignity throughout, especially when presented to the king and queen after Matilda's coronation. I believe this meeting important to your future and must convey it fully.

When the countess went before the king, a hush fell on those in attendance. All eyes studied William as he watched her cross the room. At first, he seemed most taken by her appearance. She approached the dais, knelt in obeisance, and with deep solemnity, proclaimed her fealty.

The king narrowed his eyes and, in a low voice, said, "Did your uncle forget all I have done for him?" His gaze raked slowly over everyone in the chamber as if he meant the question for all.

To the countess, he said, "I gave him rich English lands. I've sent soldiers to protect his borders, ships to strengthen his ports against Vikings. I reconciled a conflict between him and my father-in-marriage!" He rose from his throne, and some knights scattered as his voice boomed.

"Eustace swore before God an oath, a promise of fealty to me, as you do now. Does your promise shimmer in the light of my torches and sputter in the dark passageways of deceit?"

Alaric cringed as he heard the description. He knew William well. His brutal temper could terrify his most ferocious soldiers—himself included. He skipped another pebble as the monk continued.

I confess that I shook. Sweat trickled down Gilbert's temple, and I thought the king would have her slain there before us.

The countess neither blanched nor quaked at his question. Instead, she simply stated in a clear, unwavering voice that she deplored Eustace's betrayal, believing he did not know the value of the friendship he had frivolously discarded.

The king strode threateningly toward her. He demanded she look at him, and when she raised her face, it showed no fear. Not one tear.

Matilda stepped beside William. She asked the countess if she missed Fontenay.

Lady Stafford smiled and told the queen that she missed the blue flowers in the fields. She looked at the king and told him she expected such flowers to grow in Engleland if he would but command it to be so.

The king remained silent. His eyebrows twitched, then he threw back his head and burst out laughing. "Rise, Lady Stafford," he said, giving her his hand. "The Black Wolf's mate is as potent with her words as he is with his sword. Is she not, my queen?"

At the time, we did not know she referred to a Norse legend about a powerful and sage king. Where he ruled, blue flowers grew in the spring. In the land of blue flowers, there were peace and prosperity, justice and wisdom, and each of the king's commands resulted in another blue flower.

"Read that passage again," Alaric said, skipping stones on the river. His father had related the Norse tales, but he could not recall hearing such a story. How had she known it? He felt a trickle of admiration for the clever way she had turned the king's ire. His own experience had taught him that few could withstand the king's fury. The monk came again to the end of the passage. Alaric motioned him to read the rest of the letter.

During Whitsuntide, the countess engaged in conversations and private prayers with the queen and Abbot Juhel de Ponthieu of Clarion. She spent many hours in the new abbey. She and Dreux Marchand de Ville spoke together, briefly, about his castle at Thetford.

King Philip of France sent his envoy—Count Roland de Rennes, your new brother-in-marriage. Lady Stafford and her sister's husband dined in full view of Gilbert and me. Although we were not privy to their words, we believe no plots were contrived and are certain that no missives were exchanged, for Marguerite's spies found none in the countess's chamber or clothing. In the end, your wife was well received by William and especially by Matilda, having spent much time with the queen.

Marguerite was not well received. She sought to trick your wife into an amorous intrigue, but the rendezvous did not happen. Some people among the court may wish to tarnish your reputation, and Gilbert and I thought it best to keep the countess unblemished. We have resumed our daily patterns. Lady Stafford shows respect to all—even to Marguerite, who tries to provoke a brash retort.

I have seen to the enrichment of your London and Winchester manors. A new freeman miller will join us before harvest, and we returned with four boys, sons of your peers, who will foster with us. Gilbert already detests training his charges.

Alaric watched the monk lift his robes and hop over a mud-filled ditch heading back to the encampment. Johan had wisely thwarted Marguerite's schemes. As inexperienced as he with courtly intrigue, he wondered if the countess had counseled Johan and Gilbert about his enemies slithering among the king's favorites. William had not imprisoned her. The queen and Malet favored her. Why? Had she learned his intention to null the marriage? Had she sought royal favor to oppose it?

Alaric stood atop the ramparts of the newly built Warwick tower, watching two dozen riders approach.

"Check the gates," he said to Roderick, who pounded down the steps, taking a couple of sentries with him.

"Etienne!" Getting his man's attention, Alaric motioned to the archers. Etienne de Buci ran across the bailey shouting orders.

Alaric did not think these riders intended to attack, for they were riding too fast, and they were too few. He scanned the horizon for evidence that a larger force followed. Seeing none, he quickly glanced at the most vulnerable curtain walls, yet to be fortified, and the unfinished fosse, undetectable by the riders from the direction of their approach.

Shielding his eyes from the bright overcast sky, he watched the riders near. They slowed, and three men moved from the pack to the lead positions, flanked by standard bearers. He recognized the pennons.

"Satan's Curse," he said, signaling Roderick to open the gates before descending himself to the base of the tower to wait.

"God's Peace, Richard," Alaric said to the first knight who rode up to him.

"Stafford," Richard de Rupierre said, taking off his helmet and tossing it to a squire. "We bring a message from King William. I sincerely hope you have displeased him. It would give me great pleasure to see you drawn and quartered, my *lord*."

"Don't listen to him, Alaric," another rider said, dismounting. "He'd rather see you flayed alive."

"Picot!" Alaric grinned. "Did you bring wine?"

"Not for you," the third rider said, slowly walking his horse toward Alaric.

Alaric turned his gaze to Count Alain le Roux de Brittany. Since Alaric stood on the steps of the motte, he and Rufus, as Alaric called him, still mounted, were at eye level, meeting as equals, an advantage Alaric had planned.

The grooms and squires situated the horses and the rest of the retinue. Alaric ushered the three nobles into the tower, still fragrant with fresh cut oak. Roderick joined them. With a glance, Alaric cautioned him to hold his tongue no matter what these messengers said. Roderick stood behind Alaric, his legs spread and arms crossed as the others took their seats.

Alaric's favorite, Picot de Cussy, a young highborn noble with wealthy estates in Coutances, had joined William's venture for the joy of it, for he did not need more land or wealth. Richard de Rupierre had fought with Alaric at Hastings and maintained a harmlessly contentious acquaintance.

Le Roux, King William's advisor and Alaric's most vocal foe, tossed his mitts onto the table. "I am to hold you until the king arrives," he said.

"*Hold?*" Alaric asked. "Am I under arrest?"

"No," Richard said. "Though I await the day William throws you into one of his towers."

Le Roux's expression concurred. "The king arrives in a day or so. He has urgent questions," he said.

"About?"

"Edgar."

"The Atheling?" Alaric said.

"As only an English lover would say."

Alaric stared le Roux down, seeing his thick, red eyebrows slam together, forming a bar across his brow. Despite the count's proximity to the king, le Roux's brazen words revealed rather than concealed his weakness, evident now as his pale, freckled face reddened almost to the same ox-blood hue as his hair.

"What has Edgar done?" Alaric asked, supposing le Roux had initiated the rumors linking him to Edgar.

"He and his family fled to Scotia."

Alaric was not surprised. Edgar had no future in William's kingdom. Grandson of Edmund Ironside, he was the last surviving heir to the Wessex royal house of Cerdic, and Edward's nephew. After Hastings, the Witan chose him, a boy then barely fifteen, for their king. He was never crowned. To this day, the English called him prince and he remained the only credible rival to William's throne. Alaric knew the boy had no wealth, no soldiers, no command—and no support beyond the dreams of a disorganized, demoralized, defeated race. Unless . . .

"Has Edgar raised arms?" Alaric asked. Had King Malcolm of the Scots given Edgar troops to harass Northumbria for the summer?

"Picot and I will find out," Richard said, scratching lice at the edge of his scalp with his sword hand, which bore the mark of Thor's hammer. "We ride north tomorrow."

"You could have saved them the trip," le Roux said. "You were in York. You should have reported troop movements. Unless you were too busy inciting people to throw off their Norman shackles."

Alaric smiled. "Modesty requires that I refrain from taking such credit."

"My *lords*," Picot said as le Roux nearly lunged at Alaric. "The *king* will discover all when he arrives." He turned to Alaric, "Are there any women in this castle? I'm in need of entertainment."

Alaric grinned at Picot, a renowned ladies man, and ordered up food, ale, and slave girls. Awaiting sustenance, the travelers removed their armor, set their squires to polish their chainmail, and settled down to a relaxing night. As they ate, the conversation turned to their travels across the kingdom.

From couriers, Alaric had learned that the calm and unity displayed during the week of Matilda's coronation festivities ended abruptly when the earls Morcar and Edwin suddenly left the court. Afterward, William had sent his men throughout southern and middle shires to gather information about the state of his kingdom.

Now, nearly six weeks after the queen's coronation, his guests entertained him with tales of their unbroken travels. Richard had escorted various clerics to monasteries and churches throughout the south. Picot had escorted nobles north along the Severn. Le Roux remained silent, although Alaric had heard the count had traveled the southern coast. His guests did not reveal what Alaric already knew: unrest simmered all over the kingdom.

As night deepened, Roderick and several knights entertained the travelers with song and rhyme. Eventually, the travelers drifted to their pallets.

After making his last rounds, Alaric climbed atop the tower and spoke to the sentries. He sighted the squirrel constellation blinking between fast-moving clouds and gauged the wind speed and direction. Gazing slowly along the night-darkened horizon, he saw no moving lanterns guiding riders or an army on foot. The village was quiet, save the occasional barking dogs. In the bailey and along the fosse, people worked in the light of bonfires. He scratched his chest through his tunic and yawned.

"I'd like to skewer him," Roderick said, joining him.

"He'd like you to try, Roddy," Alaric said. "Raising arms against Rufus or anyone in the king's inner circle is a sure way to have me gutted."

"He resents William's regard for you. Will you take his place beside William?"

"Hardly," Alaric said. "I am one of William's workhorses, a knight with a company of experienced builders and a talent for getting villagers to swear allegiance."

"Since the beginning, le Roux has challenged your loyalty and your authority," Roderick said.

Alaric rubbed the crusted smoke from his eyes and sighted the silhouette of a distant landmark through a slit between the boards. He should ease off, he knew. Le Roux was too easy a target, too easy to rile, and Alaric took perverse pleasure in prickling his fragile skin.

"He wants to destroy you," Roderick said. "Can he?"

"Rufus is dangerous to anyone who gets in his way," Alaric said.

Recognize your true enemies, Malet had told him in York.

He and le Roux had been at each other since the eve of Hastings. It did not matter that Alaric's knowledge had saved many of le Roux's men. What mattered to le Roux was that Alaric, then a lowly, unknown mercenary, had contradicted him, a highborn count, and that his men had followed Alaric's counsel instead of le Roux's orders.

He bit off the ragged edge of his thumbnail and spit it over the parapet. Rufus cared nothing for the people, the land, or for the kingdom's future. He sought only personal enrichment. As William's guard dog, Rufus attacked anyone edging too close to the king. Thus, when le Roux learned that Alaric was William's blood kin—and his own—when William gave Alaric land and titles he had not yet given to others, le Roux's hatred became deadly. With the king's favor and attention, Alaric was closer to William than le Roux—a fawning flatterer with brawn instead of brains.

"After you left, le Roux said your wife was annoying as a boil on his arse. Richard teased him, saying it was because she waved your banner in his face."

Alaric did not want to think about her but inwardly smiled, pleased she had gotten under le Roux's skin.

"I've won another purse off Neel," Roderick said.

Alaric laughed. Neel, Picot's man, and Roderick had an ongoing, semi-friendly competition, betting on any number of things: how many bees in a hive, how many men a whore could take in one night, how far either could spit, throw their lances, and so on.

"William has not been this far north before," Roderick said.

"He has not."

"Maybe he wants to see what he has won."

"Or what he has to lose."

The words surprised him as well as Roderick. "The desertion of Morcar and Edwin blurs our future." The earls of Northumbria and Mercia had renounced their fealty a few weeks ago. An ending? Or a beginning?

Roderick stepped into the bowman's niche and loosened his braies. "William should have spiked their heads at Lud's Gate," said Roderick, pissing through the slit. "Isn't that how it's done? Kill the leaders?"

"He hasn't done it yet. The only person he's threatened to execute is Eustace if he ever returns. Besides, he made a vow. Have you forgotten?"

"No," Roderick said, adjusting his clothing. "I just don't agree with it,"

Neither did most of William's followers, thought Alaric. Since becoming king, he had prohibited execution or mass killings, and last Christmas, he banned pillaging. Churches and monasteries remained safe and untouched. Although Normans conscripted villagers for hard labor and appropriated existing slaves, he prohibited his men from enslaving or selling the vanquished English.

William's constraints disgusted and angered his own followers who took liberties in their lust for more land, more wealth, more power.

Chapter Forty-Three

William arrived two days later with Henri de Beaumont in tow. "I've given Warwick to Henri. Brief him," William said to Alaric. He added, "Join us in Council this afternoon."

Alaric watched the king depart, troubled by William's abrupt manner, and turned to Beaumont.

"Your counsel is unnecessary," Beaumont bristled.

Alaric knew Beaumont had never been to Englelond before the invasion, and had spent the intervening months in or near Westminster. He'd never built a castle, had no Saxon language nor cared to learn. Despite Beaumont's hostility, Alaric shook sand over a table and drew a map roughly showing him the castle's location.

"These are the King's Roads, the main roads," he said, pointing to where the Fosse Way and Watling Street crossed. "They must be patrolled regularly and remain open at all times."

"I know my duty as castellan, Stafford. Better than you."

Alaric ignored the jibe and told Beaumont about the people, the surrounding territory, the rivers, Arden woodlands, villages.

"No different from Norman land," Beaumont said. "And I need no reminder that I rule over inferior people."

Without comment, Alaric cleared the sand and drew a layout of the timbered castle, the largest he had ever built. He pointed out the gates, the bailey, kitchens, bakehouse, storage sheds, armories and such, and told him about the palisade needing completion.

"These should have been finished before I arrived," Beaumont said. "Your incompetence is staggering."

Just then, Roderick arrived with a breathless, richly dressed noble. The man glanced at Alaric and creased his brow in confusion.

"Why is this maggot polluting my castle?" Beaumont asked, glaring at Alaric.

"I invited him," Alaric said. "He is a prominent burgess. He governs the village, owns large estates, and ranks above the thegns, the noblemen-warriors, other men of property who provide military service to the king. He and the *gerefa*, the village reeve, are important men who can assist you."

"*Men of property?*" Beaumont said. "I rule above them. They will keep their land if *I* so wish."

"By William's grace," Alaric said. "Only those earls and thegns who fought against him at Hastings, or who raise arms against him now he is king, will lose their lands. The men in this shire hold land of the old kings. They did not fight against us, and unless they resist you with arms, they are to retain their lands."

"Is that so?" Beaumont strutted around the old man and drew his seax. "Tell me," he said to Alaric, using the tip of his short sword to lift up the villager's knee-length, gold-embroidered tunic. "Do you think this lazy, ignorant *English* cur will do my bidding?"

"I do," Alaric said, although he did not think the villager lazy or ignorant.

"We shall see." Beaumont turned to the burgess. "Kneel before me, you reeking turd. And *kiss* my boot."

The villager blinked and turned to Alaric.

"Obey *me*, not him!" Beaumont's anger exploded, and he thrust his sword at the man's gut.

Alaric blunted the thrust by shoving Beaumont off balance into Roderick, who righted him. Beaumont's men all stiffened, hands on their hilts. The castellan's face reddened in fury as he whirled, grazing the tip of his sword across Alaric's tunic.

"He does not understand our Frankish tongue," Alaric said, watching Beaumont's jaw saw back and forth as if deciding whether to slay him or not. Without taking his eyes off Beaumont, Alaric repeated the command to the elder in Saxon.

After the slightest hesitation, the elder fell to his knees and bent to kiss Beaumont's boots. Beaumont kicked the elder in the face, sending him sprawling. Alaric's glance checked Roderick's reaction. Beaumont's armed men outnumbered them.

"Round up all the villagers," Beaumont ordered his men as he sheathed his sword, "for hard labor. Including this . . . burgess." To Alaric, he said, "These churls will obey their Norman masters whether they understand our French or not. The whip is *all* they need to understand."

Alaric turned to leave.

"One more thing, Blackwolf of *Ewyas*," Beaumont said, mockingly. "Were you not under the king's protection, I would have you whipped for putting your hand on me."

"I'm a knight sworn to defend the king and his *kingdom*," Alaric said. "Even from Normans who forget the king's wishes."

"God gave Normans the right to rule the English," Beaumont said.

"You tarnish God's gift," Alaric said. "The people will submit from good sense and loyalty, not from terror. They will revere William for bringing peace to the land."

"My lash will bring peace," Beaumont said.

Alaric shook his head. "You rode with us to Exeter. Even after the village resisted, William showed us how to be generous to the people, how to acknowledge ancient practice and traditions and gain the people's abidance. We can do no less in our own shires."

"And we butchered all those armed forces having the audacity to rebel. We built a castle to control the villagers, and I can assure you that the castellan rules the people as I intend to rule my land—with the lash, the sword, and heads posted at the gates. Now, get out of *my* tower, Stafford."

Alaric stared at Beaumont for a count of three. "May God's peace be with you, Henri," he said softly before departing.

Alaric and Roderick crossed the bailey together and gathered his company commanders. "Pull our men from the work gangs and have them prepare to march," Alaric said. "Pack your own gear and be ready to move as soon as we receive orders."

"The master builders," one of his men said, "have questions about the main gates."

"Have them turn over construction to Beaumont's men, and tell them to refer all questions to the castellan," Alaric said. "He's in charge now. Have the builders collect, pack and load their rods, plumbs, pulleys—especially the ropes—and all their tools."

After dispersing his captains, he and Roderick continued to the garrisons.

"Can't get out of here fast enough, eh?" Roderick said. "Where to next?"

"We'll know after William's council."

"Will Beaumont squawk to the king?" Roderick asked.

"Like starlings defending a nest? No. The Beaumont brothers support the king, but neither agrees with his methods for pacifying the people. Both would rather cut off the noses of the people who will feed them than acknowledge the benefit of keeping the villagers alive and well."

"William's soldiers say we may be fighting in the North," Roderick said.

"It's been a while." Alaric whistled to a couple of his men, motioning them to the garrisons. "We've not met armed troops or killed anyone for months."

"I'm getting rusty," Roderick said, kicking chickens aside. "We've been on the march for more than a year, and all we've done is build castles along the way. Except for chasing Edric last fall and the December siege at Exeter, it's been quiet. And since William's prohibition, we can't even go a raiding anymore."

"Perhaps we're to settle the land, Roddy," Alaric said. "Even the Danes who invaded in years past knew to stop killing and pillaging and to start plowing and harvesting."

"You don't think it's over," Roderick said.

"No. I don't."

Alaric joined William and a dozen of the king's magnates, including Alain le Roux and Henri de Beaumont. From the moment he entered the room, Alaric felt William's eyes tracking him, and once settled, he glanced at the king, unable to read his expression. Curious? Annoyed? Furious? Alaric approached the boards with caution and sat on a bench along the back wall, opposite William.

"Since my coronation," William began, "the scattered rebellions, mostly in the southland, have all been suppressed."

The counselors applauded with grunts.

"Castles built along the borders have secured the kingdom. Eustace, who failed to take Dover, is hiding in Boulogne. Edric, the so-called Wild Man of *Shropshire*, Stafford's neighbor, lives in trees."

A few men chuckled, others glanced at Alaric.

"Harold's bastard sons seek alliances abroad. Except for the annual spring raids, the Welsh are subdued, and although longships patrol the coasts, they seem to have forgotten us."

William smiled, and several men laughed.

"Nearly all of the old kingdoms are mine," William said. "But I was told once," he looked at Alaric, "that Edward King could not keep York loyal or free from raiders."

Impressed by the king's recollection of his warning, Alaric nodded. None of those present knew York's hostility, the fierce people, confident that their ancient kingdoms exempted them from Norman rule.

"Queen Matilda and I will travel to York. We will demonstrate the advantages of kneeling to our royal prerogatives. I will build a strong castle and also confirm the new earl of Northumbria."

Someone hissed.

Alaric tried to discern the king's thoughts. His prized English earls, Morcar and Edwin, had revoked their fealty. Their sudden departure would have stung William. He had let them retain their wealth and earldoms, and kept them at court as his *guests*. He'd taken the earls and anyone else who might stir rebellion with him to Rouen on his victory voyage, where they stayed in bejeweled captivity until they all returned last December. Perhaps William hoped they would see resistance as futile, that their only future was to accept Norman dominance and his generosity.

Their flight did not surprise Alaric. He knew the proud, strong people, the ancient lineages, the blood of the old kingdoms pulsing throughout this land. The earls would have watched and waited for the moment when they could trade riches for freedom.

Where were they now? Alaric wondered. Thegns would flock to them. If they again proffered Edgar Atheling for king, they could amass a large enough force to counter William. Where would they gather? Northumbria. But he knew little about the province, nothing of the western moors or the lands called Cumbria.

"I am told," William said to Alaric, "you are acquainted with Edgar of Wessex."

Alain le Roux snorted.

"I know *of* him," Alaric said, ignoring le Roux.

"Tell us about him."

Alaric related the boy's lineage, his family, guessing his age at sixteen.

"Have you met him?"

"No. I saw him from afar once. Three, four years ago."

"Describe him."

"Tan hair, a small frame . . . " He shook his head. "Nothing else."

William studied him a moment. "Perhaps it is time for you to meet this . . . *prince* as you are known to call him."

Meet him or kill him? Alaric wondered.

Chapter Forty-Four

Alaric hated this kind of mission, he thought, as heavy rain beat down on his thick leather cloak. Summer in Scotia land. He shivered and turned in his saddle to glance back at his entourage: a long line of mounted men, packhorses, warhorses, and one carriage. Alaric smelled moss, fetid grasses, musky, wet wool . . . and danger.

Roderick and Etienne rode silently beside him. He felt their increasing unease as they all trekked farther north than they had ever been. Unused to this territory, he had been tense, listening, watching as they traveled through the densely wooded lands—Ghost Country, he had been told. He knew it to be true as giant, misty shadows appeared in the thickets and disappeared suddenly, making their trained horses skittish as young colts and compelling the bishops to wave their crosses and chant prayers against the trolls and elves and demons.

Besides the specters, summer offered thick leafy cover for those intending ambush. Along the journey, they had passed few travelers. Merchants and bandits might wait for better weather. Rain, however, would not deter armed warriors following their climb up into the colder realms. Etienne, his best tracker, had seen signs of riders following their progress, although they remained well out of sight.

Alaric's relief at leaving the woods this morning was quickly replaced by a different concern, for now they rode fully exposed through the grassy plains stretching before them to the jagged horizon. His scouts traveled a horn blow ahead of the vanguard, and Etienne's men backtracked the rear guard. Alaric glanced again at the banners bearing Alain le Roux's device and those bearing holy crosses and knew neither would give them safe passage through Alba, for he had little confidence in the dubious protection of royal messengers.

Le Roux and two bishops, all appropriately neutral ambassadors, carried William's message to King Malcolm. William had put Alaric and Alain le Roux in an awkward situation. Because he held English estates and a related title, Alaric outranked le Roux, who had yet to receive either. Although the count and his men answered to Alaric, the king had put the delicate mission entirely in le Roux's hands. Alaric would accompany him everywhere: when he met Malcolm, when he mingled with Malcolm's royal court, to the privy. He would even sleep in le Roux's chamber.

"Jesu!" Roderick cursed and spurred his horse forward.

Alaric looked ahead, barely able to see the advance guard through the rain. To ease the blow of being outranked, Alaric had given le Roux's steadfast captain, Jagu the Tall, the honor of leading the vanguard. Now, he saw the lead horses slow their pace and watched Roderick racing past them to meet the scouts galloping back.

A few moments later, Roderick and Gawain, Alaric's Welsh scout, reined in beside Alaric.

Gawain pointed to the ridge they approached. "The road winds through a narrow pass. Armed men block the far end of the passage. The vanguard awaits your orders."

"Malcolm's forces?" Alaric asked.

Gawain shook his head. "Rogue warriors."

Alaric had hoped to avoid such an encounter. He tipped his head at Roderick, who immediately rode back along the line of soldiers whistling signals. Several dozen riders broke rank and split up. Alaric and the main body of men continued along the road with a new formation. The horns signaled instructions to both the vanguard and the rear guard.

Le Roux left the center of the pack and joined Alaric. "What is amiss?" he asked, watching the knights shift their positions.

"We have company." Alaric gazed at the ridge.

"We are in Scotia. Our orders are not to engage. No hostilities!" le Roux said.

"My orders are to protect you and the bishops. If they attack, we kill them." Alaric turned to his squire. "Bring up the black." He would ride his warhorse for this task.

Alaric, with Roderick beside him, joined the vanguard just as they entered the narrow passage. It had stopped raining, though the clouds lay heavy in the sky, dragging misty fingers through the rocky crags.

After conferring with the vanguard's captain, Alaric took the lead, and quickly scanned the area. Their challengers had selected this place, perhaps, for its perceived advantages: a passage no wider than eight horses abreast, a sheer wall of rock on one side, on the other, a river raging down a steep ravine. A good site if both sides were on foot. Far better to force a skirmish in a field prepared with hidden traps, or stage an ambush in the woods, where hidden archers could easily kill horses unable to maneuver. Experienced warriors would know that in this small, narrow space, warhorses have the advantage.

At his signal, his retinue stopped. He walked his horse slowly toward the soldiers blocking the passage. By facing them alone, he insulted them, a ploy to provoke an angry, careless response. He studied this band of bedraggled warriors and recognized their woolen caps and round shields distinguishing them as English. He measured their threat: fewer than fifty, on foot, no archers, no lances, but they would use their deadly axes skillfully.

"*Blaecwulf*!" a gruff voice shouted out from the warriors bunched together, blocking the road. "*We es waitan fur ye. Well cuman to Scotya.*"

"To whom do I owe this gentle greeting?" Alaric answered likewise in Saxon, knowing his translators would keep le Roux and the bishops informed.

A burly man stepped out from the group. "Beardlong," he said.

An apt name, thought Alaric, seeing the man's long brown beard, twisted and oily like unraveling rope.

"God's peace, Edgar of Wessex," Alaric said to the only mounted warrior in the center. He saw tan hair, a sparse short beard on young cheeks, and a shield bearing the unmistakable arms of Wessex.

The boy jerked in his saddle. The soldiers around him tensed, and their shields clattered as they jostled to protect him. Alaric realized immediately that these soldiers had fled with their prince to Scotia. Here he received asylum and might gather enough military strength to challenge William for the crown.

"Your greeting mocks our rightful *King* Edgar," Beardlong said.

"Have you come to escort us to King Malcolm?"

"We've come to kill you." The leader grinned.

Alaric nodded, a smile on his lips. "Single combat?" he said to Edgar, daring him to engage.

Edgar edged his horse through his men toward the front.

Beardlong intervened. With sword raised, he roared and ran straight at Alaric along with four or five others.

Alaric charged. His black stallion, with mane whipping the wind, sped surefooted toward the warriors. They paused as the stallion's hooves thundered toward them. Someone screamed. Alaric wheeled his stallion, bucking and kicking at those trying to surround him, leaving sharp cries in his wake. The warriors fell back, even as more joined the pack. Alaric's sword hacked at several men, his long shield blocked the axe, and his stallion, now in blood thirst, bit an unprotected arm. Alaric slashed Beardlong down and wheeled again. Those still standing backed away. Beardlong lay vanquished, his hand clawing the ground as he tried to raise himself.

Alaric lowered his bloody sword. "Come, gather your dead and wounded." He backed his horse, feeling his stallion's flesh quivering for the next bout.

A handful of men cautiously looked to a pale Edgar, who nodded. They ran forward, grabbed their comrades and dragged them back behind their line.

Their best fighters, now dead or dying, Alaric surmised, seeing blood streaking across the narrow combat field. At his signal, Roderick joined him.

"Capture Edgar on the next round," Alaric said, watching the warriors regroup.

"With pleasure!" Roderick grinned and returned to the waiting retinue.

As the English shouted insults, boasting their prowess, Alaric sat on his warhorse in silence. Their shield wall clattered into place before they moved in close order, and stepping in a jerky, uneven pace slowly toward him, they created a broad bar, three men deep, spanning the width of the pass. He let them come, noticing the men on the ends slowing their pace to narrow the center. The geese formation, intended to drive a wedge through the middle of Alaric's retinue, push the mounted knights into the river or against the cliff—an action Alaric and his men had anticipated. Alaric wiped his bloodied sword with his horse's mane before sheathing it.

He identified the leader whose shouts set the pace and called for a lance. The instant it slapped into his palm Alaric spurred his horse forward and launched his spear into the leader's eye. The blow knocked the commander back, creating a slight break in the wall. Alaric and two knights who had joined him moved into the break, quickly killing those in the advance position, widening the breach and cutting a swath through a dozen men. At the same time, parallel columns of Alaric's knights charged, flanking the English, squeezing them into the center where they had no room to fight, where they fell atop each other. Edgar's men were soon surrounded and found they could not retreat for the mounted soldiers blocking their rear.

With a twist, Alaric yanked his lance from the fallen body before pulling back, leaving room for another charge. He saw that Roderick had Edgar's reins and now led him over writhing bodies, forcing his horse to skirt the edge of the ravine.

Alaric faced the English. Would they stop now? These warriors, no match for him or his men, had died foolishly. He seethed, blaming Edgar for it, and Malcolm, who might have encouraged the boy to provoke this skirmish, an exercise to cut his teeth.

"Who else seeks to join our Maker this day?" Alaric roared.

The English glanced at each other, more frightened it seemed by Alaric's rage than his sword.

"You, there," Alaric pointed his lance. "You look reasonably awake, Man. Come forward so I can take your scabby head to Malcolm."

The combatant did not move.

"Who will meet me now?"

"I will," said a boy, perhaps fourteen winters, shouldering through the warriors.

Alaric glared at the boy, at the others, and back. "Your name?"

"Cedric of Marden."

"You are a brave man, Cedric of Marden." Alaric looked again at the men standing behind the boy, seeing them avoid his gaze. "Live to fight a different battle," Alaric said. "Lead these men from this place. Train them."

"We have sworn our allegiance to Edgar," the boy said. "Our English king, chosen by the Witan."

"A valiant pledge," Alaric said, glancing at Edgar surrounded by Alaric's men. "Your liege lord would not want you to fight a losing battle. He wants you to retire and prepare to fight another day. Is that not so?" Alaric looked at Edgar.

Outnumbered, surrounded, a step away from the steep ravine, Edgar had no other choice. He glared at Alaric before nodding to his warriors.

"We are sworn to protect him," the boy insisted.

"By my saints," Alaric said to the boy. "I swear before these bishops, he will be delivered unharmed to King Malcolm."

Cedric looked to Edgar and back at his companions, all silent, bitterly acknowledging with shifting, lowered eyes that their will to die had waned with Edgar's capture. The boy looked at both ends of the narrow passage.

Alaric saw that his men blocked the English from retreating in either direction. "Make way. Let them through."

They settled that night on a hill, sheltered from the wind by rock outcroppings, yet able to see attackers moving in on them. The sky cleared, the full moon rose, and it became colder, more uncomfortable for the bishops. Despite complaints, Alaric forbade fires to impede anyone from detecting their location.

He had entrusted the night watch only to his men. Now, his gaze swept carefully over the bishops talking together beside their tents, a sullen Edgar refusing the dried meat offered by a guard, his men settling down on the periphery. Gawain caught his eye and nodded. Etienne and the others were alert at their posts.

Le Roux and his captain approached him.

"Edgar wants to speak with you. Alone," le Roux said.

"I have no wish to speak to *him*," Alaric said, still angered by the men he'd killed for Edgar's folly. "He's in your custody. Keep him under strict guard."

"You have no right to take Edgar to Malcolm," le Roux said. "By God's will, Edgar fell into our hands. You must kill him. It is your duty to William, your *leal* duty to your king!"

"I swore to take Edgar safely to Malcolm."

"Yes. Before witnesses, you swore an oath to those witless vermin. You need not honor that oath."

"My oath stands," Alaric said, rubbing his aching shoulder.

"What about the oath you swore to your king? We all know you love the English. Do you love them so well that you will uphold your oath to *them* over the allegiance you swore to your cousin, to your king? You must kill this boy who contends for William's crown. You must stop him from raising arms against our king as William himself wishes."

Alaric knew better.

When you find Edgar, give him this, William had said in private, giving Alaric a small packet. *And give this to Malcolm.*

Both packets were marked carefully so he could not mistake one for the other. *Am I to bring you Edgar's head, or the boy himself?* Alaric asked.

William smiled. *Keep him safe and very much alive. If you bring him, it must be of his own will. Some of my followers are more impatient than others. My reign, my dynasty, has just begun. Take care that those wishing to see hurried results do not gamble with our future.*

Now, to le Roux, Alaric said, "We take Edgar to Malcolm. If he is harmed, if he is rescued, escapes, or leaves your care, I will give you fifty lashes. Get back to your charge."

As night deepened, the travelers settled down and his squire began to snore. Alaric stepped softly to his tethered traveling horse. He nodded at the guard before taking the horse and slipping away from camp.

Once away, he mounted and walked his horse until he could lope, then canter, then slow again to an easy walk. He did not know where he went, only that he rode . . . away. He had been struggling against the fatigue following combat, and now as his horse rocked him at a steady pace, his eyelids dropped, and sleep slithered gently beneath his armor. He jerked awake and rotated his left shoulder, feeling the persistent ache from the injury he'd received at Hastings, and inflamed today. He stopped, sniffed the air for smoke, and smelled none. His horse nibbled on the grasses. He listened: nightjars, scurrying mice, a soft thump as something–or someone–crept near and stopped.

He shook his head, acknowledging Roderick's presence. His childhood friend, his captain, his shadow. Roderick had sworn to protect him, to ride with him, to serve him as he had for years. They had no need for words. Roderick would wait in the high grasses, listen and watch.

Alaric dismounted and guided his horse between the rocks toward the sound of running water. As his horse drank, he stared at the creek glistening in the moonlight. He removed his helm, hood, and padded cap. A cool breeze rippled through his hair. He knelt in the soft, wet bank and sluiced his head and face with cold water, moved to a rocky ledge and leaned back against a boulder. He slipped his hand through the tear in his mail, through thick-leather padding, through his woolen braies and picked out a metal rivet embedded in his skin from a wayward blow. Staunching the blood on his thigh, he gazed at the water, seeing a glassy, haunting vision of Beardlong rippling in the moon's reflection. Before he could finish his prayer for the men he'd killed this day, he fell asleep.

Chapter Forty-Five

June 1068, Dunfermline, Scotia

After crossing to Inverkeithing, they rode another half day beneath a fickle sun to the gates of King Malcolm's fortress, a large timbered wall surrounding the peninsular outcropping of rock. From atop this crag, Alaric saw the steep ravine, the village Dunfermline nestled below. He wondered why William had sent them by land when they could have come by sea to the port called Edinburgh nearby. Scanning the broad view of the surrounding land he knew that scouts would have spotted their party and recognized their banners. Malcolm himself would already know this was a royal envoy and that they'd captured Edgar Atheling.

To the guard's challenge, Alaric, gesturing toward his entourage, introduced the bishops and Count Alain le Roux of Brittany as envoys from King William. Alaric did not mention Edgar.

"And you are?"

"Alaric of Ewyas, lord of Staffordshire."

"Black Wolf howls at our gates!" someone within yelled. Several people ran to the ramparts to look him over.

Roderick, mounted beside Alaric, snorted.

The gate opened. Alaric dismounted and led his horse into the walled fortress. His retinue followed. The bailiff, an elderly man with a toothy grimace hobbled toward him.

"I will see to your comforts. We have prepared quarters for your stay. King Malcolm invites you to the *Toun* when you have settled." He motioned to the grooms who approached to take Alaric's horse.

Alaric handed his reins to his own squire.

"As you wish," the bailiff said, his lips twisting into a bitter scowl.

Le Roux and his men helped the bishops alight from their carriage and, with grand ceremony, followed the bailiff who took them to their quarters. Alaric stopped le Roux's captain, who had led the vanguard.

"Well done, Jagu," Alaric said. "It's an honor to have a good man."

"At King William's command, I owe you obedience during this journey, Stafford. Your tribute will not win my allegiance," he said. "*That* belongs to Count Alain."

"As it should," Alaric said. "Join your liege, and remember we *all* serve William."

Roderick joined him, and Alaric shrugged away Roderick's unspoken question.

Turning to see Edgar, Alaric recognized the boy he himself might once have been: young, impulsive, eager to forge his future, landless, impotent. Cruel fate had teased the prince. His kingdom had blown into his hair, fluttered his elegant cloak, and vanished as quickly as it had come, leaving only a trace rippling across the grassy vale of his life.

Edgar stopped before Alaric. Despite a humiliating defeat and capture, he held Alaric's gaze—proud and direct.

Alaric took a packet from his inner cloak and handed it to him. "From William."

"What is it?" Edgar asked. "A bribe? My . . . kingdom?" The boy's eyes sparked with fury.

Alaric saw Edgar flush, embarrassed at his outburst. "Choose wisely, Edgar of Wessex."

The boy turned away and crossed the courtyard.

"He or his men will try to kill you," Roderick said.

"Perhaps."

"One of Malcolm's grooms is telling tales about you. Seems you killed a hundred men with one slash of your sword and changed into a black wolf the size of your horse."

Alaric glanced around the courtyard at the people watching them. One man's hard stare caught his attention: an old mucker with shorn hair unlike the Scots.

"Rotate the men to guard our horses."

"How long will we be here?" Roderick said. "I want to find me a willing woman, or two, and see if they brew a decent ale."

"We'll have a few weeks, enough time to do both," Alaric said with a grin. "William wants us back by Lammas Day. Tell the men to be cautious with their boasts. Malcolm spent his exile years in Edward's court. He and his men might be as fluent in Saxon and French as we are. Have Gawain and his brothers mingle. They know the Gaelic tongue better than we do."

After they removed their mail and travel gear, Alaric followed le Roux to the stone tower, and, as customary, all relinquished their swords before entering.

Dunfermline's hall was crowded, hot and steamy, and the smoky room smelled of sweating men, spilt ale, and burnt hair. The Scots milling or sitting around the shadowy room were all large and loud, as large, Alaric thought, as Roderick, a giant among men. They had long shaggy hair and beards, and wore woolen blankets wrapped about their bodies toggled with broad belts. Their strange words began to cease as Alaric and le Roux walked toward Malcolm, obvious strangers in their tunics, leggings, and mantles, with their clean-shaven faces and short hair giving them the look of tonsured priests.

Edgar Atheling stood near a wall in conversation with someone whose profile seemed vaguely familiar to Alaric. One of the bishops nearly pushed Alaric into le Roux in his haste to join the other bishop and the king's priests, all arguing among themselves.

When the crowd parted, Alaric saw Malcolm. A large, robust man, mid-thirties like William, more grizzled and broader. He had a full head of thick red hair streaked in yellow and a long, dark-red beard. His hair was pulled back, revealing a high forehead, creases between pale, keen eyes, now turned to watch them approach.

As they neared the king, someone in the back began to sing a Gaelic tune, the jumbled words garbled and unintelligible except for a single word: *Blackwolf*. Malcolm's cheek twitched as if he passed gas, and his fingers ran down the length of his beard. He turned his intense gaze on Alain le Roux, who took the lead as Alaric stood back.

"Lord King," le Roux began in French.

Immediately the bishops and priest began translating into various languages. From the first greetings and customary platitudes, Alaric realized William had chosen a worthy envoy. Le Roux's family were kin of King Philip, Malcolm's ally. Francia and Brittany had together shared a mutual regard for Scotia—*against* Normandie.

Malcolm gave le Roux many compliments, stating that Brittany's alliance with Scotia was a much-valued result of long friendships and mutual support. Surprisingly, le Roux, a blunt, insipid brute in Alaric's opinion, seemed little swayed by flattery and demonstrated a surprising alacrity until he got to the core of their mission.

Malcolm raised his eyebrows. "I've been *summoned* to York by your presumptuous king?"

"Invited, Sire," le Roux said. "William, our consecrated, blessed, and anointed king, invites you to York, so you and he may join hands in mutual grace and sanctity to demonstrate the peace between two great and wise kings. We would be honored to escort you."

"Think I don't know the way?" Malcolm smirked. Everyone in the hall laughed.

"We will see to your safety."

Several of Malcolm's men roared in Gaelic or banged on the boards. Some stood abruptly, stepped forward aggressively as if issuing challenges. Alaric cringed inwardly. Le Roux had just insulted Malcolm's prowess and ability to keep himself safe. Malcolm, long a friend to the English, especially now after sheltering Edgar Atheling, had more guarantee of safe passage throughout all of Englelond than William or any Norman could provide. Besides, he knew his uncle's court in York well.

With a wave of his arm, Malcolm quieted the hall. "What are the terms?" he asked.

"The usual," le Roux said. "William gives you hostages. Blackwolf and fifty of William's finest knights."

What? Alaric thought but said nothing despite le Roux's shocking statement. Kings usually chose hostages from among their unimportant relatives, those whose death mattered little. By custom, Alaric and his men would be executed if *any* harm came to Malcolm or anyone under his protection—including Edgar. Ripe with lethal possibilities, this situation gave le Roux the advantage of killing both Edgar and Alaric with one arrow—if he had the balls.

Malcolm studied Alaric.

"Are you disposed to become *Edgar's* hostage, Blackwolf?" Malcolm asked, testing Alaric's willingness to be placed in the hands of the English prince he had recently bested.

"I and Count Alain," Alaric said without pause, "serve King William in all things." Reaching into his mantle, he pulled out a packet, stepped forward and handed it to Malcolm's page. "William would give you this, and his most valued subject to signify his good faith." He stepped back. "I am honored to assist Count Alain. My king intends you no harm."

"Excellent," Malcolm said, fingering the packet bearing an elaborate seal. "You shall remain at liberty until we leave."

Le Roux turned slowly to Alaric, his eyes blinking, confused perhaps by Alaric's acquiescence and a royal packet he knew nothing about.

Alaric glanced at Edgar Atheling and again caught a glimpse of the familiar man stepping back into the shadows. A commotion arose suddenly in the back of the hall. The crowd hushed and gave way as two women walked slowly toward Malcolm.

The first—tall, bony, richly dressed—sailed through the smoky room, creating a chilling draft in her wake. She slowed as she neared Alaric. Her brilliant blue eyes pierced him with hatred. Surprised, Alaric frowned and saw the lingering appearance of a splendid beauty: an erect posture, a firm chin, clear though lined skin, and still full lips. Without a word, she moved to the dais, and a young woman, a silent beauty, followed as she joined Malcolm and Edgar, now standing beside the king.

"Greetings Agatha of Wessex," Malcolm said. "And to you, dear Lady." He smiled at the young woman.

"I won't have him in my presence," Agatha said to Malcolm. "My son is the rightful English king, chosen by the Witan. *That* . . . ," she gestured at Alaric, "inferior challenged him to single combat. A capital offense in Scotia, is it not? Arrest him immediately!"

The bishops gasped and looked nervously between Alaric and Malcolm.

Alaric watched the frown between Malcolm's eyes deepen as his gaze swept over the young woman whose head remained lowered in the pious stance of the cloister. The demand, Alaric knew, created a dilemma. Malcolm could not arrest William's envoy without exacerbating tensions between the neighboring kingdoms, nor could he ignore Agatha's demand.

Before Malcolm answered, Alaric said, "*A Rìgh.*"

Malcolm's eyes narrowed in speculation at Alaric's Gaelic. He nodded and Alaric continued in Gaelic, requesting permission to leave the hall.

Malcolm's fingers drummed over the sealed packet. "Why did you spare Edgar?" he asked in Gaelic.

Alaric hesitated, unsure he would say the proverb correctly. "*Bithidh na geòidh as t-fhoghar.*" The geese return at autumn: we will know all in good time.

Malcolm smiled and dismissed Alaric. As Alaric began to depart, he called out, "Blackwolf."

Alaric looked up at the king.

"On behalf of all those present," Malcolm said in Gaelic, "I wish to convey our thanks for . . . escorting Edgar back to our humble home. We have learned that you swore to keep him safe and did so despite the wishes of certain noblemen who want to give his severed head to William." Malcolm stroked his beard. "It will be our pleasure to give *you* safe passage to York." Malcolm raised a single eyebrow slowly.

Le Roux frowned, as the bishops translated Malcolm's words. Alaric bowed and turned to leave. A smile played on his lips as he passed Roderick, who followed him. In the courtyard, Alaric bent over and laughed, staggering across the bailey.

Roderick, trudging through the mud with him, shook his head, perplexed. "There is nothing funny in being held hostage!"

Alaric struggled to control his relief and looked at his captain. He burst out laughing again and walked on. "Malcolm will not hold us hostage. We're going to York."

"What? How do you know?" Roderick asked, tying on his sword.

"Practice your Gaelic, Roddy. Malcolm just said so." Alaric slapped

Roderick on his back. "If God wills it, and if Rufus becomes insuffer-able, Malcolm just might hold *him* hostage instead."

"Praise God's will!" Roderick said. "Then what?"

Alaric sobered. He shook his head, recalling William's words to him.

You have been on the march with me, and on my behalf, for more than a year, far beyond the normal knight's service. Occasioned by serving me directly, of course. I need you yet, Alaric. But after making a pact with Malcolm, if all is calm, you may return to Tutbury. Matilda would have you bring your wife to us at Christmastide.

As he and Roderick walked toward the cookhouse, Alaric felt what he had not felt for a long time: loss. He'd fought for William to secure the birthplace he had once called home. But without his family, he had no home. For an instant, he thought of Marguerite, and the thought fell flat and hollow like a heavy leather boot on a dusty road.

He tried to recall the vague, indistinct image of Genevieve de Fontenay. He could not. Eustace's niece was the blood price delivered by the man who had probably watched his family die in their pyre.

Alaric swirled suddenly in his tracks, gazing intensely about the courtyard.

"What?" Roderick asked, reaching for his sword.

"Dubec!" Alaric said. "Brian Dubec, Eustace's man. He's here. I saw the son of a hairless mother's whelp talking with Edgar Atheling. He does nothing without Eustace's orders. We have to find him."

Chapter Forty-Six

Aware that someone tracked his progress, Alaric scanned the people weaving around him and listened for someone coming up from behind. Entering the stables, he stepped aside and cautiously measured his surroundings. His men guarded their horses as stablehands and grooms moved around the stalls with water buckets. An old mucker shoveling dung into a cart raised his head when the distant crowd cheered the horse racers.

King Malcolm had sequestered William's party inside the fortress and entertained them with food, drink, slave girls, and games of strength and cunning. The roar ended, and Alaric recognized the unmistakable sounds of heavy carts moving armaments outside the gates. As Malcolm prepared for his royal journey to York, the Scots prepared for war.

Alaric headed toward his charger and wondered if Eustace had sent Dubec to woo Edgar and Malcolm. Any such intrigue would further complicate Alaric's relationship with King William and renew le Roux's warning about Alaric's treasonous relatives. But despite searching for Dubec, he had been unable to find him. Alaric began to wonder if he had been mistaken in thinking he had sighted Dubec in Malcolm's *Toun.*

Alaric ran a hand over his stallion's neck. The black stamped and rolled his eyes. Alaric spun, his seax drawn, pointing at the mucker who had crept up behind him.

The old man recoiled.

"Have you business here?" Alaric demanded sharply.

The man opened his mouth and then shook his head and began to turn away, his shoulders slumped into a dispirited curl.

"Do you know me?" Alaric asked in Gaelic, halting the man's retreat.

The mucker turned back to Alaric and nodded. "*Oui, mi knowen ye.*" He mixed French, Gaelic, and Saxon. "Ye were a *bairn*, son o' Simeon. He lives still?"

"No," Alaric said, seeing tattered clothing hung on a thin frame, rags wrapped around bowed legs. He'd noticed the man's scrutiny when they'd first arrived, and every time he hobbled across Alaric's path, stooped over, leather straps digging into his shoulders, pulling a cartload of dung. "How do you know my father?"

"I were at Ewyas, nigh a score year ago, 'til *cuman* here. Riding for me life. Near starved, no packhorses, *nihl* but our wits 'n our swords."

"With Osbern the Pentecost," Alaric said, vaguely remembering the castellan who had abandoned the outlawed Normans to bounty seekers.

"*Oui. Ri Alban,* the Red King, gave us shelter. We gave him our swords—until Osbern betrayed him for gold as was his like."

"You stayed here in Scotia."

"Me glory days ended when Osbern left his wounded behind for Scots to butcher."

Lines furrowed the man's brow, thick eyebrows shaded deep-set blue eyes. Alaric recognized the long Norman face and saw full cheeks flushed by the crisp morning air and a two-day-old grey stubble covering the lower half of his face, probably hiding a dimpled chin. The man's eyes crinkled in humor under Alaric's gaze and his grin exposed missing upper and lower front teeth.

"A Frankish knight now a groomsman." He rubbed his lips with a gnarled finger stub, a familiar battle injury. "Ye'll no remember when Welshmen spiked yer sisters."

Alaric's heart tumbled. The buried memory sparked alive, filing him with sudden intense grief. He was six then.

"Osbern provoked the Welsh, and he ill-willed Simeon, yer pater. 'Twas Simeon saved the garrison an' skewered the raider *cuman* to *quellen* me." He scratched his neck. "Good man, he were, to all."

Alaric nodded as stark, long-forgotten memories hit one after another: Osbern torturing a Welsh hostage, his father defying Osbern to release the boy, the girls, limp and bloodied after the retaliatory raid.

"Ware, Alaric of Ewyas," the mucker said. "Normans are untrusted here. Ye may yet pay for old injuries." He glanced over his shoulders and back. "Ware the Breton whose pride leads him to folly."

"What folly?" Alaric asked, sheathing his weapon.

"He thinks to snatch Edgar under Malcolm's nose and send him to William ahead of yer journey. 'Tis Agatha's trap he'll spring tomorrow."

Corning dew dripped from the trees. Moss softened the boulders and blunted sharp edges. Alaric held his breath as he rode his horse a leisurely walk through swarming midges. His cloak reeked, his stomach growled. Without armor, shield, and sword, he felt naked despite the bow and quiver toggled to his saddle and a seax strapped to his thigh. Swatting his neck, he watched fresh hounds pick up the scent. They moved ahead, their backs arched, pulling their handlers forward, outpacing the fatigued dogs retiring from the course.

Malcolm and Edgar followed the hounds closely along the path chosen by the huntsman. Riders in pairs or straggling in single file accompanied them. Le Roux and Jagu rode a few paces behind them with a dozen men, Alaric in the rear. Alaric saw his men back along the trail, deliberately surrounded by le Roux's men, all riding unhurriedly, pressing his men farther behind, unable to come to his aid.

Alaric moved his mount through the horsemen to le Roux's chestnut.

"Rein your horse!" le Roux scowled over his shoulder as Alaric rode up behind. Alaric kept the chestnut's rump in his sight as the path twisted again. The hunting party bunched up when the trail narrowed, closed in by thick, thorny brambles, windfalls, and giant ferns.

He stiffened when two riders emerged from the misty shadows. Edgar's men flanked him, stirrup to stirrup, their horses jostling against his. He let his horse nip and kick out, back and forth, pushing the pair into the underbrush until they eased back. Ahead, he caught a glimpse of sunlight slanting through the trees and Malcolm's red cloak.

The dogs began to bark. Alaric's horse bolted forward, and, with others, he rode wildly, following the dogs, the horns. Trees whipped by. He ducked beneath a low branch, his horse careened into another, the mounts leaped apart. Bellowing hounds guided the mob galloping head to head, passing Alaric and surging through the woods. Malcolm and Edgar disappeared around a bend as horns blasted again. The hunters followed the dogs up a steep, rocky hill. At the top, they burst into full morning sunlight. The hounds streaked across a small stream above a waterfall. Men whooped as their horses splashed through the shallow ford. The dogs snaked back into the shadowy woods, Malcolm charging at their heels. Edgar followed the king, but Alaric saw neither le Roux nor his man, Jagu the Tall.

They came to a long meadow, where the hounds, low to the ground, ran through the tall grass. Riders veered right, then left in front of Alaric, surrounding him. Horns blasted again. Alaric saw the hunters split, herding him from his men. He glanced back as Edgar's men closed in.

"Catch him," he heard.

Cheek against his mount's mane, Alaric gave the gray its head. He cut across the meadow and leaped into the underbrush, over fallen trees, through the brambles until he came to a small clearing. He turned to face the pair—English warriors unused to mounted combat. Before their horses skittered to a stop, Alaric spurred his horse and rammed into the colt, nearly knocking it off its feet. The rider flew from his saddle and rolled under the gray's hooves as the young horse bolted. Alaric whirled a half turn away from the other assailant who had tried to grab his reins. Wheeling in the opposite direction, Alaric slammed the gray into the gelding's rear, making it buck. Spurring his mount, Alaric leaped over a mossy downed tree and rode through dense woods, escaping his attackers. Gauging his position from the filtered sunlight and echoing horns, he headed to the old hunting lodge the mucker had described.

He found le Roux's chestnut tethered in the woods, out of sight, and led it down to the ravine behind the lodge where he'd left his own horse to graze. Climbing back up, he circled and sank below the mossy rocks to study the area. He noted fresh dung, tracks of three horses, and heel marks of someone dragged to the lodge now overtaken by the wilds. He could barely make out thatching beneath the overgrowth or the timbered walls arrested in partial collapse. The portal, like a cave opening, hid behind large, flat leaves.

No other horses. No sounds. No guards.

He drew his seax and ran quietly across the clearing. Ducking, he entered the dark hollow space, stepped aside, and paused. He smelled damp earth and rotting wood, as his eyes adjusted to the dimness. A faint light came through the thatching. He turned toward a muffled sound and spotted le Roux tied and gagged on the floor, struggling against the ropes. Alaric put a finger to his mouth, signaling silence, and crouched to cut the binds. Le Roux's eyes flared.

Alaric pivoted on his haunches. His seax blunted the blow as he fell back against a wall. A man, silhouetted against the gray light, raised his sword. Alaric sprang up and lunged, sending him back into a post. The attacker dropped his blade. Thatching fell in damp clumps, timbers creaked and shuddered. Alaric plunged his weapon hard into the man's soft underbelly and up. Eye to eye, he recognized a shocked Jagu in the dim light and inhaled his last breath. He twisted the blade and yanked it out in one movement, shoving the body away from him, letting it fall face down into the rat droppings.

He slashed the ropes binding le Roux and sheathed his seax. Hearing horses coming toward them, Alaric dragged him out of the hut and into the underbrush.

"Wait," le Roux said. "They'll aid us."

"They'll kill us," Alaric said, angling them down a hill, away from their horses. They stumbled and skidded in the loose soil. Le Roux tried to break free. Alaric tripped him, and he fell, rolling down, landing hard against a rock. Alaric heard the crack. Le Roux did not cry out, though by the time Alaric reached him, the pain on le Roux's face betrayed the agony of a broken arm dangling at an odd angle. Alaric grabbed le Roux's uninjured arm under the shoulder and heaved him to his feet. Le Roux, his face now pale and dripping in sweat, cradled his broken arm. Together they ran to an overhang concealing them from the riders galloping toward the lodge on the trail above them.

"They'll start searching as soon as they find you gone," Alaric said, ripping the wide embroidered hem off le Roux's tunic. He quickly tied le Roux's broken arm to his body.

"We're dead on foot," le Roux said.

"We're not dying in Scotia," Alaric said. With le Roux's good arm over his shoulder, Alaric half carried him down the hill to a wide stream. They hobbled along the bank and waded into the water. Moving against the current, they ducked beneath overgrown trees and around a curve as if traveling through a shadowy green tunnel. Le Roux hissed when his arm hit a branch. Alaric stopped and looked back through the dappled light. Although he could not see their pursuers, he heard them atop the wooded knoll.

"Circle around!" Edgar of Wessex ordered. "Don't let the Breton and Blackwolf get away!"

"Blackwolf!"

"Who else would free the Breton?" Edgar said.

"Move, Rufus," Alaric said. They traveled as quickly as they could, from rock to rock, over downed trees. Within moments, they heard a shout. "Tracks!" Horses slipped and slid down to the stream, hooves hit the graveled bank.

"Dismount! Dismount!" Edgar ordered. "Search the rocks and underbrush. They move upstream."

Rounding another bend, Alaric spotted a crevice in the sheer stone wall. He pushed le Roux past a vine curtain into the niche, barely large enough for the two of them. Drawing his blade, he listened hard. Behind him, le Roux breathed heavily. Men staggered in the water toward them.

"Listen!" someone yelled. "Stop! Listen!"

A long, low bellowing sound wound through the woods.

"Malcolm!"

"He must not find us here," Edgar said.

"We have them!" someone shouted. "They're trapped. Look, tracks near the boulder—"

The faint cacophony of the hunt—yells and horses and horns—penetrated the woods.

"My lord?" someone asked.

Alaric heard river rocks clatter as someone stepped from one stone to another toward them. The stagnant pool before their cleft rippled as boots waded slowly through shallow water.

The hunting horns shifted toward them.

"Swive my holy saints!" Edgar cursed. "Retreat! Mount up. Now! Cut back. Try to rejoin the hunt. If not, get back to Dunfermline."

Alaric watched the waves sloshing over his boots as someone splashed quickly through the water back to the horses. He heard the mounts struggling up the hill and the men riding away, but no barking dogs.

He grinned and sheathed his weapon.

Alaric eased le Roux out of the crevice, and they traveled back the way they'd come quickly downstream. When they reached the ravine, Gawain and Etienne waited with their horses. Gawain packed away the hunting horns they'd blown to divert Edgar and his men.

"We heard shouting," Alaric said, handing le Roux off to Etienne.

"Roddy and the others."

Almost immediately, Roderick skittered down into the ravine. He laughed, seeing Alaric. "Edgar fled like a startled hare!"

Le Roux, dazed and sweating, asked, "What happened?"

"We've slipped out of Agatha's trap," Alaric said. "Set his arm, Roddy."

Roderick bound le Roux to a tree, freed and exposed his broken arm. "If you were a better man, I'd regret causing you pain." He grabbed le Roux's arm at the elbow and wrist and pulled slowly, twisting, and all heard the grating sound as the bones moved into place. Le Roux groaned but did not faint. After splinting and binding the arm, Roderick untied le Roux and let him sink to a squat, his back braced against the tree.

"Drink," Alaric squirted wine from the goatskin into le Roux's mouth.

"What trap?"

"The trap set when Jagu, on your behalf, accepted Agatha's coins for my life."

"How did you . . . ?"

"Agatha's demand for my arrest should have warned you."

Le Roux blinked.

"Don't feign a girlish blush," Alaric said. "Agatha wants her son on Englelond's throne. She wants to kill me for besting him, and you to prevent a truce between Malcolm and William."

Le Roux frowned. "I don't—"

"As you and she agreed, her men would have taken me to the lodge. You intended to betray her by snatching Edgar when he came to kill me. Instead, Jagu trussed you like a Christmas goose for transport to Malcolm. For abusing an envoy's privilege and attempting to abduct his royal guest, Malcolm would have spiked our heads on his gates, ending any possible truce with William. And he would give arms to Edgar to reclaim the English throne."

Le Roux glared at Alaric. "Did you contrive with Agatha or with Edgar—your Wessex *prince*—to trap me?"

"If so, I would have killed you. William sent me to protect you. I will do so until we leave Scotia." Alaric exhaled loudly. "Think, Rufus! She paid Jagu for your head. Who encouraged you to capture Edgar? Who else could have captured you?"

Le Roux clenched his jaw and nodded. "Nothing is more bitter than a disloyal liegeman."

"Except a woman's revenge. Until we leave Dunfermline, do not underestimate Agatha. She is a formidable woman."

"Like Eustace's niece?" Le Roux sneered.

"Take care when speaking of my wife," Alaric said softly, letting le Roux hear his threat. "Despite her uncle's treason, the king accepted her oath. The queen champions her. You snipe because I've saved your arse. You are not indebted to me, Rufus. You are indebted to King William. Meanwhile, squirm when recalling my wife. Did she corner you in King's Hall and make you stammer?"

Seeing le Roux's face turn red, Alaric laughed. "Mount up."

Riding back to Dunfermline, Alaric glanced at his stiff-jawed enemy. Their tentative alliance would last until York. Would Rufus cease spreading doubts about his loyalty, unchanged since the moment Alaric chose William over Harold? As Alaric hoped, William had begun to secure Alaric's birth land from predators. A truce between the two kings would stop border incursions and end Scotia's support of Edgar—for now.

Frowning, Alaric thought about Agatha of Wessex, a woman who knew the value of deception. Had she met with Dubec, had she sought Eustace's support for her son? That thought led Alaric to his wife, another woman said to be skilled at kingcraft. It pleased him that she had vexed le Roux at the queen's coronation. But her cunning was dangerous. When released from his knight's service, he would return to Tutbury and take the woman's measure.

Chapter Forty-Seven

Atop the ramparts, Johan shielded his eyes from the morning sun and watched a company of knights leaving the castle. "I'm glad to see Richard de Rupierre depart," he said to Gilbert. "His dislike of Alaric irked me."

"Dislike?" Gilbert said. "They're allies."

"Allies do not curse each other."

"These do," Gilbert shrugged. "Richard and Alaric are two rocks in the same river. They crash into each other, but both roll downstream side by side. At least we know Alaric is in Scotia. Richard thinks he will meet the king in York by summer's end."

"I hope Dreux's not there. I didn't warn Alaric that Dreux tried to compromise the countess."

"Why not?" Gilbert demanded.

"He would assume she'd enticed Dreux or suspect her motives for spurning him."

"She had to rebuff him," Gilbert said. "Dreux set the court astir with his lingering gazes, and Marguerite spread rumors of a tryst. Her ladyship's rejection quashed the rumors."

"And provoked Dreux's malice. Along with blaming Alaric for Clare's death, he now despises Lady Stafford for her public rejection."

"What *exactly* happened?"

In a flash, Johan recalled the moonless night, a lighted, glowing tent tucked between festive pavilions. "As you and her ladyship attended mass with the queen, I fed a young pig enough ale to make it sleep. I dressed it in a silk chemise, and left it in Dreux's tent, snoring contentedly on a bed of furs. Soon, courtiers filtered into the shadows to witnesses the rendezvous."

"Dreux?" Gilbert asked.

"Came dressed in gold and silver. He stood before the tent, aware of his hidden audience and swirled his sable cloak. 'I make my case, gentlefolk,' he said, 'the lady is mine.'"

Gilbert gasped.

"Yes! I wanted to gut him!" Johan said. "With a flourish, he turned to the tent and spoke to the silhouette of a reclining figure, 'Oh, lady! I am humbled that you await my embrace.' He mentioned love and things beautiful, stars and seas. He entered the tent, 'Come, let me kiss your sweet lips.'"

Johan cringed. "A moment later, Dreux yelled and fled the shelter, tripping when the squealing pig ran between his legs dragging the garment."

"God's breath!" Gilbert crossed himself. "He'll never forget this insult."

Johan nodded. "Witnesses stepped forward, laughing and repeating Dreux's love words. He turned the incident to jest. With his broad, infectious smile, he said, 'I accept the lady's refusal.' He clapped one knight on the shoulder as they laughed together. But," Johan shook his head, "when he caught me watching from the shadows, his eyes turned deadly as if vowing: *Alaric's wife will die as did my Clare.*"

In silence, they walked around the ramparts and spotted Lady Stafford and Jeoffroi riding beside the fields.

Gilbert asked, "Will Dreux hurt her? Can he?"

"I don't know. If Alaric would only give her a chance. Damn his obstinate heart!"

To Elise's relief, Richard de Rupierre and his knights headed toward Burton Road. From the moment they arrived yesterday, the boisterous group, led by the loud, hulking brute, had dominated the hall, brawling with Gilbert's hearth guards, grabbing female servants, drinking and dicing, whooping and singing. And she disliked Rupierre's eyes tracking her as she and her women had left the great room to their raw pleasures.

"We'll stay in full view of the spotters," Jeoffroi said to Elise, riding beside him. "It will take a few more days before we can slip unnoticed into the woods."

"Yes," she said. She had not seen Frigga in nearly two months and longed to ask about the things she'd heard whispered among women at court. What were dewale and sleep-apples? Was it true that midwinter falling on a feast day foretold a harsh winter? Did bramble tea cure warts, and could someone rid a malady by burying his nape hair?

As they rode back toward the castle, Elise mentally repeated Frigga's song, reassured she had not forgotten how to find plants in the wood and meadows and along the riverbanks. Approaching Castle Road, she asked, "Did you enjoy being in charge of the garrison when Gilbert was away?"

"No, my lady," he said. "Those duties left little time to entertain your aunt during her illness."

"Hortense is stronger than ever," Elise said. "Perhaps your scant attentions helped her flourish."

"Taking charge of the hall in Marguerite's absence restored her," Jeoffroi said, grinning.

Elise smiled, recalling the moment they entered a newly white-washed hall, saw the fresh rushes on the floor and smelled the spicy, inviting aromas. In response to Marguerite's fury, Hortense struck back: *No worries. Now that you are back, the hall will again fall to ruin.* With that, the hostility between the two women sharpened.

After the noon meal, as Elise and Brother Herluin walked to the kitchen garden, Marguerite accosted them.

As usual in Herluin's presence, she spit on the back of her fingers to ward off evil. "This creature casts a shadow on your soul and tarnishes your husband's reputation. I have enjoined Brother Derrick to expel him. Moreover, your aunt may no longer enter the storerooms without my permission, and she is forthwith prohibited from leaving the castle. See to it that she conforms to my orders."

Elise, unwilling to recognize Marguerite's reinstated authority, merely gazed at her.

"Are you deaf, too, Lady Stafford?" Marguerite said, glancing at Herluin and back. "Can you not speak?"

"Mind your shrewish tongue!" Hortense chided behind Marguerite, startling her. "Servants might think you a common wench."

Before Marguerite could respond, Hortense said, "Brother Derrick answers to God, not to his lordship's whore. You have no authority over me. I go where I please."

"One day, you will go too far!" Marguerite vowed.

"Make haste. Johan summons you," Hortense said. "Perhaps he sends you away."

Marguerite glanced at the hall and back at Hortense. "Never," she smiled, departing.

"Come," Hortense said, turning Elise and Brother Herluin toward the garden. "I overheard Richard de Rupierre telling Gilbert that your husband is far north. He says William may not release him for months."

"God will it!" Elise said, making Hortense laugh.

Elise remained cheerful as the trio worked their way slowly across the kitchen garden. Near eventide, the sound of a horn drew her attention to Southgate. She dropped a hand full of leeks into Herluin's basket and stood up to watch the commotion.

A priest entered the bailey. People gathered around him reverently. Some reached out to touch his garments, many knelt, and all crossed themselves. When Johan and Gilbert greeted him, the priest gestured to Derrick's monks leading a mule carrying his baggage. Elise noticed the priest's green cassock, embroidered along the hem and sleeves, and his mantle hanging casually over his shoulders. From his head held high and his dark, tonsured hair, he appeared young, and she admired his slow, majestic walk as he entered the hall.

"Lady Hortense," Serilda called, a few minutes later. Out of breath, she ran toward them, speaking in Saxon. "Johan has offered the priest respite for a few days. He's going to bless the chapel at vespers and dine with us."

Elise smiled, seeing Serilda's dimples twinkle in excitement as she told Herluin with gestures.

"Is he passing through?" Hortense asked.

"Yes. He's visiting several villages to see which ones need priests. He came from Normandie."

"Excellent! Tutbury needs a good blessing," Hortense said.

"Yes, but he saw that we have no church," Serilda said. "Brother Derrick explained that his lordship had set aside land for one, but he has not yet started the design or sought proper builders. The priest offered to help Brother Derrick with those plans."

"Perhaps he can stay a week or more." Elise hoped he would read aloud from her scriptures, or speak of Rouen or Rome, or engage her in learned conversation. She wondered if he played *talf* or chess, knowing that a Norman priest would enrich all their lives. She imagined Tutbury having a priest and a church, the masses, the richness of festive and solemn feast days.

"To have a priest, even for a short time, would gift us with God's favor," Elise said. "We'll meet him after we trim the marigolds."

As she worked, she smiled, happier than she'd been since marrying the stranger whose angry mark had nearly shredded the betrothal documents. Despite her husband's efforts to demean and confine her, despite her uncle's treason, Elise had thrived.

Along the way, she'd learned patience, which the nuns could never teach her, and had won Gilbert's and Johan's trust by quietly, calmly asserting herself. Her efforts won fewer guards, a dozen servants, more tasks and freedoms, and invaluable allies. Never before had she cherished secrets, but now she hid and savored the rigorous mental challenges of learning Frigga's forbidden arts and the Saxon tongue. Surprisingly, she'd found more courage than she'd known before, which led her to face the king's fury and to speak openly of pagan worship. And yet, she thought, filling her basket, even if her husband returned, she could recede back into her shadowed life and wait, quiet as a still pond. And one day he might accept her alliance.

Elise looked out over the bailey glowing in the late afternoon sunlight, mirroring the warmth in her heart. She had made a place for herself in this foreign land. In Black Wolf's absence, Tutbury was hers, and she would use it to strengthen the new Norman kingdom, now her home.

Acknowledgements

Many people, too numerous to name, read my manuscripts over the years. I wish to express special thanks to Anne Hayes, an English historian, who declared on the occasion of our meeting, "I am a Saxon." She and her husband, Norman (the irony did not escape me), provided tea, enthusiasm, and local details. I am most grateful to Liza and Chris Klein, Jack Eldridge, and Joseph Mihelarakis for their unique support. Martha Hoffman of Cuidono Press provided keen insights and invaluable encouragement. Thank you all.

Particular elements in this book demand special recognition of sources. Alaric's battle memories and the story of the bloody sheets were inspired by Barbara W. Tuchman, *A Distant Mirror: The Calamitous 14th Century*. Alaric's comments regarding an unseen wife are similar to those expressed in *Life in the Middle Ages*, selected, translated and annotated by G. G. Coulton, Volume IV, Monks, Friars and Nuns, excerpt No. 4, "The Monk's View of Womankind." Marguerite's story is inspired by a similar event noted in Amy Kelly's *Eleanor of Aquitaine and the Four Kings*.

Author's Note

When my children left home, I took a job dealing with the aftermath of natural disasters. At the same time, I challenged myself to learn something new and decided to study the Middle Ages. I learned how to make poisons, how people prepared bodies for burial, about feast days and diets, how chess went to England via Normans in Italy, and so much more.

Despite my research, I could only retain the information when I invented characters who lived in those times, so I began writing vignettes of daily life. When I focused on the Norman Conquest of England, my university studies in political philosophy came into play, and these scattered pieces of information congealed. Eventually, it became clear to me that I was writing a book. I went to England to see the places my characters traveled, to follow their journeys along old Roman Roads and nearly extinct waterways.

Serendipity accompanied me each trip. Entirely by chance, I was allowed to climb a dark spiral staircase to Westminster Abbey's archives. Amid stained glass windows and blackened oak furniture, as my white-gloved hands caressed ancient texts, I wove my way into the past. Driving for the first time in England, I got stuck on a roundabout. After circling it several times, I managed to spin off in the wrong direction—and met a historian of the period, who shared knowledge and insights, while packing for a month-long journey beginning that same afternoon. Magically, it seemed, I met caretakers who guided me to one adventure after another.

I searched for Alaric's birthplace among the Norman castles predating the Norman Invasion. I found it at the base of a grassy mound—the only thing left of Ewyas Harold, which I call Ewyas. I found the Thames at Cricklade, a brook. But Cnut and his 160 warships landed there fifty-one years before my character, Genevieve (Elise).

One March night, I got lost trying to find Tutbury Castle. Pulling onto a dirt road, I drove into an isolated field and got out of the car. Alone, in complete darkness, I spotted a comet. Someone standing in the same place in April 1066 would have seen Haley's comet. Did they shiver as I did from the chilly night—or from fear? When I stood atop Tutbury's motte, I decided Alaric would build Tutbury's first Norman castle a year or so before historians think it was built. Like me, Elise would look out at the forest, at River Dove, and beyond.

In the evenings and on weekends, I found writing about knights or English rebels less stressful than my day job surveying collapsed freeways or buildings toppled over from an earthquake. Imagining my characters crossing the Narrow Sea seemed less precarious than navigating steel twisted by a massive hurricane, or searching for whole towns washed away by a 30-foot wave. One January, while in tropical Saipan after a typhoon, I wrote about a freezing Yorkshire winter, then flew back to England for more research. Years later, I had a rough, horrible, 2000-page tome, from which *Knight's Pawn* emerged.

As a novelist, I made adjustments no historian would. The Medieval calendar began on December 25th or March 25th. In *Knight's Pawn*, the year starts on January 1st. England, as we know it today, barely existed then. The dominant peoples were the Angles and the Saxons, but they were scarcely the only groups. I call them all "English." Likewise, I use the term "Norman," although the invaders and occupiers included people from elsewhere. Englelond is a 13th-century term for the land and people, including all occupiers. I refer to the English language as Saxon, the Norman-French as French, and use modified Old English words and modern Gaelic. I chose Hewisa, a spelling variation for the name of an actual person, and

"William" to distinguish the duke of Normandy, king of England, from others having the name Guillaume.

My apologies to the descendants of Harold Godwinson, Archbishop Robert de Rouen, and Count Eustace de Boulogne II. I gave them fictional relatives to link my characters to the competing factions of the time. Excepting his fictional involvement with my characters and the dubious charge of mutilating Harold, Eustace's actions noted in this novel are well documented, including his conviction for treason.

I hope you enjoyed my recreation of a long-gone era. I wanted to share my reverence for those resilient people who experienced the same love, fear, pain, and joy as we do. For more information about my research and other books, see my website at: www.alkucherenko.com.